VELVET DUSK

The Velvet Chronicles – Book 3

Claire L. Wilkinson

Claire L. Wilkinson

Velvet Dusk, The Velvet Chronicles – Book 3

Independently Published 2019

Amazon Publishing

Copyright © Claire L. Wilkinson 2020

Dedications

The Serious One

For Kerry

Even though we are not related by blood, you are the family I chose and I could not imagine my life without you now. You are my best friend, my partner in crime and my team mate in the zombie apocalypse. You are one of the very few people in the entire world who can know what I am thinking and feeling without having to be anywhere near me. You are an amazing woman and an inspiration to me and I thank the universe for you every single day

xx

The Fun One

For Myself

I know that sounds egotistical but bear with me on this one... This is my way of finally giving myself some credit and praise. Or possibly more of an acceptance that I have actually done something half decent in writing some little story. Anyone who knows me, knows I don't take compliments at all, so this is me giving myself one... a compliment that is. I know how your dirty minds work...

xx

Chapter One

They say that everything happens for a reason...

First of all, who is this "they" that say this? Because they sound like a bunch of fucking idiots. And secondly what possible reason could there be for my life to be so utterly mind fucking me at the moment? I mean, what the actual fuck did I do that was so bad that I managed to piss off the universe enough for me to find myself in the middle of a growing war and everyone around me is destined to screw me over? My life has completely gone to shit. Everything I knew, or thought I knew, was a complete lie and the only person I can now trust is myself.

The entire world is against me. I was so happy being miserable in my normal every day life, I loved my crappy little office job because I didn't have to worry about anything, I loved being able to walk down the fucking street and not have someone point a gun at my head. Why could my super powers not include time travel so that I could go back and avoid any of this ever happening? Why on God's green earth did I have to go out to that stupid rock club that first night? If there was ever a night for an early bed time, then that was it, then I wouldn't have been attacked and attracted Gideon's attention and I would not have awakened my abilities and then become the number one person that all the shit gravitates to.

I think that I swear and drink far too much and I'm starting to accept the fact that I think I have some serious anger issues. I am losing my mind and I want to throttle everyone I meet. There are several people I can think of just off the top of my head that deserve a well-placed chair to the face.

I take a deep breath and try to relax, I don't know why I bother though, relaxing isn't something I'm very good at, as is quite evident by my past experiences. I am destined to live the rest of my days constantly in a state of anxiety and anger.

After what happened with Bertol and Claudia and then what I subsequently found out, I kind of had a mini meltdown and everything got a bit too much for me to handle, so I did the only thing I could think of to control the situation... I bolted. Instead of sitting down like adults and talking through everything, I just ran. Whenever things get hard and I feel so overwhelmed that I just don't know what to do or I can't cope with the all the emotional shit, my brain takes over and says "Nope, not today, fucking get out whilst you can and avoid it all".

I keep running over everything that happened in those last few moments of my life, when I actually thought I had finally got a grasp on everything and I knew what was going on around me. And then BOOM! My entire universe imploded on itself and I suddenly realised that I knew fuck all about anything. Everyone around me are manipulating lying bastards, not once did any of them consider how I would feel... No! They just all thought about themselves and their secrets and promises were more important than my friendship and loyalty.

I have hardly slept and I've been pissed off for 12 whole days. I could have probably handled the Kerry thing, I thought I was doing OK with finding out who she was and that she had known all along who my mother was. I could even handle the fact that I knew Gideon was keeping a secret, there were still some reservations about the whole killing my dad thing, but I thought I had actual feelings for him after the last time we had sex. But now that I have the realisation that Gideon didn't actually kill my dad and that he is alive, that he did not once in the last 27 fucking years try to find me or that he just let me think I was unloved and that he was dead... I need to calm down because if I don't I am going to explode. Gideon knew that my dad was alive, he looked in to my eyes and let me think he was dead and that he had murdered him.

I also still have remnants of my time with Claudia in my head. I said things to Gideon that I would never have spoken out loud, but the more I think about what I said to him when I told him that I hated him, the more little bits of truth filter through. Honestly though, I can't decipher what is fact and what is fiction in my head. I felt things for Claudia that I have never felt for anyone and it scares me because in my head I know it wasn't real, and she forced me to feel that way, but in my heart... But then I thought I felt things for Gideon then Claudia pushed that out of me and made me hate him. I am so confused. Should I be following my mind or my heart? Because either way I still feel like I will be completely fucked up. So, I've come to the conclusion that this is who I am now, a pissed off loser who can't stand people because they all fucking suck enormous hairy donkey balls.

I close my eyes and lie back in the bath, I let the boiling hot water consume me. I know, however, that no matter how much I try to zone out, my mind will go through everything again like it has done a million times before. I know it's foolish of me, but I kind of hope that one of these times I'll wake up and it will all have been a bad dream...

...

"Gideon? What's going on?" I ask. The military man notices Gideon looking towards where I am standing and turns to face me. I freeze on the spot as his eyes meet mine, my heart starts to pound as he looks at me. I know that face. It can't be him, out of everyone on this earth, how can it be possible. I swallow hard and I only manage to get out one word... "Dad?"

I suddenly feel like I can't breathe. I drop Bertol's head and it bounces slightly as it lands on the floor, his blood splashing up my leg as I stand in shock. I look back to Gideon, but he puts his head down, not wanting to look at me.

"What the fuck is going on?" I force myself to say. Rick looks as shocked as I do though.

"The TV said you were dead," Rick says, his eyes transfixed on me.

I almost laugh at the situation but I feel myself go light-headed again, I have lost a lot of blood and I can still feel it falling down my chest from the wounds on my neck left by both Bertol and Claudia. Why didn't I consider this before? As soon as Kerry told me that the Osiris blade was used in resurrection rituals, I should have known that there would be more to this pact between him and Gideon than what I had been told, or not told... as Gideon basically told me fuck all about it.

"Velvet?" Gideon finally speaks, but I am too preoccupied with the fact that the man I saw murdered in my vision, is now standing in front of me. "Velvet?" Gideon says slightly louder to try to get my attention. I look over at him but I don't know what to say. I suddenly have all these very overwhelming feelings that are fighting inside of me to burst out and the only thing I can do is stand here, open-mouthed and stare at them both like I am some crazy person.

This can't be happening. I can't be here, I need to get out!

I drop the knife and swiftly jump off the side of the raised area and step over Bertol's dead body without giving it another thought. I can't even look at them any more, so I just make my way straight for the loading bay doors. I hear Gideon try to come after me, to calm me down as he can clearly see that I am struggling to just keep breathing as my body has gone in to overdrive with all the thoughts, questions and scenarios in my mind. Luckily his injuries slow him down, so I can get away from him and have a bit of space to deal with all of this before I have to face them.

"Hey! What's up?" Kerry asks as I approach the doors, but I shake my head and walk past her. I wouldn't even know what to say, my mind can't even process what is happening around me right now, never mind trying to explain it all to Kerry. As I get outside it's freezing cold and pitch dark. I have no idea of the time or day, I don't know how long I have been here and I can't remember if I have slept or eaten at all whilst being with Claudia. I head a bit away from the building and out in to the street, then I close my eyes and place my hands on my knees and try to breathe slowly. I know that there are people around me, I can feel them watching me, wondering what I'm doing and why I look like an idiot trying not to have a panic attack in the middle of the road. I just need a moment to chill out and get my head around things before I explode.

Eventually, I open my eyes and stand back up, I'm standing in the middle of a city street, but I have no idea which one as I don't recognise anything, I was brought here whilst unconscious in the back of a van.

"I'll bring the car around!" Kerry says cautiously as she smiles at me slightly then heads off down the street. There are quite a few people milling around outside, a mixture of vampires and what I now know to be Rick's hunter unit, or whatever they are, I don't really know. The night itself is unusually quiet and I notice that none of the other buildings on the street have lights on. I laugh at the thought of Claudia and Bertol literally taking over a full street just to try to stay unnoticed so that they were not found as easily.

"Velvet?" I take a long deep breath as I hear Gideon speak behind me. "This isn't the way we wanted you to find out."

I can't even look at him. All this time of him letting me believe that he killed Rick, and he couldn't just tell me the truth. He couldn't even give me the tiniest of hint that he was alive, he watched as I walked away to find out about my own father that resulted in me facing the General for the first time, when he could have just stopped me and told me the truth. I shake my head as Gideon walks around and stands facing me, but I just look at the ground. I don't want to have him anywhere near me.

"I can't deal with this!" I say as my voice quivers. I can feel myself panicking. I briefly glance up as Kerry pulls up in my car and gets out. She can see how uncomfortable I am, that I am almost screaming inside, that I need to get away from them all.

"Do you want to leave?" Kerry asks me and I just nod my head. She knows exactly what I want to do. I start to head straight for the car, if I leave now then maybe I won't erupt with anger.

"Wait!" Gideon says as he grabs my arm, but I pull away and force myself to step back.

"Don't touch me!" I say firmly. I look up at him and finally connect with his eyes. I can see that he is desperate to tell me everything will be OK, that what I saw wasn't true and that everything is fine and it will all be like before. But we both know it's all lies and that everything I believed has been smashed to bits and I will now never put all those pieces back together in the right place. Everything will be different between us and I don't know how much longer I can hold back all the emotions that are accumulating inside of me.

"We should talk, all of us," Gideon says cautiously and nods over to the group of hunters standing to the side. I see Rick nervously watching us, he looks as unsure as I do, but at least he knew what was going on, whereas I grew up without a family or a father. He walked away from me when I was just a tiny innocent baby. How could anyone do that? He abandoned me.

I pause for a moment and think about things logically. I do need to know why. What was the purpose of him being killed or not killed... I'm so confused. It all has me second guessing myself about what I saw in my vision and if I really did see him die. Or is this one of Claudia's games, and she still has control of my mind and is making me see all of this so that I will hate Gideon even more? I guess there is only one sure fire way of finding out.

I walk over to the car and take the keys off Kerry. I turn back to Gideon who stands watching me, his eyes pleading me to stay, I take a deep breath to calm my nerves.

"Get in the car!" I say bluntly. Gideon looks at me unsure who I am referring to. "Both of you... Now!" I flash Rick a look then get in the driver's side. I sit by myself and silently wait to see what they do.

Gideon and Rick speak to each other for a moment, I see Rick nod his head and sigh before turning away from Gideon and talking to his men. Tristen tries to stop Gideon from just leaving as he's lost as to why there are hunters helping him. He has no idea who Rick is and what is going on, but I see that Gideon gives him orders and Tristen eventually heads off down the street with Greg. Kerry gets in the passenger side and doesn't say a word. After a few minutes of sorting things out, both Gideon and Rick get in the back of the car. I silently reach over to the glove box as everyone sits quietly and I take out the Sat Nav and set it up, then grab a half drank bottle of water and some pain killers and take a few. My head is pounding and the wounds on my neck are restricting my movements but now is not the time for me to be in pain, I am far too pissed off to be dealing with that shit as well.

"Velvet, where are we going?" Gideon asks quietly.

"Home!" Is all I say. I start the engine and drive away without looking back. After a few miles, Rick finally speaks.

"This isn't how I imagined us finally meeting," he says quietly, but I shake my head. I don't want to listen to anything he has to say to me right now. I know I need a distraction to stop myself going crazy, so I turn on the MP3 player that is attached to the cars speakers.

"This is a silent car journey, so I'd appreciate it if no one speaks to me, because if they do, I will lose my shit," I say bluntly as the music starts to play.

"What is this music?" Gideon says after a few seconds.

"Slipknot," Kerry informs him.

"It sounds like shouting murder music," Rick says trying to lighten the increasing tension in the car.

"Then it fits perfectly with the mood I'm in right now!" I snap back then turn the music up louder.

We were only a couple of hours away from the bunker but as I pull up I can already tell it's close to dawn now. We managed the full trip without me shouting or losing my cool which I personally think is a massive achievement for me. I get out of the car and hand the keys to Kerry after she takes a bag out of the boot, then she heads over to open the front door. My feet are sore as I've not worn any shoes for a while, and they are cut and scraped from the rubble in the basement. I'm desperate to change out of this shitting outfit and pretty much every part of me is covered in now dried blood and my skin feels like it is on fire.

Kerry opens the door, Rick and Gideon follow her inside with me close behind, but as soon as I walk through the doorway I stop. I think for a moment and shake my head... just when I thought things couldn't get any worse.

"You have got to be fucking kidding me!" I say through gritted teeth as I look at Gideon. I'm fuming, I try to take a few deep breaths to keep it in. Gideon looks confused then looks at the door, he realises that I didn't invite him to come in.

"Oh!" Gideon says as he looks slightly guilty.

"Fucking, oh?" I snap back. I look at Rick as he makes his way to the sofa to sit down then back to Gideon. "Just how good of friends are you two? You are obviously close enough to have been here before, you know, this safe house that's protected from everything that's not human and that no one is supposed to fucking know about!" Gideon puts his head down and joins Rick on the sofa, where they then sit in silence.

Kerry places the bag she took from the car down next to Gideon and takes out several bags of blood, I'm guessing she found Greg and Tristen, and they had her bring supply's just in case. Gideon takes a couple of blood bags from her and rips one open with his teeth and starts to drink it as Kerry stands to one side. I slowly walk around the sofa to face them and take a deep breath before I speak.

"Right, this is how this is going to work!" I try to say calmly as I look at Gideon and Rick. "I am going to talk first, I'm not going to lie I'm probably going to vent and get a little loud. I'll try not to shout but I can't promise anything. Then when I'm done I am going to get changed out of this wanna be Greek stripper dress and then it will be your turn to speak... Understand?" I pause, waiting for them to reply.

"Why can't we talk now?" Rick asks nervously.

"If this is anything like when she found out that I was still alive," Kerry says to him, "then I find that it's best to just let her get it all out in the open first." Rick and Gideon both nod and the room falls silent. I had so much that I wanted to say in the car but now I'm here I don't know where to start.

"So..." I try to calm myself, "I'm going to start with the obvious, that you, Rick, Patrick, Dad, or whatever you are calling yourself these days, are not dead... Wow, this is hard to take in, see a little while ago, just after I found out who I was and who my parents were, I had a vision and in it I watched Gideon kill you!" Rick and Gideon glance at each other and Gideon nods to confirm that what I am saying is true. "I specifically asked you, Gideon, to explain and all you gave me was a cock-and-bull story about a blood pact and that you were forbidden from speaking about that day. Was that even true?" Gideon goes to speak but I shake my head. "Don't answer that, I don't want to know, not yet anyway... So instead of you just saying something along the lines of, oh I don't know... what you saw wasn't real, he's alive. You just let me believe that you had killed him." I pause and take a deep breath and then laugh slightly. "Every fucking thing that has happened since that day... I'm now putting down to being your fault!" I say directly to Gideon.

"My fault? How is that exactly?" Gideon chimes in.

"If you hadn't made me believe that you actually killed him, like, if I had known the truth when I asked for it, then I would never have left that night. I wouldn't have walked away from you... I felt surprisingly happy that day, being with you... but you told me to leave even though you knew the truth... then I wouldn't have driven to Scotland to find the hunters base..." I say.

"You did what?" Rick asks shocked.

"I drove to Scotland to find out why Gideon killed you and why it was so important for him to keep it a secret from me, so I went to find answers in the only place I knew that you had a connection," I continue. "Following swiftly on, I then wouldn't have got in a car crash and woke up handcuffed to a bed, I wouldn't have pissed off the General, then I wouldn't have found out about my link to Camelot, or had to escape, or been on the most wanted list because the General took an interest in me..." I pause briefly to catch my breath.

"You were at the base? Do you know how dangerous the General is?" Rick asks concerned but I can't help but laugh at him.

"Do I know how dangerous he is?" I reply trying to keep calm, but I am literally fuming. "Are you having a fucking giraffe? I went into hiding because of that bastard, only to hand myself over to him to save the lives of some friends of mine, then I spent days being tortured, subjected to electroshock treatment, experimented on... He had a Doctor attempt to surgically remove eggs from my ovaries to create his personal super army, I was drugged, violated and my only way out was for me to fake my own death!" I flash Kerry a look for support but I can feel myself tipping over the edge, my whole body shaking. "Then after all that I wouldn't have found out about the Osiris blade and went back to Gideon with it, for answers..."

"You have the Osiris blade?" Rick quickly interrupts. Kerry pulls it from the bag and throws it in front of him on the table before I continue. Rick stares at it and can't believe what I am saying.

"The Osiris blade..." I say, sarcastically presenting it to him. "So, because I went back to Gideon, I was then kidnapped by psychotic vampires, mind controlled to forget who my friends were, I was treated like meals on fucking wheels, I was vampire date raped in a pool resulting in my first girl on girl encounter. Then I was fed on by Claudia and Bertol whilst Claudia made me her shitting bitch..."

"You did what, with Claudia?" Gideon asks. He seems clearly shocked that things got sexual between us.

"That's not the point Gideon!" I snap back. "He's not dead." I shout, pointing at Rick. "That's the focus here, and can I remind you that I nearly killed you tonight, this fucking close because I had no control over myself. But it's all OK though because you were keeping a promise of not telling anyone my fucking father was actually alive... so everything I've been through happened for a reason, right?" I stop and breathe deeply, the silence fills the room after I stop shouting.

"I'm sorry," Rick says gently, "I never meant for any of this to happen the way it did." I run my hand through my hair as I listen to what he has to say. "I knew the day you were born that you were special, that you alone would be the one to bring everyone together and end the war before it begins fully. But I also knew that you would never be able to do that if I was around." I swallow hard, trying to calm myself again. "I needed a way for you to discover your own path but I couldn't do that as leader of the Hunter's Council and it's not exactly a job you can just leave, so with a little help from an old friend we faked my death and vowed to never tell anyone the truth. That's the short version of it anyway."

"And what about what I needed? I needed a dad... All this because you were trying to fulfil some prophecy?" I ask. I don't understand why he would do this. "What happened to us just being a family? You don't have any idea what it was like for me growing up thinking that I had been abandoned and that I wasn't even loved... I guess you only came back to see Gideon tonight because you thought I was dead and that you were safe to show your face again."

"It's not like that..." Rick replies.

"Then what is it like?" I ask loudly. "Call me a sceptic, but it's more than a coincidence that you turn up now." Everyone goes quiet, I'm not sure what else to say right now as it's a lot to deal with. I take a deep breath and calm myself down again. "I'm going to go have a wash and get changed," I say eventually. There's an awkward silence then I head towards the bathroom.

"I'll make you some food!" Kerry says gently as I pass her. "You kind of become a massive douche bag when you're hungry." I force a smile at her and nod

13

my head as I walk away.

After I've had a quick wash and got most of the blood off me, I change into some comfortable clothes and head back into the sitting room. As I enter they are all talking amongst themselves, all smiling and acting like there's nothing wrong, that everything is perfectly normal. I listen to Rick and Gideon reminisce about old times and it's all just a bit overwhelming.

"Hey!" Kerry says softly as she sees me and I nod at her. "There's a pot noodle on the bench for you, sorry we didn't have anything else in."

"Is it edible?" I ask jokingly. "You know in all the galaxy an edible pot noodle doesn't exist, right?" Kerry smiles at me and I smile back but secretly I am dying inside. Am I supposed to just sit down next to them all and act like everything is fine now that I've vented? Am I suddenly supposed to start calling him daddy and have a happy little family unit? Am I supposed to forget about all the lies and move on with my life and bury the anger and darkness that is brewing inside of me? There's so much going on in my head and my heart that I don't know if I can cope with this right now.

"Why don't you sit down and join us?" Rick asks gently, I smile at him and nod my head but inside I'm having a breakdown.

"Yeah, I will do, give me a minute, I'm just going to grab some fresh air and then I'll be right back," I reply. He nods at me happily then I walk towards the door.

Luckily no one noticed that I'm carrying a duffel bag and that the car keys are in my jeans pocket. I can't stay here right now, it's all a bit much for me to handle. I walk outside and inhale the fresh day breeze, the sun is shining brightly and there is not a cloud in the sky as I head to the car. I throw the bag on the back seats and get in then put the key in the ignition and start the car before looking up, my heart drops as I see Gideon standing in the doorway trying to stay in the shade. I can see it in his eyes that he doesn't want me to leave, that he has a million things that he wants to say to me, that his heart is hurting already, but after everything that happened with Claudia, I just don't know how to move forward from that just yet.

I look into Gideon's eyes and mouth the words "I'm sorry" before turning the car around and driving away. I didn't really have a plan of where I was going to go, but I had a bag full of clean clothes and money. I knew I had to keep my head down with the whole being dead thing and I couldn't face talking or trying to explain how I felt to anyone.

So, I ended up at a hotel in Wales in the middle of nowhere. They do room service and have TV so the past 12 days have been spent lying low and trying to figure out what I am supposed to do with my life.

After I get out of the bath I put on my comfortable pyjama's and wait for my pizza to be delivered. The hotel isn't anything flash but it's nice enough for the price and I'm not bothering anyone. All I needed was my own room and a bed. At this time of year, they don't get much business anyway, so I've been told I can add on nights as often as I want and I don't have plans to leave any time soon.

I've been trying to avoid the news as much as possible but the reports are everywhere, actual real-life witch hunts are happening all over the UK now, groups dragging unsuspecting woman from their homes and judging them unfairly then hanging them in the street. Because of this, there have been increased missing persons and a new string of gruesome murders where the victims have all been members of the extremist group the Hammer of Light and their bodies have been found skinned and mutilated. I can't shake the feeling that Helana and the Midnight Church coven are responsible for those deaths, kind of like payback for the witch killings.

Everything throughout the country is turning mental, I'm actually quite glad everyone thinks I'm dead and that I'm just keeping myself to myself. I don't even like my own company sometimes so right now being alone is perfect for me. It has given me time to think about all the things that are inside my head, granted, I have yet to work through my issues and I still have not accepted why everyone around me are arseholes, but I do feel a little better just being away from all of the drama.

There's a knock on the door and I glance at the time, I do a little happy dance... is it bad that I'm a little too excited that it's room service with pizza? Food makes me happy, it's reliable, it doesn't lie to me or abandon me and it makes me not be a dick sometimes. I jump off the bed and open the door, but my smile instantly drops.

"Hi," Gideon says awkwardly as he stands outside the doorway with my room service pizza in a box. He seems a little nervous and doesn't quite make eye contact with me. I am rooted to the spot in total disbelief that he is actually standing in front of me, and we both just stand in silence for a minute. He eventually gives me a slight smile then I take the pizza from his hand and close the door in his face. "Velvet, please, come on, let me in!" Gideon says softly through the door. I've had a blissful 12 days of not having to deal with all my life shit, I definitely don't even want to deal with it now. There's a gentle knock on the door again and I sigh.

"Please?" He says again. I know I have to face this at some point, I just didn't want it to be now. I look at my food and reluctantly put the pizza down on the bed then go back and open the door. Gideon stands silent. He looks different, more casually dressed in a pair of black jeans and a black hoodie. He looks in great health compared to the last time I saw him, and he smiles slightly at me when I open the door. His eyes are captivating and gently, but I need to ignore all of that because even after all this time away I am still so angry with him. My thoughts and emotions have been all over the place, and I am struggling to keep everything in line in case I go insane.

"How did you find me?" I finally ask, trying to ignore the fact that he is pleasing to the eye, so I purposely don't look at him. I tried to cover my tracks so well to enable me to have some alone time.

"Kerry managed to locate you after much persuading. She seems to think you two have a sort of psychic and empath link, something about her being connected to you as your familiar," he says cautiously. I nod my head in understanding but I don't say anything else. We both stand awkwardly for another minute until Gideon speaks again. "So... are you going to invite me in?" He asks coyly.

"A hotel is a public place so you don't need me to give you an invitation," I reply quietly. Gideon nods at me then takes a deep breath.

"I guess I thought I'd risk asking if you actually wanted me to come in though," he says trying to force a smile at me, he puts his hands in his pockets and quietly waits for an answer. I have a million things running through my head and I already feel very uncomfortable about having him near me. I don't know if it is because I am still trying to avoid dealing with the lies and having an actual real life father or the fact that every other time I have been around Gideon, I have not been able to control myself enough to resist him. After a very long pause I step away from the door then go and sit down on the bed, Gideon cautiously enters the room and closes the door behind him. "So?" He says looking around the room, I don't say anything, instead, I pick up a slice of pizza from inside the box and start to eat. Food will distract me. "Nice room... I guess!"

"What do you want Gideon?" I snap, he obviously tried to find me for a reason. He stands for a moment and thinks about what to say, he seems nervous and the air between us is thick and tense. I honestly did not mean for it to come out so abruptly but my emotions are all on high alert and I can't contain them.

"You left the bunker without saying anything... Rick was worried about you," he finally says. I laugh slightly at his statement.

"Rick was worried about me? So you came to find me? He didn't seem too worried about me the past 27 years when he just let me think he was dead," I scoff, I'm not in the mood for this at all.

"Yeah, that sounded better in my head," Gideon says to himself, he looks up at me and smiles. "I understand that you are upset..."

"Upset is a bit of an understatement," I interrupt him. "I am so fucking angry with all the lies, I feel betrayed, I'm confused... most of all, right now, I feel so fucking alone..." I force myself to stop talking because I know if I don't, I will tip over the edge.

"I'm sorry," Gideon says gently. "A lot has happened to you and I feel responsible for that, but it was never my intention to hurt you." I take a bite of my pizza as he talks. "I wanted so much to tell you he was alive but I just couldn't, I couldn't betray our blood pact. The strong magic that was used to bind us, forbid me from revealing the truth to anyone... I guess what we did made sense to us at the time, we felt that it was the only way to ensure the outcome of this war within the supernatural world would eventually turn in our favour. But I had no idea that he had a child and that Rick's plan involved you."

"What plan Gideon?" I say wearily. I just want to enjoy my food and for him to shut up then fuck off. But I also want to know why all these cloak and dagger secrets that they shared were so important.

"Rick told me that he believed that there was a person who could unite all forces in the supernatural world. Someone who could bring together the witches, hunters, vampires and so on. Someone who would be strong enough to lead us all to a new and better life. I didn't ask more questions, maybe that is my downfall because I should have known everything before I agreed to help him, but I trusted him and did what he asked of me. He just told me that it wouldn't be possible for his plan to work if he was the head of the Hunters Council and the only way for him to disassociate himself with them would be if he died." He pauses for a moment before continuing. "Then I met you... and when I found out your lineage it all made sense." I watch him as he sits on the end of the bed and for a second I feel like I really missed seeing him... I need to ignore it, it's not real.

"What all made sense?" I ask, urging him to continue. This is the most open about Rick that he has ever been with me.

"You have a rightful claim, because of who your parents were, to both as leader of the Hunters Council and the High Priestess position in the Midnight Church. Myself and your father always saw eye to eye and just wanted peace between all people, so I instantly knew that you would want the same and I knew that I would stand by you as leader of the vampire clans as the third position when the time came." The room goes quiet as I try to take it all in. But instead of understanding what he has just said, I laugh to myself.

"You are out of your mind!" I say quietly. "I don't want any of this. I don't want to lead people, fuck man! I don't even like people most days." I pause to take a deep breath. "So you are telling me that Rick killed himself in the hopes that when I grew up I would overthrow the General and Helana to take power, then with your help, we would unite everyone and then live happily ever after and try to make the human world forget anything bad ever happened?" I get up from the bed and walk over to the chest of drawers against the wall, I didn't hide out in here for 12 days with only water. I fill the pint glass that stands on the top with a mixture of Pepsi and rum and take a long drink before turning back to Gideon. I watch him sit in silence for a moment, unsure what else to say to me. "What is the real reason that gave you the overwhelming need to find me, Gideon? You certainly didn't come here to talk about Rick," I ask bluntly. I know he didn't come all this way to discuss my dad and his secrets. Gideon stays silent for a while longer as I drink more, eventually he sighs and stands up from the bed.

"The things that happened with Claudia and Bertol..." He pauses trying to find the right words.

"No!" I stop him. "I can't discuss that as well as my father right now... my mind is so messed up that I honestly don't know what parts of that were real... I mean, I felt things that I shouldn't have and..."

"That was not the real you," Gideon says softly. "Claudia did some unbelievably evil things, and I am so sorry that again, what happened was because of me. What she did to you, what she made you do... it was payback and you were the unwilling victim in the middle of it all." I look away from him. I feel like I was too weak to resist her or maybe that I didn't want to resit her. I am just not sure of anything any more.

"I nearly killed you," I reply. "I didn't know who you were and all I wanted to do was drive that stake through your heart so much, because I wanted to please her, I wanted to make her happy," my voice quivers slightly, I am trying to stay calm but there is too much going on inside of me.

"Speaking of that..." Gideon sighs. "And what I said to you, right before..."

"I know," I stop him. "I know that you only said that to make me try to wake up, to try to do anything to save your own life... all for show and that... Right?" I say, watching him, expecting him to smile and agree that everything that happened was all to get back at Claudia. But instead he shakes his head.

"No, Velvet, I said it because I meant it." I stand for a moment, not quite sure what to say or do.

"Why?" That's not the word I was looking for in my head but it's a response at least.

"Why? Why did I say that I loved you and that I meant it?" He asks confused, I just nod my head at him. "I said it because at that moment I truly thought I was going to die and I didn't want to leave you without telling you how I felt." I take another drink and think. He can't possibly have actually meant it... could he?

"But you can't," I reply, "the feelings or whatever, it's all because of the link you have with my father, not with me. You said it yourself that you were drawn to my blood because of the pact you made, that the connection we felt for each other was fabricated... Don't get me wrong I enjoyed the sex a lot, but we don't even know each other very well, it just isn't..." I can't find the words. Gideon moves in front of me. The closer he is to me the more static I can feel between us, my body yearning for him to touch me and I don't understand why.

"I know I said that, I thought by me saying those things that it justified the reasons why you had to leave me. That because of the blood pact, I couldn't trust my own feelings and the more you were around me the more out of control of myself I felt..." Gideon stops and thinks about what he should say next. I watch him, he doesn't look like he is lying to me. "The longer you were away from me the more my heart began to hurt. And that had nothing to do with your father or your blood... It was because I was starting to fall madly in love with you."

"But it's not real, Gideon," I say cautiously.

"I swear that it is real for me," Gideon replies. I search his eyes to see if he is lying, to see if he is just trying to put these thoughts in my head just like Claudia did, but all I can see is him and I'm so torn. When I was under Claudia's control I felt like she would never hurt me in any way and it made me realise that Gideon has done things to me that still haunt me now, so I am a bit reserved. I have a lot of things in my head that I need to deal with and adding this on top as well is too much.

"I... I don't know what to say," I manage to get out. "I am still so angry and upset with everything that's happened... Maybe it's best if you leave."

Gideon slowly steps forward, takes the glass out of my hand and carefully places it on the drawers behind me. He reaches out to take hold of my hand and I pull back and look away. I can't let him touch me because Claudia did that and look what happened.

"Velvet?" Gideon says gently. "Velvet, look at me, please." I am hesitant, I don't know what to do for the best.

"I can't," I force out. I swallow hard and concentrate on looking down at the floor.

"Talk to me," he pleads.

"I am scared that when I look at you, I won't be able to resist... just like when I looked at her..." I feel my heart rate quicken under Gideon's watch.

"I promise you, all the times we have been intimate... I have never forced myself on you, I have never made you do anything you did not want to do. That was the real you and you need to let go of what happened with her and start listening to your heart instead of your mind," Gideon says. I think about his words. I didn't feel under his control when I went after him that night I had come back to see Tristen. I acted on my own will when I went back again when he thought I was dead. When I was away from him, I craved him, I wanted him near me, I wanted to be close. I sigh and look up to him, my gaze meeting his. As soon as I look at him, he smiles. "I missed you," he says gently. Deep down inside I have missed him too. I feel stupid for letting Claudia get to me so much.

"I missed you too," I reply nervously. I have to stop myself from jumping in to his arms and kissing him, as just his smile makes my heart skip a beat. "I, erm... like I said, I just don't know what to say."

"You don't have to say anything, but I would like to think that maybe you feel something for me too?" He asks softly. I don't know, I don't know how I feel, he has hurt me so much in the past. Plus I just can't get what happened with Claudia out of my head. Her touch drove me wild and she used her abilities to control how I felt about her, so I instantly assume that Gideon could be doing the same... Even though I know he didn't.

"Gideon... I'm sorry but I can't say those words back to you. I don't even know what they mean," I reply. He watches me closely. If he was controlling me, then that is not the answer he would want, so at least I know what I am saying is all coming from me. "Honestly, I don't know what love is Gideon. No one loved me when I was growing up and lost in this world, I felt abandoned, no one even liked me much never mind loved me. And now I'm older I don't know if I ever thought that I would get close enough to someone to say something like that, because lately every time I think things are going great, shit happens... And it scares me, that if I was to be that close to someone and I lost them... I don't know how I could ever move forward." I pause and think for a second then take a step back from him. "I guess the thought of love scares me a little."

"Why?" Gideon asks softly. I look in to his eyes and feel like I am being swept up in them all over again.

"Because it's new and unknown, I don't understand why anyone would love someone like me," I say then look away from him. "I am a no one, I'm a total bitch, I swear too much, and I am a fucking weirdo... I mean look at me! I'm standing here in no make-up, my hair is a mess, I'm wearing the same pyjamas I've been wearing for the past 3 days. This is the real me Gideon, the real moody, sarcastic, alcohol-loving me. That's why love isn't real, because it's based on fake looks and romance and that isn't me, not one little bit... I am sorry but I think I would only say those words if I actually truly meant it... and I don't know if I ever can," I explain. I stand watching him, expecting him to shout at me saying I've been wasting his time or to storm out and slam the door. But instead he steps forward and takes my hand.

"You are amazing!" He says gently. "You are beautiful and powerful, I am so in love with your fire. I don't care about what clothes you wear or what make-up you cover your face in... it's your soul that I am attracted to. I've been alive for a long time and though I've experienced many women, there has only been a couple of times I've felt this crazy about anyone... even after such a short amount of time, you make me feel alive." I swallow and go silent. I don't quite know what to say to him, I am stunned.

"Gideon I... This is a bit... Overwhelming. I mean, I've never said that I loved anyone except for Kerry, but that is in like a best friend kind of love, whereas this, what you feel might be between us... I don't know what that is, erm, it's, I don't know," I stumble over trying to get my words out. I know inside myself that I like Gideon, I do feel an attraction to him... I must have felt something otherwise I wouldn't have slept with him again. But even though I am unbelievably drawn to him, love is a strong word to me.

"I am sorry if I've put you on the spot, if you still want me to leave, I will," Gideon continues. "Just tell me that you don't feel anything at all, tell me that there isn't even the tiniest of chances that one day you might feel the same way for me." Gideon grips my hand tighter and steps closer till his body is almost touching mine and my back is now pressed against the drawers. "Tell me to leave and that you don't want me!" My breath hitches in my throat as I listen to him, I suddenly feel extremely nervous. Just because I can't tell him that I love him, doesn't mean that I want him to leave.

"I know that you are hoping that I am going to tell you I love you Gideon, but I can't. What I do feel is that I am really attracted to you," I say as I place my hand on his chest, "you are fucking amazing at sex, your strength and dominance is such a turn on that just thinking about you makes me horny. I do like you a lot, I think, but there are a lot of things holding me back and those are my issues, not yours... I just don't know what parts of how I am feeling, are real right now." Gideon smiles at me slightly.

"Then I can wait. I've already waited hundreds of years to find a woman like you, I am sure I can live with just knowing that you at least feel... something." He holds up my hand to his lips and kisses the back of it gently.

"I just want to be totally clear with you," I say, "I don't know if I will ever be able to say that I love you with any kind of meaning because I don't know what love is supposed to feel like." All I know is that there is a strong attraction to him and my body aches for him every time he looks in to my eyes.

"Then please, let me show you what it feels like for me," Gideon says gently then places his hand on my cheek and pulls my face to his, I feel it as soon as he kisses me, that tingling sensation in my loins. Gideon's tongue slips between my lips and explores my mouth. My body yearns for him, it wants him completely, but my mind and heart are so closed off. I think that someday I might want to feel that pure connection with a man, possibly even with Gideon, but I am scared of letting go.

"Gideon?" I say as I pull away, and he looks down at me. "Please don't think that I am just leading you on, because I am not, I've never even been in a proper relationship or anything. It's just weird for me, you know. I've always just been happy plodding along and having a bit of fun. All these emotions are a bit too much, they are so intense and I don't quite know what I should be doing. I was never keen on making anything I had in the past in to something serious. And now I have a lot of stuff going on in my head after everything that's happened, and I am so confused," I take a deep breath and sigh. "I'm sorry, I am waffling." Gideon laughs at me slightly then sighs.

"Why don't we start again then," he says softly as he looks down at me and smiles. "I don't want to make you feel uncomfortable around me, so let's just say I came here because I missed you and that I just wanted to make sure that you were OK. I like having fun with you too and I think that you have an unbelievably fucking attractive soul. And let's just say... I like you a lot. Nothing more, nothing serious and if you just happen to want to fuck me then..." He tilts his head and smiles cheekily. I laugh at him then look down at myself and how frumpy I look standing in front of him. "What's wrong?" He asks as he notices that I seem deflated.

"I look like complete shit!" I laugh at myself. "You sure do know how to make a surprise entrance and catch me off guard."

"Yes, I suppose I do!" He laughs slightly, I can see Gideon watching me, waiting for me to do something. "What do you want me to do now?" He asks gently. I am honestly so confused, putting aside the love and feelings thing though, I just want him. This strong, masculine vampire could have anyone in the world that he wants. I mean, come on! He's the fucking vampire King! He could be anywhere in the world right now, but instead he is here with me, and he is telling me that he wants me too.

I don't say anything back, instead I lean over my shoulder and grab my glass and drink the rest of it in one go then place the glass back down and slowly remove my top. Gideon stands watching me, his eyes falling on my naked breasts. I hear him exhale sharply then his gaze moves to meet mine, and he smiles.

In one slow move he removes both his t-shirt and hoodie, and we both just stand taking each other in, then I watch him as he kicks off his boots, my eyes trail to his tattoos that surround his perfect figure and I realise that I am very lucky that he wants to spend his time with me. Gideon steps forward until our body's almost touch and runs his hands down my arms then entwines his fingers with mine.

"Oh, and another thing!" I say out of the blue. "About those things I said, that I hated you and stuff. Please know that isn't how I feel now, Claudia got in my head, I had no control over what I was doing and..."

"Shut up!" Gideon says playfully, interrupting me. He leans in and our lips touch again. It's not the usual frantic lustful kisses that I've experienced before with him, this time it's slow and gentle. His tongue playing with mine in a sensual dance, I close my eyes and let myself enjoy the touch of his body pressed up against mine. He wraps his arms around me and his fingers stroke down the centre of my back, I can feel that my skin is so warm compared to his, but I don't care. After a few moments of closeness, he steps away from me, takes my hand and then leads me towards the bed. He swiftly moves my pizza box to the floor and positions me so that I am able to lie back on the mattress.

Gideon slowly leans down and removes my pyjama bottoms and fluffy slipper socks then pauses for a second and smiles down at me.

"What?" I ask quietly. I feel my cheeks blush with embarrassment as he looks at me so longingly but Gideon's smile broadens, and he bites his bottom lip.

"You are so fucking beautiful!" He replies. I smile back at him, I am a little bad at taking compliments so don't know how to respond. He moves to lie between my legs and then runs his hands across my thighs, slowly kissing my skin, starting just below my breasts and moving down across my stomach. Every touch of his lips on my skin making my heart beat faster. He trails his way towards my apex until I feel his hand between my legs, and he starts to slowly tease my clit.

His lips quickly take over and his tongue caresses my bud softly, circling my clit and relishing in having complete control over me. His hand grips my thigh and I feel myself becoming wet for him already, wanting him to touch me more firmly and just take me on the spot. I quickly find myself wanting him to make me cum but he takes his time, making me wait. I moan slightly as the feeling starts to slowly build inside of me then he moves his hand from my thigh and trails his finger tips around my opening. I lie here, waiting for his fingers to penetrate me, to experience the feeling of bliss from having some part of him inside of me and being so close to him that our bodies almost feel as one, but he holds off, I'm squirming beneath him as I want more, but he continues to tease me slowly. It's almost too much to bear as the anticipation is killing me.

I gasp when Gideon eventually slides his fingers inside my pussy, I can feel my juices flowing as his hand just slips in to me. I moan louder as his fingers move inside of me and stimulate all the right places as he begins to suck and excite my clit more. My breathing gets heavy and I get louder under his touch. As if he knows how close to the edge he has me, so quickly in to his playing, he intensifies the friction caused by his mouth and I feel like he is suddenly trying to suck me dry. My clit is throbbing beneath his lips as it aches for a release from his teasing and I cry out as I feel so close to climax.

"Gideon... Holy fuck!..." I say between gasps until the pleasure inside of my core rises so high that I welcome it with open arms and it is released and washes over every inch of me. I grip on to the bed sheets as I enjoy the moment that had been building within and has finally taken me over completely.

Gideon begins to slow as my orgasm starts to subside. I lie on my back and watch as he stands up from the bed and removes his pants. I can already see he is rock hard as he playfully climbs back towards me, his body pressing down slightly on me as his lips find mine again.

Our tongues play together, I can taste my own juices in his mouth as I close my eyes again and I let myself experience him. His skin touching mine sending me reeling as I love the closeness of having him pressed against my naked body. I move my legs to enable him to get closer and I can feel his member nestling close to my sex. I move my hands across his biceps as he moves his hips, his dick slips between my now moist lips and I groan beneath him, just in anticipation, as I feel his tip tease my entrance. Gideon kisses me deeper, his tongue now delving further in to my mouth as I return the gesture, I run my fingers across his shoulders and around the back of his neck, holding him on to me as our mouths become one, then he penetrates me and I inhale sharply as his length fills me up.

I moan against his lips, my sounds of pleasure getting louder again as Gideon grinds his hips and glides in and out of me, both of us now locked in passion, only us two existing in the moment. I hear Gideon groan as he thrusts a little deeper in to me, my pussy soaking wet for him, I know he is enjoying being inside me.

"Gideon?" I say through breaths, he pauses momentarily and moves his lips from mine then looks down at me. "I want you to bite me." As soon as I say the words I feel so turned on, I know how it feels and honestly I think I crave his fangs in my flesh. That sensation of both pleasure and pain, almost like magic, is far above anything else that I've ever experienced and it's as though it's a drug that I need to enable me to get my fix.

"Are you sure?" He asks, I nod my head, and he smiles before returning to kiss me again. His lips move against mine as we start to give in to the passion between us. I can feel him getting more aroused as he thrusts a little quicker, making my skin feel flush as my hands begin to tremble as I hold on to him. Then his mouth leaves my lips, and he moves his head, trailing playful kisses across my cheek then starts to play with my neck. I know Gideon is trying to hold back, trying to prolong the wait before he bites me so that we both want it more, but as he begins to fuck me harder, I can't help but moan louder. He groans in my ear, the pleasure building in him also and it is only a matter of time before he can't hold off any longer from taking me completely. I run my fingers up and through his hair as his lips caress my neck then he moves back for just a second and I know what he is about to do.

The expectations of knowing how it feels when a vampire feeds from me in this way makes me even more aroused. I think it is the pure adrenaline rush that has me hooked and makes me beg for more. Gideon's lips make gentle contact with my neck and I feel the sharp tips of his fangs tease slightly before they pierce my skin. It's that first sheer pain when his teeth enter my flesh that makes my body feel totally alive, then as my blood starts to slowly flow from my wound as Gideon drinks, the pleasure feeling takes over, then grows stronger and stronger the more he continues.

I cry out and grab his shoulder as Gideon digs in to my neck more firmly, the pleasure/pain mix is intoxicating and teamed with him fucking me is unbelievably satisfying. His cock delves deeper and harder as I feel another orgasm quickly build inside of me. Gideon moans on to my neck as the pleasure takes him over also.

"Oh... shit!" I cry between gasps as I suddenly cum extremely hard. Gideon raises from my neck and hooks his arms under my legs and forces them back to enable him to thrust deeper, my back arches under him and I can feel my legs start to shake more with every dominating thrust. I quickly orgasm again before the previous one is finished as he fucks my pussy more, and he groans loudly as I feel him explode inside of me, our eyes locked, unwavering as we cum together.

When we both finish, Gideon leans back down and kisses my lips gently then smiles as he looks in to my eyes.

"I fucking love... Sorry," Gideon stops himself and shakes his head slightly, "I mean, I fucking like you a lot." I laugh at him and groan with satisfaction.

"I like you a lot too," I reply.

Chapter Two

Another night of restless sleeping and I feel like utter shit. I am exhausted and no matter how tired I seem to be, when I close my eyes my mind goes in to overdrive and it keeps running through everything that has ever happened to me in my life. The night I was first attacked by Gideon, those hunters at the orphanage attempting to rape me, those little faces of the children that were slaughtered, being tortured by the General and then being controlled by Claudia where I had no will of my own. It's enough to drive anyone in to a full-blown mental breakdown and some days I feel like I am just hanging on by a thread, as though at any second all these feelings and thoughts are going to erupt, and I am going to turn in to a full-blown mess. My mind is totally broken and no matter what I try to do it's not going to let me escape.

I think I finally fell asleep around 4 am, Gideon lay by my side all night even though I know he doesn't need much sleep, he stayed holding me close to him until I passed out with sheer exhaustion. My dreams were no better either, they have all been nightmares really and over the last week or so I've found myself waking up covered in sweat and my heart pounding nearly every night.

When I wake up it's still morning and I only managed a couple of hours sleep, I am knacked and my eyes are burning because I am still so tired. I sit up in the bed and look at the time on the small clock that sits on top of the bedside cabinet, it's only 8.15am, I suppose I had slightly more sleep than I feel like I have. I look around and notice that Gideon is not in the room, I can see his hoodie is folded neatly on the armchair that sits near the window and the room key is not on top of the drawers where I left it.

I sit for a few minutes in silence and contemplate what happened last night, Gideon just turning up out of the blue and the things he told me about Rick. Maybe

I am being paranoid but I can't shake the feeling that something isn't quite right. I told Gideon last night that I didn't know why he loves me, that I am a nobody compared to him. The more I think about that, the more I am doubting the real reason he is here, he said that he would stand by me if I were to take power of the Hunters Council and the Midnight Church, but what if that is the reason he came to find me instead. He's here because he needs to keep me close. If I was to gain power of those two massive groups then I could be a threat to him and his people. What if he sees me as his potential enemy and his way to keep control, is to control me? Then everything he told me would be lies, this could have been his plan all along.

My mind is so confused. I know he is dangerous, his power is immense and I don't even know how many people he rules over or how many humans he has killed. He told me that he wanted to protect me and that he would never hurt me but everything he has done has been the total opposite. In fact, out of everyone I've know in my life, the one person to tell me that they loved me is the person who has hurt me the most, both physically when he left me for dead and tortured me, and emotionally with all the lies and deceit. Is this love thing all just mind games? I mean, it can't be real can it?

But I feel so strongly attracted to him that maybe it's just me trying to find an excuse not to get too close. Maybe I am trying to push him away because I am so scared of getting hurt. I feel like I am going crazy, as though I could literally snap at any minute, I need to try to sort my head out to figure out what is real and what isn't.

I get up and have a shower, everything just keeps repeating over and over in my head and it's horrible. I hope I am being stupid because I do really like him even though I know I shouldn't, he's the bad boy that all the girls want to be with and right now maybe that's bad for me. I am, after all supposed to be dead and keeping a low profile from everyone and Gideon is not exactly the low profile type of guy.

After my shower I get dressed in to a t-shirt and black jeans, then put on some make-up. I am not an everyday make-up kind of girl but I like to think of it as my war paint and I have a feeling that if Gideon returns my mind won't let me relax around him. I have things I need to get off my chest, eventually.

I turn as I hear the door open behind me just as I am putting my boots on, Gideon smiles at me as he enters carrying a small brown paper bag and two take-out coffees.

"Great, you are awake, I thought you might like a decent coffee instead of the crappy hotel stuff that you have been living on," he smiles broadly and I nod my head at him as I stand up. He hands me one of the cups and continues speaking. "I didn't know if you fancied anything to eat, so I grabbed you a muffin and a bagel just in case, I wasn't to sure what you liked." I smile slightly at him and then climb on to the bed and sit crossed legged in the middle.

"Thanks, I'm not too hungry just yet," I say quietly. I don't know if I should talk to him about the things in my head, he might think that I am fucking mental or worse, what I think could be true and then I think I would be devastated. He said he loved me, the first man ever to tell me that and if that was a lie then I would honestly be crushed, even if I don't think that I feel the same way.

"Did you sleep OK? You seemed to toss and turn all night, I was kind of worried that you are not as alright as you seem on the outside," Gideon asks, he seems quite happy this morning as I watch him take the other cup from its holder and sit down on the armchair near the window.

"I haven't been sleeping great lately, I've just got a lot on my mind that's all," I reply. I take a sip of the coffee, it's scalding hot on my lips but it's really nice.

"Are you OK?" Gideon asks, I glance up at him and force a smile then nod my head.

"Yeah, I'm fine." I don't think that my tone of voice was very convincing, I've never been any good at hiding my emotions.

"What's wrong?" Gideon asks me, I can see he is trying to figure out whether there is something going on or not.

"Nothing," I say bluntly, maybe I am just being daft, it's just all in my head now. I can't shake this strange feeling about him, but it could be just because of Claudia.

"That's a lie. I can tell there is something you are not telling me," Gideon's tone changes slightly. I try not to look at him as I can feel myself getting more worked up.

"Just drop it Gideon, it's nothing," I say more forcefully. I take another sip of the coffee he brought me, and we both sit in silence for a few moments. I can feel Gideon's eyes burning in to me as he watches me.

"Velvet?" He eventually says quietly. I glance up and meet his gaze. "What's going on?" I grit my teeth slightly and exhale slowly. I don't know how to explain everything to him without potentially starting an argument.

"There's just some stuff in my head, it's making me feel crazy that's all and I'm struggling to deal with it," I stop for a second and seriously consider whether or not I should continue.

"What stuff?" Gideon asks, I force a smile and shake my head. I know if I start talking now that it will all come out wrong.

"It's stupid, just forget about it," I try to brush it off.

"Velvet, tell me," Gideon says, pushing me for answers.

"Is that a command?" I snap. I didn't mean to but I can already feel myself starting to become very anxious and it just came out. I notice Gideon raises his eyebrow at my statement.

"A command? Velvet what is going on?" He asks again, I can see that he is already on alert. "Please tell me that you don't think me asking for answers is anything like... We spoke about this last night. I promise you, I would never try to control you like that." But he did though. He has done it before, I didn't know what was real and fake when I was under Claudia's thrawl so how do I know that this is the truth now? I know I keep going over the same things but my mind is utterly fucked and I can't help what it thinks.

"This... this thing between us," I stutter. "What do you... I mean, what are your intentions? Why are you here, really?" I can see Gideon's eyes narrow slightly as he tries to understand what I'm talking about.

"My intentions? What do you mean?" He says slowly. I swallow and try to stop myself from jumping off the bed and leaving now before I have to tell him what's on my mind. Before I actually have to open up to someone, and they see how truly broken I am.

"My mind is so fucked up Gideon, something inside of me feels wrong. I don't even know what feelings that I have are real. It's as though I shouldn't trust anyone but myself, that includes you and Kerry." I look up and Gideon is still just sat patiently watching me from the chair.

"Then tell me everything. I can't help you if you don't talk to me," he replies so casually, sometimes him being so calm is alarming for me. I can't tell what he is thinking as he usually hides his emotions so well.

"Promise you won't flip out? Just let me vent and get it all out in the open, it will clear the air and my mind," I say cautiously.

"Well that doesn't sound good," Gideon replies.

"I didn't say it was good, but I need to get it out." I already feel so nervous. Gideon nods his head and sits in silence.

"OK," I take a deep breath and decide to stare at my coffee rather than have to look at him. "I don't want to say that what happened between us last night was a mistake but... I don't think it should have taken place, not at this moment anyway..." My hands are starting to shake. "I'll start by saying that I do like you a lot, probably more than I have liked anyone before you, that is not a lie. But if I am being honest, there is also a small part of me that knows it should dislike you and I can't get rid of that right now, no matter how much I am trying to... The first time we met, if you can even call it that, you used your persuasion on me, much like what Claudia did..."

"That was nothing like what she did and what you did with her," he snaps.

"Gideon please, you said that you would let me talk," I say, still not looking at him. I hear him sigh and then fall quiet again.

"You tried to force yourself on me, you tried to get me to go with you so that you could... so that you could take me against my will and then when I fought back you nearly killed me." I pause and take another deep breath trying to centre myself and push the emotions back. "The second time we met I was in quite a state, I had already fought with some of your men and again I was nearly killed, then you tortured me and tried to force your will on me to get information... That is something that still haunts me, even to this day, especially now after almost being raped by hunters, being tortured by the General and then being controlled by Claudia. Everything that they did to me, you tried to do to me first. If you had got your way, and I was unable to keep you at bay, you would have technically forced yourself on me and I would have been helpless to stop you. Although I don't look hurt or in pain... on the inside I am screaming. My soul has been torn to shreds and I no longer know who to trust, as nearly every single person I know has lied to me or screwed me over in some way." I look up at Gideon, and he still sits in the chair but his calmness is starting to slip.

"Are you done?" Gideon replies, he seems slightly agitated.

"No," I say bluntly. "There is more. After all that, you then tell me that you love me, which I admit freaks me the fuck out. I can't quite get my head around how you have managed to developed strong feelings for me in such a short amount of time. Like I said, maybe my head is just fucked up, or I am being overly sceptical or cautious, but after what you told me about how I was destined for power, I can't help but feel that your intentions may not be all that innocent." I clear my throat then stand up for the bed, I know that what I say next may cause him to become very angry and I honestly do not want to upset him.

"Care to elaborate on that point," Gideon almost snarls at me, but he still doesn't move from the chair.

"I'm going to be blunt..." I reply. "Are you only interested in me because if I do take control of the Hunters Council and the Midnight Church, I will become a threat to you? Is that why you are trying to keep me close? I ask this because as soon as you found out who I actually was, when you found out who both my mother and father were, your attitude towards me changed instantly..." I can see he is gripping the arms of the chair as I talk. As soon as I've got all of that off my chest I begin to second guess myself again. It is all in my head, isn't it? By saying all that I think I've just made things worse. I want to take it all back, I have made a massive mistake. "But I really hope that I am wrong," I continue. "Everything I have just said was all just sat in my head and it was eating away at me. I need it all to be wrong because after everything that's happened, I don't know if I can survive being let down and lied to again." I pause and take a deep breath. "I think that I do have extremely strong feelings towards you, I have never felt like this before, maybe I might... Maybe it's me just putting up barriers because I don't want to be hurt again or maybe... you are trying to get me under your thrawl, just like she did." I look at him and catch his eye. "But 'Ive never wanted to be wrong so much." I stand in silence for a while. Gideon and I just stare at each other, I have no idea what he is thinking. I can't read him, I don't know if he is going to understand or be angry. "Are you going to say anything?" I eventually ask trying to break the growing tension. I watch him, waiting for him to react, to say something as the silence is worse than anything else.

"So, let me get this right..." He finally says. "I've tried to be honest with you as much as I was able, I opened my heart to you and told you that I love you and you still don't trust or believe anything that I have to say?" He grits his teeth and I can see that he is struggling to keep calm.

"I didn't say that," I reply nervously. "I am sorry if it all came out wrong but I just wanted you to understand how I was feeling, I wanted to be completely honest with you about everything I felt and..."

"Fucking bullshit!" Gideon snaps, he stands from the chair and I see his eyes burn almost like they did that first night when he attacked me and I feel slightly scared of him. "Is all this because of Rick? Is him coming back the reason you have changed your mind? Before the whole Claudia and Bertol thing, I thought things were going great between us, you seemed to want to be around me... I couldn't give a shit if you ran the whole fucking world or if you decided to spend all the rest of your days locked in this shitty hotel room," Gideon starts to raise his voice as his anger grows. "You know what?" he continues. "I feel like a complete fucking idiot. I honestly believed that you truly liked me..."

"I do like you Gideon," I interrupt, "it's just..."

"No!" He stops me. "Let me speak for a change, you have had your chance... You want the truth? I love you so much that it hurts when you are not near me... You drive me wild... When I heard the news that you had died in military custody, my first thoughts were not of revenge or even that you were out of the way and I could try to take power for myself... My first thoughts were that after all these years of being alive, of watching the world change around me and enjoying the life style I had built, that I no longer wanted to be a part of it any more." I swallow, I take a step back as I watch his anger grow. "I knew then that I loved you, that I couldn't bear the thought that you were gone and that I would never see you again. And yes, I might only have known you for a few months, but I was heart broken and I mourned you... I mourned you more than I did my own parents when they were killed." He goes quiet for a moment but I can see his chest is heaving trying to remain relatively calm.

"I'm sorry..." I say quietly.

Gideon grabs hold of the glass that is still sat on top of the drawers and launches it towards the wall. I cower as the glass shatters across the carpet, and I am suddenly consumed with fear.

"You are not sorry. You obviously don't give a shit how I feel at all. Yes! I've done things I am not proud of, but you knew all about that before the first time we fucked. You knew I was a blood thirsty vampire and capable of terrible things. So what has changed?" I stand silent, my heart beating faster as he stands in front of me, I can feel my breathing quiver as my entire body starts to tremble. "Everything you are accusing me of, happened before you came back, before you gave yourself to me willingly, that was not control. That was not my doing, you wanted to fuck me and I did not force you. But now suddenly everything has changed, and I am the bad guy again. Is this what you want to hear?" He shouts at me. I step back more as his anger boils over, I am not sure what to do or say... I feel terrified of him. "Here I am Velvet, I am a fucking monster," he continues "I've slaughtered full family's, I've killed thousands of humans and do I regret it? No! I don't, because I am a vampire and this is who I am. You wanted the truth, so I am going to give it to you," he snarls, stepping towards me. "I've only been in love twice in my entire life on this planet and that is a very fucking long time. The first time was Claudia, and she turned out to be a fucking psycho, the second time is with you." He pauses and laughs at himself. "And it would seem that's my type, because you are so fucked up in the head that no wonder no one has ever loved you before, why would they? You are a fucking head case!" He spits. I start to feel annoyed by what he is saying and without thinking I just snap back.

"How fucking dare you!" I try to shout as my voice quivers. Gideon stops and looks at me. "You wanted honesty from me and I gave it to you. Would you have preferred that I lied to your face?" My body starts to tremble more as I get increasingly angry. "You are a monster Gideon, I knew you were, and for some unknown bastard reason I am totally attracted to you, just your slightest fucking touch makes me go weak at the knees... But you know what? As much as Claudia was a psycho, she made me feel wanted and never once was I scared of her, unlike I am of you." At the mention of Claudia, Gideon moves forward and stands right in front of me, I can see his teeth are bared and my back is pinned up against wall, but I am not the kind of person to back down even though I am beginning to regret ever opening my mouth.

"Don't you dare talk about her that way, she's a monster," Gideon snarls.

"And so are you. You think you are the big bad vampire boss? Then why don't you show me your true colours? You are clearly trying to intimidate me, so instead of being just all bark, show me your bite... Go on, bite me!" I grab the collar of my t-shirt and pull it to the side, exposing my throat to him. "Go on," I shout. "Fucking bite me, give in completely to that blood-lust that I can see in your eyes." As much as I am trying to stand strong, he is so intimidating and all those images flash back in to my mind. I can feel my whole body panicking as my breathing starts to get erratic and I feel my eyes burn. I think about the first time he was consumed and wanted to drain every last drop of my blood from me, I think about when I was with Claudia and even though he loved me, he drank from my wrist and let his blood-lust take over. "What are you waiting for?" I ask. "Bite me, show me the true monster that is inside of you... Do it... Do it and this time finish the job you started that first night, just fucking kill me." I scream. I can see he is taken a back slightly by my words, but they are out there now and I can't stop them. "You should have killed me that night, some days I wish you would have... it would have been easier." My eyes start to fill with tears as I continue. "Everything would have been simple and I could have died happy, I would have been at peace instead of constantly reliving every second of being tortured and beaten, nearly being raped and violated every single day. My life is a complete disaster and I honestly do not know what I did to deserve any of it."

"Is that what you want? For me to kill you?" Gideon asks sarcastically, I can see pure evil flash in his eyes as his gaze roams down to my throat. I know my heart is beating a million miles an hour and with his senses, my blood pounding in my veins is probably near irresistible. I nod my head as tears start to flow down my cheeks.

"Yes," I reply at almost a whisper. "Kill me. I can see it in your eyes that you want to. Everyone would have been better off if I had died that first time, you all would have been happier." Gideon leans in close to me and places his hand on the wall next to my head. My breathing is so shallow now, I know I am terrified of him, I feel weak and useless, every situation I am put in to, I am not strong enough to fight my way out of. I feel like I am a nobody, and maybe it would be better for everyone if I was really dead. It's not like I actually have a future any more. I stare at Gideon, his eyes almost aflame as I lose control of myself and all my fear and emotions come flooding to the surface. My face filled with tears as I try to stifle my sobs, then suddenly Gideon's face changes, and he steps back.

"I'm sorry," he says quietly, he puts his head down and turns his back to me. He takes a deep breath and exhales slowly then places his hands in his jeans pockets. I just stand still, I am not sure what's going on.

"What?" I ask.

"I am sorry that I hurt you," Gideon says softly. "I didn't realise that what I had done to you before I had got to know you as a person, had affected you so much... and until now, I didn't even think that I hadn't actually apologised for it properly." Gideon turns back to face me but avoids making eye contact with me. "I have been a complete arsehole. When I looked in to your eyes right now, you know what I saw?" I shake my head. "I saw fear. You are terrified of me and you have every reason to be." Gideon walks over and sits down on the side of the bed.

"Erm..." I try to speak but no proper words come out.

"You seem so strong and powerful, that I forget how much pain and suffering you have had to endure in such a short amount of time, more than most people experience in their entire lives." He pauses, thinks for a moment then finally looks back up at me. "If I was to ask you some questions, would you promise to continue being honest with me, if I promise to not be an arsehole?" I am slightly hesitant but my body starts to relax and I nod my head. "You have just said something that has got me thinking. When you were taken to the Bird Cage," he starts. My heart skips slightly at just the mention of the place. "What happened to you was horrific. Kerry told me what that bastard did to you, what he tried to do... but when you returned you had marks... On your wrists." He pauses thinking of the right words to say next and I already know which marks he is on about. "Were they off the General as well? Did he give you those marks?" I don't answer, I can't get the words to leave my mouth, instead I just shake my head. Those scars that he is referring to were self-inflicted. "Were things that bad for you that you wanted to kill yourself, that you would rather die than continue on? Did you feel like you literally had no hope left in the world at all and the only way out was for you to take your own life?" I swallow hard as I feel more tears fall down my face.

"Yes," I say quietly. Gideon nods his head then asks another question. I have to force myself to not completely break down crying just at admitting that to him.

"When I was taken and Claudia had you under her thrawl, what did she do to you?" He asks. I shake my head, I can't tell him that. Out of every question in the world, I can't tell him. "Velvet please, you promised," he says gently. I think for a second then nod. If I don't tell him then we can't move forward.

"At first I could feel myself fighting her in my head, the more I tried to resist her, the more I could feel her forcing her way in and the pain was unbearable. She put thoughts and images of you in my mind that are still there now, that's part of the reason why I can't think straight. I can't tell what was real and what was because of her. I don't know what is reality sometimes." I take a breath and wipe the tears from my face as Gideon patiently watches me. "I didn't want to hate you, you saved me from those men at the orphanage and you showed me passion and respect. I was so drawn to you as I saw a deep kindness in your soul and I craved to know everything about you. But she made me see you as the monster, and she made me fall for her, I didn't even know who you were any more by the end of it." I pause, thinking that Gideon will say something and that would be enough information for him, but he nods his head and encourages me to continue. "She made me want her, she did things to me that I wouldn't have done in reality... And I did things to her that... the worst part is though that when it was happening I enjoyed it. I couldn't get enough of her, when we played with each other, when she drank from me, when we had sex... But now I hate myself for that, I feel dirty as I know she was doing it to get back at you. She used me to feed on, Bertol also, and I had no self-control over any of it. It's like my body and mind were not my own and it scares me that it could happen again and that I would do unspeakable things."

"You had sex with her?" Gideon asks quietly, I nod slowly expecting him to flip out again, but he sighs and looks down at the floor.

"I'm sorry Gideon, the things I did and said..."

"I know," he interrupts. "It wasn't your fault. None of this is your fault and you have nothing to apologise for. You have every right to hate me, I guess I didn't realise any of this. It's no wonder you are so guarded and you are so afraid to get close to anyone." Gideon looks up at me and smiles slightly. "Last question, I promise. How can I help you? Tell me what I can do to make you feel batter, to make you trust me or just not be so scared of getting close to someone." I shake my head as I continue to stand with my back against the wall.

"I don't know. I just wanted you to understand what was on my mind, I am sorry for doubting your intentions or accusing you of things. I guess, over time things might get better, so I just need you to be patient with me and know that I am fucked up a bit." I try to force a smile as I remain rooted to the spot. Gideon sighs and nods his head.

"I can do that. As long as you are always honest with me, if you have any doubts about me or you think I am being a douche bag, then please tell me. Don't bottle everything up, I want to help you... I care about you too much that I don't want to see you hurting." Gideon stands up and looks at me. "I know that you don't like the words, but I do love you, that is not going to change any time soon and that is the complete truth."

"OK," I reply. I feel a bit stupid in thinking that he wanted power and was using me, but I am glad I told him what was in my head and got it all out in the open. Just saying all that feels like a massive weight has been lifted off my shoulders.

"What do you want to do now?" Gideon asks cautiously. Maybe he expects me to ask him to leave, but I still feel so strongly about him even though we just had a massive fight. Just looking at him right now, I can't deny the feelings I have towards him.

"Did you say there was a muffin and a bagel?" I ask.

Gideon smiles and nods then heads over to the drawers and picks up the small brown bag with the food inside. I sit on the side of the bed and pick up the coffee that I put on the bedside cabinet and take another drink, it's a bit cooler now so it no longer burns on its way down. He hands me the bag, I take out the bagel and take a bite as Gideon returns to sit in the chair.

"I guess after all that, finding out Rick was alive tipped you over the edge?"

Gideon asks as he picks up his coffee. I just nod, I am very torn about Rick. On one hand I have a parent who's alive but on the other I am apprehensive about learning more, as I don't know where things will lead with him. "When you are ready I'll tell you whatever you want to know. No more secrets and lies between us." I nod my head again, I am not ready to talk about Rick yet, maybe when I've dealt with other stuff first I'll be ready to know more. "Is there anything else you want to say or ask whilst we are getting everything out in the open?" Gideon asks whilst he drinks. I think for a moment before answering.

"What happened to Claudia? Is she still out there somewhere?" I feel a little bad at mentioning her name again but I want to know if she is a threat to me. Gideon nods at me and sighs.

"After you punched her in the face she must have slipped out without anyone noticing her. I'm going to guess she will be pretty pissed off that Bertol is dead though... Speaking of Bertol, you cut his fucking head off and just stood there holding it covered in his blood," Gideon smiles to himself.

"Yeah, I bet that made a great first impression of me in front of Rick," I laugh nervously and Gideon smirks at me.

"Can we continue the honestly thing?" I nod my head, curious as to what he is going to say. "Seeing you like that, watching you literally destroying him... Was pretty damn hot. I know that will probably sound vile, but I am a vampire after all and watching you murder him... it kind of turned me on... A lot. So much so that these last few days that you have not been around, I have fantasized about fucking you whilst we were rolling in his blood. I wanted to lick his life force off your naked body and revel in his death." The room falls quiet and Gideon doesn't take his gaze off me, I can already see the glint in his eyes as he speaks about this. That's a hell of a lot to take in, far beyond anything that I would consider kinky. After a few moments I shake my head and laugh.

"You are a fucking weirdo," I say playfully.

I can understand slightly where he is coming from though. After I killed Bertol I felt powerful and it was as though nothing could stop me. It was totally thrilling. I'm not going to lie but feeling like that is so euphoric, however it's still an unusual thing for me to get my head around as it frightens me how much I enjoy the kill.

"Don't tell me that you don't feel it also, the excitement and thrill of the kill, being totally in control of the situation. The power that runs through you as you take a life is intoxicating," Gideon says slowly. I see his eyes flash with lust and I just sit silent on the bed staring at him. I do feel it, I've felt it every time and with

Bertol it was amazing and I loved it.

"I suppose," I manage to say, I'm trying to play it cool.

"Tell me how it felt killing Bertol," Gideon grins, I watch as his breathing starts to get heavy just thinking about the sight of me clutching his bloody head. "Tell me how taking his life made you feel inside." I place my cup on the bedside cabinet and get up from the bed as he watches my every move.

"Are we still doing the total honestly thing?" I ask.

"Always," Gideon replies quickly, eager to hear what I have to say. I stand for a moment and think, then I sigh and just let it all out.

"When he attacked and bit me I felt my flesh rip from my throat and I thought I was going to die, he was determine to kill me and that was all he was focused on. But also in that moment I had clarity and I knew that if I killed him first, that I would survive... Plunging that knife in to his neck felt like a release, as though all my worries had gone, then when he fell to his knees in front of me I leant down and told him I was going to kill him. I told him exactly what I was going to do to him and that he had no way of stopping me. At that point he couldn't fight back, he couldn't hurt me any more and that made me feel invincible. I felt every second of the blade hacking away at his spinal cord, then when I detached his head and kicked his body away I felt complete, as though that was who I was truly meant to be... And I liked it. I like the kill, I enjoy feeling their blood flow over my hands and feeling their life force cover my skin..." Gideon stands up from the chair and walks towards me as I continue. "I liked watching the life disappear from his eyes, but he isn't the only one, it's not the first time that I thrived after a kill. Even if it was in self-defence I welcome the feeling of killing someone with my hands... Life is a miracle and taking that away from someone makes me briefly feel like a God." Gideon stands behind me, he wraps his arm around my waist and starts to gently kiss my neck whilst I speak. "The amount of power I felt coursing through my veins when I killed Bertol was amazing."

"Does it scare you?" Gideon whispers in my ear.

"Yes," I reply. "But it also excites me. I know I should be scared of the things I could do, I feel like the more I learn about myself, then the more I feel like my power comes from darkness and that scares me because I am afraid that if I let go completely that I won't ever be the same again. I do want to know more, I want to feel that sheer dominating power inside of me when I take a life. Because I know that if I can hurt them, then maybe I won't hurt as much inside any more." Gideon unbuttons the front of my jeans and starts to play with the edges of my underwear beneath.

"Does that feeling you get when you kill, turn you on?" He asks. I can feel his icy breath cascade down my back as he continues to tease my neck with his lips, his body pressed against my back as I feel my heart rate increasing more with every slight movement.

"Yes, it does," I reply truthfully. Gideon slips his hand down the front of my panties and quickly, his fingers find their way towards my clit. I moan slightly under his touch as my legs quiver. "The thrill of doing that makes me feel so fucking horny."

"Then you know how it felt for me seeing you do that to Bertol," he whispers.

I moan again as his fingers play more firmly and I feel myself getting immensely turned on just by talking about this subject. I thought that this feeling was something I had to ignore, that it was wrong of me to like it, but maybe I should be embracing it instead.

"Watching you take his life, this vampire who had slaughtered multiple thousands of humans with no regrets, who took innocent lives, who only wanted to control human kind for food. Was killed by you, your soul burns brighter than any I've ever seen and watching you take his head made me want you so much it hurt," Gideon says as he slips his fingers down towards my pussy. I can feel his cock pressed against me as he plunges his fingers inside of me, the feeling of pure lust rising in me, making my knees almost go weak.

"Shit," I moan as he roughly stimulates me, making my entire body shake against his hand. "And talking about it, remembering how powerful I felt and knowing how much it turned you the fuck on... it makes me want you to fuck me right now," I say confidently.

Gideon pauses for a second to process what I just said then forcefully pulls down my jeans and underwear. He pushes me forward so that I can lean on to the bed then I hear him unzip his trousers from behind me as he places his hand on my back making me bend over for him. Gideon runs his hand over my ass then slides it between my legs, briefly going back to my clit, but this time it is not playful, his firm touch making my breath catch. I moan again as it aches to be played with then his fingers move and slip inside my opening, checking that I am already soaking wet for him. He moves closer to me and his fingers are quickly replaced by his now rock solid dick, there's no more teasing now, instead he rams his cock in to my moist hole.

"Oh fuck!" The words escape me as he catches me off guard, the sudden penetration setting my loins on fire.

Gideon places his hands on my hips and begins to fuck me hard, every thrust he makes getting deeper and stronger. I am so turned on right now that I am begging for that quick release, I grab the sheets on the bed in front of me and almost cry out as Gideon pulls me towards him more forcefully. His cock dominating my pussy as the overwhelming sensation of pleasure grows fast. I can hear Gideon groaning behind me as he gives in to his lust, his fingers digging in to my hips, sending little pangs of pain through me that only make me want him to go harder.

"Oh... My... Fucking... God!" I manage to say between gasps for air, I am already so close to the edge that it becomes super intense, the louder my cries of ecstasy, the more aroused Gideon seems to become which only makes him fuck me faster, giving in to those carnal urges. I feel myself start to tighten around his cock as I explode and orgasm hard, I cry out, my legs start to shake and my entire body bucking as Gideon holds me in place.

"Fuck," I hear Gideon groan through gritted teeth as he cums hard inside of me, he continues to fuck me until we can't take it any more, and we are both feel spent and satisfied.

In that moment a quick fix is all we needed to relieve the sexual tension between us and clear the air after our argument. Gideon steps back and takes a moment to sort himself out as I get up from the bed, pull my jeans up and head for the bathroom without saying anything.

I clean myself up and fasten my jeans then look at myself in the mirror. I definitely have some trust issues and I still have some things that I need to work through but Gideon has been so honest and open with me today that it's so hard to not like him. I sigh deeply and smile at myself, there is no denying that he makes me feel alive and totally wanted. There's a definite magnetism that draws us to each other and maybe it might be fun to see where that all leads. I leave the bathroom and Gideon is sat on the edge of the bed waiting for me to return, he looks over and smiles as I enter.

"Well that was unexpected," I say smiling back at him.

"Does that count as make up sex?" Gideon replies playfully, he holds out his hand and gestures for me to go over to him, as I approach, he grabs me and pulls me towards him, making me straddle his lap. I giggle slightly and lean down to kiss him as his hands gently squeeze my ass cheeks. I playfully nibble on Gideon's lip as we hear a low buzzing sound coming from the top of the drawers then I pull back and smile at him as I move and let him get up from the bed. He grabs his hoodie and answers the mobile phone in his pocket. "Hello?... Yeah I'm fine, how did things go at the meeting?" Gideon watches me as I head over to the other side of the room and start to pick up the shards of glass that are scattered across the bedroom floor. "That's not good, we will need to try to control the situation before it gets out of hand... No, don't worry about it, it's OK, I'll deal with it... I'll head back soon and I'll get the ball rolling... OK, bye." Gideon hangs up the phone and puts it in his jeans pocket.

"Is everything alright?" I ask him as I continue to pick up the glass.

"Just some business I need to take care of." Gideon pulls his hoodie over his head. "I'd like it if you got out of this place." I look up at him and think for a moment, now that I've talked things through with him, I don't feel as bad. I've had some time away, so I suppose I should head back home and see what is going on in the world.

"I suppose I should really head back to the bunker and check in with Kerry," I reply.

"No, I mean, I want you to come back with me, back to Newcastle. I want you close and I don't think I could spend so much time away from you if you went back to the bunker instead," Gideon grins at me.

"OK." I nod. "Why not? I was kind of getting board of looking at these hotel room walls anyway and it would be nice to spend some proper time with you, I guess," I smile at him. "If you need to leave then go ahead, I have to pack my stuff, check out and I can follow you up." Gideon nods his head as I stand up, he walks over towards me and places his hand on my cheek.

"Is everything OK between us now?" He asks and I nod my head, I've got what I wanted off my chest. And thankfully it has cleared my mind, I don't feel confused or stressed any more so whatever happened during that argument seemed to work wonders for me. Gideon leans down and gently kisses my forehead then turns to leave. "I'll see you later then, hopefully." I nod again then he exits the room and closes the door behind him.

I take my time and clean the room up before I check out, I thank the owners for allowing me to stay then head to the car with all my stuff. It's raining as I leave the hotel, and I am already exhausted with the lack of sleep. I did contemplate trying to get some rest before I drove back, but I am actually feeling quite excited about getting to know Gideon better and chilling out without any distractions, like people wanting to kill us and things. I throw my stuff in the boot and get in the car, as much as I am excited I am also a little nervous about heading back to the North

East. I don't want people asking loads of questions and stuff about where I have been and what happened to me, I am sure I will be fine though. I turn the key in the ignition and the car makes a strange noise, I try again but the engine just ticks over and doesn't start.

"Fuck my life, stupid shitting car," I shout at myself. I give it a minute and try again but the engine ticks over and refuses to start. I sigh and place my hands on the steering wheel then close my eyes. This could only happen to me, it's like I am attracted to crap cars. I am the shit car woman, and I am also the place old cars go to die. I jump slightly as there is a knock on the driver's side window. I open my eyes and look to see Gideon standing in the rain watching me. I roll down the window and smile.

"Car troubles?" He asks trying to keep a straight face.

"I thought you had left already?" I reply.

"I did, but then I came back because I wanted to make sure you were actually alright," he smirks and looks at the car. "Plus you drive a piece of shit and I am not surprised you're having problems starting it." I shake my head at him.

"You mean compared to you who has a limo drive him everywhere?" I tease.

"Will you let me give you a lift?" He smiles at me waiting for an answer then I nod my head, and he goes around the back of the car and gets all of my stuff out of the boot.

"Stupid fucking car." I say as I get out and slam the door. I quickly head to his car that is now parked behind mine as the rain is getting heavier, I look up and stop in my tracks. "Holy shit!" I say looking at his car.

"What?" Gideon asks, confused.

"No way is this your car?" I look at the classic muscle car. I recognise it instantly.

The front of the car is a blood-red colour, as it goes further back it gets darker and changes to black, the alloy wheels are cherry red and the whole thing is sexy as fuck. I know that I have seen it before at the club, but I didn't even think that this thing of magnificent beauty could be his.

"Oh yeah, It's a 1969 Chevy Camaro, I had it imported when it was first released then gave her a custom paint job. I also customised her interior and layout, even though I have been driving since cars were invented I never could get away with a left-hand drive. I don't always travel in the limo, you know," Gideon laughs as I stand staring at its gorgeousness. "Are you going to get in? You are getting soaking in this rain." I nod my head as Gideon casually gets in the car, I walk to the passenger side running my hand along its bonnet, admiring her curves, she is amazing. I open the door and climb in, the seats are covered in dark red leather and every inch of the car looks like it's been specially designed to match Gideon's favourite colours. I smile as I see a set of black and red dice handing from the mirror.

"Are you OK?" Gideon asks as he watches me sit wide-eyed.

"I think that I am in love with your car," I say looking at the black dash board and up to date sound system.

"Do you like the car more than you like me?" He asks playfully.

"Yes, most definitely," I reply as we both laugh. Gideon starts the car, the engine revs, and he sets off for home.

Chapter Three

"You OK?" Gideon asks. "You've been very quiet this whole way up, you look quite exhausted and I think you managed to sleep a little, you kept nodding off." I nod my head, I've been lost in my own thoughts for most of the journey that I kind of forgot to speak. Plus I am exhausted, I have felt tired constantly since I found out Rick was alive and now I think the lack of sleep is starting to catch up with me.

"Yeah, I'm fine, just a bit tired and day dreaming a little," I smile at him as he continues to drive. I readjust my position and sit up in the chair, I yawn and rub my eyes before looking around to see that we are not too far from home already, I must have slept most of the journey without realising it.

"Care to share those day dreams of yours?" Gideon asks. I am not sure because I don't want him thinking that I'm stupid with all my weird questions, but we did say that we would be totally honest with each other.

"So, you know, vampires?" I say. I already know that my words sound idiotic, but they make Gideon chuckle slightly.

"Yes, I know vampires, in fact I think I know them quite well," he replies whilst trying to hide his smirk.

"I know that you, Tristen and Emily were all born this way... but is it true, like in the movies, that a human can turn in to a vampire?" I feel a little embarrassed asking, but he wanted to know what was in my head.

"You have a lot of strange questions running through your mind," Gideon smiles then nods his head at me. "It is possible, but the majority of the time, the changing process is deadly and very few people survive the transformation."

"Obviously you don't become a vampire just by being bitten, so how does it work?" I ask more.

"Why do you want to know?" He glances at me perplexed.

"Just curious. I have a lot of questions and the books that I have can only give me so many answers," I say curiously.

"Well, erm..." Gideon struggles to find the words. "It's been quite a while since I... it's not something that is common practice these days." I give him my best innocent looking face to encourage him to tell me. He smiles and nods then thinks of what to say. "Doing it, it's not easy. A vampires blood would have to flood their system, and when I say flood I mean they would have to drink a large quantity of vampire blood at the same time that the vampire would drink from them. It's kind of like exchanging life forces and it must be done mutually, so with consent. It is very difficult to force a human to consume pints of blood when it is against their will. Doing it in this way is sort of like transferring a virus, the vampires blood would consume their system, it is painful and the majority of people don't survive it. Even some of the ones that do get through the initial process can go insane or lose their minds... That is the basic answer, anyway."

The car falls silent as I nod my head and think about his words, I guess that would explain why the vampires don't just turn all the humans and build an army. They probably don't want to risk killing off their food source.

"Are you hungry? I can get Rose to make you something when we get back if you like?" Gideon says after a few minutes trying to change the subject. I hadn't thought about it, but now he has mentioned it I am pretty starving.

"That would be great," I reply. I'm still not sure how things are going to work here though, I don't think that I am ready for a relationship, so I hope Gideon doesn't expect me to move in with him or anything. I like my own space and there are still things I need to work through.

Once we get closer to Gideon's club I start to feel a little nervous, as though there is that pressure being placed on my shoulders again to be that person everyone wants me to be. All I want is a quiet uneventful life but I don't think that will ever happen now. Gideon drives straight past the front of his club and I look around confused.

"Where are you going?" I ask. Gideon smiles at himself as he turns down a small alleyway.

"You don't think that I am just going to park out front again, do you?" I sit back and think about that, I remember when I came back after Gideon thought I was dead and I saw his car, basically dumped outside the club. I dwell on that for a moment, I wonder if he heard about my death when he was out and literally abandoned his car when he got home. That would explain the several parking notices and fit with him mourning me.

We pull up to a large set of steel security doors, Gideon pushes a button on the dash board and waits a few seconds, the large doors start to open and Gideon drives inside. We drive down a dark ramp in to a brightly lit garage, I am in awe as we are greeted by multiple cars and bikes. I notice Tristen's black porch to the left amongst different sports cars and muscle cars.

"Are all these yours?" I ask in amazement.

"Mine and Tristen's, we both have our own taste in cars but it's a beautiful collection." Gideon pulls in to a space near a lift and swiftly gets out.

"These must have cost an absolute fortune," I say as I get out and just stand looking at them all. The garage is big enough to hold 40 maybe 50 vehicles easy.

"Good thing I have multiple fortunes to spare then," Gideon smirks as he opens the boot and grabs my bags then starts to make his way to the lift. "Are you coming in or are you going to spend the rest of the day looking at all the cars?"

"Is that an option?" I smile wildly at him, then just stand for a moment and take in the amount of beauty that surrounds me. Gideon shakes his head, I give him a fake sad face then reluctantly head over to the lift, and we get in. This lift is slightly different to the one I've been in before, there are a lot more floor selections, Gideon notices my puzzled look and explains.

"There's not just one lift that goes up to the apartment, in fact you have only seen a fraction of it. I'll give you a tour later on." He presses the top button as he talks. "I think you have literally only seen my bedroom and the living room so far, we have a games room, conference suite, mini spa..."

"You have a spa?" I interrupt.

"Yes. Complete with hot tub and steam room." The lift doors open and I follow him out, we are in a part of the apartment I have never been before but the decoration matches the scheme in the living room. I follow him up a couple of stairs and along a corridor until we are in the main room.

"The place can be a bit of a maze," Gideon says as he dumps my bags on the sofa then I hear the kitchen door open.

"Velvet?" Kerry almost squeals at me, and she runs over then gives me a hug. "I've missed you, Gideon phoned ahead and told us that you were coming back."

"Us?" I ask confused, I glance up and Greg and Tristen are stood behind her.

"Nice to see you again Velvet, hope you are well?" Greg asks in his usual manner.

"I'm fine thank you," I reply nodding my head slightly. I notice that Tristen still seems a bit awkward around me, but I look over to him and smile. He stands back and glances at Gideon as thought needing approval, then smiles back at me.

"Right!" Gideon says as he claps his hands together, breaking the tension. "What do you want to eat?" I smile and look at Kerry before turning to Gideon.

"Actually, I could murder a kebab," I reply. "With garlic sauce and a few drinks?"

"Night in and a catch up, it is," Gideon smiles. "The club is closed tonight, we only open 4 nights a week now as we are getting too busy and I have other things I need to do, so whatever you ladies want to do, we will do." I smile at Gideon and look around the room.

"We need drinks first," Kerry says excitedly as she grabs my hand and pulls me towards the sofa, we sit down as the boys stand looking at us.

"OK then, Tristen would you mind grabbing some bottles and stuff from the bar, Greg it looks like the ladies want a takeaway, so that's your job... I'll get Rose to get the guest room sorted, I assume you will want to stay the night, Kerry?" Kerry nods her head as I lean forward and grab the remote from the coffee table and turn on the TV then we let the guys do their stuff.

"Things got a little awkward after you left the bunker," Kerry says once everyone leaves the room. "Rick seems nice enough though, for being your dead dad and all."

"Yeah, sorry about that," I say quietly.

"Don't be, I could feel how uncomfortable you were. I am not surprised you left, I probably would have done the same," Kerry replies. "Anyway let's change the subject, what's happening between you and Gideon? Because I'm not too thrilled about him at the moment, everything you told me about him, how much he hurt you and stuff, he sounds like bad news."

"He told me that he loved me," I say cautiously. I know Kerry doesn't really approve of him, but she doesn't know him like I do.

"And? Do you... You know." I can see she is fishing for information, but I am not sure what to say to her.

"I told him no," I inform her. "But I do like him, very much and I know that you have your reservations about him, I had them too..."

"I just don't want to see you get hurt, especially not by a man like him," Kerry cuts me off. I know what she is saying but I do have strong feelings towards

Gideon. I can't just ignore that.

"I'll be careful, I promise," I say trying to reassure her. "Just give him a chance, maybe if you got to know him a little better you will see he isn't all bad."

"I can't make any promises that I will just magically like him overnight, but I am willing to possibly get to know the guy." I can hear the reluctance in her voice. "But mind, if he hurts you in any way, I will kill him. I am not even joking, I will ram a wooden stake where the sun doesn't shine." I laugh at her comments, I know she means well, and she is just trying to protect me, but I am a big girl and I can make my own choices in life. Kerry thinks for a second before changing the subject again.

"You would have been well impressed with me finding you in Wales, I figured after I managed to find you and Gideon it was worth a shot and it was so weird," she explains. "It's like I could sense where you were, I've been reading up on some of the books I found in the bunker and apparently the closer a witch is with their familiar the stronger bond they have. It mentions a psychic and empath link, which makes sense because I've always been able to feel when you are sad or happy and I always knew when there was something wrong even thought you never spoke about it." We both look back over towards the kitchen doors as Gideon and Rose come out, Rose smiles at me then heads towards the bedrooms as Gideon joins us on the sofa which signals the end of that conversation.

We quickly lose track of time. We have a really fun night, we watch crap movies, there is a lot of drinking and laughs, it is nice to just kick back and have fun instead of worrying about the real world. Tristen finally seemed more relaxed around me and Greg and Kerry seem to be getting on very well, considering the fact he did actually kill her, she seems quite fond of him. I must remember to mention that the next time she pulls me up about Gideon.

"I am so tired, I'm done... need to sleep," Kerry says slumped in the corner of the sofa, I get up and help to pull her to her feet. "I love you," She says slurring her words slightly, I just smile as she starts to walk towards the rooms. She stops for a second and looks back at Greg. The whole room knows exactly what that look means, Greg notices her and nods.

"I'll make sure you get to your room safely," Greg's says as he stands from the sofa and walks over to take Kerry's arm. I flash her a look, and she makes a frowning face at me.

"Don't look at me with those eyes," She says, "all judging me and stuff."

"I didn't say anything," I tease and smile as they head off to the bedroom together. I turn back to the sofa, trying to stay on my feet then pick up my glass from the table and take a drink. Gideon and Tristen both sit at opposite sides of the sofas, then Tristen suddenly jumps up.

"I should leave, stuff to do... and things," Tristen says awkwardly.

"You don't have to go," I say as I stand drinking.

"No, I do. I'll give you guys some space." He doesn't look at me again as he heads out of the room. I feel really drunk, but I am not ready to go to sleep just yet. Gideon sits with a near empty glass of whiskey in his hand, watching my every move. He does that a lot, just watches. I wonder what goes through his mind, he is always so difficult to read.

"So!" I say breaking the silence. "Are you going to show me this hot tub of yours?" Gideon smiles slightly and shakes his head.

"It needs time to be prepared, by which time I am afraid you might be asleep because I can see you are already looking exhausted and you have drank a lot," he says casually.

"So, you are saying no to me?" I tease him, I notice he raises an eyebrow at my statement. "I might have drank a lot but I have these amazing super powers that I have found counteract the effects of alcohol very quickly... I don't even get hangovers any more... and don't worry about me looking exhausted, I promise I have all the energy you would need." I flash him a cheeky smile. What I said was true though, ever since I have gained my new-found abilities, I have noticed alcohol having less of an effect on me. I still get mortal drunk but it doesn't last as long. I think it might be something to do with the healing abilities.

"Well then, what did you have in mind?" Gideon asks as he smiles back at me. I nod my head then walk over to the side where there is full bottle of champagne in an ice bucket and 2 glasses, Gideon looks confused as he doesn't remember bringing those in earlier. I pick up the bottle and the glasses and turn back to him.

"I was really very interested in your hot tub... Good thing I asked Rose to sort this out before she went to bed then. So are you going to show me where it is or am I going to have to go find it myself and drink this alone?" I tease. Gideon smiles and then gets up from the sofa, I playfully bite my lip as he walks over towards me and takes the bottle from my hand.

"It would be rude of me to say no," Gideon says softly then leans down and gently kisses my lips for a brief second then looks in to my eyes and smiles. He takes a hold of my hand then leads me out of the room.

He was right about the place being like a maze. We head away from the direction of the bedrooms and past the kitchen, he leads me in to a small room that is lined with wood and then through it and on to a small balcony over-looking the city. The large hot tub sits in the centre and it bubbles away, the steam rising in the cold night air. I place the glasses on the side of the tub and step away from Gideon slightly. I feel really playful right now and because I am so drunk I lose all my inhibitions. I make eye contact and slowly start to undress in front of him, I see him swallow hard as he watches me without saying a word, taking in every curve of my body. Once I am undressed fully, I stand naked in front of him, I let his eyes roam over my body then I turn away, climb in to the tub and lower myself in to the warm water.

"Care to join me?" I ask playfully as I smile at Gideon. He slowly nods his head and I watch him as he nibbles on his bottom lip in anticipation. He quickly gets undressed and joins me in the water, he pops the cork from the bottle and pours two drinks then hands me one of the glasses. Gideon sits opposite me on the carved out seats and smiles.

"I like this version of you," Gideon says softly.

"What the seriously drunk version?" I laugh at myself as Gideon shakes his head.

"No, the version of you that seems happy," Gideon smiles at me as I take a drink, I don't usually drink this sort of thing because it goes straight to my head but it seemed like a fun thing to do at the time.

"Well I have my moments," I reply smirking at him. I down the rest of the glass then lean over to the side and fill it back up before returning to my seat. The warm water flows over my skin as I start to enjoy the ripples, watching them splash over my breasts. Gideon doesn't take his eyes off me, even when he takes a sip of his drink. "Do you eat normal food?" I say out of the blue, the thought just crossed my mind and came straight of my mouth.

"Sometimes, but it is not essential to survival," Gideon replies.

"Then why? And why do you drink?" I am really inquisitive all of a sudden but thankfully Gideon just smiles at me.

"Why not? I still enjoy the taste of fine food and drinks. And if I consume enough alcohol sometimes it dulls my pain... Like the time I thought I had lost you," Gideon says then takes another drink.

"Well I am here now," I say playfully. "I'll try not to die again." Gideon laughs at me slightly.

"I don't get you sometimes," he says gently as he watches me. "You say you don't want anything serious, that you are scared to get close to someone... but yet you are so playful and like this around me. You are so fucking sexy and you know that you drive me wild." He doesn't take his eyes off me as I drink the champagne again and place my glass down on the side then slowly wade towards him until I am almost stood between his legs.

"Can a girl not just have a bit of fun?" I say as I lean forward and run my hand up his thigh towards his crotch.

"You know I want more than just a bit of fun, Velvet," Gideon sighs. "I want you to be mine, completely. I don't want to just play games, I want what is between us to become serious, I want you as my partner," Gideon tries to explain as I lean closer to him, my hand skimming his manhood.

"Is me saying that I like you a lot, not enough for you?" I ask playfully. Gideon licks his lips as I bend forward and seductively kiss his chest.

"For now it is, but I want you to love me, the way I love you... I need you." I look up and stare in to his eyes. My feelings towards him are extremely strong but I don't know what it all means yet.

"Then for now, at least... we have fun," I smile at him and lean in, my lips meeting his. My hand starts to play with him beneath the warm water, making him grow for me, making him want me. Gideon pulls away slightly before speaking again.

"You are very drunk, Velvet. Maybe we should discuss things more tomorrow... I don't want you to think that I am taking advantage of you," he says gently. I smile and shake my head as I run my hand up and down his shaft. Even though he is holding himself back from me, I know he is getting very aroused as he starts to get hard.

"I'm horny, and I am the one taking advantage of you," I say as I hear Gideon moan slightly at my touch. He smiles as he watches me lean in more and slowly kiss his neck as I work his cock with my hand under the water. His head falls back as he relaxes and enjoys the experience then I playfully bite his neck, and he groans louder, he trails his fingers across my shoulders as I caress him. After a few minutes Gideon shuffles under my touch, starting to tire of the teasing and speaks to me.

"Come here," he says breathy. I look up at Gideon, and he smiles then places his hands around my waist and pulls me towards him. I straddle him as he positions me in his lap and makes me slowly ease myself down on to him. He looks deep in to my eyes as my pussy envelopes him fully. "Oh God, you feel so good," he says as I slowly start to rock my hips back and forth on his cock.

Gideon grips my hips and takes control of the motions as I moan, he leans his head forward and kisses my breasts then takes my left nipple in his mouth and gently nibbles on it. My breath hitches as a tiny shooting pain ebbs from it beneath his lips. Gideon moves one of his hands around to my lower back and pulls me closer towards him, making his dick go deeper inside of me. I lean back in the water as I fuck him, letting his shaft rub inside, making me grow more sensitive with every thrust I make.

As the passion starts to build between us, I can feel Gideon becoming increasingly restless. I know he likes to be in control, and he is forceful as he always likes to get what he wants. I continue to grind on him, then without warning Gideon wraps his arms around me and moves, still holding me on him, he kneels in the water. I wrap my legs around his waist as he pushes my back up against the side of the hot tub. Gideon starts to fuck me as his lips move to mine, his tongue slips inside my mouth and explores every part of me. My hand trails up the back of his neck and plays through his hair as we kiss deeply through moans of growing pleasure.

I gasp as the feeling of Gideon inside of me starts to grow more intense, my chest begins to heave, he stops kissing me for a second and just watches me become consumed in the moment. When I look back to him, I can see his eyes burn with lust, I can feel it with the way he drives his cock in to me deeper as he tries to divert his thoughts to just screwing me instead of thinking about tasting me. I know exactly what he wants though, so without saying anything I tilt my head to the side and give him free access to my neck. I think I like the feeling of having him bite me as much as he likes to do it. Gideon grins at me then leans in and starts to caress my neck gently with his lips. I can feel the tip of his fangs skimming across my skin then his mouth gently kisses his chosen spot.

I cry out as Gideon finally bites me, a fresh wave of pleasure and pain washing over me, my skin suddenly feels very sensitive to the touch, I can feel my own blood start to flow as my entire body becomes flush and I feel increasingly warm.

"Oh fuck, Gideon." I breathe as he thrusts a little harder, my head starts to spin and I close my eyes, my whole being shaking.

I let Gideon take over me completely, allowing him to do exactly what he wants, he dominates my mind and body as I give myself to him. All the sensations swirl and play together making me quickly hurtle towards orgasm, intense pleasure both building in my core and from him drinking from me is all consuming. I grab on to Gideon's shoulders to steady myself as he senses that I am getting close and starts to thrust more forcefully against the side of the tub. The room starts to spin around us as I go light-headed and try to ignore how drunk I am and instead focus on the feelings I am experiencing inside.

I cry out again as I feel my core burn, Gideon raises from my neck and watches me cum as he continues his rhythm, that in itself makes him more turned on as I can see him getting close also. I almost hold my breath, feeling euphoric as I orgasm for him, surrendering to him completely. Eventually Gideon groans loudly as he explodes, thrusting more fiercely as he empties himself in me.

When he stops my chest heaves through trying to control my own breathing. I close my eyes again as I go dizzy, the alcohol is starting to kick my ass and I lean forward slightly and rest my head on Gideon's shoulder as I start to relax, I am so tired, I don't think Gideon drank too much from me, maybe I am just exhausted.

He just holds me close for a few minutes, letting me rest, enjoying having me close to him then I feel him gently run his fingers through my hair.

"Hey?" Gideon says softly after a little while, I am so comfortable that I just moan at him to acknowledge his words. "You can't fall asleep here."

"I'm just resting my eyes," I say wearily. I am suddenly really sleepy and my eyes are as heavy as lead.

"Come on, I think it's time for bed," Gideon says as he stands up and lifts me out of the water. "Try to stand here for one second." He lifts me over the side and places me on the ground as I struggle to keep my eyes open. I have to force myself not to fall asleep as I stand on the spot. He quickly pulls on his boxers then grabs a big towel from the side bench and wraps me in it, then scoops me up. I cuddle in to Gideon as he carries me back to his room, but I think I fall asleep before I get to the bed because I can't remember anything else after that.

The next thing I know, I'm lying naked in Gideon's bed and my head is pounding. I groan as I roll over and feel sick. Fuck my life! How much did I drink last night? I can't even remember half of the night and have no clue how I got to bed. I open my eyes and squint, it's not bright in the room but my eyes hurt and every time I move my head I think that I am going to throw up.

I manage to drag my ass out from between the blankets, throw on my jeans and T-shirt that have been left on the bottom of the bed for me and head to the bathroom in Gideon's room. I turn on the light, stop, close my eyes and then turn it off again, it's far too bright. I do what I need to do then give my face a wash to try to wake myself up before heading towards the living room. The apartment is empty, so I flop on to the sofa and just lie there trying not to die from my hangover, although this would just be my luck after I bragged to Gideon last night about how I don't seem to get hangovers any more. It must be karma.

I hear a groan and look across the room to see Kerry stumble in holding her head.

"Do I look as shit as you do?" I say as I notice her. Kerry looks at me then nods before slumping on the opposite sofa.

"Yes, in fact I think you look more shit than me." She tilts her head back and closes her eyes.

"Awesome," I say yawning.

We both just wallow in silence for a while, I think I must have fallen back to sleep, which isn't a bad thing, but my eyes dart open as I hear someone move in the room and look up to see Gideon standing over me. He tries not to laugh as I wipe drool off my chin, I must have dribbled whilst I slept.

"Good afternoon," Gideon says as he sits down on the coffee table in front of me. I just groan at him, I look over to Kerry who is also now awake again and rubbing her eyes.

"What's so good about it?" I ask sarcastically as I try to sit up, my head is still killing me but at least I don't feel as sick any more.

"What happened to you saying you don't get hungover?" Gideon smirks, I groan at him again and give him the dirtiest look in the world.

"You are enjoying this aren't you?" I say whilst I roll my eyes at him.

"Slightly," he smiles more. "We need to talk though."

"What's wrong?" I ask, I am a little worried what he wants to speak about.

"Well for starters I'm kicking you two out," Gideon says bluntly, I seem to sober up very quickly at those words, I feel like I have done something very wrong. "Don't worry, I can see the look on your face but I have my reasons so just hear me out. I'm not saying that you are cramping my style, but I have too much work to do and I don't have time to deal with hungover ladies lying around my home," he smiles as he takes some folded up paper out of his back pocket and hands it to me.

"What's this?" I ask as I unfold it and try to read what it says, but my eyes are still blurry and the words look like tiny squiggles. Gideon hands me a pen and turns the page then points to a line near the bottom.

"Just need you to sign there, please," he instructs. I can't be bothered to argue, so I do a bit of a signature and hand it back to him. He nods at me then gets up, places the paper back in to his pocket then places a set of keys on the table in front of me.

"What are they for?" I ask, I glance to Kerry as she sits watching him.

"I have a couple of empty properties, the bunker is a little cramped and far away from here, so I thought you might like to use this one of mine. It's only a few streets away and it's your own space, you can do what you want with it," Gideon smiles at me. I'm stunned, I lean forward and pick up the keys and look at Kerry.

"Erm, wow, thank you. That's pretty awesome," I manage to say. I hadn't thought about moving back here, in fact I hadn't thought about living anywhere. Me and Kerry hadn't even discussed living at the bunker full time.

"This is essential," he continues as he places a brand-new mobile phone down on the table. "I've already put some numbers in for you, I know that you attract trouble so you can call us if you need anything." I nod at Gideon and sit shocked, he's giving me stuff and it's weird and I can't think of words to say.

"OK," I say slowly.

"And lastly, these," he holds out a second set of keys. "Your car is a piece of shit and it is only worth scrap, so you need something that actually works." I look at the keys in his hand, as soon as I recognise the keys I jump up from the sofa and grab them.

"Shut your whore mouth!" I shout excitedly. I know what those keys belong too.

"I have my eye on something new, so I need the space anyway, plus I know you liked it a tiny bit," Gideon smiles. "Of course if you don't want it..."

"Fuck off!" I interrupt "No take backs." I stand looking at the keys in my hand as Gideon watches me.

"If you ladies would like to get your stuff together, I'll take you over to your new apartment." Me and Kerry nod in disbelief at Gideon, and we quickly grab our stuff. I look over to Kerry, and she mouths "What the fuck?" at me and I just shrug. I have no idea what is going on.

Gideon takes the car keys out of my hand so that he can drive us over to our new place. After only a couple of minutes of driving we pull in to a private car park then myself and Kerry follow Gideon through the lobby and in to a lift, he presses the top button, and we all go up in silence. Honestly, I have no clue what to say to him.

After a few moments the lift doors open, there is a small landing and then another door, he unlocks it with keys on the bunch and then pushes it open and signals for us to head inside. As I walk through the door, my jaw drops.

We enter in to a large open-plan apartment, very modern in its colour scheme but still has those Gothic touches around the room. There is a large breakfast bar and the kitchen is black and white with an amazing coffee maker sat on the counter top. A large black leather corner sofa sits in front of a flat screen TV and I can see that the far side of the room is all glass that over looks the city below.

"The apartment has 3 bedrooms, 2 of which are en suite and then a large family bathroom," Gideon says as he hands me the keys and carries my bags in to the room then places them on the sofa.

"Gideon this is all too much, I don't think we can afford this," I say looking at the amazing apartment.

"Did I mention rent at any point?" Gideon replies, I shake my head at him, I can't believe that he is letting us stay here for free and that he gave me his Camaro. "That's sorted then, I will let you two settle in. Velvet, I am sorry for just dumping you in here and leaving but I may be away for a couple of days as I have some business to attend to. I'll check in on you when I get back if that's OK with you?" I nod as Kerry goes exploring towards the bedrooms.

"I don't know what to say Gideon, this is mental." I am in shock. He smiles at me and takes my hand.

"A thank you will do," he says grinning then leans down and kisses me, his touch soft against my lips. As we part I look up at him and smile.

"Thank you," I say gratefully. I think I am falling for him all over again. Gideon nods then turns from me.

"If you need anything, anything at all, just send me a message. You have my number," he calls back as he heads for the door. I nod and watch him leave then stand in the middle of the room and take a deep breath. Wow, this is crazy.

"Kerry?" I shout. "Are the bedrooms truly awesome?" I head towards them to find her and spend some time just taking it all in.

...

Me and Kerry spend the next couple of days just chilling out, it's not like I can go find a job or anything with having to remain dead and all. Although I didn't really have that many people who knew me when we used to live here before so going out isn't really an issue as no one recognises me anyway. After we both got mortal drunk at Gideon's the other night we have tried to avoid alcohol for the last couple days so that we don't kill ourselves. I've had fun just hanging out and not having to worry about stuff, although the news gets more and more depressing every time I watch it. I know I should just ignore it all but Kerry has it on all the time.

These witch hunts that the TV reports keep going on about are getting out of hand, and I am starting to see more occurrences of murders and what the news is calling terrorist attacks, but I'm thinking it's the Midnight Church in retaliation to the archaic followings of the Hammer of Light. The attacks on certain people and places don't seem normal, they scream magic and possible alterer motives. I'm sure the TV is trying to cover up the existence of powerful witches like Helana as to not start mass panic. It's bad enough that the general public are aware of vampires without having to get their heads around actual magic and supernatural forces as well.

I can't help wonder what kind of business Gideon is away doing, I know he has meetings with the heads of county's throughout the UK but now that Bertol and Claudia are no longer a threat I don't know what he is so concerned with. Unless it has something to do with the General and trying to fight his men...

I get a weird thought and try to shake it away. He wouldn't do that though, surely?

My thoughts flash back to things that Tristen said to me when we first met, about building an alliance between the vampires and witches. What if that is what Gideon is working on now? He knows the history I have with Helana, what if he lets slip that I'm still alive? That's all I would need, her trying to find me again. I try to get those thoughts out of my head, I know what happened last time I had random thoughts about Gideon and it didn't go too well when I talked to him about them. I don't want to fight with him again, I think things are going really well between us.

As soon as I try to not think about Gideon, I think about Rick instead. Now that everything has calmed down my mind is consumed with knowing that I have a dad who is out there somewhere. I didn't really give him a chance to explain anything after we both found out each other was alive, I know why I was alone growing up, it was for my own safety. I even understand why he didn't try to find me when I was younger, so as to not draw attention to me. I just don't understand how he could live with himself knowing he had a daughter and that he didn't want to know the real me and show me this world that both him and my mother brought me in to.

"Hey, you OK?" Kerry asks snapping me out of my thoughts.

"Yeah, just lost in my own mind," I reply as I just sit on the sofa watching TV.

"Anything I can help with?" Kerry says as she comes and sits next to me. I sigh and think for a moment.

"I think I want to find out more about my dad," I say quietly. I don't know if I have questions or anything, it's just that I want to know who he is and what he does. I know he's not the leader of the Hunters Council, but he had men, and they were like a hunter unit, it's all a little confusing.

"Give Gideon a call," Kerry says bluntly. "As much as I don't like it, he will be able to give you the info you need."

"You still don't like him?" I ask.

"Well the apartment and car are making me like him slightly more, but I feel like he is paying you like a prostitute. Look at all this! People don't just give away cars and property. You are his call-girl now." She gives me a look, and we both burst out laughing.

After a moment I get up and fetch the phone that Gideon gave me and scroll through the contacts. Why do I feel so nervous? I haven't spoken to him at all since he left here a couple days ago, maybe I do miss him a little bit when he's not around. He said he would call in to see me when he got back, but he hasn't been, I take a deep breath and press call.

"Velvet?" Gideon's voice sounds happy when he answers. "How are you?" I don't quite know what to say.

"Hi, I'm good thanks. I was wondering if we could talk... Face to face?" I ask nervously. He said he would be as honest as possible when I was ready to find out more about Rick but I can't talk about it over the phone.

"Sure, of course. I'm just finishing up something and I'll be right over... I'll see you soon," Gideon says then the phone goes dead. I know that as soon as he starts talking and telling me stuff about Rick that I won't want to sit around here any more, I need to prepare myself for the fact that as soon as I'm finished talking to Gideon, I'm going to want to go and find my dad.

Chapter Four

"Hi!" I try to say casually as I answer the door. Gideon stands dressed in a smart black suit and waistcoat, something I haven't seen him wear in quite a while, but a look that I'm definitely not adverse to. As soon as I see him my heart skips a beat.

"Hey, sorry I haven't been over, work is a bit crazy right now," Gideon says smiling at me. I leave the door open and walk over to the sofas then sit on the arm of the chair, Kerry sits silently watching from the other side. I feel super nervous about talking to him now that he is here, I am kind of lost for words and feel sick to my stomach. I don't know if it is because I think I have missed him whilst he has been away or that I am anxious about his reaction to me wanting information about Rick.

"You need to invite me in!" Gideon says coyly, I frown slightly as I don't understand why.

"It's your apartment Gideon, you are free to come and go from it as you please," I reply confused.

"Technically... it's not mine anymore," he says smiling. I look around to Kerry to see if she knows what's going on but she just shrugs, so I turn back to Gideon for answers. "The forms you signed the other day, were the deeds to this place. I told you it was yours to do with it as you wished. Took me a day to transfer everything over but it's all done now."

My jaw nearly hits the floor. Did he seriously do that? Maybe Kerry is right, is he is trying to buy me with lavish gifts?

"I... I don't know what to say," I stumble over the words, I thought just crashing here for a while was a massive bonus, but this?

"How about something like, Gideon please come in?" He smirks. I sit in shock but after a few seconds I nod.

"Yes, sorry then, erm, come in... I guess." Gideon walks in and closes the door behind him, he gives Kerry a small nod and then awkwardly stands waiting for me to speak.

"You said you wanted to talk?" Gideon finally says. I nod my head and take a deep breath, that revelation has totally thrown me.

"Yeah, of course I said that... I want to know where my dad is," I try to say confidently, but I am still a bit gobsmacked. "I can't just sit around in here all day, watching life go by, I thought I could... but it's a bit boring." Gideon nods and then walks over to stand in front of me. He is close enough for me to smell his scent, the hint of expensive aftershave making me want to dive in to his arms.

"I don't know where his exact location is right now," Gideon explains, "but I do know what he's... No." He stops himself from going any further and shakes his head. "I know that look, I know exactly what you are thinking... you can't go. What Rick does is dangerous..."

"And what is it that he does exactly?" I ask as I cross my arms. He can't stop me finding out the truth.

"He's kind of a free lance hunter... Bounty hunter, now, I suppose," Gideon clears his throat before continuing. "He also runs the underground rebel groups that do what the Hunters Council don't."

"What do you mean?" I ask. Is he still technically one of them, I can't imagine him being like the General in any way.

"He is still trying to unite and protect the innocent and kill the bad guys, that's the only way to explain it. The normal Hunters Council don't give a shit about anyone but themselves, especially now that the General is in charge. Your dad, Rick continued doing what he believed in, he still follows the codes of the old ways, just without many people knowing."

"So he's a good guy? Even though he's a hunter, he's not like the General and his arseholes?" I ask, I just want to be sure. I watch Gideon as he smiles slightly at me.

"Rick is a good man. I am not saying that everything he's done has been righteous, but we have all got blood on our hands. That doesn't make us bad people," he explains.

I nod my head, Gideon has just stood there and told me not to go look for him, which just makes me want to go even more. It sounds like Rick is fighting to try to bring peace back, he came to save Gideon from Bertol and Claudia as well, so he can't be that bad if he just wanted to help. I stand up and grab my phone from the table and put it in my pocket. I got ready before Gideon came over and I have a bag packed already to go.

"Roughly where will he be?" I ask Gideon as I pick up the car keys and turn back to him.

"You're serious aren't you?" He asks surprised. I nod my head at him as he runs his hand through his hair anxiously. "He said he was following a lead just across the boarder, some demon or something that had contacts with Claudia." I freeze when I hear her name.

"He's hunting Claudia?" I ask nervously. Gideon pauses and sighs, he knows he shouldn't have said that.

"Honestly, we don't think she is still in the country, but she has a mine field of demons, vampires and God knows what else covering her back." Gideon stands watching me as I start to pace the floor.

"When did you last speak to him?" I ask, but Gideon stays quiet, not wanting to give me more information. "Gideon, please? We promised to tell each other the truth." Gideon sighs again and nods, he knows that I won't back down, and he can't go back on his promise to me.

"Yesterday," he says quietly, "he told me he's just north of Liddle castle, I swear I don't know the exact location though."

"You sure about this?" Kerry says quietly from the sofa.

"Yeah," I reply. "You know me, once I get something in my head, I can't shake it." I pick up my bag from the sofa and head towards the door, Gideon follows me.

"Can I walk you out?" He says cautiously. I nod my head at him and turn back to Kerry.

"Are you going to be OK here by yourself?" I ask, she smiles wildly at me.

"I'm sure I can find some way of entertaining myself," she grins. I laugh at her as I open the door and head for the lift.

"I don't like it when you go away, bad things seem to happen," Gideon says as we head down in the lift.

"Do you trust Rick?" I ask. Gideon nods his head without hesitation.

"Yes, I trust him with my life," he replies.

"Then I'm sure I'll be fine," I say, trying to avoid his eyes. I can't have him distracting me when I am trying to leave.

The doors open and I walk out then head straight to the car. This feels like deja vu, me walking away from Gideon to go find hunters, but this time I am stronger, I know I need to speak to my dad eventually and now feels like the right time to do it.

"Do you want me to come with you?" Gideon asks as I put my bags in the back of the Camaro.

"No. You said you had a load of work to do, so I wouldn't want to keep you from that." I shut the door and stand for a second, not sure what else to say.

"Please be careful, the last time you went..."

"I'll be careful," I interrupt. "I don't know how long I'll be gone, but I have the phone you gave me in case anything happens." Gideon nods his head then steps forward, he stands right in front of me and looks down, his eyes connect with mine and I instantly get lost in them.

"I love you," he says gently. "I just don't want to see you get hurt again." I sigh and force a smile.

"I know, you keep telling me," I reply.

"I keep telling you, because I mean it... When you get back, I'd like to spend some time together, just us two away from all this, I was thinking Paris maybe?" Gideon strokes my cheek lightly with his fingers. Why does he always do this to me? Just as I feel like I am happy just being kind of single, he pulls me back in to him and it's like my entire soul can't resist his charm.

"Gideon?" He smiles at me, encouraging me to continue. "What is this? This thing that is between us? It feels relationship like from your side, and I am a bit confused as to what I'm feeling." I say but it sounds like it all came out of my mouth wrong.

"Do you want to be in a relationship with me?" Gideon asks gently. He watches me, silently gazing at my face as though he is taking in every feature.

"Honestly? I don't know. Maybe... But then I'd be like someone's actually girlfriend and that's pretty weird and you are... Not exactly the standard boyfriend type material." I shake my head and sigh. "I always thought if I ever became ready to get serious with anyone then it would be with someone normal... sorry. That sounds wrong, I'm not saying you're not normal..." I pause and think for a second, I don't want to say the wrong thing. "If I got serious with someone, what would be the ultimate outcome for me? I guess I would eventually want to have kids, a real family and grow old together... But you are a vampire and none of that is possible." Gideon's eyes seem to go sad as I speak, he takes hold of my hand and tries to force a smile.

"Then you have the same dreams as a lot of people. I'm not going to lie, I do want a family someday, I want a happy life, I know I have a long life... But I also want you." I feel emotional for some reason as he speaks, I do like him, it's just... Shit! I don't even know. My chest hurts the more I think about him.

"How old are you Gideon? Because I'm guessing my 27 years on this planet are nothing compared to your life," I say.

I think about my parents and my mind flashes back to the nursery they created for me and my heart sinks because that's not something that should be taken for granted. If I was to want a life with Gideon then, even though kids have never crossed my mind till now, they would be totally out of the picture and could I really live my life knowing that's one thing that I would have to sacrifice.

"Can you even have kids, Gideon? I mean, if we were to do the whole relationship thing then what will happen? Will I just live by your side and you can watch me get older every day until I'm frail and gray and you still look like you do now? One day I might want more from life... I might want things that I can't have with you." I feel bad for bringing this all up as Gideon looks down at the floor, I can see he is upset.

"Not many vampires are blessed with children and are able to truly find love... My parents were together nearly 400 years before I was born and then Tristen is almost 600 years younger than me," Gideon explains. I knew he was old but that's literally hundreds and hundreds of years and that blows my mind.

"Wow!" Is all I manage to say in reply.

"My parents were lucky, Emily is a miracle, the majority of vampires will never be able to conceive children, let alone three... And it's never been known to happen with a human... it's just not possible," Gideon sighs and looks in to my eyes. "That doesn't mean that I can't love you, I can give you the world, take you anywhere you want to go... I could make you so happy if you would only let me. I need you in my life." I go silent and think for a minute. I need to figure my head out, I do really like him, but eventually I'm going to get hurt because I may want things I can never have. All this time I just kept saying that all I wanted was a bit of fun, now I am the one thinking about all the serious stuff. Am I just finding excuses to just not say yes?

"Can we talk about all of this when I get back?" I eventually say, Gideon nods in response to me. "I'm sorry, that got a little heavy with the whole relationship and family talk, we are not even dating or anything, it's all just fun right? We said nothing serious," I'm so torn, my mind is all over the place. "But maybe when I get back we can discuss... I mean, if you wanted to take me on an actual date, just to see how things might go, then I wouldn't say no. I think I might really like it." Gideon smiles as I nervously bumble my way through that.

"OK," Gideon replies. "Today there is nothing serious, we are not in a relationship, we are just having fun. But when you come back I am taking you out, I'll do things properly, no more just casual sex." I raise my eyebrows and smile "You know what I mean. I promise I'll show you that I can make you happy, I will show you how much I love you."

"And I think I would like that, a lot," I say nervously. "I do really like you Gideon... more than I have with anyone else in this world. I will consider things whilst I am away, I suppose there are worse guys that I could take a chance on." I try to not smile but Gideon chuckles and I can't help but grin.

"I promise you will not regret it. I already can't wait for you to come back to me," Gideon strokes my cheek again and I lean my head against his palm. "I will give you anything your heart desires and shower you with so much love..."

"Then hold that thought," I stop him. "When I get back, it's a date. And then we can take things slow... Very slow, maybe, and see what happens. I am very open to the possibility of spending a lot of time with you, if that's OK with you of course?"

"Yes, that is more than OK with me," Gideon replies. "And it's a step up from nothing serious so it's heading in the right direction," he smiles wildly at me then leans in and kisses me, I forget sometimes how gentle he can be despite his strength and dominant persona.

"I should go," I say as we part.

Gideon steps back as I open the driver door and get in to the car. I smile at him and start the engine, I don't have anything else to say to him but I have a lot to think about when I'm gone. He gives me a slight wave as I pull away, I need to focus on the task at hand now. I get a few miles outside of the city and realise I don't even know where I am going, so I pull over and Google the location Gideon mentioned. If I can get in the rough area I'm sure I'll find something, my instincts are usually pretty good.

After a few hours of driving I arrive at what the Sat Nav says is Liddle castle, I get out of the car and have a look around but I must be in the wrong place because this looks like a field with some stones in it. Fuck sake! This is the place that Gideon said, wasn't it? It's not even enough to be classed as ruins, it's literally a hill and nothing else.

I get back in the car and just sit for a while, I am not feeling this at all. Maybe Rick has done what he came to do and isn't even in this area anymore. It's starting to get dark, so I decide to follow the road north and see if anything jumps out at me, I am a bit dubious driving on all these country roads after what happened last time I was in Scotland, I swear to God if I crash this car I am going to cry. I am attached to this car so much that if a wolf runs in to the middle of the road in front of me this time, I am going to knock it the fuck out, rather than swerve and hit a tree.

After a few miles I come across a little village, there's not much here, a row of houses, a small shop and a pub. The shop is still open, so I pull up and grab a few snacks and some water and stuff then get back in the car. I decide to drive out of the little village as this car draws a bit of attention and I definitely don't need attention right now. I keep forgetting that I am dead to everyone in the normal world. I park up at the side of the road surrounded by sheep and have something to eat. When I went to find out about my mum something drew me towards Ethel and I ended up being exactly where I needed to be, but this is just nothingness. I am literally just sat in my car in the middle of nowhere.

I decide to close my eyes and try to concentrate, maybe if I clear my mind then I can sense something. I take a few deep breaths and yawn then relax.

I almost jump out of my seat as a truck passes me and makes the entire car shake. I look at the time and see it's 8am, that couple of minutes of trying to relax turned in to a pretty good sleep, but I am still knacked. I start the car, I can't just stay here all day, this trip has been a bit of a let down if I'm honest. I put the car in gear and go to pull away but stop, I suddenly feel really ill, I swiftly put the hand brake back on and sit for a moment trying and take a couple of deep breaths as my head starts to spin, I quickly open the car door and battle to take off my seat belt then try to get out but stumble then land on all fours.

I get a sudden immense pain behind my eyes, just as I realise what's happening, everything around me goes still, and I am stood in front of what looks like an old farm house. It seems like early morning, the sun is not too high yet but it's chilly. I notice a couple of black SUVs parked down the road and suddenly I hear shouting from inside the building. I turn to go in and have a look but in a blink of an eye I am stood in the middle of a group of people fighting. I quickly duck out of the way as a gun shot goes off close by and echoes around the room. I huddle in the corner and try to make out what's going on, I see what look like hunters fighting, there's black blood everywhere, so I instantly assume they are demons of some kind, I have had very limited experience with demons so don't know much about them other than the colour of their blood.

One of the hunters stumbles past me and drops to his knees as I notice a large gash across his chest, then more shouting as my head goes foggy again and then I am stood in silence. I blink a couple of times and try to slow my breathing, remembering to take everything in as I know this is a vision and details are key.

"Give us the information we want, and we won't kill you," I hear a familiar voice behind me, I turn and see Rick standing in front of a demon who is being restrained by two of his men, I watch as they tie him to a chair and wrap him in chains so that he can't move. Rick has a team of around six men with him now, I can see a lot of them are bloodied and bruised from the fighting.

"Fuck you!" The demon spits at Rick. He has black oozing from his nose and his hair is shaved on one side in a kind of punk style. "Kill us, and we will only find a new host, you fight us for nothing." I get closer to see what's going on until I am almost stood next to Rick, his face is cut, and he looks tired, but he smirks at the demon.

"We have our methods, and from your smart ass mouth, it seems you don't know who we are," Rick replies. One of Ricks men steps forward from the side carrying a book, he is dressed in the same all black get up as the others. The demon notices the book in his hands and just laughs.

"You think you can perform an exorcism on me?" He laughs louder. "That only works on the scum of our kind. I am too high up, it's just words. You do not have the power to kill me."

"Tell us how to find Claudia," Rick demands but the demon just continues to laugh then stops suddenly and smiles, his teeth almost yellow.

"It's too late for you now," the demon says as a gun shot rings in my ear and I almost jump out of my skin, no one saw the man standing behind us with a shot gun.

I watch as rick falls to the floor at my feet, his skull bust wide open, I look down, and I am covered in blood and brain mush from the impact. I hear his men start to shout as they tackle the unknown shooter then one of the men punches him, I see bright red blood from his mouth, so I know that the shooter was human. They pin him to the ground, but I am just transfixed on Rick's body. There is so much blood, bone fragments scattered across the floor, it doesn't even look real. I heave and try to swallow to stop from being sick but I lose it.

I am instantly back at the side of the car and I throw up, I gasp for breath through vomiting. My whole body shakes and sweat is pouring from me. After a couple of minutes the sickness subsides and I sit down, leaning against the wheel arches of my car on the dirt. I try to steady my nerves, I don't want to think about what I just saw, that was quite vile and very unexpected.

After a few minutes I push myself back to my feet and breathe in the morning air. That didn't feel like a vision of the past, so I can only assume it's like the time I saw Dee, maybe I can stop that from happening but I still have no idea where that was. I get back in the car and get the suspicion that something bad is already happening, so I need to go, now!

I drive for a good 40 minutes, past other little villages and farm land until I come to a fork in the road. I sit and try to decide which way to go before following my instincts and turning left. The sun is already out and I feel as though I'm so close that I can sense him near to me. I notice a small dirt track and take the turning leading down through the fields and then I see the black SUV's parked down the side of the road. I feel I might be already too late but I quickly pull in and get out of the car, I can't hear any shouting from inside like I did in my vision, so I know the fighting part is already over.

What if he's already dead?

I don't even think about the consequences I just run inside, I quickly look around and try to take in my surroundings but the room is empty apart from a few demon bodies that lie across the floor and then I see the man from my vision who looked like he had a wound across his chest, his eyes are still open but there is no life in them. I hear voices coming from a room upstairs, so I try to make my way across to the staircase and slip slightly in the black blood that oozes from the skull of one of the dead. I know I've got very little time, I am going to be cutting this close. I've only just found out that my dad is alive, I can't watch him die again.

I can't risk being seen as I climb the stairs, so I try to be as quiet as possible, as I reach the top I hear people in one of the rooms down the hallway.

"You think you can perform an exorcism on me?" I hear the voice of the demon that Rick is talking to say then laugh. "That only works on the scum of our kind. I am too high up, it's just words. You do not have the power to kill me."

"Tell us how to find Claudia." Rick demands.

I make my way towards the end room as fast as I possibly can, my heart feels like it is beating straight out of my chest, the door is open slightly as I get close.

"It's too late for you now," the demon says.

I push the door open, it swings and I spot a tall man dressed in denim standing in the shadows behind Rick. Everyone in the room is focused on the demon being held that no one sees him. I watch as he silently raises the shot gun, the barrel inches from the back of Ricks skull.

I act quick and focus on the man with the gun, I know he is human from what I saw in the vision, so I know he can be killed. I breathe slowly as I feel the power course through my veins for the first time in weeks and in a heartbeat the snapping of his neck echoes around the room, his lifeless body falls to the floor and the gun clatters on the wood. My heart is still pounding with adrenaline as I tried to get here as fast as I could to save his life and my chest heaves because I feel so out of breath now. There is a sudden commotion around the room as the other hunters realise what has just happened, they all quickly draw their guns and point them directly at me. I instinctively put my hands out to the side to show I am not armed then I stand frozen to the spot.

"Wait!" Rick shouts as he turns to face me and orders his men so stop. "Lower your weapons." The men all look at each other as Rick looks down at the man that now lies at his feet.

"I saw that you needed help," I say cautiously as the room feels uneasy. I swallow hard as I wait for Rick to say something, but he just stares at me.

"Sorry sir, we must have missed one, nearly killed you the bastard," One of Ricks men say as they check the man's body and then they throw his shot gun to one side. Rick nods at him then turns back to face me.

"You saw?" He asks me and I nod my head. "As in a vision?"

"Yes," I reply nervously. The whole room goes quiet then Rick laughs.

"Was it a pretty death for me at least?" He asks smirking.

"Not really," I say shaking my head, "although your brains did get some good splatter coverage." I can't believe I just said that. At least Ricks care free comment has put me at ease.

"Sir?" One of Ricks men gets his attention and then nods at me as though wanting to know what they should do with me. Rick smiles at me and scratches his head.

"Don't mind me," I say nervously. "I'll just keep out of your way whilst you try to find out where Claudia is." I shuffle to the corner as all the men watch me, unsure of who I am or what I am doing here. Rick laughs to himself again then turns back to the demon that sits in front of him to continue his questioning.

"Where were we?" Rick says to him, still smiling.

"Do your worst human, I'll never tell you shit!" The demon spits at him.

The man with the book starts reading the words that are written in it, I can't quite hear what is being said, but I am going to guess it's some Latin shit, that's usually something they read when trying to do an exorcism, right? I watch, expecting some magic demon non possession thing to happen but instead he just laughs.

"Is that all you have? It doesn't even tickle. Like I said your holy words won't work on me," the demon smiles wildly as he cackles. I hear Rick sigh and shake his head.

"Peters?" Rick says and instantly one of his men steps forward. "This isn't working, we need another lead and fast before the trail goes cold." Peters nods at him.

"No human can kill me," the demon continues. "It takes true power to destroy evil and humans are too weak." The men all ignore him. But I suddenly get a crazy idea and step forward.

"Hi again," I say nervously raising my hand slightly, kind of like the way you would do in school to get the teachers attention. Rick looks over to me and nods to give me permission me to speak. "Mind if I have a try?"

I hear a few of his men scoff and laugh under their breaths at my suggestion but Rick nods and moves out of the way leaving their prisoner sat on the chair in chains. I slowly head over to the demon and grab my own wooden chair from the side of the room and place it only a couple of feet in front of him then I sit down.

He looks at me as though I am some sort of joke, I know I'm nothing special but I'm not a joke.

"The men can't do it, so they send this pathetic human girl. What do you want whore?" The demon grins at me. I see Rick out the corner of my eye get angry at what he called me but I place my hand up slightly to stop him coming over. I can fight my own battles and I have probably faced worse guys than him on a Saturday night out drinking in Newcastle.

"I just walk to talk," I reply calmly. "I am going to be honest though, I don't know much about demons," I say as I casually place my boot up on to my knee and sit back in the chair. "So let's call this a training experience for me, you can be my tutor."

"You can experience my cock in your pretty mouth if you come a little closer," he grins. I don't react, I just smile and keep my cool.

"You must be a pretty big deal for a demon, the big bad who can't be exorcised or killed? I am sure that is not something one would come across every day," I act interested whilst the demon watches me, trying to figure me out.

"These other demons were scum compared to me, my essence is too powerful to just die. Like I said to these pussy's, all they have to do is kill this vessel and I'll just find another," he smirks, clearly proud of himself.

"Impressive!" I reply. "You are not immortal though, are you? I am sure there is something that could kill you in some way?" The demon starts to laugh again.

"You humans don't have the ability to kill someone like me. Try it and my essence will just escape, do a real exorcism and again I would just escape. You have no leverage, I won't give you jack shit," his laugh echoes around the room and I can see that Rick's men are getting restless, clearly board that I am talking to their captive and getting the same results that they already have.

"Tell Rick where Claudia is!" I say firmly.

"Suck my dick," the demon snaps back. I smile wildly and laugh at him which startles the demon slightly.

"Thank you," I finally say.

"For what?" The demon asks puzzled.

"For giving me all the information I need to kill you," I reply calmly.

I ignore the watching eyes around me and pull my chair closer to the demon until my legs are touching his. He looks down confused as to what I am doing. I quickly glance to Rick who just stands watching me then I smile again at the demon.

"No human can kill me," the demon snarls, his yellow teeth bared.

"Who said I was human," I say softly, his face changes and tries to work out who I am.

"Who are you?" He asks, suddenly intrigued.

"Me? I am a nobody," I smile. "Here is what I have learned in this lesson. Please, correct me if I am wrong, but if someone was to... Say, stop your essence from escaping this vessel," I watch as his eyes go wide as I talk, "then manage to... crush it. You would die for real, right?" The demon falls silent. I can see Rick smile out the corner of my eye. "So, do you want to talk about Claudia?"

"You're lying, what you speak of is not possible for a whore like you to do. I am not telling you anything," he finally replies.

"OK," I sigh. "It was worth a shot, thought that I may as well give you a chance... Guess I'll just kill you then."

I reach out and place my hand on his chest, focusing on what he said about his essence and try to visualise it in my mind, picturing this physical thing that could possibly be manipulated and controlled. He starts to laugh at me then slowly his face changes, almost twisting in pain. I can feel pure energy flow through me and it's intoxicating. I watch as a tiny amount of black blood starts to flow from his eyes like tears then I hear him gasp as he tries not to cry out in pain. I concentrate on what he called his essence and I picture it in my head as almost like a black heart, which if I hold it in place, I can squeeze the information out of him.

"What... what are you... doing?" The demon tries to say through the pain but I ignore him and push his essence, as he calls it, harder causing him to cry out. I notice Rick's men take a step back, clearly they have never seen this happen before.

"Where's Claudia?" I hear Rick ask forcefully as he comes to stand beside me, the demon shakes his head not wanting to say anything, not wanting to betray his master. I smile and make his pain worse, I feel so strong that I know I could kill him in seconds, but I am starting to have too much fun just playing with him.

"I don't know where she is!" The demon cries out. I pull back slightly to allow him to talk.

"Why don't I believe you?" Rick replies.

"I swear!" The demon says whilst trying to gulp air. I've given him a few seconds of rest, that's enough, so I push again, I feel his whole body shake under my palm as more black blood drips from his nose and eyes.

"Please!" He yells and I stop again. "She's planning to leave the country in a few days, she had a few loose ends to sort out first."

"Where is she now?" Rick asks, but the demon shakes his head again. I can see he is in pain, but I don't care, I can feel his black soul deep inside of him, it's trapped, and he is scared. His body goes ridged as he screams in pain again as I focus on ripping his essence to shreds, he starts to cough up black goo and I smile as I enjoy his pain, I enjoy feeling invincible.

"She will be heading to Glasgow in a few days," he spits, I stop again and let him talk. "She is flying from Glasgow to Budapest, she has security details posted around the city to stop any interruptions to her plans." I look up to Rick.

"If she gets on that flight we will lose her," Rick says to himself. He turns back to the demon. "Do you know where she is now?" He asks again but the demon just shakes his head. Rick sighs and then nods his head before talking to his men. "We at least now know where she's going to be, get the teams ready, we will meet at the base to sort out a plan. Peters? Call the Doc in to the base to patch you guys up, we will need to also sort back up, as taking on Claudia won't be easy." Peters nods and heads out of the room.

"I told you what you wanted to know," the demon looks at me as the men in the room start to gather their stuff. "You said you wouldn't kill me if I gave you what you wanted, so let me go." I smile at him as Rick stands by my side once more. I slowly push the chair back that I have been sitting on and stand up.

"Unfortunately, he said that, not me," I inform him as I point to Rick and correct him. "We had no such deal."

The demons eyes go wild as I smile at him, without touching him this time I exhale slowly and then watch as he writhes in pain, I hear him choke on his own blood as he tries to get free, gurgling noises filling the room as he desperately tries to fight me, to escape my grasp on him, but after a few seconds his body goes limp and I stand mesmerised by the black blood as it flows down his chin and I smile. When I spoke to Gideon about how I felt when I killed I wasn't lying. It fells amazing and dark, I could so easily be drawn in.

I am snapped out of my thoughts and back in to the room when Rick clears his throat, I look up to see all the men just standing staring at me.

"Sir? Who is this woman?" One of men says cautiously. Rick smiles and gives me a friendly look.

"This is Velvet... She is, my erm... my daughter," he smiles more. The room is silent as the men look on in disbelief then slowly one by one they start to filter their way out of the room until only myself and Rick remain. "I see that you inherited your mothers power," Rick says breaking the silence between us. I nod my head and smile.

"I'm still learning," I say awkwardly. There's another silence before Rick speaks again.

"Was this a flying visit or..." Rick asks.

"I thought I might hang around a while," I reply. "If that's OK with you?" I add quickly then Rick nods.

"I'd like that," he says without hesitation.

"So... I guess we're leaving then," I say nervously and start to head towards the door. Rick doesn't say anything but follows me down the stairs and outside. I can see his men are getting in to the SUV's, a couple of them seem injured from the fighting.

"Is that?" Rick says as soon as he steps outside, I turn to look at him and notice he is staring at the car. "I haven't seen that car in a while."

"You and Gideon were close?" I ask and he stops in his tracks.

"Yes, a long time ago... How did you two become... friends?" He fishes for information and I smile at him as I open the car door.

"He tried to feed on me then left me for dead, quite romantic really," I say sarcastically. I can see that Rick doesn't know whether or not I'm telling the truth, so I just laugh at myself and get in the car.

Rick rides with me to give me directions back to his base. It seems like we head to the opposite side of Scotland to where the Generals base is, but I'm not quite sure where exactly as it's all those stupid country roads and dirt paths. Eventually we come across what looks like deserted factory's and Rick tells me to pull up behind the SUV's in front.

"Excellent, looks like Seamus is already here, best Doctor around he is," Rick says as he gets out of the car and heads towards a small brown pick up truck parked a little way in front. I turn off the engine and get out as Rick goes to great a well-built man with white hair, he looks mid 50s. As I approach I hear Rick tell

Seamus which of his men need medical attention.

"No problem," Seamus says, "any help I can give to you, I will."

"Thank you," Rick nods. "Did you convince him to join you this time? I know we keep asking but, having him on board could be good for the cause." Seamus nods and looks over to his truck.

"It wasn't easy, but I tried to explain what you are doing here and that it can only benefit our people to build an alliance," Seamus seems hesitant. "Be warned though, you will have your work cut out trying to persuade him. He's too stubborn for his own good, and he doesn't take well to outsiders." I stand back as I feel a bit awkward right now, I don't fit in here and it sounds like it's all military talk and politics. "You will be lucky if you get a brief conversation out of him if he doesn't know much about you, doesn't trust many people, that one."

My head feels a little weird again and I get a strange ringing in my ears, then my arm gets itchy. Must be the adrenalin off finding Rick and all the dust off this dirt road. I rub my forearm through my jacket as it starts to annoy me. What the fuck is going on?

Seamus waves towards the brown truck as I remove my jacket and look at my arm, that's weird, It's almost as though the wolf mark is burning. It's not painful, just irritating. I look back up as the man they have been discussing climbs out of the truck and reluctantly starts to make his way towards Seamus and Rick.

"This is our pack Alpha..." Seamus explains to Rick.

"Conall!?" I say excitedly as soon as I see him.

He stops and looks up, his ginger hair slightly longer than when I last saw him, it takes him a second to recognise me before a broad smile covers his face then he runs towards me and scoops me up from the ground, hugging me tight. After a moment he puts me down but doesn't leave go, his arms still wrapped around me, his smile beams, and he just looks at me.

"You changed your hair," he says happily.

"Yes, kind of had to with being dead," I reply laughing.

"Yeah, Ben told us... When you left I thought..."

"I know!" I interrupt him. "Me too... How is everyone?"

"Good, everyone is good... I'm lost for words, I never thought I'd see you again," Conall laughs, clearly very happy to see me.

"Me either, how's Dee? After... You know." I didn't get a chance to see if she was OK after she woke up. I know Ben briefly told me everything was fine but it's nice to hear it from Conall.

"She's great, thanks to you, what you did was amazing. You totally made me a believer." I laugh at him, it's so good to see him, that I am almost giddy.

"I am glad, I bet Tiffany will be reeling if she knows you have seen me again," I say as Conall brushes some stray hairs off my face.

"Tell me about it, I'll never hear the end of it... I can't believe you sacrificed yourself like that, Ranulf had to stop me going after you, I didn't want you to get hurt trying to save us," Conall eyes roam my face as he gently strokes my cheek.

"I know, I saw when I was taken away that you tried to get to me... I am glad Ranulf stopped you though, you would have been killed," I reply.

Seamus and Rick both stand awkwardly watching us, I totally forgot they were there. Me and Conall smile at each other when we finally realise then turn to face them, trying to keep a straight face and be serious.

"You two know each other?" Rick asks as he raises his eyebrows.

"Yes, we... erm... Yes," Conall replies, I can see both Seamus and Rick notice that tattoo on my arm and I almost blush in case they somehow know what happened between Conall, Ranulf and myself to enable me to unlock its abilitiesk.

"Are you the girl that my son told me about?" Seamus inquires. I look at him and think for a moment, the white hair, the Doctor...

"You must be Ranulf and Dee's father. It's nice to meet you," I say nervously, I can't help but wonder exactly what Ranulf said to him.

"I heard what you did for both my daughter and my son, my understanding is that they would both be dead without your help," Seamus says, I nod at him to confirm that it is me that did those things. "From what they were telling me, I didn't think that I would get a chance to thank you in person." I suddenly feel quite shy, and I am not sure what to say.

"Velvet?" Conall says, I look up at him, thankful for the change of focus. "What are you doing here?" I smile at him and then look to Rick.

"Conall this is Rick... I told you his name was Patrick Elwin and that he was dead, it's a long confusing story, but he's my dad," I smile and suddenly everything feels very surreal. I am actually introducing people to my father, like actual family.

Chapter Five

"Hey!" I say nervously as I stand in the door way to the office. "Do you have some time spare to talk?"

"Of course," Rick replies from behind a large wooden desk. Things have been a bit weird since I got here, after I saw Conall and briefly spoke to him, he was whisked away for meetings with Rick and his men. I got the gist of things, Rick wants the pack to join forces with him if he goes up against the General in the future, so he is building his own underground army and trying to ensure that Conall is on his side.

I am totally out of place here though, it feels like a male dominated operation and I haven't seen any women here at all in the last two days. I've just tried to stay out of every ones way. I was shown to my own room just before Rick got back to work, it's definitely nothing flash, basically a mattress in a small room with a door. I assume I was put in here as they don't want me sharing the bunks with any of the men. I had a bit of a wander around the first day I got here just to see where I was, it's literally an old factory site surrounded with wire fences and security posts, it's pretty well secluded and set back so it's not somewhere that you would just stumble over if you were driving around.

There's a small canteen on the site, I say canteen, it's like army rations and slop. I decided against eating anything from there as it made me feel sick just looking at it, so I got the rest of the snacks out of my car and have been living off chocolate and crisps. I've seen a lot of men come and go in units, I'm not sure where they go or what they are doing, but I found it best to just sit in the room and play on my phone until I got the opportunity to speak to Rick again. I don't feel comfortable looking around more. The guys on the base here must have been talking about me because everywhere I go I get weird looks, as though they know that I am different, and they are not sure what to make of it. This morning a load of men seemed to arrive all at one and I noticed Rick was alone, so I thought I'd see if he had time to finally talk to me.

I walk in to his office and close the door behind me then take a seat opposite him, I watch as he continues to fill out paperwork and keeps glancing at the laptop screen in front of him.

"I was thinking I might leave soon and go home," I say nervously, Rick stops what he is doing, puts the pen down and looks up.

"Oh!" He says then sits for a moment and sighs. "I haven't been a very good host have I?"

"No... I mean it's OK, I can see you're busy. It's just I've been here two days and haven't spoken to a single person, I don't think coming here was such a good idea," I explain. We both sit in silence, I don't know how to talk to him, everything just feels so awkward. Do I talk to him like he's my dad, or do I call him Sir like his men do?

"Sorry," Rick finally says. "You deserve better than this from me." He closes the laptop and sits looking over at me. "We haven't really had a chance to talk just us two." I shake my head at him, I am not quite sure what to say.

"I shouldn't have just walked out on you at the bunker, I didn't really give you the opportunity to talk back then," I say quietly.

"You had every right to be pissed at me," he replies. "I didn't intend for all this to happen. I assumed one day I'd find you and introduce myself properly but life has a way of screwing over your plans. I didn't expect to meet my daughter for the first time in over 27 year, holding the severed head of one of the most notorious vampires in the UK and being covered in his blood. Things just got a little off track I suppose, after Lena was killed..." He pauses slightly, he seems like he hasn't talked about this is many years and just mentioning her name is upsetting. "Your mother knew as soon as she found out that she was pregnant with you that we would all be in danger. She kept her pregnancy hidden for as long as she possibly could and originally she was going to leave the coven, so we could all be a family." I listen to him, it's strange to hear about all this. "But then Helana found out and just before you were born Lena went to stay with an old friend who could hide her."

"Ethel?" I interrupt. Rick smiles slightly and nods his head at me.

"Yes. The day you were born was both the happiest and saddest day of our lives because we knew then that you would be hunted and that we wouldn't be able to keep you safe the way normal parents should. So everything was put in place and you were hidden in the human world." Rick stops again, his face is sad as he thinks about what to say next. "Less than a month after you were born, we had planned to leave the country together, even though we didn't know where you were, Helana still wanted Lena to pay for her betrayal to the coven... It seemed like a normal day, I had been back to the hunters base and told them I was going out on a mission and when I got back I found out that Lena had been taken whilst she was getting supplies. I searched for her for days, trying to find where she was being held, but by the time I finally got anywhere close she was already dead... I shouldn't have left her alone, I should have insisted she stayed protected in the bunker, but she was too strong willed to take orders." I feel tears start to fall down my face as I listen to him explain.

"It wasn't your fault," I say quietly. "The only thing you both were guilty of, is loving each other," I smile slightly and wipe my eyes.

"She didn't deserve to die and you didn't deserve to grown up without us," Rick takes a deep breath and exhales slowly. "This is heavy stuff."

"Yeah..." I say quietly, and we both go back to sitting in silence.

"I would like it if you stayed a bit longer... I have 27 years to catch up on," he smiles at me and I sit and think for a moment.

"If I am going to stay, then I am not just going to sit in that room. I want to know what you guys do here and I don't want to be treated differently because I am a girl... No offence but I'm sure I can stand my ground pretty good against the majority of your men," I say confidently. Rick laughs and nods his head.

"Tell me?" He says. "What did you inherit?... I mean, what can you do?" I think for a second before I reply.

"You want the list?" I ask and he nods, encouraging me to continue. "Guess I'll start from the beginning then. I can heal quickly, I read in a book from the bunker that that was a hunter ability?"

"Yes, accelerated healing runs in our line, so what kind of time frame are you at? Are you as advanced as me, cuts and stuff in a few days, broken bones week and a half?" He says seriously but I almost laugh.

"No," I say smiling. "I broke my ankle at Christmas after being thrown through a bar window and it was fine in two days, I think it was. And I died after drowning, but I was fine about 10 hours later." Rick watches me in amazement. "Then there was that car crash I had before I was taken to the hunters base, I was told I was in a pretty bad way, but I was in a coma for a couple of days so not sure how fast I healed then as I was fine when I woke up."

"OK," Rick says slowly. "Anything else?"

"I feel like I am getting stronger, it took a bit of effort to cut Bertol's head off with that little knife and my instincts are usually on point which helped a lot when I came to find you." Rick just nods and listens. "I don't think I've got the speed reflexes thing but I do know I can slow my surroundings, but I assume that's from my mums side maybe."

"What do you mean?" Rick asks.

"There's been a couple of incidents when I've managed to slow things enough to stop a knife mid-air or be able to out dodge a bullet, but I'm not sure how that works exactly, it just happens. As though it's a defence mechanism that just kicks in without me trying," I try to explain.

"What else do you have, that you know of from Lena?" Rick asks.

"The visions, I am not too fond of those though, because every time I have them it's always about seeing someone die. I saw my mum tortured and murdered by Helana, I saw you killed by Gideon. When I was with the wolf pack I saw Dee shot by hunters and then a couple days ago I saw you get your skull blown to pieces." Rick's face goes white.

"You... you saw Lena?" He swallows hard.

"Yes," I say gently. "I watched and experienced every second of what Helana did to her. It was bad and I still get nightmares sometimes because of it." I move my hand and start to play with the necklace around my neck. "Then I saw Helana take this from my mother and I managed to get it back when I went to the Midnight Church."

"Helana knows you're alive?" He says concerned.

"She did, but everyone else thinks that I am now dead, so I don't think she will be any different." Rick nods his head as I talk. "Then apart from the visions, I can move stuff with my mind, I caused a concrete ceiling to collapse and crush someone, I can start fires which comes in handy when fighting vampires, If I focus enough I can kill people by snapping their necks, I found that out for the first time after I had been tortured at the Bird Cage... Oh and now that demon killing thing, which I was unsure if it would work but it was worth a try, and it was fucking sick." Rick looks shocked at what I can do.

"How long have you known about your powers?" He says after a short silence.

"Erm... Since I was first attacked by vampires, so... 3 and a half month maybe," I shrug.

"You developed all that in only 3 months? That's crazy... And amazing," Rick says in disbelief.

"Yeah, just imagine how awesome I would be if I'd known about my powers and ability's from being a kid," I laugh but then remember something else. "Oh and another thing, this thing with me and Conall."

"What thing?" Rick looks intrigued. I look down at the mark on my arm and smile.

"I'm connected to the pack, I was granted the role of Guardian and in return I presented them with a new Elder," I explain. "So I kind of have a psychic communication thing with his family of wolves now and can harness the power of their Founding stone, but I am not to sure how that works either." Rick looks down at the desk and laughs.

"All this is 3 months? We knew you would be powerful but... Shit!" Rick shakes his head. There is a slight knock on the door, and he looks up. "Yes?" Rick calls over. The door opens and Peters stands looking in.

"Sir, sorry to interrupt but you're needed in the strat room." Rick nods at him then Peters leaves and closes the door.

"Ill leave you to it," I say as I stand up and head for the door.

"Wait!" Rick says, I stop and turn back to him. "You said you wanted to know more about the place, so let me show you, you are now my official shadow, if you want to be." I smile and nod at him as he gets up from his desk and heads for the door.

I feel slightly under dressed as I follow him in to a large open room filled with men in black uniforms, I look down at my ripped jeans and geeky t-shirt and know that I massively stick out here. The room looks like an old warehouse with a load of chairs set out facing a table and a couple of standing boards, however the space is so big that it hardly takes up any room at all. There are about 40 men in the room, and they all fall quiet when Rick walks in, he heads straight to the front as the men sit down and wait for him to talk. I hang back and stand behind them all not wanting to get in the way.

"Afternoon," Rick says addressing the room as he turns to face them all, he pauses for a second and looks around as though he's lost something then spots me at the back, he raises his hand and waves me forward. I grimace slightly then slowly wander towards him.

"A few of you have seen that we have a visitor," Rick says to the men.

I walk towards him and one of the men at the back wolf whistles at me then laughter starts to spread throughout the group. I take a deep breath and try to ignore it then I notice the doors at the far side open again and Conall walks in, he smiles at me when he sees me and stands at the back with his arms crossed.

"OK, calm down," Rick continues. "I know it's unusual to have a woman on the base, but I am going to say this now. Every single one of you in this room wouldn't stand a chance against her in a fight." There's another wave of quiet laughter and I stand awkwardly beside him unsure of where to look.

"I bet anyone in this room £500 right now that she could easily take on a group of you arseholes and win," Conall says loudly from the back. I shake my head at him and think what the fuck is he doing?

"Trust me?" I hear in my head, as Conall smiles at me. I sigh and reluctantly nod my head.

"I'll take that bet," a large man in the front row stands up, I can see he is squeezed in to his t-shirt, as he has muscles on top of muscles. I glance at Rick to try and get some back-up, but he just puts his hands up and steps back.

"Anyone else?" Conall says to the men. "One on one seems a bit too easy to me."

He laughs at himself and I shoot him a look that could kill which makes him smile more. Two other men stand up and head to the front, I realise what Conall is trying to do. The only way for the men to respect me is if I prove myself. I don't recognise any of these men though, so I don't think they were there when I faced that demon, so they don't know who I am. I watch them as they now all stand a couple of meters in front of me.

"She doesn't look too tough," the muscle man says in a gravely voice.

"This will be too easy," says the second man with blond hair. I glance at the third man who stands smiling at me, he has a scar across his face and for a slight second I think that I may be in deep shit.

I look back to Conall and say "you are such a dick head" in my mind and I see that he tries not to laugh as he hears me. I take a step back from the men and wait to see what they do. I am not overly enthusiastic about this at all.

"I'll go first and get this over with quickly," the man with the scar says, he steps forward and pulls a knife from his belt.

"Wooh!" I say taking a few more steps back and putting my hands up in defence. "No one mentioned weapons." I keep walking backwards trying to put some distance between me and him whilst I work out a plan, but he just stands and smiles as I feel all of the men in the room watch what I am doing. I glance to Rick again and I see concern in his face, but he doesn't step in to stop it, he lets the men carry on. I take a deep breath and calm myself.

OK, I say to myself, I've faced worse. It's not like they are going to try to actually kill me...

I was so focused on the scar man with his knife that I didn't notice the blond guy flank me and grab me from behind, he swiftly wraps his forearm around my throat and tries to choke me out. I quickly react and grab his hand to try to get it away from me, he's strong but I know if I combine my hunter abilities and my witch powers I can get him off me, he is definitely not as strong as a vampire.

As I concentrate on removing his grip, I feel the bones in his fist snap as I force his arm from around my neck, he groans as pain shoots up his arm but I can see in his face he doesn't understand why it's happening, why just the grip of this small woman standing in front of him is causing damage. I turn to face him, and he goes to throw a punch with his other hand but I duck out of the way quickly then, without thinking, I force the heel of my boot in to his shin. I surprise myself when his bone snaps under my foot, and he cries out, the noise echoing around the room as he crumples to the floor clutching his leg.

"Sorry!" I say to him, feeling a little guilty.

I am more used to fighting vampires, demons and witches that I didn't notice myself growing in strength so much until I fought a human again. I turn to look at the other two guys just in time to see the scar guy throw his knife towards me.

Without even thinking, I blink and the blade stops in mid-air about a foot in front of my face, I hear gasps around the room as they see the knife frozen, that was quite close. At least my reactions are getting faster and more instinctual. I take a deep breath and smile.

"Hmm, I could do with a weapon, thanks for that," I say sarcastically as I reach forward and pluck the knife from the air then look at it in my hand.

I smirk and look up to see both the muscle guy and scar man bolt towards me. I am not sure if I can take them both at the same time, so I need to split them up. I raise my hand towards the big muscle man and lightly flick it to one side, concentrating on controlling the motions of my power, he is swept off his feet and is launched in to the group of men watching with such force that he wipes out another 6 guys when he hits them, knocking them off the chairs and making a pile of bodies on the floor. The scar guy stops in his tracks and looks at me unsure if he should continue.

"What are you?" He asks cautiously. I just smile at him and play with the knife in my hand.

"Apparently I am just a weak girl who looks easy to fight," I reply sarcastically. I hear Conall and Rick both laugh.

The scar guy shuffles dubiously then decides to run at me anyway. I shake my head at him then focus on him alone. He stops again but this time it is by my will, I slowly walk towards him as he is lifted off the ground by his neck and I watch his feet dangle and dance below him. Fear starts to show in his eyes as I hold the knife up to his chest, the point of the blade skimming the fabric of his shirt.

"Do you give up?" I ask playfully as he struggles to breathe. I watch as he tries to nod his head then I let him go. He drops to the floor and quickly backs away from me before I toss his knife towards his feet and it clatters on the ground. I look up and see the entire room silently staring at me.

"Well!" Rick says loudly from behind me. "I think that's all for that impromptu demonstration." I turn to him and smile nervously. "Now if you will allow me to continue?" The men all attempt to retake their seats as a couple of them pick up the blond guy and help him out of the room.

"Sorry about him," I say quietly as Rick comes to stand beside me again.

"Don't be. They should have listened to my warning," he says smiling then turns back to his men. "As should you all. I want you to show her the same respect that you show me. Anyone steps out of line will have me to answer to, understand?" The men all nod. "Her name is Velvet, she's..." He glances at me and smiles.

"I'm his daughter," I say loudly, the men in the room all look around at each other. "I know that I don't have training, I am not a real hunter and I don't have as much knowledge as most of you in here now. But I am here to learn and I won't take any shit. I am not your typical girl and I've had my fair share of run-ins with power hungry cunts, so please don't think that I am a push over." I look back at Rick, and he stands with a massive smile on his face. He takes a deep breath and continues.

"Now down to business," he says to the men. I take this as my opportunity to shuffle out of the way, making my way towards the back of the room then stand next to Conall as Rick starts to put the men in to small teams and gives them missions and leads to follow.

"Hi," Conall says quietly as I approach him.

"Hi," I reply trying not to smile at him, I cross my arms, and we both face the front.

"Nice moves up there," Conall smirks. I can't help laughing slightly, his smile is very infectious.

"You are such a dick head," I say playfully.

"Yep, I know," he laughs at me. "This meeting has gone a bit down hill now that you are not kicking ass up there... You want to go and grab a bite to eat?" I glance at him and think for a moment. I am pretty hungry.

"Yeah, why not," I reply, we both stand nervously for a second then Conall nods and quietly heads towards the door whilst I follow him. We head outside and Conall turns to me, making me stop in front of him.

"I don't fancy the crap they serve here, so if you want... there's a place I know that is not too far, I know the owner and the food is good," he says awkwardly. I smile at him and nod, I am getting sick of chocolate and crisps so some actual real food sounds pretty awesome right now.

"Sounds good, I'll drive if you can direct me from here, I have literally no idea where we are." I start to head for the car and Conall follows me.

"I have a pretty good sense of direction, you know, with being a wolf and all," Conall replies as I unlock the car door and go to get in. "Is this yours?" He asks looking at the Camero.

"It is now," I say smiling as he gets in.

Conall gives me some basic directions, I take a couple of wrong turns but eventually after about an hour, we pull up outside a country pub. It's mid-afternoon and although it's still cold the sky is bright and there's only a light breeze. The pub itself sits on a country road but there are no houses or anything else around, it's nice and quaint with its lush garden that surrounds it and stone walls. We both get out of the car and I follow Conall inside, as soon as we enter I hear a voice boom around the room.

"Conall! My man!" A large man with a long dark beard comes out from behind the bar and shakes Conall's hand then pulls him in for a hug, his Scottish twang is very evident in his accent. "What are you doing in our neck of the woods?"

"Just looking for some good food Douglas, if you know anywhere that has some," Conall replies jokingly.

"Come... Sit," Douglas directs us towards the side and in to a booth, then quickly brings over two menus. "Whatever you want, it's on the house for you and your lady friend," he smiles and heads back over to the bar to give us a couple minutes to look. I look around the room, it's very warm and cosy, there's not many people in here, but they seem like the sort to keep to themselves, and they are all locals, so I get comfortable and enjoy my surroundings.

"He seems... Nice," I say smiling at Conall over the table.

"He has his moments, I am very involved in the community... My pack is unusually large and I have people all over the place," Conall glances down at the menu and has a look to see what he fancies to eat.

"So he's a wolf?" I ask quietly. Conall looks up and smiles then nods his head. I open the menu and have a look at the food options. I am instantly drawn to the steaks, oh, I haven't had a decent steak in ages, I didn't realise how hungry I was.

"So, how have you been?" Conall asks casually. "We never really got a chance to talk properly the other day." I look up at him and smile.

"I've been good, considering everything that has happened... I don't really feel like going in to too many details, if that is OK," I force a smile.

I don't want to think about the Bird Cage, the torture, the beatings, the whole trying to kill myself because I thought I had no hope left thing. Then how would I possibly ever try to explain being controlled by vampires and almost used as a sex and blood slave. I glance up and notice that Conall's face has changed to concern and I flush with embarrassment at the thought that he probably heard me thinking about what happened in my head.

"Sorry," Conall says gently. I look back down at the menu and try to ignore my feelings.

"Don't be, it's not your fault... How about we change the subject?" I say quickly. "How have you been?"

"I have been remarkably well, thank you," Conall smiles at me. "Although I didn't realise how quiet life was for me until your sparkling personality no longer graced our presence."

"Awww, did the big strong wolf miss little old me?" I laugh more. I don't know what it is about Conall, but he has a way of making me smile.

"Oh shit!" Conall says under his breath then tries to hide behind his menu. I look up at him confused and go to ask what's wrong when I hear a woman's voice from behind me.

"Conall? Is that you?" A woman about my age approaches us and Conall puts his menu down on the table then gives her the most fake smile I've ever seen.

"Beth? Hi. I didn't see you there," Conall says through gritted teeth. I look up and instantly think she is stunning. She's tall and slim with long wavy brown hair, her eyes are a piercing baby blue.

"You never called me," Beth says as she glances down at me and gives a sort of disgusted look, she clearly thinks that she's better than me.

I thought she was pretty but I guess she is just another stuck up tramp. I fight the urge to cunt punch her. From this position it would be quite easily accessible. Conall glances at me and almost bursts out laughing and then I remember he can probably hear me saying that as well. I have not mastered the art of closing off my mind to him yet, he can pretty much hear everything that I think.

"Yeah, sorry," Conall replies to Beth. "I lost your number, you know how it is. I wanted to call but life just got in the way."

"I can give you it again," Beth says overly flirting with him.

"Now is not a great time," Conall nods in my direction, trying to give her a hint to leave. I smile at him as this is starting to become quite amusing for me to watch as he squirms under her gaze in his seat.

"Are you two... On a date?" She asks, looking down her nose at me again.

"Actually," Conall says nervously, "yes, yes we are..."

"No. No we are not," I cut in. Conall glares at me and I just smirk.

"Then if you are not on a date, you could hand me your phone and I'll pop my number in, it will only take two seconds," Beth says playfully, she places her hands on the table and leans down slightly, I watch as Conall's eyes fall right down her cleavage, they hover there for a few seconds, and he goes a little opened mouthed then he shakes his head and looks up to the ceiling instead.

"I would Beth, honestly, but I left my phone at home," Conall tries to make excuses, I can see how uncomfortable he is, so I decide to help... Kind of.

"Conall, don't be silly your phone is in your back pocket," I smirk. This is payback bitch for what you did to me at the base today, I say in my head and smile at him wildly. I know he heard me as his face drops, and then he reluctantly reaches in to his back pocket and pulls out his phone.

"I hate you," I hear him say in my mind as he unlocks his screen and reluctantly hands Beth the phone.

"There we go," Beth hands the phone back to him after a few seconds. "I sent myself a message, so I can save your number now too." I try to contain my laughter but it doesn't work so I raise the menu and hide my face behind it.

"Awesome," I hear Conall say through gritted teeth. I see Beth lean right in to him, Conall moving as far away from her as possible before she speaks again.

"I'll call you later. We will arrange to meet up soon... and I'll do that thing you like with my tongue," she says seductively before giving him a wink and walking away. Conall sits almost in shock for a few seconds before speaking again.

"What just happened?" He says slowly, I can't help but laugh again.

"I think Beth had those "I'm going to rape you eyes". Seemed like a classy bird," I say casually as I look at the menu and giggle to myself.

"Are we even now?" Conall asks, I just look at him and do an overly exaggerated thinking face.

"Hmm..." I say playfully. "Possibly?" I smile at him and he shakes his head.

"You are such a bitch," he says under his breath trying to stifle his smile. "That would have gone miles better if you had cunt punched her though." I burst out laughing at him.

We finally order and the food is amazing. The next couple of hours were very pleasant. We talk about random shit, I probed him about his unwanted lady attention and all together it is a really good day. It is nice to just chill out and forget about everything else, I haven't been this relaxed and care free in a long while.

Conall says his goodbyes to Douglas and I thank him for an amazing meal before we leave the pub. I walk ahead slightly towards the car but Conall suddenly grabs my hand and spins me around to face him then holds me close and starts to kiss me deeply.

His lips are as soft as I remember and his body is strong and firm against mine, the rest of the world seems to disappear quickly as I get lost in his arms and give in to him. I am reminded of what happened when my mind first opened up to him, and I am instantly swept back up in that feeling again. Conall's hand roams across the bottom of my back then down and gently cups my arse cheek, he squeezes playfully as I moan at his touch...

I can't do this. The thoughts just pop in to my head and I gently push Conall away... He stands looking down at me confused.

"What's wrong?" He asks concerned. I shake my head, his arms still wrapped around me.

"I am sorry, Conall. I am sorry if I gave you the wrong impression but I can't do this, not with you," I go to step away from him, but he grabs my hand gently to stop me.

"I don't understand," he says watching me. "Is there someone else? Are you in a relationship or something?" I think for a moment as I am unsure what to say.

"No... Maybe, I don't know... It's complicated," I try to get the words out. I left things so open with Gideon that now I am not sure what to do.

"Relationships are not that complicated, Velvet. It's either a yes or no," Conall's eyes search mine, his face is so sweet and welcoming. I know that I like him, and I know that he is an amazing lover. But Gideon...

"Who's Gideon?" Conall asks. I look at him and suddenly don't know what to say.

"Are you always going to be in my head?" I ask quietly.

"You are the one who is so open to me, I can feel that you want to be close to me again," Conall says gently. I swallow hard and feel my face go flush, my mind flashes back to that night with both him and Ranulf. How connected I felt to them, how freeing the experience was and the pleasure...

"I should get back to the base," I say trying to change the subject. "Thank you for the meal." I go to leave and head towards the car but Conall quickly moves and blocks my path.

"Tell me you don't feel it then?" Conall says smiling down at me.

"Feel what?" I ask, playing innocent.

"This thing between us. We are connected on a higher level, and I am crazy about wanting to get to know you more," he says. I can feel my pulse start to race as he speaks. "I would have sacrificed myself if it had meant saving you that day in front of the General." I am slightly taken aback by how open he is. "I knew the moment Ranulf spoke about you that you were special. There's something different about you to everyone else and my body aches to know you more... I can't hide how I feel."

"You have girls throwing themselves at you, literally, you don't want to be crazy about me, I am nothing but trouble," I try to persuade him. Conall steps closer and places his hand gently on my cheek, his body is warm next to mine and I get the feeling of butterfly's in the pit of my stomach when he looks in to my eyes.

"I don't want all those girls... I want you," he says softly. I stand nervously for a minute trying to think of something to say but nothing comes to my mind, so I just nod at him slightly and walk away.

The drive back to Rick's base was awkward to say the least. I was just starting to think about the possibility of more happening between me and Gideon and then Conall comes back in to my life and everything is blown up in the air again. I know I have a connection to Conall and his pack, I am obviously attracted to him or I wouldn't have done stuff with him and Ranulf when I was at the Lookout. And I know he had feelings for me even when I was with him previously as I heard him say he liked me. But at the same time I am also attracted to Gideon and although we are not officially at couple status, it would feel wrong doing anything with Conall right now when I promised Gideon we would talk about more serious matters when I got home.

Why does this always happen? I was just starting to settle and think about moving things forward with Gideon and now I am all confused again. It's all these fucking bastard feelings and shit, fucking everything up for me.

"Are you OK?" Conall asks quietly as I pull up and turn the engine off. I haven't spoken at all since I got back in the car.

"Yeah, I'm fine. Sorry I have not been too talkative," I reply, it's so hard right now because when I look at Conall he makes me smile and I feel so happy just being around him. We both sit in the car in silence for a while, the air is thick between us and the tension is unbearable.

"So, who is this Gideon?" Conall asks eventually.

"He's just... Someone I, erm..." How the fuck do you explain to someone that you have been fucking the vampire King?

"He's what?" Conall says shocked.

"Please stop being in side my mind," I plead with him. "It's bad enough that I have to deal with my own thoughts without having you raking around in there as well," I sigh and shake my head.

"Gideon is a vampire?" Conall asks nervously and I nod my head to confirm it. "Do you love him?"

"I don't know," I reply, I have strong feelings for him, but not like that, I don't think so any way.

"But you two are not... Together?" He quizzes me further. I shake my head at him. "Then what's the problem?" I look at Conall and frown.

"I don't know, it would just feel like I am betraying his trust in me. Before I came here, we talked about things and although I left it quite open between us... I... I know he loves me, and he's done a lot for me lately," I try and explain.

"This is his car isn't it?" Conall says with almost a tinge of sadness in is voice. I just nod my head and go quiet. "Hmm," he grunts to himself eventually, lost in his own thoughts.

"What?" I ask, wanting to know what he's thinking.

"If you actually loved him and wanted to be with him, then you wouldn't have left him to come here," Conall forces a smile and goes to get out of the car, before he shuts the door he bends down and looks across to me. "You are such a mystery Velvet... And I am a massive flirt who is definitely up for the challenge in trying to win your heart. The vampire King doesn't stand a chance against my charm," Conall smiles broadly then closes the car door. I watch as he walks away and I just sit for a moment, contemplating what kind of mess I have got myself in to.

Chapter Six

"Recall all units and send to confirmed location," I hear shouting as a group of men run towards vans and start to drive away, they are in full tactical gear and heavily armed. I was in a world of my own, still just sitting in my car by myself and suddenly it looks like something big is happening. I see Rick walk out of one of the side buildings, so I quickly get out of the car and run over to him.

"Hey, what's going on?" I call to him, he looks up and stops for a moment to talk.

"We think we have found Bertol's second in command, so we are hopeful that if we capture him, he could lead us to Claudia's location. We are tying to divert all units there now, unfortunately we are quite spread out so it will take some time," he quickly says and goes to walk off.

"Is there anything I can do to help?" I ask. Rick stops again and shakes his head.

"No, it's too dangerous. I want you to stay here," he says firmly before jumping in the back of one of the black SUV's just before it drives away. I didn't even get a chance to protest before I am left standing by myself. I turn around and see another group of men head towards one of the parked vans and I notice Conall is with them. I hesitate for a moment after our conversation earlier but then shout over to him any way.

"Conall?" He looks up and nods to acknowledge me as I run over, he has changed his cloths, no longer in casual jeans and T-shirt but instead, now dressed in black cargo pants and black jacket. "Where are you going?" I ask casually.

"There's a location a couple hours north that Rick thinks a target is at. He's asked me to come along, so I can see the operations side of things before agreeing to a merger," Conall goes to walk away with the other men, but I am not prepared to be left behind, it's already dark and I didn't realise how long I had been sat in the car, if it's anything like what happened before I found Rick I probably fell asleep without knowing it again. I have been doing that a lot lately, being exhausted is no fun.

"Do you have the location details?" I ask him quickly. He looks down and pulls out a piece of paper with some coordinates written on it.

"Yeah, we were all given the details... I am sorry Velvet, I'll see you when I get back, I really need to go," Conall goes to put the paper back in his pocket but I lunge forward and snatch it from him then run as fast as I can back to my car.

"Velvet? What the fuck are you doing?" Conall calls after me.

I open the car door and quickly put the details in the Sat Nav, start the engine then go to pull away and look up to see Conall standing in front of the car with his hands on the bonnet.

"Conall move!" I shout at him, but he shakes his head and quickly makes his way around the side of the car then gets in.

"You can't go," Conall says firmly but I don't listen and just pull away with him beside me.

"I don't have time to argue with you, so I suggest you put your seat belt on," I say confidently.

As soon as I am clear from the base I put my foot down, I briefly glance at the black SUV with Rick in as I overtake it, luckily the place I am headed isn't all country lanes so as soon as I get on a decent road I just let rip. I am not just going to sit by and let the boys have all the fun, I didn't come all this way to see what Rick did to be the good little girl and sit in my room. Fuck that shit! I want a piece of the action.

"You need to slow down!" Conall shouts over the sound of the engine, I just smile at myself and go a little faster just to freak him out.

"Tell me everything you know about this vampire guy we are going to find," I say to Conall as I start to drive a little less erratic so that he can calm himself down.

"Apparently his name is Julius, he was spotted arriving in Scotland last night and followed to this location. The Intel they have suggests that the location is a large farm house sat within its own land, it's unclear at the moment how many vampires are there but Julius is vital in finding this other vampire Claudia that Rick is after," Conall explains.

"OK," I reply as I take a turning and follow the direction the Sat Nav gives. "What's so special about this Julius guy? I know who Bertol is, and he doesn't seem the type to rely on others too much."

"The men were talking saying he was some old vampire from Greece, at one time Julius was quite close to Bertol's sister or something like that." I listen to Conall. That kind of makes sense, if Julius is an old lover of Claudia's then Bertol would have had no choice but to keep him close in case he upset his sister. Hopefully if the team manage to capture him now, we can get the location of Claudia before she leaves the country.

After a good drive we arrive at the coordinates given and I pull up behind a van, within minutes the SUV with Rick in pulls in alongside us. Rick jumps out and heads straight over to us, I can tell he is angry with me before he even opens his mouth.

"I told you to stay at the base," Rick shouts as I open the car door and climb out.

"You can't stop me doing anything, I am not a little girl and you have no right to speak to me like one," I say to Rick as his team try not to watch the unfolding drama.

"Velvet please, this is different. A vampire nest is no place for..."

"A girl?" I interrupt him and he looks at me frustrated.

"My daughter," he finishes his sentence. "Please just stay here and stay safe, I can't do my job if I am too busy worrying that you might get hurt." I sigh and nod my head, these guys are the experts after all. But this is the only time I'll do as he asks, the last time I fought vampires I wasn't strong enough to defend myself fully when I faced a group of them so that is the only reason I am stepping down now.

"OK," I say quietly. Rick nods and before I see what he's doing he places a hand cuff around my wrist and attaches it to the handle on the van door. "What the fuck?" I say bewildered.

"Stay here," Rick says firmly again and then turns to his men. In teams, they all start to head towards the location on foot. Altogether there seems to be about 12-15 men being led by Rick to the house. The sun is just about to start to rise and I can see already that it is going to be a clear and bright day, there's not a cloud in the sky which is probably why they wanted to wait until morning as any vampires in the farm house will be less likely to try to run without shade. How long was I asleep in the car? I can't remember falling asleep, so I must have just passed out with exhaustion again.

The couple of units of men start to filter their way to the location whilst I stand by the side of the road looking like an idiot handcuffed to a van. Conall's group is the last to head out and I see him hover for a moment before telling them that he will follow in a second. He casually walks over to me and smiles.

"Your grand plan to kick ass didn't go so well this time did it?" Conall smirks at me as he looks down at the handcuff around my wrist.

"Shouldn't you be going to play soldiers like a good boy?" I ask sarcastically, Conall laughs slightly and nods his head. But he doesn't leave, instead he stands looking at me with a cheeky grin on his face.

"You know I could kiss you right now and you wouldn't be able to run away from me," Conall says playfully, I smile at him and shake my head.

He has great timing with this, doesn't he? Conall steps closer to me and places his hand on the SUV beside my head, I lean away from him until my back is pressed up against the van, my heart rate increases as he raises his other hand and gently brushes away hair from my face as he watches me contently.

"You would be taking advantage of me," I say softly as Conall smiles down at me, his fingers brush my cheek and I quiver under his touch. "Because I am all helpless and I can't move."

"That's what I am hoping for," Conall smiles more and leans down, I close my eyes as his lips touch mine, briefly parting to allow his tongue to slip in to my mouth and play. I keep forgetting how sweet he tastes, and how gentle he can be, everything about him makes me relax. "God you are so fucking beautiful." I hear him say in my mind as his body moves closer and presses up against me, his kisses getting deeper... and then it hits me, just because I told Rick I wouldn't go in to the farm house doesn't mean I can't know what's going on. I quickly shift my focus on to the hand cuff and feel it snap off my wrist then I push Conall off me.

"I have an idea," I say quickly. Conall looks down at my hands on his chest and seems startled.

"How did you?..." He says noticing that I am not cuffed to the van any more. "Never mind." He shakes his head.

"If you go in to the farmhouse you can walk me through everything," I say quickly. "That way I might be able to help you and I won't feel left out." Conall looks down at me then nods slowly.

"OK," he sighs. "I guess I am going to the farm house then." He seems a bit deflated that I pushed him away for a second time but I have already told him that things are complicated.

"Yes, I am going to try to focus all my energy on staying connected to you over this distance, it will be like you have a mini me in your head," I smile wildly at him. I don't know if I can do anything that I've just said but it might be fun to try. Conall laughs then turns to walk away leaving me standing by myself in silence and just concentrating on him, I close my eyes and breathe deeply then just think about Conall.

"Can you still hear me?" I say in my mind as he approaches the farm house.

"Yes ma'am," he replies jokingly.

"Awesome, keep thinking and walk me through everything, I want to know what's going on... And that Rick is OK," I think.

"OK," I hear Conall reply. "I am just heading in through the front doors now, it's strangely quiet in here," his words trail off and then there's an extended silence, I start to panic that I've lost him already.

"Conall?" I say to myself.

"Yeah, I'm still here, sorry, I obviously don't talk to myself as much as you do." I smile slightly at him. "I can hear people upstairs... Oh, shit... Fucking arsehole vampires." He sounds like he is possibly fighting but it's hard to work out when I can only hear his voice in my head, even then it's fragmented, and I am only picking up bits.

"You alright?" I ask.

"Yeah, I'm good. They just took me by surprise that's all," he continues. "Crap!" He goes silent again. I wait for him to say something, I don't want to seem too needy, so I just give him some time. I get a little nervous, I don't like not knowing what is going on. "Velvet, are you still with me?"

"Yes," I reply and let out a huge sigh of relief.

"This looks pretty bad," I can hear a slight panic in Conall's tone.

"What's wrong?" I say to him.

"Some of the men are dead, they look as though they have had their throats ripped out... Everything looks as though it's happened so fast, they didn't stand a chance as soon as they walked in through the door..." His voice quivers and it is making me very anxious. "I am outside a large room, I don't think I've been noticed but I can hear things are not good inside..."

"Conall what's going on? Can you see Rick?" There's a silence again and I start to think that something doesn't feel right. This should have been a straight forward raid for Rick's men, I know that there were only 15 max of them here, but they should be trained to kill and restrain vampires. What Conall is describing sounds like a massacre. "Conall?" I try again but get no answer. "Conall, please tell me you are OK." My head goes a little dizzy and I try to hold my concentration.

"Velvet?" I hear Conall say quietly in my mind. "There's something wrong, I can't..."

"Conall?" My head starts to ache and I feel a sharp pain in my temple. "Conall? Talk to me please!" I almost scream as I get an overwhelming pressure trying to push away my connection to him.

"I... I can't resist, she's wants me to go to her," I hear then instantly get knocked back before everything around me goes black.

I open my eyes and see that I am lying on my back by the side of the black van. I sit up and realise I can't sense Conall any more, it is as though something interrupted my connection and physically pushed me out of his mind...

Oh my God... it's Claudia, she's here!

I jump up and start to run towards the farm house, I don't know how long I have been out for but if Claudia is in there then there is no knowing what is going on. I only saw a small amount of her power before, I know she can control multiple people at once and if she has the hunters trapped...

I don't want to think about it. I head towards the front doors and stumble up the couple of stone steps and then bundle my way through the doorway. The entrance is empty but I remember that Conall said he went upstairs, so I cautiously head up, it doesn't take me long to find half mutilated bodies of some of Ricks hunters. It looks like they were out numbered and totally unprepared for what they found in here. As I reach the top of the stairs I have to step over Peters, his throat has been ripped out as though it was done for fun rather than food. I pause for a moment and take the wooden stake from his lifeless hands then look around and see there is another body on the landing. I lean down and pick up another stake and shove it in my back pocket then grab his handgun and slide it down the back of my jeans. I have no idea what is going on but if all these guys were outnumbered then I know I am going to be in for a world of pain if I try to help... that's if there is anyone left to help at all.

"I recognise you," I hear the voice of a woman say from a room at the end of the corridor and it instantly catches my attention, "you were there that day when Gideon got away."

My breathing hitches as I recognise Claudia's voice. I creep closer to the room, trying to stay unseen behind the door frame as I force myself to remain calm, I can't be scared of her now, that won't help anyone. I glance through the crack in the door and I can see possibly 5 or 6 hunters all being restrained, some with bite marks already on their necks and others who have been beaten senseless and covered in blood. The room itself has been cleared out, there's no furniture or anything, it seems like the house is abandoned. The windows are blacked out with thick paint and I can see a man standing, holding Rick from behind, over the far side.

"What do you want me to do with this one?" The man says, his accent is unusual and I can't place it. His hair is almost silver, and he is ruggedly handsome, I assume that is Julius. I watch as Claudia steps forward to look at Rick, his nose is bust, and he looks dazed as though he has been hit hard in the head. She raises her hand and gently strokes his face.

"He interests me," she says slowly then looks down to her side, that's when I notice Conall kneeling behind her. She turns to Conall and smiles, waves her hand, and he stands to his feet then steps forward, never once does he take his eyes off her.

"And him?" Julius asks as Conall stands in front of Claudia, hypnotised by her gaze. She steps close and I watch her lean in and smell him, inhaling his scent.

"Who would have thought a wolf would fall in to my lap today?" She takes another deep breath. "Not just any wolf though, you are an Alpha. I can smell your scent, it's strong and masculine." Her eyes almost flash with excitement as she runs her fingers slowly down his chest, feeling his firm body beneath her touch. "Oh, I am going to have so much fun with you." Claudia smiles then turns back to Julius. "I'll keep these two for now," she points to Rick and Conall. "The rest of them you can kill."

There are about 10 vampires including Claudia and Julius, I am hesitant to go in as Rick told me not to get involved and I promised I would stay by the van... but if I do nothing they are all going to die. Claudia places her hand on Conall's shoulder gently as he kneels in front of her again at her wish, then she turns back to Rick.

"Are you going to kill me?" Rick says between painful breaths. Claudia steps towards him and looks him up and down.

"More than likely," she grins, even from here I can see her teeth bared. She places her hand roughly in Rick's hair and tilts his head back exposing his throat. I can see it in Rick's face that he is out of options, Julius is too strong behind, holding him in place, his men that are still alive are all pinned down and Conall has been brain washed to follow Claudia's every whim. I stand with my back against the wall around the door, I know I need to act quick, I look down at the wooden stake in my hand and take a deep breath, I will let my instincts take over because if I think too much it will just slow me down. I exhale slowly and then move, I whip around the door frame and push the door fully open as I throw the stake towards Claudia in one fluid motion, propelled with a little of that added power I have to give it some oomph. She realises there is someone else here almost instantly and moves... but not fast enough as I watch the stake hurtle through the air and embed itself deep in to her shoulder.

Claudia cries out and leaves go of Rick as Julius drops him and turns to run directly at me. I grab the gun from the back of my jeans, aim it as best I can and quickly pull the trigger, the gun shot rings out in my ears as Julius stops in his tracks and looks at me bewildered. Then I see a trickle of blood flow from a bullet hole in the middle of his forehead, I can see that he is in pain and confused, so I grab the stake from my back pocket and run towards him, driving it deep in to his heart. I only wait a second to make sure it has the effect I want it too, before I push my foot in to his abdomen and kick him away, ensuring the stake remains firmly in my hand.

I look up at the same time Claudia realises what's going on, she reaches up, grabs the wood and pulls it out of her flesh then throws it to the ground. She makes eyes contact with me and I can instantly see the surprise in her face, she clearly was not expecting to see me today. A couple of the vampires drop their hunters and come towards me to protect their master.

"No!" Claudia bellows, and they stop, she doesn't take her eyes off me, searching my face, my body... "No one touches her but me."

I quickly glance around, I can feel the tension in the air. Rick pushes himself away from her and backs off to relative safety as he holds his side and tries to breathe through the amount of pain he is in. I look to Conall, but he doesn't even notice me, he doesn't even recognise me any more, instead he just watches Claudia.

"Ah... my sweet Velvet," Claudia says as she runs her tongue across her fangs, she notices that I keep glancing at Conall, so she looks between us both, trying to figure out why I am with a load of hunters, then she smiles. "Don't tell me that Gideon wasn't enough of a man for you? So instead you found yourself a wolf as well?" She signals for Conall to stand, and he does so immediately then moves to her side.

"Conall you need to fight her," I say trying to get him to look at me, but he doesn't even know I exist.

"The wolf has a name," Claudia smiles and raises her hand towards his face.

"Don't fucking touch him!" I shout at her, but she ignores me and starts to stroke his face, she looks deep in to his eyes as she exhales slowly, plucking images from his brain just like she did with me. However, Conall doesn't look like he is in any pain, he can't fight her thrawl, he is consumed by her. I go to step towards them to stop her but my feet won't move. I look down and panic, when the fuck did she get inside my head. I didn't even realise she did it, but it's just like before where I can't move my own body.

"Hmm," she moans loudly as she turns back to look at me. "You have an adventurous side. Two beautiful men.. Play your cards right and maybe we can all have a little fun... together," she smiles and runs her hand down Conall's body once more then cups his manhood in her hand as she bites her lip playfully. Conall inhales sharply, I know that feeling, the feeling of pleasure, she has him completely under her control.

"Fuck you, Claudia!" I say, but she starts to laugh at me.

"You already did," she smiles wildly. "And from what I remember, you loved every single second of it." She catches my gaze and looks directly in to my eyes, I try to look away from her but I can't move. "Come to me," she says gently. I shake my head and as soon as I do I feel that pain in my skull again. I know that the more I resist her, the more my head feels as though it's going to explode but I can't become her slave again, I can't give in to her because if I do I may as well be dead.

"I won't... let you do this... to me again," I force out, my head throbbing.

"Don't be silly Velvet, you know that resisting me will not work," her voice is soft and calm, I groan as the pain grows stronger. "It's just a few steps, just come towards me."

I try to push her out of my head, but she's so strong. My feet start to move and before I even know it I am stood inches from her. My heart is beating out of my chest, she's dressed in white again but this time she's wearing a white trouser suit which is now stained red off the hole I made in her shoulder. Claudia looks at me properly and sees I am still clutching the stake that I drove in to Julius's chest.

"Drop your weapon," she orders me but I close my eyes, the pain is almost too much to bear as I try to hold her from my mind. My hand shakes as her thrawl wants me to drop it but grip it tighter instead. "Look at me," I hear her whisper in my ear. The pain is too much, I open my eyes and look directly at her. Her gaze sweeping me up.

"Just... just let them go... Claudia, you... you don't have to... kill them," I say between breaths, my whole body shakes as the sheer pain takes over.

"Drop... Your... Weapon!" She replies firmly and my hand opens instantly, the stake falls to the floor and bounces slightly then rolls away.

She smiles at me then takes a hold of Conall's hand and pulls him towards her until he is stood by my side. With her free hand she reaches up to touch my face, I try to pull back, to stop her making that connection but her fingers gently skim my skin and I feel it straight away. The intense pleasure she can give out courses through me, my head falls back as every muscle in my body relaxes then I hear Conall moan beside me, he feels it too, she has us both right where she wants us.

"Conall?" I force out wearily. I need him to hear me, I need to break the connection.

"Say the words to me, that I want to hear," Claudia playfully whispers to me.

I try to block her out but I feel my whole body go weak beneath her touch, my breathing starts to sound shallow as she plays with both mine and Conall's minds together, making us feel things as one. We all start to get lost and it feels as though there is only the three of us left in the room. Our body's writhing and moulding together as a single entity, freely exploring each other. Claudia leans in close to me, her mouth touches mine as she kisses my lips gently, I moan again as my knees feel weak, but I can't let this happen.

I try to push all the images of Conall and Claudia's body's merging as one with mine, out of my head. It is not real, I don't want this to happen, I have to get her to stop. If I was able to open my mind to Conall and the wolf pack, then surely I should have the power to close my mind to Claudia. I managed to do it with

Gideon, I know he wasn't as strong as Claudia with this ability but it gives me hope that it is a possibility.

I try to ignore what my body is doing as Claudia slips her tongue in to my mouth against my will, I reciprocate and play with her, enjoying her completely. I think only about Conall, if I can reconnect with him then maybe I can push Claudia out. My mind and body are not working together though as Claudia places her hand around my back and pulls me closer in to her, her body pressed up against mine. In my mind I need to forget about everything I am feeling and focus on my connection with the pack, that is stronger than her thrawl, I know it is. I need to clear my mind, nothing around me is real, everything I am feeling doesn't exist.

I need to get lost in nothingness...

"Say the words Velvet," Claudia says gently to me as she pauses from kissing me and watches my face. I open my eyes and I smile at her.

"I... I want you," I say, I watch as Claudia smiles at my words. "I want you... to suck... my fucking... dick."

I lunge forward and plough my forehead in to her face, she stumbles back and leaves go of Conall's hand. He falls to his knees and gasps for air as though he has just awoke from a bad dream, and he is no longer sure what is real. I grab my own face as pain shoots through my eye then I rub it and notice blood all over my hand. There is a commotion behind me as some of the hunters take this as their opportunity to try to fight back, I know I need to give them some help so I turn and raise my hands and push my power from me, I can see it sweep the room knocking the vampires off their feet and giving the hunters enough time to get up and a chance to get free.

Within seconds, I am yanked backwards as Claudia grabs me by the hair and wraps her hand around my throat before quickly sinking her teeth in to my neck, I cry out as immense pain radiates through me, she drinks quickly, gulping down my blood, trying to drain and kill me as fast as possible. I feel myself go dizzy almost instantaneously and I can't focus on getting away.

I fall to the ground suddenly as Rick smacks Claudia over the back of the head with the hilt of his gun, I don't even look to see what is going on around me, I just know I need to get up. I try to push myself back to my feet, but struggle as my whole body is weak, my eyes blur and I feel as though the entire room spins around me. Then I feel a hand grab my arm and I look up to see Conall, I nod at him as I catch my breath, and he helps me to stand.

"Are you OK?" Conall asks me, checking my neck, I can see by the look in his eyes that the wound is bad.

"I've had worse," I say forcing a smile. Rick is fighting with Claudia now, he throws a punch and it knocks her to the ground.

"We need to get out!" Rick shouts. "We are all going to die if we stay here any longer." I see some of his men try to head for the door, but they are tackled by vampires, they are too strong and the hunters don't stand a chance against them.

"Help Rick," I say to Conall, pushing him away from me.

"No, I need to get you out, you are injured," Conall says as he looks at me concerned, he can see I am badly hurt but I need him to keep Claudia out of the way whilst I help the hunters.

"Conall, get out of my way!" I say forcefully as I push him to one side. He stops for a moment then nods and heads over to help Rick try to restrain Claudia.

My legs are shaking like mad as I try to stay upright, I take a deep breath then close my eyes and focus on the vampires in front of me, I can already hear a couple of the men screaming as they bite and feed from them. My essence starts to burn with power, it grows stronger as I concentrate solely on that until I let it consume me and I open my eyes to enable it to be released.

All around the room the vampires seem to freeze on the spot, I can see that the hunters are as confused as the vampires as to what is going on, but they waste no time in moving out of the way. The vampire closest to me starts to cough first then as though a ripple spreads throughout the room, the vampires all start to gasp for breath. My head pounds as I try to hold my power levels high enough to take out all of the scum in the room in one go. My hands start to shake and I feel fresh warm liquid flow from my nose as I watch the vampires fall to their knees and start to gargle on their own blood.

I am struggling to breathe as I push through the pain, I see some of the vampires start to change, their eyes go wide as their skin becomes like grey leather. I can't help but smile slightly as they become mummified in front of my eyes and their bodies start to hit the floor. The surviving hunters scramble to their feet, I quickly glance around and see only 6 decomposing vampires and Julius makes 7. If I ignore Claudia that leaves two that I've missed.

I brake my focus on those vampires and as soon as I stop my connection to them, I collapse to the ground. I gulp in air, it feels like doing that has just drained every bit of energy from my body. I force myself on to my hands and knees and see a bunch of hunters pin down one of the stray vampires, I push myself up more as I notice the last vampire bolt for the door. Hell no am I leaving one of those cock suckers alive, I force myself to stand and grab the wooden stake that I dropped earlier then drag my ass towards the door.

I grab on to the door frame for support as I see the vampire step over the body's on the landing and head for the stairs. I don't even think, I just run towards him with everything I have left and throw myself at him, he turns towards me to try to block my attack but the stake connects with his chest and I feel the wood shatter his ribs and hit his heart. That might have been a great plan if we weren't right at the top of the stairs, as I hit the vampire he loses his footing and falls backwards taking me with him.

I don't quite know what happened next but I remember pain, spinning and the feeling of being inside a washing machine. I finally stop falling and land flat on my back at the bottom of the stairs with the vampire dead on top of me. I groan, that is all I am capable of as every bone in my body hurts and I don't think I could move even if I wanted to. There is shouting from above then footsteps as Conall reaches the bottom and pushes the vampire off me, swiftly followed down by Rick.

"Don't try to move," Conall says quickly as he checks to see if I have any noticeable injury's.

"What the hell were you thinking?" Rick raises his voice at me. "You could have getting yourself killed, I told you to stay outside." I groan at him and give him the side eye as Conall touches my shoulder and I cry out in pain.

"It looks like you have dislocated your shoulder, I am going to have to pop it back in," Conall says trying to calm me down but I can hear in his voice that he is panicking.

"No," I shake my head. "I remember what happened last time when you tried to help me and had to break my ankle. No thank you, I'll be fine," I try to sit up but clench my teeth as my whole body feels as though it's on fire. Conall gently helps me back down and I lie for a moment then turn my head to Rick.

"Did you get Claudia?" I ask, he looks away from me then shakes his head.

"No, she jumped through the upstairs window and fled, I didn't have any men capable of going after her, so I don't know where she has gone," Rick responds. He is clearly pissed with himself, or me most likely, for her getting away. His remaining men start to head down the stairs as Conall kneels beside me.

"Right, I am going to help you to sit up and then I am going to sort your shoulder so at least you will be able to move, OK?" Conall says gently, I give in and nod my head then try to stifle my cries of pain as he slowly helps me in to a sitting position. He carefully gets hold of my arm and positions one of his legs behind my back to help me stay in place. "Just keep looking at me, OK?" I am so exhausted that I can hardly keep my eyes open and the pain is unbearable. I nod my head wearily at him and ready myself. "So... I'll count to three and then pull," he instructs me. I nod my head at him again in understanding. I take a deep breath and brace myself for his countdown. "1... 2..." Conall suddenly jerks my arm, I hear my shoulder pop and I almost scream the place down, my eyes sting with tears but as soon as my shoulder is back into place the pain starts to ease, in that area anyway. Conall holds me whilst I try to get my breathing to return to normal.

"I think I've broken my hand as well," I say shaking my head. "Fuck me! I do not miss the pain and fighting." I groan again and Conall smiles at me sweetly.

"Come on, I'll help you up," he says then wraps his arms under mine and tries to help me to my feet, as soon as I stand I cry out and Conall places his arm around my waist to support my weight as I lift my leg from the ground.

"And my knee is bust," I say laughing at myself slightly, without saying anything else Conall scoops me up, I gasp as a fresh wave of pain flows over me. My head feels so heavy that I don't think I will be able to keep my eyes open much longer.

"I'll call all units back to the base and then send teams to intercept Claudia before she gets to the airport," Rick says to Conall and then walks away outside. I sigh and place my head against Conall's chest as he nods at Rick and carries me out towards the cars.

"You don't look too good... Looks like I am driving then," Conall smirks but I don't respond. I am far too tired to even talk. Conall gently puts me in the car without making me hurt to much, then carefully fastens me in, he then picks up the keys from the chair and drives us back to the base. I try to stay awake for the journey back but I keep drifting in and out of unconsciousness.

When we arrive back, Conall gets me out of the car and takes me to my room, when we get there Seamus is already waiting for me. Conall puts me down on the bed softly then tells Seamus about my injuries, and he instructs Conall to remove my boots and my jeans then I try to ignore the pain as Seamus straps up my wrist and knee, before checking over my shoulder and cleaning the blood from my face and neck. I am so tired that I am struggling to even keep my head up as he starts applying strips to nip my skin together to stop the bleeding. Seamus finishes up then speaks to Conall, I can't even concentrate enough to know what they are saying, then he leaves me and Conall alone in the room. He helps me get comfortable and places a blanket over me, I can feel my whole body shake as I am freezing in this draughty room then he sits on the edge of the small bed beside me and gently strokes my hair as I shiver.

"Hey," Conall says quietly, "you did good today... You saved my life." I just groan in response, I feel like shit and my breathing rattles in my chest. After a few minutes Conall stands up and goes to leave.

"Conall?" I say quietly, he stops and turns to look at me. "Will you stay with me, please?" Conall smiles and nods his head then takes off his boots then climbs on to the bed behind me. He gently places his arm around my waist, spooning me, his body making me warm as he holds me close. I start to drift off to sleep, my mind filling with images of death again, racing through all the things I have been through, but I am too exhausted to care, then I hear a small knock on the door but my body doesn't want to let me move.

"Hi," Conall says at almost a whisper towards the door. "She's asleep."

"How is she?" I hear Rick ask quietly.

"Not too good, she lost a lot of blood, and she is very weak, but Seamus says she will be fine after she's had some rest, she needs some time to heal," Conall explains. I keep my eyes closed, I can't be bothered to talk to them.

"OK... please let me know when she wakes up," Rick says softly. "I think I owe her an apology... And some of my men owe her their lives." I feel Conall nod slightly then the door close again. The room falls silent as Conall snuggles in behind me then I try to go to sleep.

Chapter Seven

My body has never felt as weak as it does right now but my mind is hyper active. Everything seems to be merging together as one, I can smell my mum's burning flesh as Helana sets fire to her body, I can feel Claudia gripping me tight and drinking from me sending searing pain to every inch of my body, I can see the Generals face as he tortures me and cuts in to my flesh. It's all too much, no one should ever have to face such horrors, I feel like I am suffocating, I feel like I am going to die.

My eyes dart open and I can feel my heart beating so hard that it may break my rib cage, I try to breathe but I am hypo-ventilating and the whole room is spinning.

"Hey," I hear from behind me. "It's alright, Velvet, I am here. It's only a dream," Conall starts to stroke my hair as I realise where I am again and my eyes start to feel so heavy. "Shhh, it's OK. I promise, everything is alright. Just close your eyes, go back to sleep."

I start to relax as I feel Conall's body pressed up against my back, I'm safe here, I know he wouldn't let anyone hurt me. I can't fight the need to close my eyes again and quickly drift off, I can't ever remember feeling so tired before, but at least I can rest now. I don't think I dreamt any more but I remember being quite restless and when I finally open my eyes naturally I feel like utter shit. My head is aching and my body is weak, but I am warm and comfortable which makes me smile slightly because I can sense that Conall is still lying with me.

"Afternoon," I hear Conall say gently as I begin to stir. I move on to my back to see him and groan as I am still in a bit of pain. "Just take it easy. There's no rush for you to get up."

"Have you been here the whole time I've been asleep?" I ask, my throat is croaky and dry.

"Actually... no," he smiles at me as he lies on his side, he props his head up with his arm and continues to rest his other hand across my waist. "I managed to get a little bit of rest whilst you slept but then your dad kept popping in and then I went to stretch my legs, then I came back and you were pretty restless, so I made sure you were OK before I went to grab some breakfast and stuff." I smile at him as he waffles on. "I got a bit board of just sitting here," he laughs.

"How long have I been asleep?" I ask wearily.

"Quite a while, it's tomorrow already... Your dad was a little concerned that you were injured quite badly," Conall says, he moves his hand from my waist and strokes my face as he looks down at me.

"He didn't seem so interested when he was shouting at me did he?" I scoff before looking away. I should be pissed off at him for treating me like a child, I did save their lives after all, but I am not sure I can be arsed to be mad at anyone right now.

"You would be surprised," Conall replies. "He's all hard man in front of his men but when I was speaking to him alone he's just like you, all soft and squishy, like a little sarcastic kitten on the inside." I try not to laugh but Conall turns my head back to face him and his smile lights up the room.

"Did he manage to track down Claudia?" I ask suddenly remembering that she got away.

"I didn't ask, I was more concerned with making sure you were OK. That was my priority," he says sincerely. "How are feeling?"

"Honestly? I am fucking starving," I say, Conall laughs at me slightly.

I can't help thinking how much I appreciate that he was here to help me. He is so caring and even when I first met him at the Lookout he did so much for me when he didn't have to. He is so kind and selfless sometimes, it makes my soul happy just having him near me. What I feel for Gideon is different than what I feel for Conall. Gideon is powerful and full of lust, whereas Conall is gentle and giving. My mind is confused but my body wants to explore the present and get swept up in the moment with Conall, just the thought of him touching me sends pangs of anticipation to my core. Things just feel so strange though, I know I am safe here, Gideon would have done the same for me as Conall did if he...

"But Gideon's not here though is he?" Conall says suddenly. I keep forgetting that he can hear my thoughts, I sigh and try to force a smile. "I would never leave you or hurt you in any way, you do know that, don't you? I really like you, Velvet. I would like it if you gave me a chance."

"It's just..." I try to say.

"It's just what?" Conall interrupts. "I'm here right now, not him," Conall smiles at me then leans down and gently kisses my lips. His hand runs through my hair as I part my lips and allow him to explore my mouth as I kiss him back, surrendering myself and just giving in to the moment. I know what Conall says is right, Gideon and I are not a couple, we are not in a relationship, but he does mean a lot to me. I don't want to betray him but at the same time I don't know what will happen between us when I get back. "Shhh, stop thinking so loud," Conall says playfully as he returns to kiss me deeper, his tongue slides in to my mouth and I close my eyes as my tongue plays with his, I can't get over how good he tastes, I wonder if that's a wolf thing? I raise my hand and run it up his arm, I am reminded how firm his body feels, his skin warm and inviting to the touch. I don't know why but this still doesn't feel right, I told Gideon that we could talk more when I got home, maybe I shouldn't be doing this. Conall pauses from kissing me and looks down in to my eyes. "Velvet, you are doing nothing wrong," he sighs. I nod at him as I know he heard my concerns about Gideon. "This between us right now... is not wrong, if you and Gideon are not even together then there should be nothing holding you back," he continues gently. I force a slight smile as he strokes my cheek. He's right, I pretty much said no to Gideon but I did give him hope and I don't think I could be at ease with betraying that. Conall sighs again as we are interrupted by a quiet knock on the bedroom door, he smiles down at me then gets off the bed and stands up as I try to force myself to sit.

"Come in," I say as I raise my hand and rub my temple, my head has started to pound after I sat up. The door opens and Rick walks in, he sees that I am awake and gives me a nervous smile.

"Hi, can we talk?" Rick asks. I glance to Conall and nod my head.

"I'll go and see if I can find you some pain killers," Conall says awkwardly. "I'll leave you two to talk." He flashes me a slight smile then leaves and closes the door behind him.

"I wanted to apologise for yesterday," Rick says standing by the door. "I promised you that I would treat you no differently to any of my men and I thought I was doing the right thing by saying no and trying to protect you." I sit quietly and listen to him. "If you hadn't have come along to the location and did what you did... We all would have been killed, myself and Conall included." He pauses for a moment and thinks about what to say next.

"Forget it," I say quietly. "You were just trying to do what any dad would do, I guess."

"Well, I am sorry anyway," he replies. "You are very stubborn and you surprised me with how strong you were. You are so much like your mother..." I can see the pain in his eyes. "I am not going to pretend that you are going to just accept me in to your life or that I can even begin to make up for everything I've missed, but I hope you will at least tolerate me and give me a chance to be in your life now. I've been a pretty shit dad." I smile at him slightly.

"I wouldn't know," I say. "I've got nothing else to compare it too." Rick sighs and looks down at the floor.

"Do you need anything? I can have one of my men get you whatever you want," he replies but I just shake my head.

"No, thank you. To be honest I don't think I'll hang around here much longer." Rick looks up concerned that he has done something really wrong. "It's not you or even this place. It's just I need some time to pull myself together and I'd rather do that at home. You know in my own bed with actual real food and stuff." I shuffle to the edge of the bed and try to force myself to stand up, Rick comes straight over and takes my arm.

"Are you sure you will be OK?" He asks concerned.

"I will be, I've had a lot worse than this," I laugh at myself as I try to put weight on my leg. I get pain through my knee but it's bearable and I know I should be able to walk, even if it is with a massive limp.

I smile at Rick, and he leaves go of my arm as I attempt to wander over to my bag and grab a pair of black denim cut off shorts and carefully put them on whilst trying not to fall over and groaning again as they skim over the strapping on my knee. I can't be arsed to get changed, so I just leave the t-shirt on that I was wearing yesterday, even though it is covered in blood and then grab my boots. I gently ease myself back on to the bed, so I can put them on, which is kind of difficult with only one good hand seen as though the other is also strapped up and painful. Rick notices my phone on the side table and nods towards it.

"Would you mind if I took your number? Maybe we can keep in touch." I nod my head as he walks over and picks it up, he passes it to me briefly to unlock it then he puts his number in the phone, after a few seconds I hear his phone in his pocket ping before he hands me it back.

"Just don't be a stranger for the next 20 odd years, OK?" I say sarcastically and Rick smiles at me. I stand back up and throw the couple of loose things that I have dotted around in to my bag then zip it up. I put the phone in my back pocket and pick up my car keys.

"Are you OK to drive in your state?" Rick stands looking at me. I know I look a mess but I just nod.

"I'll be fine, it's not too far for me to get back," I reply. We both stand awkwardly for a few moments then I smile and step forward to give him a hug. He pauses as I catch him off guard, but then he wraps his arms around my shoulders and hugs me back. This is my first dad hug, and it's actually quite nice. We part after a minute or so, and he smiles at me.

"I am proud of you," he says and I smile back.

I sigh then turn, pick up my bag and head for the door, I hide how much pain I am in as I walk through the base and head outside to where my car is. I limp over and put my bag in the back, being careful not to put too much strain on my shoulder.

"You're leaving aren't you?" I hear from behind me, I turn and see Conall standing watching me.

"Yeah," I say quietly.

"Is it because of me?" Conall asks but I quickly shake my head.

"No, of course not, please don't think that at all. I just don't fancy being a burden to anyone for the next few days when I'm like this," I look down at myself, I am covered in bruises, blood and bandages... again.

"Are you going back to see Gideon?" He asks bluntly. He crosses his arms, clearly upset that I am leaving but I'm struggling with how to reply to him as I can't find the right words.

"I'm going back to Newcastle, I have an apartment in town that I share with my best friend... Gideon lives in that area, so..." I try to think of something else to say but my mind is blank.

"OK... Well have a safe drive," Conall says quietly.

"I'll try," I reply, uncertain as to what else to say.

I feel like no matter what I do now I am just going to upset someone. I don't want to leave here thinking that Conall hates me because I pushed away his advances. I don't want to hurt anyone, not him or Gideon, I feel so guilty and I haven't even done anything apart from care about them both a little too much. Conall approaches me slowly then without warning he wraps his arm around my waist and holds my head then kisses me with such passion that I just stand rooted to the spot and let it happen as I am unsure what's going on. Conall kisses me deeply, holding me close to him and enjoying every sensation of his mouth on mine. After a while he pulls away and stands smiling down at me, I feel kind of swept up and just look at him stunned.

"I could never hate you, so please, don't think like that," he says softly. "I'll be here for a few more days, then I'll be heading home... But I don't have any other plans so maybe I could... We could come and visit you," he smiles wider. "No pressure, we can just hang out, all of us, just friends." I nod my head.

"I'd like that," I reply. "It will be nice to see everyone again." I smile more as Conall steps away and lets me get in to the car. I struggle a little as my knee jerks as I climb in and Conall stands at the open door watching me.

"You sure you can drive?" He asks raising his eyebrows at me as he sees me try to hide the pain.

"I will soon find out when I try," I smile. I go to put my seat belt on and groan as my shoulder aches.

"Here, let me," Conall says as he reaches over and puts my seat belt on for me. "I wish you wouldn't go so soon, at least give yourself some time to heal."

"I'll be fine, stop worrying," I say and shake my head. Conall nods and steps back as I shut the car door. I start the engine and flash him a smile before driving off and leaving him behind.

I stop for a break about half-way home as my back, wrist and knee are killing me, I try to stretch a little, just the position of sitting in this car seat is doing my head in. I take out my phone to occupy my mind for a couple minutes before I continue home and smile as I see I have a couple of messages, the reception at the base was so crap when I first got there that I forgot to even tell anyone I found Rick.

The latest message is from Conall, it says...

- I hijacked your phone and put my number in, now I can stalk you whenever I want. -

I laugh at the message and scroll down, there is one from Kerry that just says...

- Hey bitch tits, you still alive? -

I laugh again, straight to the point and shows so much love from her. The last message is from Gideon. My heart skips as I open it and read what he said.

- Hey, haven't heard from you in a couple of days, hope you are OK. Let me know when you get back, I am missing you so much. -

I smile at his message and click reply, I think for a few seconds then type.

- Sorry I haven't text, things have been hectic and signal was shit. I'm on my way home now, I can call in and see you before I head back to the apartment if you are not busy. I would really like to see you. -

I press send and almost immediately I get a reply.

- I can't wait to see you too. I'll be waiting. -

I smile as I pull away and continue the rest of the journey home. I'm actually nervous about seeing Gideon again, I am starting to enjoy his company, and he makes me feel so alive. I'm excited to see what happens between us, the whole dating thing is totally new to me but I think that I am ready to give it a try.

I finally get in to town just as it's getting dark and pull up in the car park opposite the club, I can't remember the way to get around to the garage so this will have to do. I pull down the visor in the car and have a look at myself, no make up and my hair is a mess. I pull off the plasters that cover the cuts on my head and the wound on my neck and look at them. They have healed slightly but not as much or as quickly as my injuries usual do. I'm going to put that down to over excursion and using my powers yesterday, they drained me and it clearly shows as I look like crap.

I get out of the car and shut the door, I moan slightly and grab my shoulder, having it in a fixed position whilst driving has made it sore. My wrist is painful to even move still, so I use my good hand to lock the car then limp towards the club. It's strangely quiet, the doors are open and there are a few people milling around, although I suppose it is still really early, no normal person goes out clubbing at this time of day. I head in through the front doors and go towards the stairs that lead up to the office. There's no security around yet and no one notices me as I struggle to get up the steps with my busted knee, I almost waddle towards the lift and get in then head up to the apartment.

Why am I still so fucking tired? Claudia must have taken more blood from me than I thought, and it took so much effort to push her out of my mind. I am sure I'll be fine in a couple days though. The lift opens and I step out.

"Velvet!" Gideon says smiling wildly at me, he stands up from the sofa in anticipation. He is holding a bunch of roses, and he's wearing smart black trousers and a dark red dress shirt. His smile falters slightly as he notices all of my injuries and that I am in a lot of pain.

"Hi," I say trying to hide how crappy I am feeling.

"What the fuck happened?" Gideon asks concerned, he puts the flowers down on the coffee table. "Who did this?" I winch again as I take a step forward and sigh.

"I kind of had a run in with Claudia," I say and Gideon's face changes. "I'm OK though, just a little sore and weak, I lost a lot of blood."

"Is she dead?" Gideon asks, I can see he hates her.

"No, she got away," I say quietly. Gideon notices the bite marks on my neck and his eyes go wide.

"She didn't do..." He says nervously.

"No," I reply. I know what he is thinking, after she had me under her control last time she did things to me that, even now, makes me feel dirty. "She tried to, she got straight in my head like she did before, but I was able to block her out. She just didn't seem to like that much... hence this." I point to my neck.

"Did you find Rick?" Gideon changes the subject.

"Yes I did. We talked and I think things are alright between us," I reply and give him a slight smile then I look over at the roses. "Are those for me?" I smile nervously as Gideon picks them back up.

"Yes. I did a lot of thinking after you left and I said that I would prove my love to you when you got back... I saw these and thought you might like them," Gideon says cautiously, his eyes catch mine and I can't help but smile at how nice of a gesture it is. No one has ever bought me flowers before, as soon as I've seen him again all of those feelings come flooding back and I know I did the right thing in not pursuing things with Conall. I want to give Gideon a chance, yes there are a lot of things to work out, but I am ready.

"They are beautiful, thank you," I say. I feel my cheeks go red as Gideon walks around the sofa and comes towards me. He bites his bottom lip gently as I know he wants to kiss me, he wants to sweep me off my feet and fuck me right here and I would happily let him. I didn't realise until I saw him again how much I really do like him, my feelings for him are getting so much stronger. Gideon smiles and takes a deep breath as he approaches then suddenly stops in his tracks, I look at him confused as his face changes, he doesn't look happy any more.

"Gideon, is something wrong?" I say cautiously. He looks me up and down and gives me a disgusted look.

"You stink of dog," he says bluntly. I'm quite taken aback and just stand for a moment trying to understand what he said.

"Excuse me?" I say bewildered.

"I said, you stink of dog. I can smell it all over you," Gideon spits, he moves closer and leans in to sniff me again. "It's so strong... it's the scent of an Alpha." I take a step back and shake my head.

"You have got it all wrong, Gideon. That's Conall, he is just a friend," I try to explain.

"You are lying to me," Gideon says forcefully, he looks across my body again then his eyes are drawn to the wolf mark on my forearm. He grabs my arm and moves it to see it more clearly.

"Ahhh... Gideon, you are hurting me," I groan as pain shoots through my shoulder as he tugs my arm more.

"I saw this mark when you came back after the Bird Cage but it didn't click in my head where it came from... How could I be so stupid," Gideon snarls.

"It... it just happened, I... I made some friends and they needed help. My magic and power saved lives," I try to explain.

"Where did you say this wolf comes from?" Gideon asks forcefully, tugging my arm again as pain rips through my chest and I struggle to hold back the immense pain.

"I didn't," I snap back. "I stumbled across the pack at Christmas, they were in the Highlands in Scotland." Gideon watches my face as I speak, trying to work out why I smell the way I do.

"You fucked him didn't you?" Gideon tries to stay calm but I can see anger in his eyes. "How else would you have this mark?"

"You know what this is?" I ask nervously and Gideon nods.

"Of course I do, so what happened? His pack invited you in with open arms and just happened to make you their Guardian?" Gideon's grip on my arm becomes firmer and I moan in pain under his fingers. "Because if I remember correctly from that pack they haven't had Elders or any magic folk up there for centuries... Did they just offer you the position and wave some poncey magic wand and transform you in to their protector... because I don't recall that happening back in the early days." I don't know what to say. "So what did you have to do to complete the ritual? Fuck the Alpha? Fuck his Beta?" I try and remain calm but my body starts to shake, his eyes burn, and he is really hurting me. "Or was it both of them? One of them was just not enough for a fucking little whore like you." I swallow hard and I instantly see that Gideon knows exactly what happened.

"It wasn't like that," I try to defend myself. "That was before I came back, before I knew you loved me." I try to pull my arm away but it just causes me more pain.

"So if all this happened ages ago, why do you stink of him now?" Gideon sneers at me, his face so close to mine and his teeth on show. I shouldn't have to defend myself, I've done nothing wrong.

"Not that it's any of your business," I reply firmly, "he was with my dad forming a coalition. I didn't go looking for him if that is what you think. He helped me after I'd been hurt by Claudia and made sure I was OK. I haven't done anything wrong Gideon," I snap and finally force my arm free from his grip. "I'm not going to lie because I said I would always be honest with you... Yes, I kissed him, but I told him to stop because I had agreed to take things further with you. I told him you loved me and that I cared for you, that I didn't want to betray your trust even though we are not even in a fucking relationship." Gideon watches me, his chest heaving as he tries not to flip out.

"Then why don't I believe you?" Gideon finally says through gritted teeth.

"I don't give a shit if you believe me or not, it's the truth," I stand firm then Gideon turns his back on me. "I came back for you Gideon, I came back because I want to take things further with you, I want to see what happens between us... I smell of him because he stayed with me when I was hurt and I didn't want to face the idea of being alone. I care for you so much that I walked away from him and my dad just to get back here. I want to move forward with you, nobody else, I want a relationship. I want to make things work between us... I... I really do have very strong feelings for you and I want to..." Gideon stands silent and I'm not sure what else I can say.

"Get out!" He says quietly.

"What?" I don't understand what's happening now.

"Get out... I can't even look at you right now," he says through gritted teeth.

The room goes silent but it's almost deafening. I try to think of something to say, something that will make things right but my mind is empty. I stand for a moment as tears sting my eyes and roll uncontrollably down my face, then turn to head for the lift, before I get there the doors open and Tristen steps out.

"Hey, Velvet you're back, thank God for that because this arsehole has been swanning around like a love sick puppy, it was getting boring... Shit, what have you been up too?" Tristen looks down at me.

"Nothing!" I say quietly, the tears cover my cheeks and I put my head down as I go to step in to the lift.

"What's wrong? Has something happened?" He asks concerned but I just ignore him. I quickly step past him and get in to the lift as he looks across to Gideon then back to me.

"It was nice seeing you again, Tristen," I say almost at a murmur as I try to keep myself from breaking down in front of him then push the button on the lift, as the doors begin to close I hear Tristen talking to Gideon then the sounds of glass smashing, filling the apartment. As the lift goes down I start to feel pissed off, how fucking dare he, I storm down the stairs and out of the club as best I can before getting in the car. What a fucking arsehole he is. I didn't do anything wrong. It's not like we were in a relationship or anything, I didn't cheat on him or sleep around behind his back.

I just sit in the car staring at the steering wheel, I can't believe what has just happened. I mean I don't even understand what just happened, he just totally flipped out. I take a deep breath and as though I just opened the flood gates, I start crying, I literally sit in the car and sob my heart out. I don't care if anyone sees me, I don't care if I look like a complete loser, I just don't know what I've done wrong to make Gideon do that. Obviously everything is so fucked up now that I don't even know what to do next.

Chapter Eight

After my argument with Gideon I went straight back to my apartment and I've pretty much spent the last 5 days binge eating shit and feeling sorry for myself. I've been trying to understand what I did that was so wrong, I mean yes, I know I slept with a couple of people but as I kept telling Gideon we were not meant to be serious. When I first came home after the fight, Kerry was concerned, and she could tell that there was something wrong straight away, she always did know when I wasn't myself.

I walk through the door and stop, Kerry is on the sofa with a topless man, and I am not sure how to process everything, so I just stand still and look at them.

"Oh, hey," Kerry says as she sees me, she pushes the man off her as they were making out on the sofa, and she gets up.

"I should go," the half naked man says, then picks up his t-shirt from the floor and smiles as he passes me and leaves. I force a smile at Kerry as she notices I've been crying and my eyes are all red.

"What's happened?" Kerry asks concerned. I shake my head and look away.

"I don't want to talk about it." I am not even sure I know myself.

"This is because of him isn't it?" She says firmly and I glance up. "That arsehole Gideon has done something and now... I can feel that you're hurting." I take a deep breath and force a smile.

"Who was that?" I ask her, trying to change the subject then Kerry gives me a coy smile.

"He's... erm... Oh fuck! I can't remember his name," she laughs at herself. "He's been hanging out here for a couple of days and I know he told me it, but I just..." She shrugs and it makes me smile.

"So what have you been calling him?" I ask trying not to laugh.

"Well, I got up this morning and when he... Got out of my bed I just said, hey you, I don't think he noticed." We both laugh and then Kerry sighs. "You OK?" I stand for a moment and think.

"No, not really," I say as I feel my eyes sting with tears again. Kerry comes straight over to me and gives me a hug, I don't understand why I am so emotional. This is why I didn't want to get close to anyone, I didn't want to get hurt.

Less than 48 hours after getting back I had already demolished my own weight in junk food and watched enough Netflix to have shares in the company. My phone has been vibrating for the last few hours, so I give in and pick it up to have a look. I can instantly see that the messages are all from Gideon, I contemplate not opening them, but I am too curious to see what he has to say. I take a deep breath and open them.

- Can we talk? I'm sorry. -

Bollocks is he sorry, he went in to a rage because I smelt like someone else. Fuck me! Am I not even allowed to have friends now? I scroll down to the next one.

- I didn't mean to hurt you, I reacted badly. Can I see you? -

I sit up on the sofa and sigh.

"What's up? I know that face." Kerry sits over the other side watching me.

"Gideon text me, I'm not sure what to do," I say quietly.

"Tell him to go fuck himself. He's an absolute twat," she replies, I can tell she is angry at him.

"I know, but I liked him... a lot," I try to explain.

"Well I like junk food and shots, but I know that's bad for me. Just like Gideon is bad for you, he tried to buy you like a prostitute, everything that's happened to you and caused you pain is his fucking fault. I swear he boils my fucking piss that man," Kerry says, not holding anything back. I know she's never really liked him and I've given him multiple chances... Maybe things were my fault. If I had told

Gideon about the wolves when I first came back then he would have been fine. I don't reply to Kerry instead I scroll to the next message and read what it says.

- I love you, I don't want us to fight. I just want to make you happy. -

I sit for a moment and think then throw my phone on to the table. It's all bullshit, it's just more of his lies to keep me close.

Day four and I've had several missed calls and voice mails, although I haven't listened to them. Maybe if I ignore him enough I'll stop feeling so bad.

"Do you want a coffee?" Kerry asks as she heads towards the kitchen.

"Yes please," I'm feeling a little better today but I'm still just exhausted and feeling a bit icky. I think I am getting the flu or something as the last few days I haven't been able to stomach anything and when Kerry offers me rum I just want to be sick. She thinks it's because I liked him so much that it's now like I am having a bad break up and I need to get over myself. She even went as far as to say that she knows I love him, even if I will not say it.

There's a knock on the door and Kerry heads straight over to answer it. She opens the door, pauses for a second then goes to shut it.

"Please Kerry? I just want to talk to her," I hear Gideon say, he sounds sincere I guess.

"She not in," Kerry says bluntly. There's a few seconds of silence before Gideon speaks again.

"I know she's in Kerry, I can see her sitting on the sofa," Gideon says cautiously, but I ignore him and don't even look over.

"She doesn't want to see you," Kerry replies, she won't take any of his shit.

"Please, I just want to talk, I want to apologise," Gideon begs.

"You are not welcome here any more," Kerry says firmly and I hear Gideon sigh and take a step back. Is that like a thing? Can you un-invite vampires from your home? I guess you can because otherwise if he really wanted to he could just barge past her.

"Velvet?" Gideon calls to me from the door way. "I know you can hear me. I'm so sorry that I hurt you, please I just... Please, can we talk?" I think for a moment and shake my head.

"I'm not ready to talk to you," I say bluntly and then fall silent.

"There's your answer vampire boy, now fuck off," Kerry says and slams the door in his face. The apartment is quiet and after a couple minutes Kerry comes and sits next to me then gives me a hug.

"Are you alright?" She asks gently. I smile and nod my head.

"Yeah, I'm fine... I don't believe you just said that to him," I reply, and we both laugh slightly. I'm just feeling a bit ill and the last thing I need is to argue with him some more.

I wake up on day five of the break up, as Kerry calls it, and I feel quite good about things. I had a really good sleep, which is the first time in ages and I actually feel refreshed. I ate breakfast, granted it was left over pizza but I ate it at breakfast time so it counts, and when I looked at my phone this morning there was a message waiting to be read from Conall.

I make myself a cup of coffee and curl up on the sofa, Kerry stopped out last night, so I'm assuming she found a new man friend to play with. I pick up my phone and read Conall's text.

- Hey, so are you still OK for us to come visit? Tiffany won't let you say no -

I smile and text back.

- Oh I don't know like, don't think you guys could handle spending time in my neck of the woods -

I press send and take a sip of my coffee, within a minute I get a reply.

- Please miss? Let this poor little farm boy come and see the big city, I want to be amazed by all the lights -

I laugh at Conall's message then reply again.

- I suppose I could squeeze you an hour or so in to my busy life. When are you thinking of coming down? -

I sit and wait for a reply, I am really excited to see them all again. My phone eventually pings and I look at the message.

- Hopefully sometime soon, just tying up some loose ends up here, and we will be planning a road trip. Send me your address so I know where to send all the strip-o-grams and roly poly's -

I can't help but smile at him, I love how he is never serious and can always make things fun. I go to text back and at the exact same time my phone rings and I accidentally answer it. I freeze as it was Gideon trying to call again and I've been pretty good at ignoring him. Fuck! I've done it now.

"Hello," I say down the phone, I am so pissed off at myself for doing that.

"Velvet, it's so good to hear your voice, I didn't think you were going to pick up," Gideon says softly.

"Yeah, well, I didn't plan on it!" I say bluntly, how stupid could I be. "What do you want Gideon?"

"I was a massive dick head to you the other day and I shouldn't have been..." He tries to explain.

"Yes, you were," I agree with him.

"You were right, we were not a couple, and we are not in a relationship, so I had no right to act the way I did... I just got a little jealous that there might have been someone else who was close to you instead of me." I don't know what to say, so I just sit quiet and listen to him. "I know I upset you, and I am sure you are massively pissed off at me, but please, I'm begging you for another chance." I sigh and think about what to say. I can understand why he did what he did, and I know how fiery and passionate he is...

"OK," I reply. "But I am not going to act like everything is suddenly back to being normal because it's not. I am majorly pissed off with you and you said some pretty shitty things to me."

"I know and I regret that," Gideon jumps in. "Please, will you come and see me tonight? I want to make this right." There is a long pause as he waits for an answer. I know I shouldn't but I do still have feelings for him, I can't just switch them off.

"I'll see you tonight," I say then hang up the phone, he sounded so genuine on the call. I suppose if he had been away for a few days and came back smelling of another woman I would be a bit jealous as well and jump to the wrong conclusions.

Nothing much else happened today, I had a shower and got dressed, I refuse to make an effort for Gideon though, not like I have done before, so if he wants to see me then he's getting the jeans and hoodie me, I don't give a shit any more, if he doesn't like this version of me then he doesn't deserve any version.

It's Saturday night and I know that when I get to his club it will be busy, it's only 6.30pm when I walk over but I can see from a distance there are already loads of people around. There's not really a queue, so I wander over to the doors, the security guy goes to stop me then I notice it's the guy that I scared the crap out of when I first came back to see Gideon. He just gives me a nod and I walk straight past him, I don't look around to see if there is anyone I recognise, I just keep my head down and go towards the stairs. As I approach another security guy stops me.

"You can't go up there, it's for employees only," he says firmly, I sigh and go to explain but before I do I hear Greg shout over the music from behind the bar that I am cleared to go up. I glance at Greg and give him a slight smile as the security guy steps aside and I head up towards the apartment. As I walk towards the lift a man gets out, he's about my height but pure muscle with long blond hair tied back in a ponytail and a beard. We pass each other as he leaves and I walk in to the lift, I press the button to go up and wait for it to move.

I don't know what Gideon and me are going to discuss, I felt so ready to move things forward with him, but when he blew up it just put me straight back to that super confused me again. My mind starts to wander and I then wonder who that man was who just left. You know when you get that feeling that you have seen them before but you can't place exactly where? This is that feeling now, it was probably just one of the many vampires I've seen knocking around with Gideon and Tristen, so I try not to dwell on it.

The door opens and I step out, the apartment is empty and I just stand nervously at the side for a moment, unsure what to do. There is a new TV on the wall and the glass coffee table that was here before is now black wood, I assume those are the smashing sounds I heard the other day.

The kitchen door opens and Tristen walks out laughing, he stops when he sees me.

"Hi," he says giving me a small smile.

"Hi," I reply nervously. I don't even know where to look, so I just concentrate on the floor.

"Are you here to see Gideon?" Tristen asks me, I just nod my head. "I'll go and tell him you're here."

I smile as Tristen heads towards Gideon's bedroom. I feel really awkward, do I sit down? Do I just stand here? I don't know what to do for the best. I decide to just stand here, I don't want to look too comfortable if he walks in and I'm sat on the sofa, but then again if I am stood here it might look like I don't want to see him.

"You came!" I turn to see Gideon standing a few meters from me, I nod my head, and he gestures towards the sofa. "Do you want to sit down?"

He seems as nervous as I do, which makes me feel slightly better, so I nod again and walk towards the sofa. Gideon waits for me to sit down then sits opposite me, I don't talk, I just wait for him to say something first.

"I see your injuries have healed, are you feeling better now?" Gideon asks, trying to make small talk.

"Yeah, I'm fine," I reply quietly.

"Do you want something to drink?" Gideon asks.

"No, thank you," I say looking down at the floor.

"I erm... I want to apologise for the way I behaved. It was wrong of me," Gideon says whilst he sits watching me, I don't want to make eye contact with him as I'm currently somewhere between screaming at him and crying, I need to try to stay calm.

"You called me a whore," I say bluntly. I didn't want to start with that bit but it just slipped out. Gideon swallows and looks down as though he is ashamed.

"I did, and I am sorry for that," he says cautiously. "I shouldn't have said that to you, it's just when you..."

"It's just when I what, Gideon?" I snap at him. "Do not sit there and try to shift the blame for what happened on to me... Let's explore why you called me a whore shall we?" Maybe the calm me is not going to stay very long.

"I didn't mean it, Velvet," Gideon explains.

"Yes, yes you did otherwise you wouldn't have said it..." I know that I am very angry. "I'll break it down for you... I met a random guy in a bar, and he saved my life, I am a free single woman, so I decided that I would sleep with him. I then meet his dashing brother and although there were a few bumps in the road I found myself attracted to him and I fucked him, if you aren't keeping up that's you and Tristen that I am talking about." Gideon nods and rolls his eyes at me, which only makes me more wound up. "So we, as in us two, have like one day of fun and then you tell me to leave, so I do and I go and find out about my dad. At that time Gideon you were probably nothing more to me than a one night stand, but stupidly I liked you and I felt sad when I left."

"You can stop now," Gideon says quietly.

"No, I am going to get this all out in the open," I continue. "After my first run in with the General, I wallowed in self-pity for over a month until I got the grand idea to go to Edinburgh because I thought Kerry might be alive. At the same time I was publicly put on the most wanted list and found myself at the mercy of a hunter who had me restrained to the point that I couldn't fight back. That's when I ran in to Ranulf, and he helped me escape."

"Who's Ranulf?" Gideon asks but I ignore his question and continue.

"Ranulf took me to the pack and to his sister who was a Doctor, and they helped me," I say. "A lot of shit happened when I was with the wolf pack, I saved lives, I briefly died, I connected to their founding powers and yes, I became their Guardian. I didn't go looking for it, it just happened and things between myself, Conall and Ranulf just seemed the natural thing to happen at the time to get me in a position where I was capable of helping their pack more," I pause for a moment and glance at Gideon, he doesn't say a word instead he just sits listening. "What happened was a one time thing, just the one. I left the pack when I sacrificed myself to the General and then when I was free from being hunted and every one thought I was dead, I came back to see you... My feelings for you started to grow and I felt that you deserved the chance to get to know me more... I am not saying it's just because you said you loved me, but there has always been a connection between us and I just wanted to... maybe have more."

"So what happened when you went away again?" Gideon asks quietly. I can tell that he is already realising that he is a dick head and that he was wrong of accusing me of things.

"Nothing! Exactly what I said happened," I reply. "When I found Rick and after he took me back to his base, Conall was there. I didn't go off looking for him if that is what you think. He told me he had feelings for me and tried to kiss me, I told him that I couldn't do that with him as I was kind of involved and that I didn't want to betray your trust in me. Yes, he did say he wanted to take me out and that he liked me, I am not going to lie but, again yes I felt something, I don't know what exactly it is I feel for him though. Then we had the run in with Claudia, and I was badly injured, Conall took me back to the base and because I was freezing and hurt, I didn't want to be alone, so he just lay down next to me and stayed by my side all night. Apart from a kiss there was nothing more because I left there to come home to you... I wanted to be with you." I think that was everything, I don't know what else I could possibly say.

"I'm sorry," Gideon finally says after a long silence. "I just love you so much that jealously took over, I couldn't bear the thought of him being near you and wanting you."

"And you should have trusted me and listened to what I had to say instead of attacking me with accusations and being a total bell end," I snap then take a deep breath. "So if all that makes me a whore to you, then I guess I am."

"I told you I didn't mean it," Gideon replies firmly trying to get his point across. "What can I do to make this situation better?"

"Try not being an arsehole for once and sticking to that promise we made to always be honest with each other," I say. I'm actually quite proud of myself for not losing my head with him.

"I promise," Gideon gives me a small smile. "Do you still like me at least?"

"I shouldn't because you are a dick head... But I do," I say reluctantly. I can't just switch off the feelings I have for him.

"Can you give me another chance?" He asks almost pleading. "I promise I won't flip out again, I won't be an arsehole and I'll listen to you instead of jumping to conclusions, and lastly I promise not to get jealous just because you have friends."

"OK," I say and nod my head then smile slightly. "So... What happens next?" Gideon smiles at me and stands up.

"Next? You take my hand." He holds out his hand towards me and I reach up and take it. "Then you stand up and let me kiss you." Gideon stands in front of me hoping that I do just that, but I let him stew for a few seconds before I smile at him and get to my feet. I feel a little nervous as though it's the first time all over again, he pushes away some hair that was in my face and tucks it behind my ear then leans down and gently kisses my lips.

"I missed you," Gideon says softly when our lips part, he holds me close and looks down at me with loving eyes.

"I missed you too," I reply as he leans in and kisses me again, this time deeper and with passion. The kisses that could sweep you off your feet and make you want to get lost in his arms. I feel my phone vibrate in my back pocket but I ignore it, I just want to stay in this moment, blissful and happy. Then my mind wanders and something pops in to my head, it bugs me so much that Gideon stops and looks confused.

"What's wrong?" He asks concerned. I think for a second before I answer.

"When I got here there was a man leaving the apartment." I still can't shake the feeling that I know him. "Who was he?" Gideon smiles sweetly and takes a step back.

"Just a work colleague, people come and go all day in this place, some days I can't keep track myself," Gideon says gently then places his hand on my arm and pulls me in to kiss him again, before my lips touch his I lean back slightly, and he stops.

"I just could have sworn I've seen him somewhere before that's all," I say trying desperately to remember because it's driving me nuts.

"He's probably just been in the club before when you have been here," Gideon reassures me.

No! That doesn't sound right, I would have realised he was a vampire. He seems so familiar, as though... Then it hits me and I pull away from Gideon's grip and shake my head.

"That can't be right," I say to myself.

"What are you talking about Velvet? You're being paranoid," Gideon tries to convince me but I don't think I am.

"I don't know his name, but I am almost certain of where I've seen him before," I say nervously. "You said you wouldn't lie to me not 2 minutes ago, you promised to be honest with me, no matter what."

"I am being honest with you," Gideon says acting confused.

"Then why don't you explain to me why a member of the Midnight Church, whom I watched help drag an innocent girl in to their basement then hold in place whilst Helana slit her throat in a sacrifice, has just left your apartment?" I demand, Gideon freezes and I can see guilt in his eyes.

"It's not what you think," he says quickly.

"It's not? Because what I think is that even after everything that has happened, you are still trying to maintain an alliance with Helana and one of her minions has been here talking terms." My heart start to beat faster. "You knew that I was coming here tonight and you still ran the risk of someone who follows that fucking bitch recognising me and telling Helana exactly where I am." I'm fuming, why does this keep happening, am I destined to just argue with Gideon until I die.

"I didn't think," Gideon says nervously.

"You didn't think? Are you fucking kidding me? Next you're going to tell me that all these meetings you have been having have been with her." I am trying so hard to not raise my voice but Gideon looks down, guilt all over his face. "You do remember that she murdered my mother, right? That even as a baby she wanted me dead and that given the chance she will kill me. But yet you still invite her people in to your home and pander to her... What? Threats? Requests?... I don't even know, all this to form a greater bond against the hunters? Is that the aim here?"

"I did what I had to do to protect my people," Gideon finally snaps back "Regardless of who she is to you, I couldn't have her as a threat."

"But she is a threat to me," I shout. "Don't you get that? No matter how much you say you love me or what kind of truce you and her have, she will kill me if she knows that I am alive."

"I wouldn't let that happen," Gideon says through gritted teeth. "If she lay one finger on you then I'd kill her myself, but you have to understand that I have obligations to my people." I stand looking at him, I don't know what else to say. I do understand why he has to do this sort of thing but I don't like it, and I am scared that she will already know that I am here if he recognised me. Silence fills the room as we both just stand waiting for the other to make the next move.

The lift pings behind us and opens, the security guy from the bottom of the stairs walks in then stops when he spots us. Gideon gives me an apologetic look then glances to the security guy.

"Sorry to interrupt you Sir, but can I have a word?" He says. Gideon nods just as my phone starts to vibrate again in my back pocket.

"What is it?" Gideon asks the security man.

"There may be a possible situation down stairs, but we wanted to run it by you first," he replies.

I glance at my phone and I see that Conall is calling me, seen as Gideon is a bit occupied now, I answer it.

"Hello?" I say trying to stifle a smile, if he's calling then they must be making plans to come visit and honestly I am looking forward to seeing Tiffany.

"Where are you?" I hear Conall shout over loud music. "We came to surprise you but you weren't at the address you gave us, someone called Kerry said you were at some club, so we are here now." My heart drops, they can't be in here, in Gideon's club. I glance over to Gideon as he continues to talk to security.

"What do you mean the bouncers think they smell unusual?" Gideon asks him confused. This isn't good, Gideon flipped out just because he could smell Conall on my clothes, never mind him being in this club right now.

"You need to leave," I try to say down the phone without Gideon hearing. "You shouldn't be here."

"What do you mean? I thought you might like the surprise," Conall shouts down the phone. My heart starts to race as I panic, Gideon can't know that Conall is here, he will flip out.

"I'm coming down, I need you to leave though," I say quickly then press the button to open the lift doors.

"Wolves?" Gideon says to security. "There are wolves in my club?"

The security guy nods as Gideon starts to get angry, he looks over to me just in time to see the lift doors close. I pray that I am being stupid, I hope so much that my mind is over reacting and Gideon is cool but as soon as I get out of the lift the doors close and heads back upstairs where Gideon is waiting. I shove my phone in my pocket and run, I almost slide down the stairs as I notice Conall near the front doors. I barge my way through the now packed club and Conall turns and smiles at me as he sees me approach.

"Hi," Conall shouts as he beams, I quickly notice he's not alone, Tiffany, Ranulf, Dee and Ben are all here. Oh great, not only two of the wolves I fucked but the Generals hunter son is here as well.

"Get out!" I shout at him and try to push him towards the exit.

"What's going on?" Conall looks puzzled but I don't have time to explain.

"It's not safe here, for any of you, you need to leave now," I demand.

"OK, we will go, whatever you want," Conall says and turns to leave, but he stops as he walks in to someone who is standing behind him. "Sorry man, I was just leaving," Conall apologies and smiles then goes to walk around him but is stopped again as a hand is placed on his chest and I know without even looking up that it's all a bit too late.

"What are you doing here?" Gideon asks firmly, his unbridled authority is back in full force. Conall looks confused and just shrugs.

"We came to visit a friend," Conall says pointing over his shoulder at me. I can see the others are as confused as Conall. Gideon is full of anger, so I quickly move and stand between them both.

"They were just leaving," I say calmly to Gideon, but he doesn't even look at me, instead he stares down Conall.

"Velvet what's going on?" Ranulf asks from the side.

"Nothing, everything is fine, isn't it?" I shove Gideon slightly to try and get his attention, but he continues to ignore me.

"This is weird... so we are just going to leave now," Conall says slowly then carefully pushes Gideon's hand off his chest and goes to walk out.

"How dare they come here," Gideon snarls down at me.

"Gideon please, I thought we got past this?" I ask pleading with him to let it drop. "You promised." I notice Conall stop out of the corner of my eye and turn back towards me.

"Is this him?" Conall asks bluntly. I glance at him and nod but my eyes are begging him to walk away. "Hmm, he seems like proper wanker to me."

I don't even have time to blink before Gideon turns, he grabs Conall and pushes him up against the wall. Some of the party goers move out of the way as a couple of security guards come running over.

"What did you say?" Gideon is furious, even from here I can see his eyes start to burn. Ranulf goes to pull Gideon off him but Conall shakes his head and Ranulf stops then steps back. Conall looks Gideon dead in the eye showing him no fear.

"She may not have told me much about you, but I heard things in her dreams. You don't deserve her, not after everything you have done," Conall snaps back. There's a moment of rest before Gideon grabs Conall's neck and quickly forces him towards the front doors then throws him outside. We all follow fast, just as I get outside I see Kerry heading over towards the entrance.

"What's going on?" She shouts over the road and I shake my head. Conall picks himself up from the ground and stands, facing Gideon.

"You think you're the hard man?" Conall shouts as he gets up close to Gideon's face and shows him that he's not scared. Tristen and Greg come out behind us as Gideon turns to them and tells them to back off. It seems Conall and Gideon have some issues with each other, and they don't want anyone else involved.

"You made a mistake coming here mutt," Gideon snarls back. Tiffany stands by my side, I can see she is worried for her brother.

"Gideon stand down!" I shout as I step forward to try to break them up.

"I'll fucking kill you for touching her, your scent was all over her when she got back," Gideon steps forward, his and Conall's chests almost touching trying to out man each other.

"You can try arsehole, I've been wanting to fuck you up all week," Conall growls at him.

I step in to push them apart, to try to defuse the situation but Gideon grabs my arm and shoves me away with immense force, I fall backwards and land hard on the concrete clutching my arm, rolling slightly as I hit the curb, my cheek is sore and feels as though it has scraped across the ground. Ben and Dee come straight over to help me as Conall pushes Gideon but Gideon quickly reciprocates and pushes Conall hard, knocking him off his feet and back a good 10 meters. They are both so powerful. Conall growls and then gets up and runs. It all happens so fast that I hardly see him change, all I know is that it is not Conall that tackles Gideon to the ground, but the wolf.

The air around us is filled with shouting and screaming as people watch this large ginger wolf fight a vampire in the middle of the street. Tiffany shouts at Conall to stop as Greg holds Tristen back from getting involved. Kerry runs over and helps me up then tries to make sure I am OK but I don't even know if I am any more, I am hurt, both emotionally and physically. Dee carefully helps me remove my hoodie and I look down and hold my arm as it is consumed with pain, and blood falls down my cheek.

Gideon grabs Conall and throws him to the ground, Gideon's shirt is ripped, and he has claw marks across his face of the fight so far. Before Conall can get up Gideon jumps on him and the wolf howls as Gideon plunges his fangs in to his neck to try to cause him damage. Conall rolls and manages to get away from Gideon's grip then runs at him again, snarling and I see that both of them are willing to kill tonight, both focused solely on destroying the other.

I act quick and focus my power on the both of them before they have a chance to lock on to each other again. They are amazingly strong and it takes everything I have inside of me to force them apart. They are both pulled backwards as though by an invisible bungee cord but I feel that was the easy part as I can feel myself struggling to old them from each other. They both quickly get to their feet, or paws in Conall's case, but I don't let them move. It takes me all my energy to keep them rooted to the spot. They are furious to get at each other, they want to rip each other apart. Tristen and Ranulf realise what I am doing as I start to shake then I feel my nose begin to bleed as I desperately try to hold them in place, they run over and try to calm Conall and Gideon down.

Tristen pushes Gideon back and points over to me to show him that he has hurt me as Ranulf places his hand on Conall's head and I can see them talking telepathically. Conall bows his head in submission and Ranulf grabs his trousers from the ground for him. Gideon eventually looks over towards me as he realises what he has done, I stand clutching my arm, I can see the shape of Gideon's hand print already starting to bruise and my skin feels as though it on fire. Tiffany runs over to Conall as he turns back in to human form and pulls on his jeans, blood flows down his chest from the bite mark, I can see his lip is bust, and he has deep red marks across his back from the fight.

"What the fuck is going on?" Kerry says to herself next to me.

Gideon heads straight towards me, he looks remorseful but I take a step back away from him, I can't deal with him right now and having him hurt me again is making me feel vulnerable.

"Velvet, I..." Gideon starts to say.

"Don't you dare touch her!" Conall shouts over, he heads towards me in bare feet. "How can you say you love her when this is what you do to her?" He says pointing at me. I reach up to my face and my fingers are covered in blood from my cheek and nose. My hands are shaking like mad and I can't control my own breathing.

"I didn't mean to," Gideon tries to explain. "It was an accident, please I can explain."

"I think you have done enough explaining, don't you?" Conall stands firm, I can see that he is wiling to defend me if Gideon gets any closer.

"Gideon just leave it, come on," Tristen says trying to pull Gideon away, but he stands still and just looks at me, I can see frustration in his eyes as I try to stay strong but everything is overwhelming and I can feel the unwelcome sting of tears.

"Velvet, I am sorry," Gideon pleads. "Come back upstairs, we can talk, it was a mistake." I stand for a moment, wanting to say something to him then I take hold of Kerry's hand, and she squeezes it for support.

"I want to go home," I say trying to hold back my emotions.

"Please!" Gideon begs. I can see his heart break in front of me, although it is nothing compared to how I am feeling. I can't just forget this happened, how can I trust him after he hurt me... again.

"This... Gideon, this is wrong," I force out. "I can't do this with you any more." My breathing quivers as Kerry holds my arm and I start to walk away.

"Velvet please! Come on, don't do this," Gideon shouts after me as Tristen tries to hold him back. The other guys walk away after us.

"Follow her and you're a dead man," Conall threatens Gideon as he bends down and picks up his shoes and t-shirt then follows me away from the club.

No one says another word until we all get back to the apartment. Kerry leads me over to the sofa and I sit down whilst she makes me a drink, I would have preferred water but instead I am handed neat rum.

"Well that was some welcome," Ben finally says breaking the silence, I smile slightly as Dee stands up.

"Kerry do you have any ice for Velvets arm? It will stop the swelling," Dee asks, Kerry nods and heads to fetch some from the kitchen as Dee sits next to me and gently examines my arm properly. "Thank you," she says to Kerry as she hands her some ice wrapped in a tea towel. "It's not broken but the bruising looks pretty deep. It may have damaged the muscle so just take it easy for the next day or two." I wince slightly as she applies the ice. Kerry hands her a damp cloth, and she starts to gently clean my face.

"Conall you need to treat those wounds," Tiffany says to him looking at his neck.

"I'm fine, it's just a scratch," he replies standing in the corner with his arms crossed, I can see he is still worked up, his brow is furrowed in a permanent scowl.

"There's some antibacterial wipes in my bag if you want to grab them Ranulf," Ben says looking over to a pile of bags by the door, I never noticed them when I first came in. They must have brought them when they came here first to see me.

"This is my fault," Kerry says sighing. "I should have known better than to send you guys to that club." I shake my head at her.

"It wasn't your fault," I reply quietly. Conall takes his t-shirt off again as Ranulf opens the wipes and passes them to Conall, so he can remove some of the blood. The room falls silent and it feels awkward after what just occurred. I put my head down, I feel personally responsible for Conall being hurt, if it is anyone's fault then it is mine.

"I'm starving," Kerry finally says breaking the growing tension. "Do you guys fancy grabbing a bite to eat? I promise it won't be from that club." Every one chuckles slightly.

"I could eat," Tiffany agrees.

"Where's best to go?" Dee asks her.

"There're loads of places with amazing food, it all depends on what you fancy really," Kerry replies.

I kind of zone out as they all start discussing what they want to eat and where they should go. I try to smile and nod along with the conversation but inside I feel so lost. I was almost sure that I wanted something more with Gideon, I wanted to be with him, but every time I get close something else happens and now with him trying to work alongside Helana, it makes me wonder if he is starting to become the enemy instead.

"Hey!" Tiffany says gently as she places her hand on my arm. "Well is it a yes from you?" I look at her confused, I totally missed the discussion.

"Is what a yes?" I ask. Conall laughs slightly as he knows I was lost in my own thoughts instead of listening, I look over to him as he smiles at me.

"Food and drinks? A night out on the town to let our hair down and relax a bit," he says smiling more. He looks like he has calmed down now and everyone seems to be getting along really well.

"You lot go ahead," I say after a moment. "I've had a long day and I have a banging headache... but you guys should totally go out and enjoy the night. Kerry is an amazing hostess, and I am sure she will look after you like royalty," I smile at them all.

"Are you sure? I mean we can all just stay in if you prefer?" Tiffany asks sincerely but I shake my head at her.

"Don't be daft, I am super tired so I'll probably just go to bed and sleep anyway. Go have fun, let your hair down," I smile to reassure her then stand up and walk over to the kitchen to put the ice in the sink.

"Looks like we're going out then," Ranulf says as they all start to get up and grab wallets and things. I drink the rum in the glass that Kerry gave me as Tiffany comes over and gives me a hug.

"Feel better soon, we can all hang out tomorrow and have a proper catch up," Tiffany says smiling, I nod and usher them towards the door. Conall quickly grabs a clean t-shirt that isn't covered in blood and follows them.

"Go, the lot of you, give me some peace," I laugh as they say bye and go.

After a couple of minutes they are all gone and I stand silently in the middle of the apartment. I put the glass down on the breakfast bar and slowly walk towards my bedroom, push open the door, walk in and climb on to the bed. It's just me alone with my thoughts now, I lie back and it just overtakes everything. I can't stop it as tears start to roll down my cheeks and I just burst out crying. There are so many mixed emotions that I no longer feel like I am able to control them and the only thing I can do is just let them all out.

I should be used to it this week, having Gideon get in my head and hurting me. I never used to be like this, I was always independent and strong willed and now I am crying over a man and I hate that I am letting myself be so effected by him.

"Velvet?" I sit bolt upright as I hear Conall from outside my bedroom door, he appears in the doorway and I quickly try to wipe away the tears from my face to hide the fact that I've been crying but my eyes are puffy and the tears are quite obvious.

"Yeah?" I reply, my voice shakes as I desperately try to stifle my sobs. He looks over to me and gives a kind of half smile.

"You're not alright, are you?" He asks concerned and I shake my head.

"No," I manage to say. He steps in to the room and sighs.

"So much for my surprise," he shrugs and I force a smile. "I didn't want to leave you alone when you were so upset, I thought having a shoulder to cry on might help, but now it just seems creepy and stalkerish." I laugh slightly, Conall has always tried to care for me. Even at the base when I told him I had feelings for Gideon he still helped me and made sure I was OK. "I should leave you alone. I'll see you tomorrow," Conall says nervously. I force a smile and nod my head.

"Yes. Have a nice night," I say quietly. I can already feel more sobs bubbling inside of me.

"Goodnight Velvet," he says softly and leaves, closing the door behind him.

I sit in the darkness in my room, I have never felt so broken and betrayed. I should never have let myself fall for him, I knew Gideon was trouble the moment I met him but I still kept going back, why was I so stupid? My chest hurts just thinking about what has happened and I feel crushed. More tears flow down my cheeks, and they sting slightly as they go across the scrape on my face. I wish things had been different, I wish that I had met Conall under different circumstances and I could have gotten to know him better instead of being foolish and running back to Gideon. At least Conall seems absolutely genuine in everything he does, whereas Gideon is a lying, manipulative, blood thirsty arsehole... and now I feel empty and rejected. Gideon was right when he said that I was so fucked up and it was no wonder no one had ever loved me before. I don't want to feel like this... I don't want to feel so alone.

I am startled by a very light knock on my bedroom door. I sit for a moment and smile to myself as there is only one person I know that could be cocky enough to not actual leave and stand outside my room listening to my thoughts just to see if I was alright.

"Am I that predictable?" Conall says quietly through the door. I smile more as he slowly pushes it open and stands looking at me.

"I thought you were going out?" I ask him. Conall smiles sweetly at me and nods his head.

"I decided that trying to cheer you up was more important. Plus I am concerned about you," he says softly and I force a smile at him. "I can't believe you walked away from me and my charming personality for that cunty bollocks vampire." I try to stifle my smile.

"I had my reasons," I reply quietly. I feel a bit awkward with Conall watching me.

"He never deserved you, you know. The amazing fearless woman that you are, he took you for granted and fucked it up extraordinarily." I look up at Conall as he speaks. "I wanted to say that his behaviour is not your fault... and stop blaming yourself for me being hurt, I heard you say earlier on that you felt personally responsible. I choose my own battles and I got in to that fight on my own... I don't like seeing you hurt." The room falls silent again, I sit and think of what to say but before I do Conall speaks again. "That's all I wanted to say. So this time I am going for real. You look like you need some rest," Conall smiles and then turns for the door.

"Conall?" I say nervously, he stops and turns back to face me.

"Yeah?" He replies quietly. I take a deep breath and think for a moment.

"At Rick's base I told you that I had feelings for both you and Gideon," I say cautiously.

"Yeah, so?" Conall replies slightly confused as to why I am bringing that up now.

"Well, I think Gideon's out of the picture now... And I don't think that I want you to leave me alone," I swallow hard as I try not to cry.

There's an awkward silence between us as Conall decides what to do. I know he likes me, he has told me several times and I like him. I don't want him to think that this is just my way of rebounding due to Gideon because it's not, it's my way of taking control and doing exactly what I want to do for once.

"And what is it, that you want to do?" Conall asks. He obviously heard that in my head again which makes me smile.

"You," I say playfully. "Unless you have other plans." Conall stands and thinks for a moment then shuts my bedroom door and shrugs.

"I had a couple of dates lined up tonight but I suppose I can push those to tomorrow," he says as he walks over to the bed then climbs towards me, I lie back as he just looks down at me, looking at me as though he's never seen my face before.

"What's wrong?" I ask him as he doesn't move.

"Absolutely nothing," he smiles then he leans down and kisses me.

As his lips touch mine it mixes with the feeling of his body on top of me and makes me relax instantly, I wrap my arms around his neck, being careful not to hurt him where he was bitten, and passionately kiss him back, our mouths opening to each other and our tongues dancing wildly. Conall moves his hand and slips it up under my t-shirt and it finds its way straight to my breasts. He skims over the fabric of my bra and gently plays with my nipple through the lace, teasing and gently pinching it, making small pangs of pleasure dart through me. I move my hand from his neck and down to his crotch, as soon as my hand touches his package he moans slightly. We continue to kiss as I unbutton his jeans, pull down the zip and slide my hand inside then he pauses from kissing me and looks down, I can see he wants me, his eyes make that perfectly clear.

"Are you sure this is what you want?" He asks me.

I nod as I slide my palm seductively along his shaft, and he inhales sharply then I bite my bottom lip playfully as he watches my face. After a few seconds he smiles and gets up from the bed, he pulls me up also then starts to undress me. He pulls my t-shirt up over my head then slowly loosens my jeans, taking his time and enjoying the sights in front of him. He watches me as I jiggle them down playfully and stand before him in just my bra and panties then he steps forward and kisses me again as he slips his hands round my back and unhooks my bra, pulling it free from my body then drops it to the floor. He then moves from my lips and takes my nipples one at a time in his mouth and gently sucks and caresses them with his tongue. I watch him intently as he teases them with his mouth and kneads my breasts with his hands.

I take hold of the bottom of his t-shirt, and he pauses to allow me to take it off him. I spend a few seconds just admiring his body and running my hands across his firm torso before I kneel in front of him and pull down his jeans. I look up at him and smile playfully as I take him in my mouth, Conall moans as my lips slide along his semi hard shaft making him all wet and making him continue to grow, I wrap my hand around his cock as I slowly tease the head with my tongue then slide him deep inside my mouth again, encasing his full length.

"Oh fuck!" I hear him moan as he places his hand on my head and strokes my hair whilst I suck his dick. Hearing him moan as I continue to run my lips up and down him makes me wet and I feel moisture start to pool between my legs. My hand and mouth work in unison, his breathing changes and his leg starts to shake as he becomes more aroused. I move a little faster and allow him to go deeper every time I move my head. I'm enjoying giving him pleasure and it's making me immensely horny.

"Stop," Conall moans. "Velvet, stop!" I look up at him and do as he requests.

"What's wrong?" I ask concerned but Conall smiles at me.

"Nothings wrong, but I am so turned on right now that if you don't stop you are going to make me cum... And I don't want that to happen just yet," he laughs slightly then pulls me up to stand.

He places his hand on the back of my head and kisses me with so much passion that I almost go dizzy then slides his free hand down the front of my panties, his fingers glide between my lips as moisture almost over flows from them. My knees go like jelly as he plunges two fingers straight in to my pussy and his thumb glides over my clit making me moan loudly as it pulsates through my loins and I know I want him so very badly. He starts to fuck me with his fingers as his thumb swirls in unison, I cry out as his movements become firmer and I can feel myself building towards orgasm very quickly.

After a minute he playfully sweeps me up and throws me on to the bed as he leans down and slowly pulls of my knickers then tosses them over his shoulder. I laugh at him as he climbs towards me again, he kneels between my legs and runs his hands across my thighs then pulls me towards him as I lie on my back, he looks down then gently penetrates me in one fluid motion. I let out a long breath as I feel the entirety of his length slide inside of me.

He starts to move his cock in and out as he plays with my clit with one hand and holds me in place with the other. He watches me as I start to moan and move beneath his touch, as soon as I think to myself that he should get faster or firmer he hears my thoughts and gives me exactly what I want. Conall tries to control his breathing as I moan louder but I can't help but arch my back as the pleasure course's through me and every small hair across my skin stands on end.

He grabs my leg, hooks his arms beneath it to change the angle of my body and pulls me closer still, his dick sinking deeper in to my hole as he trusts a little harder. His fingers flick and twirl around my clit, my breathing quickens as I feel myself give in to him completely, he locks eyes with me and smirks as he starts to fuck me faster still. I can't help the faces I am making right now because this feels amazing and I know Conall gets aroused by watching me, if it is anything like our last encounter then I am certain he is enjoying taking me. Conall grits his teeth as I see he is close to the edge, I smile back then move my leg, forcing him to the side and in one motion he is on his back and I straddle him, taking away his control.

He looks a little shocked by what just happened, but he smiles up at me as his hands move to my waist instead and gives in to me. I seductively place two of my fingers in my mouth and suck on them, making them all wet. Conall watches me with open mouth in awe as I then run my fingers down my body and slip them between my legs then start to play with myself as I begin to rock slowly on his erect cock.

"Holy shit, that's hot," Conall groans as he grips my waist tighter and I moan loudly on him. As much as Conall is a great lover, a girl knows exactly what to do to pleasure herself fully, and I am no different. I thrust my hips forward and I lean back slightly as I move my fingers a little faster, hitting the sweet spot and making me so close to orgasm already. I feel Conall push up and I gasp as it feels so deep. "Oh God," Conall moans as I fuck him, and he watches me play with myself. He is so close, so I move more on him as my clit is starting to ache for its release. Conall digs his fingers in to my hips and forcefully thrust up to meet me with every move I make, he tries to hold off, waiting for me to be ready to cum with him.

"Fucking, shit!" I cry out as I can't resist it any longer and I simultaneously orgasm from both my clit and my pussy. As though giving Conall the green light I smile at him and watch as he cums also, I feel his juices fill me up as I continue to grind on him until I cum again, tightening around his cock and exploding on him very quickly then I move my hand from my clit and place it on his stomach to support me as I slowly rock on him until every last drop is drained from his manhood.

"That was amazing," Conall says after a minute and I just laugh as I try to catch my breath.

Chapter Nine

The last couple of days have been a bit of a blur.

We did the tourist thing as none of the gang had visited the North East before, Tiffany wanted to go to the Castle Keep and visit Durham Cathedral whereas Conall and Ranulf thought that would be extremely boring, so they voted for having a day playing out at Beamish. Ben and Dee were happy just going along with the majority so in the end we did everything and much more. It's been a busy 3 days but I have loved every second of it. Me and Kerry didn't get the appeal of visiting anything that they wanted to do as we have lived here for so long we just took it all for granted but I have to admit that it was very enjoyable.

3 full days of activities, laughter, amazing friends and so much fun. I can't remember the last time I just felt so happy. I feel like I don't have a care in the world right now, my lineage doesn't matter to these guys, we have all just clicked and I can't describe it, it's just amazing. I have my best friend Kerry by my side, I have new friends that totally get me and are awesome. I have Conall, which I am not going to lie, is strange... A good strange because I find myself wanting to spend so much time with him... Like, all of my time with him, my body craves to have him near, he lights up my soul. Also there is something about being able to hear each others thoughts occasionally that means there're no secrets and lies, it's all so open and I think I am actually falling for him hard and very fast. I haven't given a thought to Gideon, I am just so happy right now that I can't believe how lucky I am to have met Conall.

I roll over in bed and stretch, I slept really well last night, I think all the fresh air and fun made me just pass out, plus having Conall here and the truly amazing sex that we have been having every day is not hurting. We have been like two smitten teenagers, we can't keep our hands off each other and I can't help but smile every time he looks at me. My bedroom door opens slowly, I look over and smile.

"Morning," Conall beams at me, he is wearing a pair of shorts and a transformers t-shirt, casual attire for him. "I made you a coffee, you know, cos you're grumpy as fuck when you first wake up sometimes," he teases me. I laugh slightly and sit up, I fell asleep in just a vest top and underwear last night, so I don't have to try to be modest, not that Conall hasn't already seen it all, but still it's a comfort thing.

"Thanks," I say gratefully as he walks over and hands me the cup then sits on the side of the bed. "Are you sure you guys can't stay for a little while longer?" I ask.

I know they said they were only coming for a short visit but it seems to have flew by too quick. Tiffany needs to get back as her husband, who has been looking after the kids, he has to leave with Seamus as they are off on another work thing soon. Ben told his father he was taking some time out and needs to get back before suspicions start, and Ranulf and Conall have a pack to run, even more so now when things are getting more unsettled, maybe him working with Rick would be beneficial in the long run. I think I will miss him more than I realise when he leaves.

"I wish we could," Conall says as he sighs. "These past few days have been... Fun."

Fun? That's a word I wasn't expecting to hear from him. That's usually what I say when I'm trying to keep things from being serious, but hearing Conall say it makes me feel weird. Do I feel hurt? Maybe he did just want to have some fun, maybe I read things wrong. I thought all the signals he was giving out meant that he wanted to spend more time with me, but I guess I was picking up on things that were not there.

"Yeah, it's been... fun," I say trying not to show that I am actually feeling a little upset. "What time are you planning on heading back?" Conall smiles slightly and stands back up.

"Pretty soon, I thought it best to leave early and then I can get straight back to work," he replies.

I force a smile and nod at him. I am not sure how I feel about all this, Conall makes me so happy and just the thought of him leaving and not being near me any more is actually devastating. I want to be close to him, I want to open my eyes every morning and see him here, I want to tell him exactly how I feel... but I am scared that he won't feel the same now.

"Cool," I force out. "I'll get dressed and give you a hand with your bags and stuff." It's a good thing we have plenty of room here, they all crashed at the apartment and it's been really nice having people around me that don't piss me off every day.

"OK then," Conall nods, he stands awkwardly for a second then turns to leave. Just as he gets to the door he stops and sighs then I look up as he turns back to face me. "Is that all you're going to say?"

"What do you mean?" I ask confused.

"I am leaving, and we had fun... and your reply is cool, I'll help you with your bags?" Conall seems a little deflated and I don't know how to respond.

"I'm sorry, what do you want me to say?" I reply.

"Why don't you just say what you're thinking?" Conall asks. "I understand that you are a little guarded and apprehensive about getting close to people. But I hear you Velvet, I hear you constantly, every single thing you say to yourself. I hear one thing in your head but then other thing comes out of your mouth and it's pretty confusing for me."

"I don't... I don't know what you're saying," I stutter. Conall sighs and looks at me.

"Just say the words," he says. "Say what you are thinking." I sit in silence for a while, I know what he's talking about. In my head there is so much I want to say, like that I don't want him to go. I like having him around and when he's close I feel safe and protected. I don't just like him, it's something more, something more intense and I don't want that feeling to go away.

"I... I don't know," I respond. Why can't I just tell him?

"OK then... I'm going to go, I need to get my shit together," Conall looks away, he pauses for a moment to see if I say anything then opens the door to leave. This is my chance, if I don't say anything now he could walk away and I might never see him again. Is that really what I want?

"Conall, wait!" I say quickly as I put my cup down on the side and get up from the bed, he stands watching me and waiting for me to speak. "Please don't leave." I can feel my heart beat get faster. "I don't want you to go. I'm sorry if I've been giving you mixed messages but this is all new for me and I don't know what I am feeling for you because I've never felt like this about anyone before... I can't describe it, when I look at you my heart skips a beat, when you smile I get butterfly's in my stomach and when you said you were leaving, I was then faced with the possibility that I might not see you again... and It makes my soul hurt." Conall listens to me, I suddenly feel so nervous. "I don't want to spend a single day away from you, I want you in my life so fucking much... I have never felt this happy," I swallow and just stand in front of him. I honestly think I would die if he turned around now and said he didn't feel the same.

"Wow!" Conall says eventually. "Well, I have your number so the next time I'm down this way, maybe I'll give you a call."

What? I stand frozen in shock, I said all that to him and that's the response I get.

"Oh!" I say quietly, the entirety of my vocabulary has abandoned me and I'm literally lost for words.

"Velvet?" I look up at Conall as he starts to smile. "You do know I was kidding, right? It's called a joke, normal people with amazing personalities like myself make them sometimes for fun and to lighten the mood." I just nod my head and listen to his words but I'm not taking them in.

"I'm lost..." I say, I don't know how to respond now. Conall laughs and steps towards me, he takes hold of my hand and smiles so brightly that I almost melt inside.

"I've just been waiting for you to tell me how you felt, so that I could say..." He pauses and takes a deep breath. "So I could tell you that... I think I love you and that I never want to leave your side."

Conall puts his arms around my waist and picks me up, I wrap my legs around him as we kiss. I feel so happy with him, I know I keep saying it but it's true. This man is truly amazing. Conall pulls back slightly and smiles at me as he stands holding me in his arms.

"Come with me," he says gently. "Apart from Kerry what else is making you stay here?" I think for a second a smile.

"Nothing, there's nothing left here for me any more," I reply as I lean in and kiss him again. Our lips exploring each other gently.

"So..." Conall smiles. "Is that a yes?" He fishes for an answer and I smile at him.

"Yes, it's a yes," I say happily as Conall carries me to the bed and lies me down on my back. My legs are still wrapped around his waist as he kisses me deeply. I can already feel his erection through his shorts as he lies on top of me, the friction as he slowly grinds his hips rubbing between my legs and making me moan slightly.

"Conall?" Ranulf says coming to the open bedroom door. We pause and look over to him.

"Great timing bro," Conall smiles. I feel my cheeks flush at getting caught making out and I try not to laugh.

"Are you about sorted? We are just about ready to leave," Ranulf smirks at us. Conall sighs and gets up from the bed, I sit and realise I am just in my knickers and a vest so grab the blanket and cover myself up a bit.

"Look at you, acting all shy," Conall teases me, I just shake my head and smile. "Why don't you guys take the truck and head home. I'll follow you up." Ranulf looks slightly confused then looks towards me and smiles.

"I will tell the others that we don't need to do goodbyes then. It will be nice having you back with the pack, Velvet," Ranulf nods at me then quickly leaves.

Conall stands trying not to smile at me as I realise they did the talking thing again without me hearing. It's strange, I can hardly ever hear what any of them are thinking or saying, and it seems that only Conall can hear everything from me all the time. I must be more open to him than to any of the others. Not that I mind, sometimes it's nice having him in my head.

"What's up with you?" I ask him.

"I'm just happy," he replies. I spend a moment just holding eye contact with him as we smile at each other then we both look over to the door as Kerry comes hurting in.

"What's this about you leaving?" She asks stunned. I probably should have talked things through with her first. "Is it true? Are you going to stay with the pack for a while?" I nod my head and then she smiles. "So does that mean I have this place to myself?" She asks excitedly.

"What? You couldn't have pretended to miss me until I left?" I smile at her.

"You know I'll miss you, but I'll come visit you all the time and I can throw an awesome party every weekend..." She says as I shake my head at her.

"I suppose I better pack some stuff then, not like I have much but..." I stand up, I am definitely doing this then.

As much as I love Kerry, and she is my best friend I don't think I need her as my familiar right now, I don't need protecting or guidance. I'm done with fighting, that's not the life I want. I never wanted it, it was just thrust upon me, and I was hurtled in to the middle of a war between the General, the witches and the vampires. Conall and his pack have a quiet life, they work on the surrounding farm land, they are now protected so the hunters can't find them and they have the whole peacefully happy life thimg... this is everything that I want. I'm even done with this place, being in the apartment just reminds me of Gideon and all the pain he caused me... I'm keeping the car though, fuck no, is he getting that beauty back. Call it compensation for putting up with all of his shit.

Conall helps me pack my belongings and I say goodbye to Kerry before we head down to the car. The others left about an hour ago, so we shouldn't be too far behind them. I start the engine and pause for a moment, this is it, I have absolutely no regrets. I came back to Newcastle for Gideon and now there's nothing that would make me want to come back again. I feel free knowing that I'll never have to see Gideon's face again, put it this way, right now I'd choose to fuck Claudia again over him.

"Did you actually... with Claudia?" I turn my head when Conall speaks, and he is sitting staring at me.

"Sorry, I don't mean to have full discussions with myself in my head. I guess I need to learn how to control that more and close my mind off to you," I smile.

"Yeah, you keep slipping and letting little bits peak out," he laughs. "You will get used to it, just takes time to control it properly. Personally I think it's cute, I like knowing when you are thinking about me... So you were saying... That psycho bitch Claudia then?" I laugh at him and pull away. We spend the entire journey talking about everything, he asks me about things that's happened to me and how I discovered my powers, how I got involved with the General and the vampires. He is genuinely interested in my life and it's nice to talk about it without anyone getting jealous or shouting at me for it.

After the journey we finally arrive at the Lookout at early evening. The place is quiet, Tiffany has gone home to see her family, Dee and Ben have their own places to be and when we eventually sit down in the den, it's only me, Conall and Ranulf. The fireplace has already been made and the wood burns and crackles to warm the house through. I know that wolves are naturally warm, so I am guessing the heat is for my benefit.

I thought being back here with Conall and Ranulf might be a bit awkward after we... You know, but strangely it feels right. There's no competitiveness between them. I think back to when I first came here, I was attracted to both of them but in very different ways. Don't get me wrong Ranulf is still hot as fuck but Conall is starting to steal my heart. It's quite a nice relaxing atmosphere and I instantly feel at home, I know that this is where I am meant to be.

"Hey!" Conall nudges me slightly, I open my eyes, and he smiles down at me. "You seem tired, you should go to bed."

I must have dozed off, I nod at him and drag my arse off the sofa and head upstairs. Ranulf made up a bedroom for me so that I could still have some personal space, it's slightly larger than the bedroom I was in last time I was here and this one has an en suit bathroom. I feel exhausted after driving all day so I get changed for bed and get in. I must have fell asleep straight away because when I next open my eyes it's morning and the sun is already filtering through the curtains.

The next couple of days are sheer lazy bliss, I literally do nothing and I love it. Everyone is so busy doing what they do, that I just stay out of the way and spend most of the time at the Lookout, I was going to have a walk to town but I've been really tired again lately, I think it was all that stress off Gideon catching up with me.

Today was the same as the last couple of mornings, I get up and dressed then head downstairs, I feel really ropey and have a banging headache again, the house is quiet and I think I am alone. I make myself a coffee and some toast and sit in the kitchen playing on my phone to keep myself occupied. I flick through the apps and play a couple of games then I send Kerry a text just to say I got up here OK and that I hope she hasn't trashed the apartment yet. I soon start to get bored and have a wander around the house, I have a look for some painkillers as my head seems to be getting worse and I keep going dizzy, it's far bigger than it looks on the outside. I counted 7 bedrooms plus an office thing, there are steps up to the attic but I couldn't be bothered to go up there and have a nosey. I can't find any painkillers, so I head back downstairs and turn on the TV.

It doesn't take me long before I am eye rolling my way through the news and seeing all the shit that's going on. I catch the end of an interview with the General, just seeing his face on TV makes shivers shoot down my spine, I saw the words "war against the supernatural terrorists" and I have to just shake my head. Someone seriously needs to bring that twat down a peg or two, he has the media and the human population eating out of his hand, it is so one sided.

Not only is he leading the badly directed hunt for supernatural beings he is now trying to run for head of the supernatural task force they are setting up to control the relations between humans and everyone else, what idiot in their right mind would want to vote for that sadistic arsehole. The news reporter asks him about his opponent in the upcoming elections, but he doesn't seem worried. No one has come forward and named his appointment yet so it will be interesting to see who it is.

I pick up my phone again as I receive a text from Kerry. I open and read it straight away.

- Shit! Gideon has literally just stopped by, he asked to speak to you and I said you were gone. I wasn't even thinking, I think he knows you're with Conall as he flipped the fuck out. FYI. p.s miss your face -

What do I care? Gideon means nothing to me and I don't give a rats ass if he was mad, it's his own fucking fault. I go to reply but as I do my phone rings and it flashes up that it's Gideon calling. I think about just sending it to voicemail but I've had enough of his shit so I answer it and get ready to tell him right where to go.

"What do you want?" I say bluntly as I answer the phone.

"Where are you?" Gideon asks, I can tell he is angry and I don't even care.

"I'm in Lapland enjoying the company of Santa's elves, we had a massive orgy last night, and I am now addicted to snorting candy canes... what the fuck has it got to do with you where I am?" I feel like crap, so I am now in a pissy mood because if him.

"I didn't give you a house for you to abandon it when it pleases you," Gideon snaps. He sounds like he is just outside of the apartment as I can hear cars going past in the background. He literally must have spoken to Kerry, left and rang me straight away.

"No Gideon, you gave me a house so that I would like you more, thus enabling you to fuck me and keep me in your control," I say. "But it's not your house any more is it? So, what I do with it is not your concern." I hear him move the phone away from his mouth and yell in anger, after a moment he speaks again.

"You can't just walk away from me, I told you I loved you, did that mean nothing to you?" He sounds slightly more calm now that he screamed the place down.

"It did at one point, but then there was lies and jealousy, you hurt me both physically and mentally, Gideon. What did you expect me to do?" I explain. There's a small pause before he speaks again.

"I'm sorry..." Gideon replies quietly.

"I'm sick of hearing those words from you. If you truly loved me you wouldn't do things that you would have to be sorry for, especially not as often as you do," I take a deep breath before I continue. "Everything that we had between us is over. It was over as soon as you laid your hands on me and tried to kill my friend... Now kindly stay out of my life, I will stay out of yours and I think we will then both be a lot happier... I'm not coming back, so don't ask me again. I'll be champion if I never have to see or even think about you for the rest of my life."

"You don't mean that, even if you didn't say it, I know deep down inside of you that you loved me," Gideon says trying to reason with me. I sit for a moment trying not to get emotional, I've already cried enough tears over him, my head goes fuzzy again and I feel a bit sick, I don't want to have to keep dealing with all the stress and worry that Gideon is causing me. It needs to stop now.

"You're possibly right, maybe I did love you," I finally say. "But now we will never know, will we?" I pause for a moment, but he goes quiet and doesn't respond. "Goodbye, Gideon," I say softly then end the call.

I sit for a while and think over what just happened. I stand by what I said to him, it was the right thing for me to do and I know that being away from his toxic relationship he thinks that he had with me, is exactly what I need. I'm more than happy here with Conall, in fact just thinking about his name makes me smile and now that things are officially over with Gideon, I feel free.

I flick through the TV channels and get comfortable, but it's not long before I am struggling to keep my eyes open again and I fall asleep. Gideon is so exhausting, he fucks with my mind.

"Velvet?" I feel a hand placed on my forehead but I don't have the energy to open my eyes. "Velvet? I need you to wake up." I groan as I realise it is Dee's voice speaking to me. I force my eyes open enough to see Conall and Dee standing over me looking concerned.

"Hey," Conall says sweetly to me. I try to force a smile, but I am so tired.

"How long has she been like this?" Dee asks him seriously then I see him shake his head.

"She's been a bit ropey for a while and constantly very tired," he explains.

"Velvet?" I look at Dee, my eyes are stinging. "I need you to answer some questions for me, OK?" I nod my head slightly at her. "The last time to got injured did you lose a lot of blood?" I nod my head as she places her fingers on my wrist and takes my pulse.

"She was bitten by a vampire, they almost killed her, drained a lot of her blood. Your dad said she was lucky, any more and she wouldn't have survived the blood loss," Conall explains to Dee.

"OK, have you been having dizzy spells and constantly feeling exhausted?" She asks and I nod again, I've been feeling like this for a while on and off.

"What's wrong?" I ask groggy. It's probably just the flu or something.

"Have you heard of something called anaemia?" Dee says gently, I nod my head, I've heard of it, but I am not entirely sure what it is.

"You think that's what's wrong with her?" Conall asks and Dee nods her head.

"Pretty much every symptom is there, exhaustion, dizziness, her skin is pale, headaches, weakness... You also said you were struggling to maintain your powers because you felt drained?" She asks me and I nod again to confirm all of that.

"What do we do?" Conall says as he places his hand on my head and strokes my hair.

"I think it's best if we get her down to my Doctor's office and I can run a couple tests, and then we can look at our options to make her feel better," Dee replies. I look up at Conall and force a smile at him then try to sit up.

"Do I have to change?" I ask wearily as I look down and remember I am dressed in Disney pyjamas and fluffy slippers. Dee smiles and shakes her head.

"You are poorly, so I am sure we can ignore the PJ's," she says watching me. I push myself up off the sofa and go dizzy again, I feel so weak and my hands are shaking.

"Here, let me help you," Conall quickly takes my arm and gently picks me up then carries me to the car following Dee. As we get outside a black SUV pulls up and Ben gets out.

"Hey, what's up?" He asks as he notices Conall carrying me.

"Velvet is not well. Dee thinks she might have anaemia or something, so we are taking her down to the village," Conall informs him.

"Mind if I tag along?" Ben asks, smiling at Dee, she nods her head and smiles back. "Anaemia, eh? Makes sense actually, considering what you've been through," Ben says to me. I nod my head at him as Conall puts me in the back of Dee's car and then runs around the other side to sit in the back with me, Ben jumps in the front next to Dee as she drives us in to town.

Once in the Doctors office Dee takes some blood samples from me and Ben gives me a few painkillers for my headache. I feel like I've been waiting here for ages whilst they check the test results. Eventually Dee comes back in to the room and smiles at me. I've been sitting in one of those big padded chair things whilst Conall sat next to me and held my hand. Ben tried to make small talk and explained what kind of things I could do to ensure I helped get my red blood cell levels back up, he used a load of medical jargon and I wasn't really listening. Me being ill feels like a waste of a day really. All this because I am a little tired?

"Ben?" Dee says quietly. "Can you double check these results for me?" She says smiling. Ben looks at her and shrugs.

"I'm sure you know what you're doing, I trust you," he says encouraging her. Dee smiles wider.

"No, Ben, I would rather you checked them for me because you're kind of Velvets Doctor now and erm... You need to, kind of... Approve them." Ben looks at her weird as she speaks.

"Is everything OK?" Conall asks, concerned about Dee's behaviour.

"Of course, it's just with Ben knowing more about Velvet's history than me, it would be best if he had a look," Dee stares at Ben and nudges her head to the side slightly to try to tell him that she needs him to leave the room. Ben nods and heads out with Dee. My heart beat gets faster as I start to think that there is something wrong with me.

"Calm down," Conall says gripping my hand tighter. "I'm sure everything is fine," he reassures me. I nod my head, Ben and Dee have only been out of the room a couple of minutes but it seems like a lifetime of waiting. Eventually the door opens again, and they both walk back in. Dee stands at the back near the door as Ben approaches me with a load of print outs of my blood works.

"So yeah, definitely anaemia," Ben says looking at the sheets. "Your results are extremely low, so I think we may do an iron infusion to try to get those levels up quickly, we also need to look at your diet," Ben doesn't make eye contact with me as he fumbles with the papers.

"So, she's going to be OK?" Conall asks smiling at me. Ben swallows and nods.

"Yeah, she's going to be fine... Just a few more questions though, so we can update your records," Ben says as he takes a pen from his pocket and starts making notes on the test results.

"Of course, anything you need," I reply wearily.

"All the symptoms you have been experiencing, when did they start?" He asks and I think for a moment.

"Erm, I don't know, a couple of weeks. I think from just after the time that I was taken by Claudia and Bertol," I answer, that sounds about right.

"And lots of blood loss then?" He asks another question and I nod my head, they drank from me often. "OK, and erm... When was your last menstrual cycle?" Ben says forcing a smile at me. I sigh and think again.

"Just before Christmas I think, my periods have been all over the place the last few month with everything that's been going on, I chalked that down to stress," I think that's right, I'm sure it finished Christmas Eve morning just before I headed to Glasgow to find Kerry.

"What's that got to do with anaemia?" Conall asks Ben, clearly confused.

"It's a loss of blood from the body and erm..." Ben stumbles over finding the right words to say. "It's best if we know all the details so that we can..."

"You're pregnant," Dee blurts out.

The whole room goes silent and everyone just sits. Ben puts his head down and doesn't look at me as Dee now looks a bit embarrassed by just saying it like that. I glance at Ben and laugh slightly.

"That's funny, because it's a joke right?" Ben glances up at me and shakes his head then looks away again. I look at Conall who just sits in shock. Dee concentrates on the floor. This can't be true, I have been taken the pill for the last 11 year, I'm always careful. Although everything that has been going on, I might have missed some...

"She's pregnant?" Conall finally says quietly. He looks at me and I literally do not know what to say.

"How?" I say, my mind is going a million miles an hour. "I mean, I know how, but we, only just..." I try to make sense of it all.

"No!" Conall says stopping me. "There was that time with Ranulf and me after Christmas..."

"But you..." I say thinking quickly about what happened between all three of us. "I mean you did, but not... there," I try to remind him without having to say that when we had sex, he came in my ass not my pussy, it was Ranulf that came there.

"So, Ranulf is..." Conall says, he pauses for a second and smiles. "It's cool, erm, it's part of the pack."

"Actually..." Ben interrupts, he has that bad news kind of look on his face. "Taking in to consideration your last known menses and the time frame for conception... Plus the fact that you had a lot of tests ran on you behind the scenes at the Bird Cage. I don't think that's when it happened."

"But we only slept together again about a week ago and that can't be right, so it can only have been from then," I say, trying to understand.

"I am sorry Velvet, but you were not pregnant when you were at the Bird Cage, I know it was only a few days after you slept with Conall and Ranulf but the drugs you were given... A foetus wouldn't have survived that and because our technology at the Bird Cage is far superior to that of a normal Doctors surgery, we would have seen the first tiny signs of conception," Ben explains.

"So what does that mean?" Conall asks him.

"It means that you conceived shortly after leaving the Bird Cage, not before," he explains cautiously. Ben looks over at Dee for support then back to me. "So we estimate you are just about 8 weeks pregnant."

He is being serious isn't he? This isn't a joke.

"But that would mean..." I pause as it finally dawn's on me. "It's not possible." My breathing quivers instantly as I feel Conall's grip on my hand falter, and he leaves go then stands up.

"It had to be, didn't it," Conall says with his back to me, I can hear the anger and frustration in his voice. "Just when he was out of our lives his fucking parasitic spawn ruins everything."

This can't be real. Everything felt so perfect that I can't believe this is happening now.

"There has to have been a mistake." I plead with Ben. "You can run the tests again, there has to be something that's gone wrong." My heart is pounding so fast as I start to panic and I struggle to keep my breathing calm.

"We checked them twice already, they are not wrong," Ben says gently and gives me a supportive smile. "This is what is causing the anaemia, the foetus is diverting a lot of your blood supply to enable it to grow. I've never come across a vampire pregnancy before, so I am not to sure how things will progress."

It's all just words, I can't take any of it in.

"Conall?" I try to get his attention as he tries not to have a melt down in the corner. "I'm so sorry," I apologise as my entire body shakes. He quickly turns to me and shakes his head then comes over. He grabs my hand and places his forehead to mine.

"You don't have to be sorry, this isn't your fault," he reassures me, but I can see how angry and upset he is... I have hurt him. He looks up at Ben. "How is this possible? It's never been heard of for a vampire and a human to have off spring. Things like this just can't happen. It's not natural." Ben smiles at me slightly before answering.

"Well technically, you're not entirely a normal human. You have blood running through your veins that's more powerful than anything I've ever seen, but like I said I am not an expert. But I'll do everything I can to help you. Whatever you decide you want to do," he says supportively.

"I need to get up," I say suddenly as I push myself from the chair and Ben tries to stop me.

"You need to rest until we can get your levels balanced, you are extremely weak," Ben tries to say but I ignore him and push him out of the way.

This can't be happening, this is all a bad dream. I don't look at any of them and just head for the door, I feel like I can't breathe in here, the air is too thick and I need to go outside. I feel claustrophobic, my head is spinning and I don't want to accept what is happening. It can't be, I left Gideon and told him I wanted noting to do with him. I can't be pregnant! I can't be having his baby... I can't breathe.

Dee, Ben and Conall all follow me, trying to get me back inside but I need to get out, I can't deal with this. What am I going to do? I can't have a baby. I can't even take care of myself most of the time without having this... thing inside of me to worry about. I try to blink a couple of times as my eyes start to lose focus. I feel my legs shake beneath me as I feel so dizzy that I am sure I'm going to pass out at any second. Everything around me goes strange, I feel myself fall and everything goes black.

I can't be a mother, I don't know how.

Chapter Ten

I don't want to wake up, because if I do I will have to face reality, and I am not sure if I can. I reluctantly open my eyes and look around, I don't recognise the room at all. It's like a small box room, the single bed I'm lying on is very comfortable though and the walls are plainly decorated as though it's forgotten about or used only once in a blue moon for guests. I feel a twinge in my arm and notice a needle attached to an IV then follow the clear plastic tube up to a dark red liquid slowly dripping through the separator.

I notice that I am alone, I feel really bad about all this. I'm so scared that Conall is going to hate me now, he opened his heart and his home to me and now I get told that I'm pregnant with someone else's baby. I swallow hard and try not to go insane with the multiple thoughts in my head, how can this have possibly happened? Gideon told me himself that even two vampires can take hundreds of years to get pregnant, that only a small percentage of blood born vampires can reproduce. So humans and vampires have never been able to... I mean we are like different species, aren't we? It's like a cat and a dog having some form of hybrid fluffy monster puppy kitten thing.

I sit up in the bed and sigh. Physically I feel a little better just from having some rest, but emotionally I am all over the place. The bedroom door opens and Ben comes in, he is preoccupied looking at more test results to notice that I am awake.

When he finally looks up he stops and gives me a nervous smile.

"Are you alright?" Ben asks me. I just shrug my shoulders, honestly I have no clue what being alright is any more. "Have you decided what you want to do? About the baby I mean." I shake my head, as much as I hate Gideon right now I can't think about getting rid of the baby. Life is a miracle and even though I am freaking the fuck out, I couldn't live with myself knowing this might be my only chance to have a real family. Well, a sort of family, no matter what conclusion I come to I know I'll have Kerry by my side, I don't even what to think about how Gideon is going to react when he finds out.

"What happens now?" I finally ask Ben. I'm going to be strong and eventually I'll know what to do.

"I'm going to monitor you closely, I've found some old books on vampire pregnancy, but I don't think they are going to help fully as they are all based on both a vampire father and mother. I don't know how your body is going to react to it," he explains for me. At least I'm glad Ben is here to help me, he's always tried to do what's best. "We have also sorted a list of medication for you, we have had to order it from a pharmacy in the nearest town as, obviously you, as a person are meant to be dead. It's not like you can go to a normal hospital or anything now." I nod at him, everything is so complicated.

"Where am I?" I realise I haven't asked him that yet.

"Dee's home, her place is next door to the Doctor's office. She had a spare room so it was best to bring you here." I nod my head at him as he talks, but I can't help but wonder why I am here and not at the Lookout.

"Where's Conall?" I ask nervously. Ben stands for a moment and gives me a look of support.

"He had to leave," Ben sighs. "As you can imagine this is a bit of a shock to everyone." My heart sinks, I know what that means, I come to the realisation that he doesn't want me around him. "I'll bring you up something to eat and then I suggest you try to rest for a while," Ben smiles at me then leaves the room.

I feel so alone and unwanted. I lie back down on the bed as my emotions all come flooding to the surface and I end up crying myself to sleep.

You know, until a few month ago I don't think I ever really cried. I was really good at having a hard exterior and not allowing anyone to see a vulnerable streak in me. That's where I got my awesome sarcastic side from because it was a way for me to deflect things. Like these stupid fucking emotions and shit. Even growing up when things were crap I never cried about it, I always saw it as a weakness, that if I cried I wouldn't be strong any more.

By the time I wake up again I am lying curled up in a ball and I notice the needle has been removed from my arm. I roll over and I can instantly sense that I'm not alone, I sit up slowly and see Conall sitting quietly in a chair at the bottom of the bed, his hands clasped together in front of him, looking at the floor. I don't even know where to begin with talking to him. Even now just looking at him sitting there he looks sad, as though I've shattered his world. I did that to him, I ruined everything. I never meant to hurt anyone, especially not Conall. I feel devastated that I have destroyed everything between us, just when I was beginning to think I could be happy with him. I contemplate going back to the bunker for a few days or even going back to see Kerry as I don't think that I am going to be welcome here any more. I can't stand this feeling inside of me, I know Conall will no longer want me here, I know he hates me...

"I don't hate you," Conall says gently as he continues to look at the floor.

I don't understand how that's not true though, I would hate me if I was on the other end of it. I don't deserve to have Conall like me any more, it's bad enough that I've now fucked up my life without fucking up his. I mean, how is this even going to work?

"We will make it work," Conall says, he looks up at me and sighs. "I want to say a few things, if you can bear with me and just listen?" I nod my head. "Firstly, you think far too much in your head, it's constant and you never stop, I can hear it all... Secondly, everything you think is wrong." I sit in silence, I want to look at him but I feel ashamed. "Let me start by reassuring you that I could never hate you," he continues. "I know that right now you're going to have all these thoughts and feelings, but I don't want you to worry about me. I am not going to just stop loving you, that's not how it works and I don't want you to leave. Yes, it is a lot to take in, the woman that I am in love with is pregnant with another man's baby, and unfortunately it's someone I despise because he hurt you... But whatever you decide to do, whether you want to keep it or not, I will be right by your side every step of the way... Even if that innocent baby's father is an absolute dick head." I smile slightly.

"I'm sorry if I hurt you," I say quietly. I hear Conall sigh again, and he thinks for a moment before speaking.

"It's not like any of this happened on purpose," Conall replies, I am surprised by how calm he is. "So if you still want me, I'll still be here for you." He catches my eye and I give him a small smile then nod my head. "Right then, that's all I had to say for now." There's another few minutes of silence as we both just sit here, not sure what to say or do next.

"What are we going to do?" I ask him nervously. Everything feels different, like I will never be able to just have a normal life.

"Well, first I thought you might like to put some actual clothes on," Conall smiles as he picks up a plastic bag from the floor and gets up to place it in front of me on the bed. I nod my head and pull out a black skater dress and my boots. I look at him and roll my eyes.

"You brought me a dress?" I say bluntly.

"No, Tiffany brought you a dress. She also brought some little shoes that looked weird, so I sent Ranulf to the Lookout to grab your boots. She thought she was helping by lending you something to wear, so I..."

"Thank you," I interrupt him.

He nods at me as I get up from the bed, I still feel a little shaky, but I am a lot better than what I was. I go to get undressed but stop as I suddenly feel embarrassed, so I turn my back on Conall and nervously change. I grab the clean underwear and bra from the bag and then pull the black skater dress over my head. It's actually quite nice, it has mid length sleeves with lace around the edges and a slightly low cut neckline which looks quite feminine. The length of the dress is a little short for my liking as I'm so used to having my legs covered, so it's a strange feeling. I put my boots on, they might not go exactly with the dress but I can rock this look if I try. When I'm sorted I stand up and smile at Conall, I feel really shy, and I am not sure what to say to him.

"You should wear dresses more often, then maybe I'll start to believe you're actually a real life girl," he teases me and I can't help but smile. I feel so lucky to have found someone like Conall.

"I thought you had left me here as you didn't want me any more," I say quietly addressing my concerns. Conall breathes deeply, and comes to stand in front of me.

"I panicked, I am guilty of that. But I talked through everything with the family, and they helped me work through things in my head. It's not like it's the end of the world. I'm so so sorry if you thought that I had abandoned you," Conall must get the sense that it is exactly how I was feeling, so he steps forward, and he wraps his arms around my shoulders then hugs me. I rest my head against his chest and fight the want to cry again.

"I'm sorry," I manage to say.

"You need to stop saying that, if anything it should be me apologising for leaving you here alone... I promise I'll never leave you again." I look up at him and give him a small smile and nod as he speaks. "Lets get you out of here, shall we?"

"Yes please," I reply.

Although I still feel a bit guilty, Conall has a way of putting me at ease that I never thought would be possible. I've still got a lot to think about and deal with, but he is not one of the things I need to worry about now. I know he wouldn't lie to me, so I know that what he says is fact. He won't leave me, he will be strong for me when I can't. Just knowing that I have his support means everything to me right now.

We leave Dee's house and walk outside. It's actually quite a nice day, I notice that we are not far from the village centre and Tiffany's house, I keep forgetting how tiny this place actually is.

"It's a nice day if you fancy a walk back home?" Conall asks me, I haven't been out of the house in a few days so a walk sounds pretty nice.

"That sounds good," I say smiling.

Conall nods and then takes hold of my hand. It's weird, I've never walked around holding hands with anyone before and for a moment I feel like a kid holding hands with her boy crush. Is this what having a boyfriend feels like? Just saying the word sounds strange, it's like so official but at the same time, so innocent. We start to walk along the street towards Tiffany's house, when I look up we can see her children playing in the garden.

"Hi Uncle Conall," Daisy shouts as she sees us coming from down the street. She quickly opens the gate and runs down the path, Conall leaves go of my hand and picks Daisy up then swings her around playing as Chad stands by the gate smiling. Daisy giggles as he puts her back down, and she runs back to the garden.

"Hey, you two," Tiffany says as she sees us, she looks like she's been sewing and comes out still carrying scraps of fabric, I can't help wonder if she's wearing one of her creations right now as she always looks fabulous and quirky. If Conall talked to his family about the reservations he had about me then she will probably know that I'm pregnant and I suddenly feel really uneasy. I have just started to get to know these people really well and I consider them as like family already as they all mean so much to me, I don't think I could stand not having them all like me any more or treating me differently. Conall grabs my hand and squeezes slightly to let me know he's here and I look up as he smiles at me.

"Everything is OK," Conall says reassuring me. It is nice sometimes when he can hear my doubts. Just his smile is enough to make me feel happy.

"Are you wanting to stay for dinner? I have more than enough," Tiffany asks as we get to her front gate.

I can't help but watch Chad and Daisy play, they seem so happy and tiny. I know that's a weird way to describe children, but they do seem so little and young, am I really ready to have one of my own? Will my child even be like this though? What if it's evil and wants to live on the blood of other children? I mean, it can't go to a normal school because it's not going to be normal, it's far from it in fact. Will it be able to play with other kids? Can it go outside in the sun? What if when it's born it comes out green or something and looks like a hybrid alien. Will it have powers like me or be a blood sucking monster like Gideon? Or both... It could be like the spawn of Satan...

"Velvet!" Conall says nudging me, I look up and Tiffany is stood in front of me.

"I asked how you were feeling now?" Tiffany smiles at me.

"I'm feeling better, thank you, I'll be back to my usual self in a few days I hope," I reply trying to seem totally normal and not give away the fact that I am freaking out inside.

"Thank you for the offer of dinner Tiff, but we are going to have a walk back home, clear our heads a bit," Conall advises her.

"No problem, you know where I am if you need anything," Tiffany smiles as she turns to head back inside the house. I take a deep breath as we shout goodbye to Tiffany then Conall briefly talks to Chad and Daisy before we walk away.

We head out of the village towards the old bridge that crosses the stream, neither of us has said anything for the past 15 minutes but Conall has never let go of my hand. The town is peaceful, it's probably the perfect place to raise a baby, even more so now that it is protected from hunters. It's the perfect life, I always thought that one day I might settle down and have kids, have a real family. I just didn't expect this to happen. Things wouldn't be as complicated if I had become pregnant with Conall's baby instead. I think about that for a moment and get sad because that might have been nice.

I saw how he is with his niece and nephew. He is the most genuine and caring person I know, and he would have made an amazing dad. He has so much love to give and I don't know of a single member of his pack that doesn't respect and admire him. And then there's me, who eats pizza for breakfast, swears too much and my go-to drink is alcohol.... Oh, shit! I can't drink alcohol any more, fuck... I have no idea what else I can't do, I'm sure there is something about eggs and... Bollocks... coffee. I don't smoke so that's not going to be an issue... I've drank in that last 8 weeks, a lot probably, what if I've already done something? I am definitely going to have to change my lifestyle a bit, I am going to be a mam, so it's not just me I have to think about any more.

"You've decided you're going to keep the baby then?" Conall asks nervously as we start to walk across the bridge, I stop and sigh.

"Have I been waffling away in my head again?" I ask awkwardly, I wonder how much he heard.

"Yes," Conall says. I don't quite know how to respond, so we just stand for a moment. The bridge itself is made of old stones and the sight of the stream flowing underneath and then alongside this picturesque little village is beautiful. Right now I wouldn't want to be anywhere else in the world.

"What do you think I should do?" I ask Conall as I look out across the water.

"That's not my choice to make," he replies, "but whatever you decide, just know that I am not going anywhere."

"OK," I say quietly, lost in my own thoughts.

"Just for information though," Conall continues. "I was born in this village, growing up here was awesome. There's a small park around the back of those houses and in the summer you can play in the stream. We do have a small school building where all the children go to learn and it's safe." I know what he's trying to do, I don't want to get rid of the baby, I am just scared. I feel Conall squeeze my hand again as we both stand. What if I am a shit mam and my baby grows up to want world domination. Sure, I might still like the kid but if it starts trying to kill people and stuff is there like, a line? At what point would I have to step in and do a mam voice thing and bitch slip my own child. I hear Conall try to stifle his laughter beside me and I look up at him.

"What?" I ask him.

"Nothing," Conall laughs a bit more. "You will be an amazing mother, I have no doubt of that." He looks down at me and smiles.

"You think so?" I say, a little unsure of myself right now.

"I know so," he replies. "It's not like your kid is going to get bullied or anything as their mummy would bring the pain down on them." I laugh at him. Conall turns to me and gently strokes my cheek with his finger. "I love you Velvet, I am completely and utterly in love with every bit of you." I can't help but smile. This man, this pure hunk of gorgeousness has the most amazing soul and heart, I can't believe he's real.

"I... I don't know what to say," I stutter.

"You don't have to say anything," Conall says softly then leans down to me, his lips warm and gentle against mine as he kisses me.

"Why are you so perfect?" I ask him as our lips part.

"Because I am fucking awesome," he says smiling. "And apparently a pure hunk of gorgeousness who has the most amazing soul and heart," he laughs then I smile back as he kisses me gently again.

After a moment he turns, and we continue to walk back to the Lookout. It's a beautiful walk along little footpaths, we are surrounded by fields and trees and it's so quiet that it's easy to get lost in my own mind here. Conall leads me off the main path and through a lush little wood, the trees are old and tall, there are slight sounds of animals going about their day, I am in awe with how lucky I feel right now.

"So, something you said in your mind earlier is bugging me," Conall says suddenly as we come to a small clearing surrounded by trees.

"What did I say?" I ask, I think a lot, so it could literally be anything.

"You were thinking about us holding hands," he says as I look down, our fingers still entwined. "And you mentioned... I mean, I would like to be, I know it's not great timing and it sounds pretty childish to say it out loud..."

"Conall, what are you on about?" I am a bit confused.

"You said the word boyfriend," he smiles nervously at me, I did say that I guess.

"I didn't mean like..." I can't think of what to say now.

"I know it's just a word, but I can't think of anything that would make me happier right now than for us to... You know," he smiles.

"Do you want to be my boyfriend?" I say nervously. I know that things have got a little more serious between us but adding the name kind of makes it all so official.

"It sounds silly when you say it out loud," Conall laughs. "But, yes. I want an actual relationship with you, you mean so much to me that I can't imagine my life without you in it now. I know it hasn't been very long but I want to make you happy... And be an official couple, I guess."

"It does sound silly," I laugh, but at the same time I am ready to take things further with him. I want to feel like this forever. Conall gets closer to me and places his hand on the side of my face, I close my eyes momently and lean in to his palm, I just want to be close to him.

"You are so beautiful," he says almost at a whisper. "Is it bad that I want you so fucking much right now?" Conall glances down to me, I look at him and smile before he leans in and kisses me deeply. His hand moves to the bottom of my back as he pulls me closer, I can feel the passion explode inside of him as Conall's hand moves down and quickly lifts up the back of the dress and finds my bum. I stop him for a second and look up.

"We can't do this here," I say feeling a little embarrassed.

"Why not? We are surrounded by nature, and I am a wolf after all," Conall smiles then grabs my waist and lifts me off the ground, making my legs wrap around him, I close my eyes and just go with it, I go back to kissing him again as I feel him walk a few feet carrying me then I am kind of half sat down on something hard. I think I'm sitting on a big rock but my mind is too preoccupied with kissing Conall to have a look around.

His tongue plays deep inside my mouth with my own as I feel him slide his hand up my thigh and roughly rub over my mound through my underwear. His fingers move under the edges of the fabric, and he pulls them down. I watch him as he leans back slightly, he removes my knickers over my boots and gazes in to my eyes, he looks at me with so much lust as he then leans in again, kissing my lips slightly before he kneels in front of me.

I can see that I am in fact sitting on a large rock of some sort surrounded by trees and lush grass. I look down as Conall parts my legs and pushes my dress up, then moves his mouth straight to my apex. I inhale sharply as I feel his lips wrap around my clit as he gently sucks it whilst his tongue flicks across the surface then I place my hand on Conall's shoulder as I try to steady myself on the rock, it's not a great position to be in but right now I don't care because he feels so fucking good.

I moan as Conall grabs my thighs and pulls me more firmly on to his mouth, my bud throbbing as his tongue stimulates it, making me feel warm inside. It feels a bit naughty doing this outside, I glance up but there is no one around, just the thought of possibly being caught is such a turn on. I know that there is a chill in the air but Conall's body heat is enough for both of us.

"Shit," I groan as my breathing changes and the entirety of my core tingles, sending little sparks of pleasure through my loins. I move my hand from Conall's shoulder to his head and run my fingers through his hair as I watch his mouth move between my legs. This is so fucking hot, I've never had sex outside before, it's quite liberating. I can feel it start to build in my core but all I can think is that I want him to fuck me, I don't care about the foreplay, I just want his cock, right here, right now.

Conall's tongue falters for a second then he looks up at me smiling and in that moment I know he just heard me. He stands up between my thighs and I see he is hard through his jeans. I bite my bottom lip playfully as I watch him unzip his trousers to reveal his manhood then I place one hand slightly behind me on the stone and the other on Conall's shoulder as he steps towards me. My pussy is dripping wet for him as he glides in with ease, I throw my head back and moan as he penetrates me then he leans in and gently kisses my neck.

"Oh God," I groan as he starts to move in me, slowly at first, but then he grabs my waist and pulls me forward, driving in to me deeper. Every thrust is long and deliberate, making me feel his entire length before he plunges is cock back in to me, each time he does it gets deeper. His movements get slightly more aggressive with every motion, and I am almost begging him to fuck me harder, to force all that tension I am feeling right out of me. I feel his breath get heavier on my neck then he moves slightly so that he can look directly in to my eyes. I move my hand to the back of his neck and pull him forward to kiss me as I feel myself aching for him.

That's what I need, frantic pure lust. The need for him to fuck me so hard that I explode around his dick is so great inside of me that I would literally do anything to get that right now. I know Conall heard that as I feel him grip me tighter and before I know it I am struggling to breath and gasping for air as he drives my cares away.

I start to almost convulse under his touch as I cry out in ecstasy, the sounds from us echoing through the trees. I get the slight feeling that if he doesn't cum soon I am going to pass out again as I go light-headed. Just at the thought, I feel myself tip straight over the edge as the most amazingly intense orgasm bursts inside of me. I have to move my head to the side and part lips with Conall as I cum hard, almost holding my breath as I can't physically concentrate on inhaling air.

"Fuck..." he moans through gritted teeth as watching me cum excites him even more. He thrusts harder, it feels so intense that it is almost painful but I don't care, I can already feel myself getting ready to cum again. I tighten around his cock once more and my loins burn as I see Conall's face change as he explodes inside of me. Within seconds, I join him again as we both share in orgasmic pleasure.

Conall thrusts a couple more times then eventually stops, his chest heaving as he catches his breath. I can't help grinning at him, I started the day thinking Conall hated me and that he wanted nothing else to do with me. But now, after that whirlwind, I am in a real relationship with a boyfriend, and I am totally gleeful.

"Fuck me!" I say as I start to breathe normally again and relax under him.

"I just did," Conall smirks. I laugh as he kisses me again before stepping back. I pull the dress down as Conall zips his jeans back up.

"Question?" I say as I lower myself down from the rock. "Where is my underwear?" Conall looks around and laughs.

"Erm... I don't know... Oh! There they are," he replies as he spots them on the grass and hands them to me. I put them on and then Conall takes my hand and pulls me in to him, wrapping his arms around my shoulders.

"Thank you," I say looking up at him.

"What for?" I smile at him slightly.

"For just being you," he smiles as I reply. Conall kisses me on the forehead, and then we start the rest of the journey back to the Lookout.

The rest of the day is quite uneventful and I find myself getting tired pretty early on. Conall and Ranulf both force me to go to bed, so I do as I am told, I throw on a baggy t-shirt and collapse in to bed. I fall asleep almost instantly but I have a really restless night. The bad dreams are back with vengeance.

I can smell burning again, but this time it's different, I am surrounded by it. I can hear people screaming and their shouts fill the air. It's hard to breathe and I turn on the spot trying to see where I am, but I am blinded by smoke. In the distance I hear a familiar voice and then I see Helana, she stands staring at me, her mouth twisted in a malicious grin. Then I see Gideon, he stands by her side as though they are partners in the war. The burning flames get closer as I feel the heat on my skin and I cough as the black fumes fill my lungs. I look down and see that Gideon is carrying a machete, it's blade drips with blood and I can tell that the surroundings are that of the Midnight Church. I try to move, to run away but I can't feel my body. Gideon grins towards me then starts to run, the knife firmly in his hand and all I can do is scream...

"Velvet? It's only a dream, come back to me sweetheart. It's not real." I feel Conall lying behind me holding me tight, grounding me and making sure I know I am safe. I lie in his arms for a couple of minutes until my heart rate slows down and I feel better.

"They are always so real though," I say quietly as my breathing returns to normal. Conall tightens his grip around me and I feel his breath gently cascade over the back of my neck.

"Open your eyes," he says softly. "This is what's real, it's just you and me." I smile to myself as I try to shake the images from my head then take a deep breath and sit up slightly. Conall gets up and smiles down at me. "Good morning," he finally says. "I made you some breakfast, I didn't really know what you would want, so I played it safe and went for bacon sandwiches... Everyone likes bacon right?"

"Thank you," I smile up at him, he hands me a plate and a glass of orange juice then I look at it confused.

"Dee and Ben dropped by early this morning and left a load of vitamins and shit for you that you need to take. I also googled things that you should avoid with you being pregnant, so I thought orange juice might be OK?" He says nervously.

"No coffee then?" I ask and he shakes his head.

I don't really feel too hungry at the minute, so I place the breakfast on the bedside cabinet and take a drink of the juice, it's quite refreshing actually.

"And... these are for you," Conall says as he bends down and picks up a massive bouquet of red roses from the floor and hands them to me. They are stunning, wrapped in black and red tissue with a large red ribbon. "And this, because I thought you might think it was cute," he gives me a small and totally adorable wolf cuddly toy. It is cute, in fact I love it.

"Wow, these are beautiful. What's the occasion?" I ask as he also hands me a card and stands back.

"Are you serious?" He almost laughs at me. "It's valentine's Day, and I thought with us... You know." I open the card and smile as I read the words to my girlfriend on the front. I feel like a teenager all giggly and shit. I open the card and read what Conall has written.

- Velvet, if you asked me to bring you the moon, I would spend the rest of my life fulfilling your every wish just to see you smile. I want to tell you how much you mean to me but no words can describe the feeling better than I love you. I love you so much, not just today, but every day for as long I breathe.-

I take a moment and then look up at him, I think the last time I received a valentine's card it was black with a red heart on the front from a 14-year-old goth boy I used to hang around with. No one has ever said anything as sweet as that to me. Conall smiles then moves the roses, toy and card from my lap and places them on the floor then playfully climbs on to the bed on all fours and crawls towards me.

"So, today I was thinking that I could show you everything I feel for you," he says grinning as he moves closer and I lie back. He straddles me slightly and looks down in to my eyes. "After breakfast I am going to run you a hot bath then I am going to spend the rest of the day naked in this bed with you." I smile at him as he leans down and kisses me seductively, he runs his hand up under my t-shirt and kneads my breast as his tongue teases mine.

Something doesn't feel right though and my eyes dart open, so I forcefully push Conall off me, he almost falls off the side of the bed as I jump up and run straight for the bathroom. I barely make it there in time before I throw up.

"Velvet, are you OK?" Conall runs to the bathroom door as I heave again. I feel myself having a weird cold sweat as I sit on the bathroom floor for a second in case I vomit more. It just came out of nowhere. "Do you want me to call Ben?" Conall asks panicking but I shake my head as I reach up and flush the chain. My stomach feels slightly queasy now but I don't think I am going to be sick again.

"I'm going to hazard a guess, that this is morning sickness," I say as Conall comes over and helps me off the floor. "Sorry about the great timing there." Conall laughs slightly and sits me on the bed.

"Just as long as you're alright." I nod at him to confirm that I am. "I'll go run you a bubble bath, just try to relax for a bit," he smiles sweetly then goes back in to the bathroom and turns on the tap.

I have a lush relaxing bath and soon the icky feelings go away, I must have been in the bubbles for over an hour as I lost track of time. I get out and get dressed then head downstairs to where I can hear Conall and Ranulf watching TV. I walk in to the living room and Ranulf quickly jumps up, grabs the remote and turns off the TV.

"What's going on?" I ask as they are both looking highly suspicious.

"Nothing, just didn't fancy watching any more stuff," Ranulf says awkwardly. I glare at Conall, I know Ranulf is lying to me and I don't like being lied to.

"There was just something on the news, that's all, you don't want to know," Conall explains.

"Show me," I say bluntly. I want to see what is so important or horrendous that they don't think I should see it. Ranulf and Conall glance at each other then he sighs and turns the TV back on. I stand with my arms crossed and watch as the news reporter talks to the camera.

"The media has been filled with much speculation as to who General Marshall will face in the polls for the leadership position. We got word this morning that a press conference was to be held which will give Marshall a look at his appointment for the first time. There is no doubt in the public's mind that Marshall is already a force to be reckoned with as he helps to keep our nation safe." I watch as the camera pans to two podiums, the General stands behind the one on the left. Every time I see him I want to wipe that smug look clean off his face. He looks fucking ridiculous standing in front of a room full of people and live TV cameras in a military uniform.

There's lots of commotion amongst the reporters and journalists in the room as someone enters from the back. The camera follows them as they head through the crowd towards the stage dressed in a very expensive black tailored suit and my heart drops because I know exactly who's face I am going to see when they turn around. He approaches the right podium and clears his throat as the room falls quiet waiting for him to speak.

"General Marshall has been in a position of power in this country for far too long," he begins, I can see that the General doesn't recognise his face so won't have a clue who he is at the moment. "He is the reason that there is so much hatred, anger and unrest throughout both the human and non-human population alike. It is pure scare mongering which is resulting in violence and unnecessary deaths occurring that are the direct result of his words," Gideon pauses for a moment before continuing. "I am here to stand up for the people who have been segregated, who are now living every day in fear because of what this man has done. Witches, vampires, werewolves and many more species have lived side by side with humans for thousands of years. I am not going to stand up here and say they are all innocent because they are not, but neither are humans. This man is creating a war that is dividing this great nation and making it weak." There is more commotion throughout the journalists and one stands up to ask a question.

"Hi, BBC," he flashes his badge. "You speak passionately about the supernatural beings that have been shown to us as evil. Why would you want to represent them?" Gideon smiles slightly as the reporter sits down.

"Because I believe that everyone deserves a fair chance in this world, and I am probably the best person to be the face of the movement that stands up against General Marshall and condones his actions," Gideon looks strong and unwavering on the podium. He doesn't even seem scared that the crowd may turn on him. "I am going to keep this very brief, so I want to finish by saying that I will not back down. I will not be pushed aside... My name is Gideon, and I am a vampire." The sounds of gasps and disbelief fill the room as you can pinpoint the exact moment the General realises what is stood next to him. The General goes to move but security rush the stage area and block his path. Gideon nods to the journalists then turns to the General and smirks before leaving the stage and security lead him out.

The news reporter from earlier comes back on the screen but I've seen enough, so I turn back to Conall and Ranulf who just sit in silence watching me.

"You OK?" Conall asks and I nod my head.

"Yeah, I'm fine," I say quietly. Surprisingly I am feeling alright about seeing him on there. What he said was actually good and beneficial to the cause but I still can't stand the sight of him. "I'm going to have to tell him aren't I?" I say nervously.

"You have 7 more months to make that decision," Ranulf says. "Or do you even have to tell him at all? It's not like he just lives around the corner and will see you." I shake my head as his statement.

"It would be better if I told him sooner rather than later. He is the father, so no matter how pissed off at him I am, he deserves a say in his child's life," I reply. Conall looks down at the floor and doesn't say a word.

I wish that there was some way to take the pain away from Conall, I know he is upset, and he will be every time Gideon is mentioned. What's going to happen when I do have this child, is it going to have a dad? Will it call Conall dad... No, Conall might not like that, or maybe he will, I don't know.

"I don't like it, but he does deserve to know," Conall finally says, he smiles up at me, but we are interrupted by my phone ringing. I take it out of my back pocket and look at the screen then freeze. "It's him, isn't it?" Conall says trying to stay calm. I nod and decide to ignore the call until I make up my mind about what to say. Within a few seconds the phone rings again. "Answer it, you can't avoid him forever," Conall instructs me. I nervously press accept and put the phone to my ear.

"Hello?" My voice shakes slightly.

"Hi," Gideon says, I can hear noises in the background after he just announced to the world that he was a vampire. "I wondered if we could talk about the apartment."

"Erm... Kerry is living there now, as far as I remember it's mine to do with as I please, so I'm thinking about signing it over to her, so she has a roof." I am so nervous, how do you just slide it in to a conversation that you're pregnant.

"I don't think so," Gideon replies firmly. "If I need to, I will get my lawyers involved, that property was a gift and if you are not willing to be with me, then I want it back." Even though he is calm I can hear anger for me in his voice still.

"I don't want to fight about this... I can't erm..." I can't find the words to say. It's as though I no longer understand how the English language works and my vocabulary has disappeared.

"Velvet, just hang up," Conall says to me as he stands from the sofa, he knows I am starting to panic and my hands are shaking.

"Are you with him?" Gideon snaps, I feel sick to my stomach again. "So it's true, you're fucking that wolf."

"Gideon I..." I can't breathe. "There's erm... Things are complicated." Conall stands directly in front of me and places his hand on my shoulder for support.

"Things are very straight forward from my end," Gideon continues. "I will need you to come back to Newcastle in four days to fill in the paper work and bring my car back."

"Four days? I don't know if I can, I'm busy." This is happening too fast, I need time to think about what to say.

"I don't give a shit if you're busy, you have property that belongs to me. This is not your show any more, you are not the centre of my universe. You are just a blip in my life that I want gone and once I get back what is mine I will be able to move on with that life," Gideon's words sound so harsh when I know I'm carrying his child.

"I'll see what I can do, there's stuff I need to..." I try to say but Gideon cuts me off.

"2pm, four days. I'll be back from London then and I'll be at my club. I expect you to be there, no excuses," he says firmly. "I have far more important things to focus on than you now."

"I saw on the TV," I say quietly.

"Then you know I mean business. Four days, then you're out of my life for good," Gideon replies then hangs up the phone.

I try to steady my breathing, why do I feel suddenly scared? My whole life has changed in a matter of days, I no longer care about all the politics and the growing war... all I want is to have a peaceful happy life with my baby. My baby... I have this amazing life growing inside of me and I need to focus on that. I place my hand on my stomach and take a deep breath. My baby is now the most important thing to me in the whole world, every decision I now make will only be for my child. I don't want the conflict or the fighting, I want to keep it safe and I want a family. I want Conall and I just want to be happy. But what if Gideon doesn't want me to have my baby?

"Then I'll be here," I look up at Conall, and he smiles down at me then wraps his arms around me. I can feel my eyes sting with tears as everything feels too much to cope with. Four days and I'll have to face my fears and tell Gideon he is about to become a father.

Chapter Eleven

I didn't want to come.

I knew Gideon would be very unlikely to find me in the Highlands with the wolf pack, so I wanted to just ignore him for a while and not give in to his demands. Why did it have to be back in Newcastle? All those memories that I wanted to forget are from there, and his club...

Conall decided that it would be best if I went and got everything out of the way so that we could all move forward. The last few days have been horrible. I can't sleep, I can't eat. I don't know if it's morning sickness, anxiety or nerves but I have been ill. Although it has given me time to think about what I am going to say to Gideon. I am so nervous but I have thought a lot and I have decided that no matter what Gideon says, it is my baby, and I am actually starting to get quite excited with the prospect of becoming a parent. I keep getting this strange feeling in my chest every time I think about bringing this little life in to the world as though my heart wants to burst but not in a bad way...

I think I am starting to learn what love might feel like. After all this time, the thought of giving birth and then holding my own little miracle baby for the first time is so overwhelming that I can't deny that I am feeling things that I never thought I would. And it makes me realise that I might have similar feelings for Conall, all the times of saying I didn't know what love felt like and now, my baby is the one showing me. I have not said anything to Conall about it yet, I want to wait for the right time, I want everything to be perfect.

I've been shitting myself for the entirety of the car journey down. Ben wanted to keep an eye on me as I've been a bit too unwell for his liking the last few days and Conall refused to leave my side.

We get in to town a little early, so I call in to see Kerry and break the news to her. She reacted better than I thought she was going to and it makes me grateful to have such amazing and supportive friends. I decide to leave the Camero in the private car park near my apartment and walk over to Gideon's club. If he wants the car he can come and fucking get it, I am not prepared to drive it in to his garage all gift wrapped and shit for him.

It's only about a 15-20 minute walk and it's not too bad a day, I wanted to go alone but Conall insists on coming with me, Ben is going to meet up with us after I've spoken to Gideon, and then we are all meeting Kerry for a bite to eat.

"You know I don't have to do this, right?" I say to Conall as he holds my hand. "I mean I could just send him a text and fuck off back up to Scotland."

"You know, thinking about it, I don't think this is going to go as bad as you presume," Conall reassures me. "I'm sure like most people he wanted a family someday, granted this will be a very dysfunctional one but it's still a family. And if it was the other way round, I would be pretty stoked to be becoming a dad." I smile at him.

We are not too far from Gideon's club at the centre of town. Ben walked with us a little way as he wanted to go gift shopping for Dee's up coming birthday so only left us a minute ago and headed up the high street. As we walk past the monument at the heart of Newcastle there's a buzz in the air, it's always busy around here with either buskers and bands or people doing little protests. I spot a banner in the crowd and recognise it as the logo for the Hammer of Light, the anti-witch organisation that many believe are responsible for pointing out witches and publicly killing them, so I quickly tuck my pentagram necklace in to my top as I don't want any bother from anyone. I've started my journey to a happy quiet life, and I am not prepared to let anyone fuck it up. I stop for a moment and stretch my back as I go a bit queasy.

"Are you alright?" Conall asks me as I seem slightly in pain.

"Yeah, I just feel a bit sick that's all, I don't know if it's nerves off going to see Gideon or morning sickness... Or both," I laugh. "Are you OK to wait here two minutes whilst I go to the bathroom?" Conall smiles and nods at me, he leaves go of my hand as I start and make my way through the people towards the coffee shop around the corner that has toilets.

"Witches are an abomination," I hear one of the men in white jackets shout as I walk through the crowd. "The only way to eliminate them from this earth is by death. Our lord, the most holy father in Christ, decrees that no witch shall suffer this life, that we as his holy vessel do his work and strike down upon anyone who worships at the foot of the devil." They are all fucking crazy, fruit loops the lot of them. Thankfully I pass them quickly, they need to be in the loony bin those folks.

Out of nowhere everything goes really weird and suddenly there's a high-pitched ringing in my ears and I can't hear anything else apart from my own heartbeat. I am disorientated and my eyes can't focus. I don't know where I am and I taste dust in my mouth. I felt some sort of explosion, I think, I don't quite know what happened.

I open my eyes and I see that I'm on the ground, there's rubble and stones everywhere, I think I've hit my head when I've fallen but I'm confused as to why I am no longer on my feet. I push myself up slightly and look around. I see people running away, there are bodies across the floor, dust and debris floating in the air making it thick and difficult to breath in. I try to move and feel something soft under my hand then look down to see a leg, separated from its body, I try to focus my eyes and see blood everywhere. There are people dying around me, body parts blown in to bits. There are members of the Hammer of Light trying to crawl to safety. Innocent people killed and injured by the unknown blast.

The ringing in my ears starts to calm down and is quickly replaced by screaming and shouting. It definitely looks as though some sort of bomb has exploded, is this one if those terrorist attacks that I saw on the news?

"Conall?" I start to panic as I can't see him. "CONALL!" I scream, I can't sense him close, I don't know where he is. I push myself to my feel and try to look through the bodies but I can't see him.

"PRAISE BE TO OUR DARK LORD!!" I hear several people chant in unison and I freeze on the spot.

The things I saw in my dream the other day come flooding back, seeing Helana and Gideon, the fire, the screaming. What if she is in Newcastle to see Gideon, what if the meeting I am going to is a trap, was he going to set me up?

"The Hammer of Light think that they can control us witches," I hear a very familiar voice say loudly behind me, I quickly duck out of sight and hide behind a large piece of rubble. "Well no more shall we be silenced!" Helana shouts. I glance around the side and see several people dressed in blood-red robes step through the see of bodies and injured people, and start to grab anyone that is still alive in a Hammer of Light jacket. "This is what happens when you try to fight our Dark Lord," Helana continues. I try to remain calm but I am struggling. I watch as the man who was shouting about holy shit before, is dragged to his feet to stand in front of Helana.

"Please, don't kill me," he begs for his life as she smiles at him.

She has an ornate silver dagger in her hand, the same kind she uses for her sacrifices. I can't get away without being seen and I don't know what to do, I am not strong enough to face her, especially not now. I think quickly and pull my phone out of my pocket, my hands are trembling as I unlock it and go to contacts. My finger hovers over Gideon's name, I don't know if I can trust him, but I need help. After a moment of thinking I scroll past Gideon and hit the call button for Tristen instead. I try to stay as quiet as possible as the phone rings.

"Velvet? Why are you calling me?" Tristen says surprised. I go to answer but hear a voice shout at him in the background.

"Is that her?" Gideon snaps. "Tell her she's late, I want her here now," I can hear that he is angry.

"Tristen, please listen to me," I say almost at a whisper. "I need help and I didn't know who else to call." There's a brief silence before he speaks again.

"What's wrong? Where are you?" Tristen says sounding worried as his voice changes instantly. I glance round the corner again just in time for the man who begged for his life to get his throat slit open, his white jacket stained red as his body falls to the floor.

"There was a bomb," I try to say quietly as my voice shivers, "I don't know where Conall is, he might be dead."

"Tell me where you are, I'll be right there," Tristen says and I know he means it because I've heard it before.

"We... we were at Monument, she's... she's killing them," I stutter.

"Who? Velvet, who is killing them?" Tristen asks firmly, if he doesn't know, then he's not part of this, otherwise he would know she was here.

"Helana, she's here, the coven is here killing members of the Hammer of Light, I can't get away without being seen. If she sees me, she will kill me." I hear Tristen shout at Gideon that they need to leave and the phone goes dead then I put it back in my pocket.

"You are our sacrifice to our father the Dark Lord," I hear Helana say. "Your lives, even though fuelled by hatred and false Gods, will grant us eternal powers and a seat next to our Master." I watch as another person, this time a woman is placed in front of Helana. "Praised be to our Lord!" She shouts and again she slits the person's throat and their body drops to the ground. The street is almost empty, no one wants to be close in case they are killed also.

"Velvet?" I hear a very distant voice echo through the air then everything suddenly falls silent.

I hear someone groan and then I see Conall push himself up from under some rubble, he has blood on his face and is covered in dust and dirt, but he doesn't look too injured. Please, Conall don't speak, just run, I beg. If he is going to hear my thoughts then please let him hear me now. I pray you can hear me... please run.

"Velvet?" I hear him say louder and my heart sinks as I know my name has been heard by everyone.

"What did you say?" Helana's voice rings out. "Bring him to me!" She orders her followers.

Conall is dazed and grabbed quickly before being dragged to Helana, he notices what is happening and goes to fight them off. He tosses one of the coven members away then I can see him snarl, but he suddenly stops as I watch him claw at his throat as in invisible force starts to squeeze the life from him. I don't know what to do, she might kill him and then his death will be on my hands. Helana stands directly in front of Conall and looks at him.

"You are not Hammer of Light, but you did say a name that I am very curious about," she says to Conall as I can hear him struggling to breathe. "I don't want an explanation, I just want to know where she is." Conall shakes his head as his face starts to turn red.

"I'll never... tell you," Conall forces out. Helana smiles and moves her arm as Conall is lifted off the ground, his feet trying desperate to find the earth below.

"I saw on the TV that she was dead, but I had hoped that was a lie because I wanted the satisfaction of doing it myself," Helana snarls. "Let's just see what happens shall we?"

"Go... to... hell!" Conall manages to say under her grip but Helana just smiles at him.

175

"Velvet?" She shouts. "I know you can hear me, I know you are here right now somewhere." I press my back up against the stone and try to stay as still as possible. "Are you really hiding from me? I thought more of my sister's spawn to be honest. I thought you might at least try to put up a fight," I hear her malicious laugh. "Very well, if you don't want to come out and play... Then I'll just have to find my own fun and kill him." My eyes go wide as I hear Conall start to writhe in agony. I can't let her kill him, I've just found him, he's my perfect future, he is the man I want to spend the rest of my days beside.

"STOP!" I shout as loud as I can then I hear Conall go quiet. "Stop, Helana," I say as I move from behind the stone, and she sees me. "Please, let him go." Helana smiles as Conall is dropped to the ground unconscious.

"I didn't think this day could get any better," Helana smiles as she raises her hand towards me and I can feel my body being pulled to her like she did before. I try to resist, but my body is weak due to being pregnant. Just like I did the first time I met her, I am dragged across the ground, unable to stop her. I am only a few meters from her when I see her grip the dagger in her hand tighter ready for my approach, so she can follow through on her threat to kill me.

"Helana let her go!" Gideon's voice booms around the open space. I stop moving as Helana looks around. I move my head to see Tristen and Gideon standing not too far away. My chest is already heaving, I am terrified of facing her right now.

"King Gideon? For what do I owe this pleasure?" Helana says to him sarcastically.

"We had a deal that you would not set foot in this city," Gideon says firmly.

"You have no authority over me," Helana glares at him.

"I have every authority over you when you are in my territory," Gideon snaps back. Helana looks back at me, hatred smeared across her face.

"Fine! I'll leave, but I am taking her," she says.

"No," Gideon replies instantly. "You will leave, alone, or we will kill your people."

Helana shakes her head then goes to step forward to grab me but Tristen moves so quick I don't even see him, he lunges for the closest member of the coven to him and sinks his fangs into their neck, the man screams as Helana steps away then Tristen drops the man to the floor. Helana hesitates for a moment then drops her grip on me and I stumble backwards. She grits her teeth, clearly frustrated that she had me within her grasp then turns to leave without saying another word as a couple of her followers go with her.

I look over and see Conall forcing himself up from the ground, I can see he's hurt slightly but it's all just superficial. Gideon and Tristen chase off a few of the last members of the coven as we hear emergency services vehicles already getting close to help the injured people following the blast. I guess my suspicions about the Midnight Church being behind the attacks on the members of the Hammer of Light are now definitely justified.

I am going to have to be extremely careful moving forward now to ensure I don't have another run in with the church, they are far too strong and I don't want any of this life any more. Now, more than ever, I just want to go away with Conall and be a family, just me, him and my baby. It's the happiest life anyone can have and that is what I want.

I turn to walk away, to head over towards Conall, when I freeze on the spot. Helana's face is inches from mine, a twisted grin emblazoned across it as she stares at me, I know I should be afraid but instead I feel a weird sensation and I look down to see her holding the hilt of a silver dagger, it's blade deep in my abdomen. I didn't even feel her stab me, I am confused as to what just happened. I slowly move my hand to where the metal disappears in to my flesh as my own blood starts to flow between my fingers. I look at Helana in pure shock, and she pulls the knife from me in one fluid motion and smiles. I hear Conall notice what is going on and scream over to me, Helana turns her head and Conall is forced backwards through the air, making sure he is not an issue for her at the minute.

"Guess you won't be a problem for me after all," Helana says then smiles wildly before laughing and running away, leaving me standing on the spot.

Conall is quickly back to his feet and runs straight over to me, my head goes dizzy instantly as I lose my balance and Conall catches me as I fall. He searches my body to see if I am injured then I see the panic in his eyes. He looks up then shouts towards someone.

"Ben!" He says desperately. Ben seems confused as to why we are here and not at the meeting with Gideon, but he sees me lying in Conall's arms and runs straight over.

"What are you doing here? I thought..." Ben ask Conall.

"I know. Ben she's hurt," Conall cuts in.

Ben moves my hand from the wound on my stomach and starts to give Conall directions of how to help. I go really light-headed and start to zone out as they try to stop the bleeding, everything around me feels like a dream and I can't concentrate properly.

"What happened to her now?" Gideon says sarcastically as him and Tristen approach us, his tone tells me he is in a mood because we have scuppered his meeting plans. "It's just another day when she gets injured and needs everyone's attention."

"Fuck off, Gideon!" Conall snaps at him. Gideon goes to step towards us in retaliation but Tristen stops him.

"Now is not the time," Tristen says trying to calm Gideon down.

"We need to get this bleeding stopped," Ben says trying to soak up the blood with his own hoodie and applies pressure to my wound.

"You're going to be OK," Conall says to me as I suddenly feel the pain kick in.

I grab Conall's hand as it hits me, an immense searing pain rips through my stomach and I cry out, almost doubling over in agony. It only lasts a few seconds but it's enough to make me gasp for breath. Ben and Conall both exchange concerned looks as I realise exactly what might be happening.

"Ben?" I say starting to panic. "Ben please... this can't happen, please."

I see Gideon give me a look of disgust from behind Ben and I turn back to Conall and shake my head not wanting this to be real as another wave of pain hits me, this one more intense than the last. Conall and Ben try to keep me still as my body starts to shake and go freezing cold.

"No. No... No," I keep saying, this can not be happening. "Please Ben, the baby please!" Tears begin to fill my eyes, please let this be a bad dream. "Please not my baby... I can't lose my baby," I beg him to help, but I can see it in his face that things are already bad.

"Conall, I need you to get the paramedics here now," Ben says firmly as the sound of sirens fills the air. Conall is reluctant to leave me, but he nods and gently lies me back on the floor to go for help. Ben looks around and sees Gideon and Tristen standing behind him.

"Gideon right?" Ben says and Gideon nods to confirm, he seems very confused all of a sudden. "I need you to apply pressure here."

Gideon doesn't understand what's going on, but he nods at Ben and kneels down next to me and takes Ben's place trying to stop the bleeding. Ben rushes around the other side of me and tries to calm me as pain tears through me again, it doesn't feel as bad now, although my body seems to be going a little numb. He places his fingers on my neck to check my heart rate and then his face changes, I feel a freezing wave wash over me then a warm wetness spreads between my legs, and I can see that Ben notices it. Gideon looks at Ben then down at my crotch, pauses for a moment then looks to me, he is utterly confused as to why everyone is panicking around me, after all, I get hurt all the time, right? I can feel my energy draining from me fast and although I feel more pain my body doesn't react to it any more, I just feel the need to close my eyes.

"She's over here!" I hear Conall shout as two paramedics come rushing over. Conall notices Gideon at my side and forcefully pulls him away from me.

"Step back!" Conall snarls at him. "Don't fucking touch her again." They both square up to each other for a second before Conall shakes his head and comes back to me. Two paramedics kneel either side of me as Conall sits near my head and grabs my hand, Gideon and Tristen stand behind him just watching.

"What do we have?" The first paramedic asks.

"This is Lucy," Ben acts quick, I am quite impressed he remembered not to use my real name, "She's 27, single knife wound to the abdominal wall, she's nearly 9 weeks pregnant and starting to haemorrhage heavily... I am her Doctor," he says quickly.

"OK, I need you to stand back please," the paramedics says to Conall, Ben nods and stands up, he places his hand on Conall's shoulder, but he is reluctant to let go of me. "Please sir, you need to give us some room to work," the female paramedic says more forcefully, Conall nods then quickly leans over and kisses my forehead.

"I love you... I love you so fucking much," he says to me, his voice panic-stricken as I struggle to breathe. My chest hurts as I try to force air in to my lungs, it is so difficult though.

Conall stands up and watches helplessly as the paramedics cut my clothing to allow access to my wound and begin to work on me, but everything doesn't seem real and I can't focus any more. I don't think I've ever had an out-of-body experience, it's not like I am floating through the air looking down on every one, it's more like I'm just not here any more. As though I can hear and feel things, but it's not really me.

"What...erm... Why did he say she was pregnant?" I hear Gideon say confused above my head.

"She was going to tell you today," I hear Conall reply trying to stay calm, his voice shaking uncontrollably. "She wanted to talk to you about what you might want to do."

I feel multiple hands on my body as my breathing becomes shallow and my heart rate decreases.

"She's going in to hypovolaemic shock, we need to get her out of here now!" I hear the paramedics say, I feel them inserting needles in to my arms but my brain is foggy and my vision is going blurry.

"Why would I care if she was pregnant?" I hear Gideon reply to Conall. "I don't give a shit what you guys do any more."

"Because..." Conall replies. "I don't get a say when it comes to her being pregnant... because it's not my baby."

I close my eyes, I am so tired that I can't concentrate on the world around me any more, I don't even feel the pain.

"She's not breathing, we need to intubate." I feel my head forced to tilt back and then something is inserted in to my mouth and down my throat but I don't care, I can't move to stop them. "She's crashing." I just need to sleep.

"There's no pulse," I hear Ben tell them.

Everything is so dark, but that's good because I can rest now, I can sleep.

"Velvet?" I hear Conall shout, but it's distant. "You need to stay awake... Please... Velvet, breathe sweetheart, you have to wake up, please... I am begging you. You need to wake up... I love you, please... don't leave me."

It's strange the whole dyeing thing. I've never really believed in anything spiritual or religious, so I thought that when I eventually died there would just be nothingness. Like, I would just fall asleep in darkness and that would be it forever more.

I read this thing once that said when your body dies your brain stays active and you see lights, it kind of goes in to over drive and your brain activity goes off the charts and that's how you see things. Maybe I am a sceptic, but is there really life after death? Or just a load of electrical signals sparking in my brain, that's all we are anyway, isn't it? Mush and bones.

Or maybe I should think on the other side of things. All the people I have met and species I've seen, you would think that there had to be something more wouldn't you? It's always amazed me how unique individuals are, we are all made of the same stuff, yes we might look slightly different but it's our personalities that define us. Do you think that we get that from our brains or that mystery entity that we call our soul? What even is that? You can't see it, it doesn't just slot inside your body somewhere, so what is it?

I squint slightly as the white light that surrounds me is so bright. It's doesn't scare me though, as just like last time, I feel calm. I look in front of me and I see Lena smiling, as if she was waiting for me again.

"Hello, my sweet girl," Lena smiles sweetly and walks towards me.

"Hello mum," I reply happily.

"He's beautiful isn't he?" Lena says.

I feel something move in my arms and I look down. I am cradling a new born baby wrapped in a white blanket. It's fingers are so small.

"How is this possible?" I say confused, I was only a couple month pregnant.

"On this plane you see what your heart desires, and his soul is so strong that he wanted to show you how perfect he is, that this is how he wants you to remember him," Lena stands looking down at the baby in my arms.

"He?" I ask in disbelief. "He's a boy?" Lena nods her head and smiles at me. "Is this real?"

"Of course it is, when you die your soul has to go somewhere." I look around as Lena speaks, but everything is just white. "This is just the entrance, everyone's experience is different."

"So you're saying that I can have my baby here? I can stay with him and be a family?" I look down at the little boy in my arms and smile at him. His eyes are green, and he has the cutest little nose I think I have ever seen, he makes my heart melt.

"You can't stay," Lena says gently. "It's not your time yet, there are big things ahead for you." I shake my head not wanting to hear those words.

"But I don't want to leave. I can't just walk away from him, he needs me," I say, his tiny body wriggling in my arms. I've just met him, I can't let him go yet.

"You don't have a choice unfortunately," Lena says softly then she smiles. "He has your eyes." My chest starts to hurt at the thought of having to leave here, that I will never see his face ever again.

"If I leave then what will happen to him?" I say not taking my eyes off my baby.

"He will be safe here with me. And we will be waiting for you when your time does come," she explains. I can already feel so many overwhelming emotions building up inside of me.

"But how am I meant to live without him? How can I go on knowing that he's gone? I can't just leave him here, he won't know who I am," my voice shakes slightly as I feel my eyes burn with tears.

"You are stronger than you could possibly imagine," Lena reassures me.

"I don't feel strong," my voice quivers as tears flow down my cheeks. "I can't live without him, my heart already hurts just knowing that I won't see him every day."

"But you will," Lena places her hand over my heart. "Because he will always be with you. This is not a weakness, love will make you stronger."

I hold my baby with one arm and gently stroke his face with my finger, his skin is so soft and I stare at him trying to remember every tiny detail of his face, I don't want to ever forget what he looks like. He looks up at me as though I am the only person in his world, I don't even know if he knows that I am his mummy, how will he know who I am if I can't stay with him?

"It's nearly time for you to go," Lena says gently, I don't want to leave yet, I haven't got to know him. "He has a powerful soul," Lena continues. "He would have been an amazing person. Full of passion and fearless like his father, compassionate and strong like his mother. A future leader of a better world, your little Prince Marcus." I look up at Lena and smile.

"Marcus?" I ask and she nods at me. "I like that name," I say though sobs. I look back down at Marcus and force a smile, I was just starting to find out how love feels, when I look at him I feel utterly consumed by it.

"Hi baby Marcus," I say trying to stifle my sobs, "I am your mummy... I'm so sorry I can't stay with you, but you won't be alone. Know that you are loved so very much... Your mummy loves you more than anything in the world." I stroke his arm, and he wraps his tiny hand round my finger. "I love you my beautiful baby boy." My heart hurts so much. I didn't even get the opportunity to meet him, to bring him in to this world and watch him grow. How can I possibly go on living without him.

"It's time," Lena says gently, I reluctantly nod my head and hand Marcus to her. I already feel like a piece of my heart is missing by just handing him over.

"What do I do now?" I say whilst crying. Lena smiles at me then with one hand she reaches up and touches my temple.

"Now you need to wake up," she says as everything around me turns black.

All I can hear in the darkness is a high-pitched beeping every few seconds, I can't open my eyes and I can't move but I can hear people moving around me and the sound of machines whirling near my head. Although I can't physically do anything I feel quite calm and relaxed, I know people have been talking to me but I can't remember what they have said or who they were. My head is quite drowsy, and everything is fuzzy as though I kind of remember what happened but now I am just consumed by the darkness.

Lena told me I need to live but I don't know how to. I don't think I truly want to, I am not ready to face the real world again without my baby. I hear the beeping get slightly faster as my mind feels like I am starting to wake up from a bad dream. My hand seems to feel weird as though someone is holding it, and they have been doing so for so long that it won't feel right any more if they were to let go. I try to take a deep breath but I start to feel like I am suffocating instead, there's air being pushed in to my lungs against my will and I have no control over it. The beeping sounds get faster as I start to panic, I still can't open my eyes, I can't shout for help. I try to move my hand, to tell whoever is there that I'm here and I need to wake up.

"I need help in here!" I hear a man's voice shout, the room around me quickly fills with noise, people talking, hands touching me. I am so confused as to what's going on, I don't know where I am. My eyes are forced open one at a time and a bright light shines in them as my lungs burn as I desperately try to breathe.

"Lucy, my name is Doctor Simmons," another man's voice says to me. "You're in the ICU at Newcastle's Royal Victoria Hospital." I try to swallow but there's something in my throat and it's choking me. "You are going to feel some discomfort as I remove the breathing tube." I don't understand what's going on, but the voice keeps talking to me calmly.

I feel hands on my face then whatever is in my throat is pulled out and my gag reflex kicks in. My throat is sore and for a minute I can't actually remember how to breathe normally, then I feel the grip on my hand again and someone close to my head.

"Come on, breathe!" The voice says to me, is that Conall? I am not sure. "Please, Velvet, breathe for me sweetheart."

As though my survival instinct takes over I gasp, the air around me fills my lungs and I take several deep breaths until I know that I am controlling it myself now.

"Stats are returning to normal," I hear a woman's voice say as I start to relax again now that I can actually breathe.

"Put her on half hourly obs, I want her monitored closely," the Doctors voice replies.

There's more movement and noises, I can't focus on it all at once then I feel a hand on my face as my head is turned to the side, fingers lightly stroking my cheek.

"Hey sweetheart, can you hear me?" That is Conall's voice, I recognise it now. My whole body feels almost paralysed and I can't tell him that I am awake. I try to say it in my head but I don't think he can hear me. "Can you open your eyes? Just anything to let me know you're in there." I don't know what I can do, I am stuck. I feel his hand gripping mine and I use every ounce of strength I have to squeeze it back. My fingers only move a tiny amount but Conall notices and I feel his lips gently kiss my forehead.

"What's going on?" I hear Ben's voice from across the room, he's probably walked in and seen the room full of doctors and nurses.

"She's awake," Conall replies, I can hear emotion in his voice and exhaustion as though he hasn't slept for days.

I try to force my eyes open, but they are just so heavy. I try to ignore all the other sounds and people then just focus on Conall, if he is here then everything might be OK. My eyes flicker slightly and then I open them, the light in the room is so bright now that I am used to the darkness. They open just enough to focus on Conall, his eyes are red and puffy, his face tired and unshaven, but he notices me look at him, and he smiles.

"Hi," he says softly, I try to keep my eyes open but it's difficult. I go to reply but my mouth is so dry and I can't form the words yet. "Don't try to speak."

"I'll make some phone calls," Ben says to Conall then he leaves the room. Conall doesn't take his eyes off me, I don't know how long I've been here but I get the strong feeling that he has never left my side.

"I thought we had lost you," Conall says, his eyes filling with tears.

"Con... Conall," I try to say, it's barely audible, but he nods at me to show me he heard me. "I... I love you." He pauses for a moment and then realises what I just said, a broad smile fills his face as he leans closer and gently kisses my lips.

"I love you too," he replies happily. I should have told him sooner, I should never have held anything back because I nearly didn't get the chance to tell him how I felt.

"I'm... I'm so tired," I whisper as my head feels heavy and I try to fight the urge to sleep.

"It's OK, you need to rest, just sleep," Conall smiles. "I promise I'll be here when you wake up."

I close my eyes and drift back in to unconsciousness as he continues to hold my hand tightly. I don't actually know if I passed out or slept but it just felt natural, it was relaxing and nice.

My mind wakes up again before my body, my eyes open and I actually see the room for the first time. I am in a side room in hospital, I'm not in here alone though as I see Ranulf sitting reading a book on a chair in the far corner, there's a window next to him, it's raining heavily and I can hear the drops hit off the glass. On the window sill are bunches of flowers and I spot the fluffy teddy wolf that Conall gave me for valentines day, that makes me smile, next to those are a couple of helium balloons that say get well soon. I look to my side and see Conall, he grips my hand tightly as he half sits on his chair beside my bed, half slumped on the side, asleep.

Then I look up and see Rick standing drinking a cup of tea, he looks weird in normal clothes instead of his military stuff. He sees that I am awake, and he smiles at me. I smile back as he walks over to Conall and places his hand on his shoulder to wake him up. Conall looks around to Rick as though he doesn't know what's going on and Rick nods towards me, smiling. Conall turns his head towards me to see what is going on.

"Hi," I croak. Conall doesn't say anything he just stands up from his chair and instantly kisses my lips gently. After a moment he smiles and moves, his forehead touching mine as he just wants to be close to me.

"I told you I would never leave you," he says softly.

I try to nod my head as he stands back up. Ranulf looks up from his book after hearing talking, and he smiles wildly. It's strange though as they all seem happy that I am awake but at the same time slightly awkward as they don't quite know what to say to me. The door to the room opens, Kerry and Tiffany walk in with coffee and sandwiches. Kerry instantly sees that I am awake and quickly puts what she is carrying down on the small table at the bottom of my bed and runs straight over to give me a hug. She hugs me so tight I think she's going to squeeze me to death.

"Kerry! Need to breathe," I say tapping her on the back. She stops and smiles at me.

"Sorry, I am just so happy you're awake," Kerry replies then steps back, Tiffany then takes her place and hugs me gently but doesn't say anything.

The next hour or so, I drift in and out of sleep, when I open my eyes properly again the room seems a lot more relaxed, I see smiling faces, Kerry and Tiffany sit chatting and laughing. Conall is being forced to eat from Ranulf, and I squeeze his hand again to let him know that I am awake. As soon as I do he looks at me and smiles, then reluctantly takes a bite of stale sandwich.

Behind Conall is the door, it has a small square of glass in it that the medical staff can see through, I glance up and see a Doctor standing just outside talking to Ben. He talks Ben through the charts and test results on a clipboard he is carrying and Ben nods along then looks over and sees that I am awake, shakes the Doctors hand and takes the charts from him. He stands outside for a second before finally coming in.

"Hey, guys," he says cautiously to everyone in the room. "Would you mind giving us some privacy for a few minutes." I look at Conall and force a smile as I can see it in his face that he doesn't want to leave.

"It's OK," I reassure him and leave go of his hand. The room empties and Ben closes the door, there is an awkward silence as Ben just looks down at the sheets.

"I am named on everything as your Doctor, so I thought it would be best that I spoke to you first," Ben says gently, he glances up at me and I nod.

"OK," I say, encouraging him to go ahead. I know what he is going to say but I don't think I am ready to hear it out loud.

"So, the stab wound you received was quite deep, I am not going to go in to full details as I am sure you don't want to hear it all, but there were several organs affected which caused you to bleed out very quickly. You went in to shock, and we lost you a couple of times just trying to get you here." I can tell he is skirting around the subject a bit but I just listen. "You were taken to surgery, where they found a rupture in the uterine wall from the blade... They did everything they could but unfortunately they... They were unable to save..."

"OK," I cut in, I don't want him to say it. I don't want him to say my baby is gone out loud.

"I am so so sorry, Velvet, there was just nothing they could do," Ben says coming to sit next to me. I look away and swallow back tears, trying not to show my emotions. After a few seconds Ben continues. "The surgical team were able to eventually stop the bleeding but it was hit-and-miss for a little while. You were clinically dead on three separate occasions and your body was unable to support itself so you were placed on a ventilation system to allow your body to heal. We didn't know until you woke up if there was any adverse effects on your brain."

"How long have I been here?" I ask him. He smiles at me slightly then nods.

"13 days," Ben says gently. "Truthfully, we didn't know if you were actually going to wake up at all." I nod at him, I've missed so much. Everyone else has had nearly two weeks to adjust to the fact that I am not pregnant any more, for me I am struggling to just keep it together as inside my heart is breaking.

"Well, I am awake now," I say forcing a smile to stop myself from crying.

"Are you in any pain? I can ask them to give you something if you need it?" Ben asks me but I shake my head, it's not physical pain I am in. "Alright, is there anything you want to ask me?"

"No," I say quietly, I don't want to know anything else. All I need to know is that my baby is gone and I can't do anything to change that now.

"I'll leave you to get some rest, I am sure Conall will be itching to get back in here, he's never left your side," Ben gives me a little nod then heads out of the room. A tear escapes me and I quickly wipe it away, now is not the time to cry, I need to be strong.

Over the next couple of hours the gang try to lift my spirits, but it's all fake smiles and awkward conversations. Eventually it starts to get late and one by one they leave to go to bed, Conall is the only constant, unwavering in his duty to stay with me, until there is only the two of us that remain. I am still hooked up to a monitor and drip as I've been out for a while, and they said that I am dehydrated and need constant observations because I was technically in a coma and died a couple of times. My body feels fine, everything seems to have healed, much to the surprise of the medical staff.

After a little while I start to get tired again, just as I do there is a slight knock on the door, I can't see from this angle who it is but Conall gets up and walks over to open it.

"You have got to be shitting me... No! Fuck off!" Conall says firmly.

"I just want to see that she's OK," I hear Gideon's voice from outside the room. "Please, I need to..." He tries to say.

"No, you are not welcome here, this happened because of you. She came back because you made her," Conall replies to him, clearly not happy that Gideon is here.

"I know, it's just..." Gideon tries to explain.

"Do you not understand the word no? She doesn't want to see you," Conall says as I see Gideon lean forward slightly to see if I am awake. "You need to leave. Now!"

"Conall!" I say to get his attention, he looks around and I nod slightly. "It's OK." I have to accept that I am not the only one who lost a child and I need to face Gideon at some point. Conall reluctantly sighs then walks back over to me.

"I'm going to be right outside, if you need me I am straight in," he kisses my forehead and squeezes my hand then I nod at him before he leaves. He stands and stares for a few seconds at Gideon then pushes past him and disappears from view. Gideon stands in the door way for a few moments then steps in and shuts the door behind him. I can see he is carrying a small bunch of tulips, as he forces a smile at me and awkwardly hovers at the bottom of my bed.

"I brought these for you," he says holding up the flowers then he puts them down on the chair in the corner.

"Thanks," I say quietly, I didn't even get the chance to talk to him about being pregnant and now I have to have the conversation about this.

"I'm sorry that I didn't come to see you sooner, I've just been... Busy," Gideon apologises, he is nervous and is avoiding making eye contact with me.

"How's the campaign going?" I ask trying to make small talk, I don't know where to start.

"Good," is all he says back on the subject. "How are you?" He grimaces at himself as soon as he asks, as though thinking to himself that he shouldn't have said that.

"I've been better," I reply quietly. I don't think we are very good at the small talk thing. I think for a moment then finally bite the bullet. "I didn't want to tell you over the phone, I thought that it would have been best said in person." He looks up at me and nods.

"I appreciate that," he takes a deep breath. "I spoke to Rick, and he told me what he knew, about things. Conall told me to stay away and I didn't know what... How to say..."

"It's OK," I replay. I feel bad about how he found out, I'd only know I was pregnant for less than 7 days and it changed my whole outlook on my life. That week of starting to think about having a little family and what I was going to teach my child made me so happy. Gideon didn't get any of that, he never got the chance.

"I should go," Gideon says after a minute of silence. He seems upset and it just makes me hurt inside more knowing that he would have been happy when I told him. If he didn't care he wouldn't be here at all. Gideon smiles slightly and turns for the door.

"Gideon?" I say stopping him, I can already feel the tears in my eyes, all the emotions bubbling up inside and I can't hold them back any longer. Gideon looks at me and nods. "I'm sorry."

"Sorry for what?" Gideon says gently.

"I'm sorry that I couldn't protect our baby." The flood gates open and I feel the salty tears flow down my face. Gideon grits his teeth to stop himself showing any emotion but I can see it in his eyes that he is devastated, his heart is breaking. He shakes his head and looks down at the floor, trying to suppress any feeling he might show before he speaks again.

"I need to go, if I am welcome I'll try to visit again in a day or two," he says quietly, I nod my head and wipe away my tears as he turns and leaves.

As I sit alone I just sob, my eyes start to sting with the amount of liquid that escapes them. After a few minutes Conall comes back, he sees that I am upset, he comes straight over and sits on the bed with me. He holds me tight as I let the emotions all take control and give me the release I need.

The next day I have a room full of visitors again and Conall still hasn't left, I am starting to feel like I want some alone time, so I order Conall to go with Kerry and get some proper sleep in an actual bed, I told him he stunk and needed a shower. It took some persuasion but eventually he left and I just sit on the bed and enjoy the quiet, I am tired, so I get comfortable in the bed and try to sleep. I have a restless night as the wards are filled with the noise of machines and people's voices. I finally fall asleep in the early hours of the morning and wake with a start, it's cloudy and murky outside but it's not raining any more.

It's still early but my mind has been working in overdrive for hours. I can't just lie here, I have to do something, anything to stop myself from going crazy. I've already been told by the doctors that they are not willing to let me go for at least a few more days, so they can make sure I am fine. But I don't have a few days because I know that tonight is a full moon and because of that I will know exactly where Helana will be.

I was so close to having the perfect peaceful life, and then she ripped it away from me. I know the only way I can live is if she dies, and it will most certainly be by my hand. I need to get out of here and somehow get to the bunker, there are weapons and things that I can use. Plus I know that I still have clothes at the bunker, I don't even know what happened to the ones I was wearing when I was brought in.

I rip the small round monitors off my chest and wince as I pull the needle attached to the IV out of my arm. The machines in the room start to make weird sounds as they are no longer attached to me and I swiftly head for the door, just as I go to put my hand on it I see Conall, Ranulf and Rick through the glass. They are talking to each other and laughing, Conall has been changed and looks refreshed. He looks up as he goes to open the door and notices me, he looks puzzled as he pushes it open and I just stand here.

"Hey," he looks at me confused. "What are you doing?" I can feel my heart begin to race.

"I was going to the bathroom," I quickly say. He searches my face to see if I am lying

"You are meant to tell the nurse so that you don't have to remove your drip," he says looking at my arm as blood trickles from the pin prick hole.

"I couldn't wait," I say nervously and force a smile.

"Here then, I'll help you," Conall goes to take my arm but I step back. Rick and Ranulf walk in to the room and move to the side as Conall blocks the doorway.

"I'll be fine, I don't need a chaperone," I explain, hoping that he believes me. He gives me a funny look then places a set of keys on the small table at the bottom of the bed, I glance at them and notice that they are for my Camaro. He must have driven it back here from the apartment car park where I left it.

"What's going on?" Conall asks, I just smile at him. If he knows what I am planning in my head then he will do anything to try to stop me going.

"Nothing, just sick of lying in bed, so I need to stretch my legs," I say looking down at my bare feet. He doesn't believe me, I don't want to hurt him but I can't risk missing this opportunity to kill Helana, I can't wait for the next full moon. I need to leave now.

"Maybe you should lie down, I'll go and get a nurse to help you," Conall says slowly, his facial expression has changed slightly.

"I'm fine," I reassure him. "I'll just go to the bathroom and come straight back." I step forward to leave the room but Conall puts his arm up to stop me.

"Tell me the truth," he says firmly. I glance at Rick and Ranulf as they just sit and watch us, unsure of what is going on.

"I am telling you the truth," I say smiling. "Everything is fine."

"Then why are you trying to leave so you can go and kill Helana?" Conall says trying to stay calm. I swallow hard as it must have flashed in my mind, and he heard it.

"It's not what you think," I reply. I step back again and my mind starts to race.

"It's suicide if you get anywhere near her. I've already nearly lost you once, I cannot go through that again," Conall says, I see Rick stand and look at me as he talks about Helana.

"Is tonight a full moon?" Rick asks me and I nod my head as he puts his hand on Conall's shoulder. "We need to support her actions," Rick encourages him. Conall shakes his head and pushes Rick's hand away. I know Rick would do the same in my position, Helana killed his future wife, my mother and my unborn baby. She deserves to die.

"No!" Conall shouts. "I won't let you go, I'd rather chain you to that bed for the rest of your life than watch you walk to your death."

"You can't stop me," I say firmly.

"I will stop you, because I will not watch you die again," Conall goes to grab my arm but I force him away, I didn't mean to but my power bursts out of me, and he goes across the room a few feet and hits the bed. I act quickly, grab the keys to the Camaro and run. I must look great running around the corridors of the hospital in just a gown but I don't care, I follow the signs for the exit and pray it's the same way as the car park.

I run outside and the ground is wet from the rain earlier on, I spot the Camaro instantly, it does stand out quite a bit in the sea of normal cars. I run across the car park as I hear shouting behind me.

"Velvet?" Conall shouts as he runs outside after me. "Velvet, stop!" He screams at me but I keep going. I get to the car and look back as Rick and Ranulf grab

Conall and hold him back from chasing me down. My dad knows what I need to do, but I can't do that with Conall trying to stop me. "Velvet please, if you walk away now I won't be able to protect you," Conall shouts across the car park as I open the car door. I shake my head as a red Ferrari pulls up near the main entrance, I see Tristen and Gideon inside the car, they can see what is going on instantly, but they don't get involved. I pause for a second then shout back.

"I'm sorry Conall, but I have to do this," I look at his eyes for possibly the last time then get in to the car, he tries to run over to me, to stop me but Rick and Ranulf hold him back firmly.

"Please, I'm begging you, if you go she will kill you!" He screams.

I hesitate for a moment, I know what he is saying but I need to do this. As I start the engine, I see Gideon get out of his car and look over to me, I briefly catch his eye before driving away, I can't let them stop me from going after Helana. I don't regret my decision to leave, I know Conall will be hurt by what I've done but I can't live with myself knowing that the person responsible for the death of my baby is out there. It might be a death wish or suicide and right now I don't really care. I will not stop until Helana is dead.

I don't look back or stop, I just drive until I reach the bunker. I get straight out of the car and open the door to the house, go inside then just stand. The last time I was here I walked out after finding out my dad was alive, I left because I couldn't cope with knowing that I had real family, now I am back because a part of my family has been taken from me. My body feels cold, I've nothing on my feet and all I am wearing is a hospital gown.

I don't have a plan for what I am going to do, I just know that in about 10 hours time, Helana will be meeting with the coven. I barely escaped with my life last time I was in there, but this time I've got nothing to lose. She took my heart from me, and she needs to pay for that.

I slowly walk towards the bedroom to get changed but instead head straight past and stop outside the room that was supposed to be my nursery. I take a deep breath and push the door open then turn on the light. The airbed that Kerry had been sleeping on is propped up against one wall and everything else in the bedroom is exactly how I remember it. I step in to the room and look at the crib, still made ready for a baby to sleep in. I run my hand along the top of it, feeling the cold wooden frame beneath my fingers as tears roll down my cheeks again.

I lean in to the crib and pick up the small teddy that will never be cuddled or comfort a child, I imagined that my baby might have slept here, comfortable and safe from the outside world. I turn and look at the draws with the small wooden toys on top and the photo of me and my mother. After experiencing those images of Lena and Marcus when I died, I smile as that could be them, the baby in the photo looks like him, he does have my eyes.

I open the drawer and look at all the tiny baby grows, the fabrics on them all soft, but will never be worn. I see one that is blue and pick it up, it makes me wonder if my parents knew I was going to be a girl before I was born or whether they just bought clothes for any eventuality, not that I wouldn't have looked amazing in this little blue suit though, I always liked the colour blue. I sit down with my legs crossed in the middle of the bedroom floor as I feel my whole body shake, I don't want to cry any more, I don't even think I have any tears left. I close my eyes, trying to picture the tiny perfect face I saw bundled in my arms, his beautiful green eyes that looked so happy and innocent. His fragile little fingers that wrapped round my own... he never even had the chance to truly know who I was.

I always used to say I didn't know what love was, but as soon as I looked in to his eyes I truly felt it. And now my heart feels empty without him, I just feel numb. I open my eyes and look up as I hear a noise in front of me in the room.

"The door was open," Gideon says quietly as he looks around my nursery for the first time. I just look back down at the items in my lap, clutching the teddy and baby grow as though if I let go of them then the images I have in my head will disappear.

"My baby was beautiful," I say thinking about him. Gideon isn't sure what to do, so he just stands listening to me. "I saw Lena... I saw my mother, she said my baby had my eyes." My face is soaking already off the tears but I don't care.

"You saw her when you died?" Gideon asks quietly. I nod my head as my breathing quivers.

"I didn't realise how tiny... She said my baby's soul was so strong, that I saw him how he was supposed to be," I say then hear Gideon's breathing hitch.

"Him? It was a boy?" He asks nervously and I nod my head. "I... I had a son?" I can hear the pain in his voice and it just makes me more emotional.

"He was perfect," I go on. "He was destined for greatness... Lena said he was a little prince and was fearless and passionate like his father." It didn't occur to me till this very second that her calling him a price was literal as his father was a vampire King. "I didn't want to leave him, but I couldn't stop him from going away... I always said I didn't know what love was, but as soon as I looked in to his eyes, I felt it. And now my heart is shattered in to a million pieces... How am I supposed to live without my beautiful baby Marcus?" I sob, I can't hold it back.

"What did you say?" I look up at Gideon and see tears fill his eyes. "Are you telling me that my son was called Marcus?" I nod my head at him.

"Lena told me his name, I thought it was nice," I reply as I see Gideon start to cry, he quickly gets overcome with emotion and falls to his knees.

"Marcus?" He asks again and I nod to confirm it. "Marcus was my father's name," Gideon explains, I've never seen Gideon cry, like fully break his heart. I didn't think it was possible for him to feel this way.

"Then your son was named after his grandfather," I say wiping tears from my face. "I wish so much we could have known him, really held him in my arms, had the chance to show him that I loved him more than life itself."

We both sit in silence for a good 10 minutes just trying to process everything and letting the intense feelings begin to subside. Eventually Gideon looks up at me and speaks.

"Conall said you were planning on going after Helana." I look him in the eye and nod my head.

"Why? Have you come to try to stop me as well?" I ask, this is something I need to do, I won't let anyone talk me out of it.

"No!" Gideon says. "I am going to help you kill her."

Chapter Twelve

"I thought you hated me Gideon, so why the fuck do you want to help now?" I say wearily, I don't want to argue with him but I don't understand why he is here.

He gets up from the floor and places his hands in his trousers pockets. I didn't notice before that his outfit it almost identical to the night we first met, black trousers with a blood-red shirt, its sleeves rolled up and a black waistcoat over the top. This is the man that started me on this journey, the one who I was most attracted to and felt such a powerful connection with. This man wanted me so much that he fought for me and then became the father of my unborn child, but yet I could never tell him how I truly felt. His face looks as though he's finished with being emotional today and is back to his usual calm expression, it was surprising to see him like that, the only emotion I have seen from him lately has been aggression.

"I never once said that I hated you," Gideon replies. He is so calm now, the pain is gone from his voice. "Yes, I was pissed off. I just made a lot of wrong choices and I couldn't stand the fact that you walked away... No..." He pauses slightly and sighs. "That's wrong of me to say, because I drove you away, I didn't know how to just be normal around you..."

"Instead of being a giant dick head, you mean?" I cut in, I don't seem to have a filter any more. It feels easy to talk to him when he's like this, no anger or jealously, just the Gideon I came to know and like... or love. He smiles at me and nods.

"Yes," Gideon sighs. "I fucked up didn't I?" I just smile at him then look back down at the items in my lap. I fold up the little baby grow and carefully put it down on the floor near the crib then sit the teddy on top. I take a moment to push back any sadness I am feeling then I stand up. I need to be strong now, I need to get my head in the game and focus on my goal.

"Things could have been so different," I say eventually, glancing briefly at the photo of me and my mother on the draws. "But this is how it is now." I take a deep breath and force a smile. I need to get changed and have a shower as I haven't actually washed properly in, what? 15 days since the incident. "I'm going to have a shower as I feel filthy, then I'll think about a plan of action," I say and then walk out of the room but Gideon quickly calls after me.

"I still love you, you know." I stop and listen to him as he comes to the bedroom door but my back is to him. "Seeing you with Conall is tearing my heart in two... because I still love you so much that it hurts... I made a lot of mistakes and I know I can't take those back, I can't make you like you again and I can't change the fact that I hurt you. I know you never loved me back, I have to accept that but you were going to be the mother of my child and that now means more to me than anything else in the world." I swallow and think for a moment before I reply.

"You're wrong," I say quietly. "I did love you Gideon, I just didn't realise that it was love I was feeling at the time... Because you were my first true love... But it's too late now, everything has changed, and I am loyal to Conall."

"Do you love him?" Gideon asks me quietly.

"I do. He makes me happy, he would never hurt me," I reply. I hear Gideon sigh deeply before he speaks again.

"Do you still love me?" He asks me.

I stand quiet for a moment, even after everything he has done I'm still attracted to his power, his passion and his lust. Conall is kind and gentle, I know he would give me the world if it would make me happy. But Gideon has a fire that draws me in, that makes me want to surrender to the darkest parts of my soul and give myself to him. I can't deny what I feel, even though I know I shouldn't.

"Yes," I reply bluntly to his question then walk away without looking back and head in to the bathroom.

I place my hands on the basin and stand looking at myself in the mirror, my face is pale, my eyes red and puffy, my hair is greasy and dull, this is the lowest point of my life. Even when I was being held at the Bird Cage I had the ability to fight back, to hold on to that tiny bit of hope that maybe things could get better. But now I don't even have that hope, my hope died with Marcus. He was my perfect life, my opportunity to get away from this fucking war and live happily. Now that he's gone I feel consumed with hatred, for Helana, for Claudia... for the General. Basically for any mother fucker that wants to stand in my way of my happy ending.

My happy ending? That's a laugh. The only way I'll ever get that now is when every single one of them is dead. I thought I wanted to get away from the war, I didn't want to fight, I wanted no part in any of this. As soon as I managed to get out they all dragged me the fuck back in, this is all their doing, I always kept saying I was a no one and I didn't understand why they wanted me dead. Well you know what? I'll show them exactly who the fuck I am, I was destined to be the most powerful being that could decide the fate of the war. So I'll be just that, I'll embrace my destiny, but I am not going to fight for good or evil, nor am I fighting for any particular side. I'll fight for me and only me, I'll do what I believe in, I don't care if that makes me a bad person or anyone's enemy.

I am the force to be reckoned with, I am the one they should all fear. They want a leader? I'll give them one, because they will all bow at my feet and if they challenge me I will rip them limb from limb and stare them dead in the eye whilst their blood covers my skin, they will die knowing that they drove me to do this. They killed themselves because now that I know how love truly feels and then had it ripped away, I know how hate feels, and I am consumed by it. They want a war? Then I'm ready to fucking give them one.

I hear a loud smash and look down to see the large stone basin cracked in half under my hands. Love makes you strong is what Lena said, I smile at myself because I know it's true, I loved then lost and now I'm going to avenge it.

I run the water in the shower and climb in, it's slightly too hot but I leave it as it is and let it burn my skin. The pain reminds me that I am alive and strangely I like it. When I'm done I head to the bedroom to get dressed, there isn't a great selection as I took most of my casual wear clothing with me, I find underwear, a pair of black leather trousers and Kerry's biker look boots with buckles up the sides, I am so glad my best friend is the same size as me, then I spot a red studded belt and put them all on. I rifle through the left over bags of clothing to find a top and realise that everything that was left here is the stuff Kerry bought when I was supposed to be dead. I am more a t-shirt and jeans person, whereas this stuff is all Gothic night club gear and wannabe bondage wear, at least there's some new make-up.

I empty the bags out on the bed and just stand looking at it. What the hell, if I am going to turn in to a bad ass bitch then I may as well dress like one. I pick up a top that is slightly fitted but thankfully not corseted because I can't even sit down in one of those never mind fight in one, then have a look at it. The bodice is black with vivid red inserts with laced up ribbon detail up the front. It has a semi sort of sleeve, leather and lace and goes alright with the pants that I am wearing I guess, I start to second guess myself instantly though, this isn't me. But then again, I don't feel like me any more. Fuck it! I put it on and quickly apply some make-up, black has always been my go-to colour and today is no different. I actually look pretty cool, it's feminine but strong at the same time, maybe if that's how I look to other people then I might believe it for myself.

My hair is still wet when I walk out in to the living room. Gideon sits on the sofa watching the TV, I can see it's showing a repeat of his announcement that he is running against the General, he doesn't notice me enter at first, so I just kind of hover behind the sofa. I see that the rerun conveniently cuts off just before it shows the General go to attack Gideon, obviously he has the media wrapped around his little finger. The footage then flicks to another day and I see the General addressing the room of journalists.

"These beings do not need a self-confessed vampire for representation. What they need is extermination, they are a blight on our people, they murder and kill anyone who disagrees with their existence. We are getting terrorist attacks against humans that are just trying to better our world, mass murders from vampires, there are things that can turn in to animals and enter our homes. This is not the kind of people we want running our country. They are not innocent, they are born and bread as monsters and in this new world we will rise up against them, we will take back our country. We are at war, I will lead us forward and eliminate any threat to the good people of this nation.

Gideon, as the vampire likes to be known as, is a monster, he has murdered thousands of people in his lifetime, he drinks the blood of human victims. These vampires treat us like cattle. Well I for one will not stand by and let it happen. It's time we all stood up for what is right and fight against this evil."

I cough slightly and Gideon turns around to look at me, at first I see frustration at the comments made by the General but when he sees me his face changes. His eyes roam my body, taking in my appearance, I can see it in his eyes that he thinks I look good but I didn't dress for him, it was more an accidental coincidence that I am in the kind of outfit that would please him to no end. I ignore his wandering gaze and go to turn towards the kitchen when I hear the news reporter start to talk about the so called terrorist attack in Newcastle. It instantly peeks my interest and I stand and watch.

"It seems that the victims were in majority made up of members from the group the Hammer of Light, reports are still unclear as to how many innocent people were killed that day, but we do know that several high ranking members were targeted in the attack. We are aware that the Hammer of Light are a group of witch hunters who have rightly unmasked several women who were accused by them of being involved in the practice of witchcraft. Originally it was believed that these attacks were random but now a group calling themselves the Midnight Church have claimed responsibility. In a statement issued to the press by their leader known only by the name Helana, she said - in the past our kind have lived in the dark, hidden from the world by the masks that we wear every day. But now that we have been exposed we will not roll over and let our kind be hunted. We will fight back, and we will kill anyone that tries to punish us for simply loving our Master too much - at this time it is not clear if any further retaliation against the Hammer of Light is planned."

I close my eyes for a second and try to take a deep breath, my whole body is shaking just by hearing her name mentioned. She needs to be killed, I will probably die trying though, but I can't just sit back. I turn and walk in to the kitchen to grab a knife, the bunker itself has been locked since I went back to see Gideon and I haven't actually been down there since well before Christmas, but now everything I need is just underneath my feet.

Gideon has been silent this whole time and now watches me as I approach the large bunker door. I hold up the knife and briefly look at it before I run the large blade across my palm, I know I only need a tiny drop but if felt good to cut in to my own flesh, to feel that pain, to feel something other than sadness. I let the blood flow from the cut as I hear Gideon stand up behind me, he's probably able to smell it. I hold my hand up and watch the crimson blood cascade from my hand, down my arm and staining my skin. My eyes are mesmerised by this liquid that plays a vital part in if we live or die. I must have been standing looking at my own blood for longer than normal because I feel Gideon take hold of my wrist, his fingers quickly getting covered in my blood then he removes the knife from my other hand.

I look down at the knife as he takes it off me then look him in the eye. Neither of us say anything but I can see that Gideon is trying so hard to control his actions and ignore the blood-lust, it must be so tempting for him, to just want that taste. He turns my hand gently and places it on the door, he waits a few seconds for it to start making noise as it begins to unlock then, still holding my wrist, he leads me to the kitchen where there is a first aid kit. I stand in silence and watch as he carefully wipes the blood from my arm and then bandages my hand.

"Tell me how you're feeling," Gideon says to me. I don't look at him, instead I focus on the floor.

"Like I am numb inside... Like I have no choice but to fight back. Like pain is easier to deal with," I take a deep breath. "I'll feel better when they are all dead." Gideon looks away then puts the first aid kit back on the bench. My mind starts to wander, thinking about how much everyone deserves to die for what they did to me, that I can't have a normal life because of them. Gideon then takes hold of my hand and I look up at him.

"Then that is what you need to do," he says to me gently. "I just don't want to see you get hurt."

"It's too late for that," I reply. "Why are you doing this? Why are you trying to help me now, after you said your alliance with the coven was more important than my safety?"

"I wanted to form an alliance to protect my people," Gideon says firmly, I can see he's trying to hide his anger. "But she just killed the one person that could have been the most precious to me." He pauses for a moment to calm himself before continuing. "I didn't even get the chance to know I was going to become a father, I never felt that joy or that love. All I had was the grief and the regret that I pushed you away instead of having you near me so that I could protect you both." We both stand staring in to each others eyes, each of us bound by anger and hatred, with one common goal.

I need to look away, I need to move because I can't do this right now. As much as my entire essence wants him, now is not the time. Gideon looks at my longingly then leans in to kiss me but I quickly shake my head and place my hand on his chest to stop him.

"What are you doing?" I ask surprised by his advances.

"I just thought..." Gideon replies forcing a smile and then steps back. "I'm sorry, I shouldn't have done that."

"No you shouldn't," I say firmly. "You and me are not a good combination, not now anyway. And I don't want to betray Conall, no matter how strong my feelings are." I have to ignore how I feel for him, I've moved on, I was happy. I pause for a second before walking away from him and over to the bunker door then forcefully pull it open. I turn around as Gideon's phone starts to ring and I get a instant bad feeling. He takes it out of his pocket and answers it.

"Tristen?... No," Gideon says on the phone, he glances over to me. "Then tell him that I don't know where she is, I haven't seen her... No, I've checked the bunker, it's empty." I smile at him slightly, the last thing I need is to have other people stopping me, or even worse trying to help and then I'll have to worry about protecting them. "Yes, OK, I'll keep looking." He hangs up the phone and sighs.

"You lied to him," I say quietly then Gideon nods.

"I did, I could tell by the background noise in the car that he wasn't alone. I thought that you would rather not have everyone coming after you," Gideon says cautiously. He's right, he knows I'd rather go alone than put other people at risk. I nod my head then head down the steps in to the bunker below.

I don't know if there is anything in particular I need, to go up against Helana, so I head straight over to the cabinets on the far wall and open them to reveal all the weapons. I'm thinking over kill might be good in this situation as I don't know how many coven members are going to be there. I see a few straps made out of sturdy material, I didn't know what they were when I first came in here but after being with the hunters and the military units I know they are holsters. I pick one up and strap it to my thigh and attach a large knife then grab a smaller dagger in a sheath and I slide that down the side of my boot.

I then look towards the drawers, I've been saying for months that I would never touch the guns but times have changed and I've used them now, it's actually scary how easy they are. I take a deep breath and slide the drawer open, the pair of guns look like they haven't been used in years and I don't even know how to load them. I pick one up and look at it, I couldn't even tell you what kind it was as I have absolutely no clue, I can just see that they have black rectangle things next to them with bullets in and it kind of looks like it goes in the bottom of the handle.

"Do you need some help with those?" Gideon asks, quietly watching me from the bottom of the steps. I nod my head and he walks over.

"I haven't really used one properly before, I fired a gun but apart from that I don't have a clue." Gideon takes the gun from my hand and quickly shows me how to use it, what to flick or press for the safety and how to quickly reload. It's not too hard once you know, he then helps me attach the holders to my belt.

"I'll put the guns in the bag as you won't be able to sit in the car with them on, is there anything else you want to take?" Gideon asks me, I am so tempted to take that axe from the cabinet but I shake my head.

"If I remember correctly from the last time I was there, to get to the meeting room we have to go through the library. There are some pretty decent swords and shit in there so if I want something a bit more hefty I'll use one of those," I inhale deeply and try to calm my nerves.

Gideon nods and picks up a couple of bits for himself. I know for me this is probably suicide, we are going to be massively out numbered, they all have some sort of powers and last time I was there they had demons helping to protect the castle. With the war pretty much being in full swing they will most likely have more people around just in case of an attack. I'll be lucky if I even make it through the front doors this time with everyone being more vigilant. But I feel like it's my only option, even if I die tonight I'll be happy knowing I'll see Marcus again. Maybe I would actually prefer to die, I'd then get to see my baby and be happy.

"Gideon?" I say quietly, he stands looking at the blade of a large knife in his hand and turns to me as I speak. "There's a massive possibility that after I walk in to the church tonight, I won't be walking out..."

"That's not true," Gideon interrupts me. "We are going to be just fine." I shake my head and force a smile.

"Please Gideon, let me talk," I reply softly. "I know that I am walking in to a shit storm, Helana is the single most powerful person I know, and I am not going to lie, but she terrifies me." Gideon goes to speak again but I flash him a look, and he stops. "No one dares stand against her, and she is pretty much unstoppable when she is with her coven... So, maybe it's for the best if you don't come with me."

"Don't be stupid, I am not going to let you go alone," Gideon snaps at me.

"And I don't want to be responsible for you getting hurt, I couldn't live with myself if you came along and something happened to you. This is my fight, if I die then I can accept that but I can't risk losing anyone else," I reply. I pause and try to remain calm, I know he shouldn't be here.

"What are you trying to say?" Gideon asks me confused.

"I don't want you to go, because I don't want to think that you might die," I say to him, I look him in the eye and continue. "I've already lost Marcus... I should have told you sooner, I should have made sure you knew how I was feeling, but I was too scared to admit it to myself."

"Velvet, I don't understand," Gideon stands watching me.

"You said to me that you loved me so much it hurt, well I am hurting because I still love you and I can't bear to lose you as well," I explain. I can see Gideon thinking about my words. Unsure of what to say back to me.

"But you said you were with Conall," Gideon says eventually.

"I am. I love him so much, he makes me so happy, and he cares for me unconditionally, he was going to be my perfect life... But in my darkest of times, when I feel like I am being consumed by the hate, when I need to forget the world and I want that fire... It is you that my soul yearns for, right now all I want is that part of you that would slaughter an entire town just to be close to me, who would kill all my enemies to make me feel alive."

"That part of me is a monster, you said it yourself," Gideon says quietly.

"That part of you is your passion and fire, it's who you are and I've always known that," I step closer to him, and he watches me, his eyes almost burn with lust. "I should have told you before now that I loved you," I place my hand on Gideon's chest. "Even if your soul is black because of all the evil you have done, I will always want you... So, if I am going to go head to head with Helana, I know I probably won't come out alive, I just needed you to know how I felt before it was too late for me to say it." Gideon places his hand gently on my face and smiles down at me.

"Thank you for telling me," he says softly then leans down to kiss me again but this time I don't stop him.

My entire being wants him, I wrap my arms around his neck as he pulls me in to him closer. I want to give in to him, to let him take me, I want to feel that passion and fire that burns deep inside of him because I don't want to feel empty and lost. Gideon pulls back as his phone begins to ring in his pocket again, he looks down at me and forces a smile then takes out his phone and steps away from me.

"Yes, Tristen what's up this time?" He says as Tristen calls again. "Why do you?... Put Tristen back on the phone," his voice is firm. I watch as he sighs and then pulls the phone away from his ear then puts it on speaker phone. "Speaker phone is on so there you go, are you happy now?" Gideon says rolling his eyes.

"Velvet! I know you are with Gideon," Conall's voice says on the phone. "I just want to know you're OK, please." I stay quiet and look away.

"I told you that I am not with her," Gideon replies.

"Well I don't believe you," Conall says firmly. "Kerry told us that she was most likely to go to this bunker place, so we are heading there now..."

"You can't!" Gideon cuts in quickly. I look up and freeze, I can't have them try to stop me, I don't want Conall to get hurt. "I told Tristen she wasn't there so you are wasting your time." The phone goes silent for a few moments, then there's a fumbling noise as though people are fighting over the phone and it goes quiet.

"Vel?" I hear Kerry's voice. "Listen, I know you are at the bunker and I know you're with Gideon."

"She's not here Kerry," Gideon tries to explain.

"Shut up Gideon," Kerry snaps at him. "Vel, we are in Tristen's car, we are literally pulling up the road and I can see your car at the top, I knew you would be here because that's the only place that you would go... Get off the phone, I am talking to her," Kerry says to someone. "We just want to help." I stand for a moment and think, even if we had managed to get sorted and leave before they got here they will only just follow us to the church, but now it's a bit too late.

"You can hang up the phone now Gideon," I say reluctantly. Gideon nods then does as he's instructed and puts the phone back in his pocket. I climb the steps back up to the house and can hear the car pull up outside, I don't need this right now.

"Velvet?" I hear Conall shout as he gets out of the car then runs towards the door, I just get out of the bunker when he pushes the door open and comes in to the house. He stops in his tracks when he sees Gideon appear behind me.

"I told you not to come after me," I say firmly to Conall as I stand with my arms crossed, however he doesn't look at me, he looks at Gideon, disgusted that he is here. Kerry and Tristen follow him inside, and we all just stand watching each other.

"What are you wearing?" Conall finally asks me. "And the weapons? The clothes... This isn't you."

"I'm sorry, Conall," I say gently. "But I won't let you stop me, I want you to leave." Conall shakes his head and goes to step towards me but Gideon quickly moves and stands in his way.

"Please Velvet, you can't do this... And you're with him?" Conall is upset and it doesn't help that Gideon is here. "You need to come home... I know you're hurting but putting yourself at risk like this is not the answer... If you go after her, she will kill you."

"Well, maybe I've accepted that," I snap back at him. "Maybe if she kills me the pain will go away." I watch as Conall takes a step back in disbelief. "The best thing that could have happened would have been to let me die that day, at least then I would have my baby with me and I would feel something more than pain."

"You can't mean that?" Conall says shocked. "You have me, I love you... Is that not enough?" I fall silent. I am not sure how to answer him. I know I love him, I know that he loves me back but I now have all these other emotions and feelings inside of me that are all battling against each other making me just numb, as though I am dead inside.

"I'm coming with you," Kerry suddenly says breaking the tension, I go to shake my head, but she just smiles at me. "You can't boss me around, if I say that I'm going, then I'm going. Plus you will need all the help you can get so don't try to turn the offer down." I give her a small smile and nod.

"I'm coming too," Tristen says giving Gideon a slight nod. I look back at Conall who stands staring at me, shaking his head.

"You guys can't be serious," Conall says starting to get angry. "Velvet come on, this is Gideon isn't it?.. He's brain washed you or something." I see Gideon get tense then go to lunge forward but I put my hand on his chest and push him back slightly as I step towards Conall.

"I love you," I say calmly to Conall. "But you have to make a choice. You either stand with me and support the fight... Or you get out of my way," I stand firm as I watch Conall debate what to do in his head.

"I just don't want to see you get hurt," Conall pleads. I smile at him slightly more and move close then gently kiss his lips.

"That's my choice to make," I reply. I can see his eyes begging me to change my mind but I just smile again and walk past him towards the front door. The others quickly follow me outside, Gideon has a bag of weapons with him, and he throws it in the back of the Camaro. "Here!" I say to Gideon, handing him the Camaro keys. "It's your car after all." He laughs at me then shakes his head as he walks to the passenger side and opens the door.

"Keep it, it suits you better than me anyway," Gideon replies. I smile at him as Tristen and Kerry get in to Tristen's black Porsche.

"What am I meant to do?" Conall calls after us. Gideon turns to Conall and throws him the keys to the red Ferrari.

"Take my car, I'll not be using it at the minute," Gideon shouts then gets in next to me. I briefly glance in the rear view mirror, Conall stands on the door step with Gideon's car keys looking very lost.

I can tell he doesn't know what he should do for the best, I do feel a little guilty but I can't just pretend that Helana isn't out there haunting me. I can't just go back to the Highlands with him and live that happy life, because I don't know if it can even exist for me any more.

Chapter Thirteen

I make the decision that if I am going to head to the Midnight Church meeting then I am not going to hide away and sneak my way in, I'm going to go in all guns blazing and show Helana that I am not scared of her, even if deep inside I'm literally shitting myself. I honestly don't care if I do die tonight though, I am at peace with that, but I will use every last breath in my body to try to take her down with me, I've never hated anyone as much as I hate her right now.

I roughly know where I parked last time to cut through the woods, so I drive up the road and hope for the best in finding an entrance road up towards the old castle, I know that there is one as I watched a car pull up with that innocent girl in last time. Tristen follows me closely in the Porsche, it's pitch black on this road, obviously if you are heading to the coven meeting you already know exactly where you need to go. I glance at the time, it's just after 12 midnight, by now all the coven members will be downstairs and Helana will be in the middle of them all.

"Are you ready for this?" Gideon asks me as I pull up a small road where I can see the castle up in front. I feel strangely relaxed as though this is what I was destined to do and everything that has happened in my life has been leading me towards this point.

"Ready as I'll ever be," I reply as I stop the car on the large drive way, leaving enough distance from the entrance so that it gives us time to prepare. I take a deep breath and pause for a moment before getting out of the car. Gideon gets out first and grabs his stuff out of the bag he brought from the bunker as Tristen pulls up behind us. Kerry gets out and I notice she is looking around and busy on her phone. "Who are you texting?" I ask her then she looks up and smiles.

"Your dad, I promised that I'd message him the details of where we were," she replies then goes back to finishing what she is doing. I nod my head as Gideon hands me the set of guns and I place them in the holders on my belt. I didn't even think about Rick, he won't want to miss the chance to take down Helana. I was so focused on what she did to me that I keep forgetting that she ripped his life apart as well.

Without saying much else we all start to head up towards the entrance, the path way is dimly lit by torches again, just as I remember from last time I was here, up ahead at the main gates I see two people. They are not dressed in robes, so I am going to guess that they are here for security purposes only, Mitchell and Laurie didn't do a very good job on watching the entrance last time, the inexperienced and no-nothing me got straight in before.

"If you lot are here for the meeting, then you are late. The High Priestess will not be happy." I look up and smile at the guy who speaks. He's average looking, dressed in casual black t-shirt and black trousers, nothing special I guess, he's stood next to a butch looking woman. She is not someone I'd like to go up against in a bitch fight and I can almost sense that they are not human. It's weird, I've never been able to just know by looking at someone before, I must be working through that hunters checklist as I get more accustomed to my powers and abilities. I realise that when I was pregnant I felt my powers growing, but I was incapable of using them as my baby needed the energy more than me, so it will be interesting to see what I can actually do now that I have nothing holding me back.

"That's a shame," Gideon replies as the man and woman start to make their way down the steps towards us. "We were looking forward to pretending to give a shit."

Gideon and Tristen move fast then the man and woman instantly know we are not here to play, so they all start fighting. Myself and Kerry have a slow wander up the path as Gideon tries to attack the man but is quickly overpowered and pinned to the ground, Tristen grabs the woman from behind, but she tosses him over her shoulder and mounts him, punching him hard in the face. I sigh as we get closer, I know vampires are powerful so these two are kind of on par with them.

"Men!" Kerry says shaking her head.

"Tell me about it," I reply as we both just stand and watch, who ever these people are they are super strong. Gideon manages to get free and tussles with the man, I notice that he doesn't try to bite him, instead opting for brute strength to try to subdue him, so I think they must be demons. I wouldn't want to have that black shit in my mouth either so it's no wonder he is avoiding that.

"Do you think they will be much longer? This is a bit of a waste of time," Kerry says.

Gideon forces his knife in to the man's chest and jumps up from the ground. The man just laughs at him and pulls the blade out, I can see it is covered in black gunk, Helana really beefed up her security, I am actually quite impressed. The man grasps the knife and lunges at Gideon just as the woman punches Tristen again, forcing him back to the ground.

"This is ridiculous," I say to myself then exhale slowly as I use my power properly for the first time in weeks. Oh! How I've missed this feeling.

I watch as both the man and woman stop in their tracks, I can hear them both fight for breath as I effortlessly target their soul, remembering what it felt like when I discovered the easiest way to kill a demon was to trap and crush their essence. I watch, transfixed on them as black blood starts to gush from their mouths, and they collapse to their knees, clearly they have no clue what is going on but I smile wildly as I watch them die. I spend a moment revelling in the sheer amount of energy I can feel coursing through me, it's intoxicating and for the past month or so it's felt stifled compared to now. Gideon catches my eye as I bend down and pick up the knife from the demons hand, I hand it to Kerry, and she makes a disgusted face as she tries to wipe off the black goo.

"If you boys are finished playing," I say to Gideon and Tristen, they are in a slight amount of disbelief, "maybe we can actually get to the real fight." I step over the man's body and head towards the gates then Kerry laughs behind me as they all start to follow me inside. The castle itself is eerily quiet.

"Which way?" Tristen asks wiping blood from his nose, he seems slightly embarrassed by taking so many punches so early on.

"To the left in here, we need to go through the library and then down the stairs at the other side towards the meeting room below," I reply confidentiality.

I push open the door to the library and have a quick glance around, it looks exactly the same as before minus the massive mirror I was thrown in to and smashed. I walk straight over and take the axe off the wall and smile, it's not as heavy as I remember it being. Gideon laughs at my choice then grabs a sword as Tristen and Kerry also arm themselves and prepare for what's to come. I look down at the axe and sigh, it is a bit chunky and I can't really do much else if I am playing with this, so I put it back. I turn quickly as the door over the far side opens and a woman in coven robes walks in to the room, she doesn't notice us at first, then eventually looks up and stops in her tracks.

"I don't want any trouble," she says quickly holding her hands up to show that she is not armed, she looks familiar to me, so I glance at the door behind her and it closes at my will then slowly make my way towards her.

"Do you know who I am?" I ask her, the others stand back whilst I talk.

"Yes," the woman replies. "You look so much like your mother." I stop, that is not what I was expecting her to say, it's actually thrown me off a bit.

"Who are you?" I ask intrigued by this person. She carefully removes her hood then I realise that she was the woman who gagged the innocent girl the last time I was here, she has the same black fringe. Her hair is medium length with a turquoise colour at the ends in an old-fashioned pin up style. Thinking about it more, I am almost certain she was also there the night my mother died.

"My name is Sharon, I am the High Priestesses advisor." I watch her as she tries to remain calm under my gaze.

"You're not human," I say very matter-of-factly. She looks around my age but I know she watched my mother die so it looks as though she doesn't age. She smiles slightly and shakes her head.

"No," I see her swallow as though my knowing she's different might cause her some problems.

"Let's just kill her and get to Helana," Gideon says bluntly. Sharon takes a step back, I can see her calm exterior is starting to slip.

"Wait," I stop Gideon then turn back to Sharon. "Tell me why I should keep you alive?" I don't know why but I get such a strong feeling that I need her for something, I just don't quite know what.

"Because your mother trusted me, I was always loyal to her. Helana is a powerful and strong High Priestess, but she took control from the blood line. She was never meant to rule, your mother was our true leader," she explains.

"You shouldn't listen to her," Gideon says beside me, "demons lie."

"And so do vampires," Sharon snaps back then she ignores him and speaks directly to me. "Are you here to kill Helana?"

"Yes," I say bluntly. "She deserves to pay for everything she's done." Sharon nods her head and cautiously walks towards us.

"Then let me help... As soon as you go through that door it will trigger a protection spell that will alert her allies to your presence here. There are far more of them than there are of you... But if you grant me life I can stop that from happening," she stops in front of me, I could easily kill her right now but I believe what she's says.

"What are you? You don't seem like an ordinary demon," I inquire, and then she smiles at me.

"I haven't been ordinary for quite some time," she laughs slightly. "Let's just say my normal day job is far more interesting than running around after our false Priestess. After so long on this earth a woman has to find some way of entertaining herself." I don't know what that means but I like the way she talks about Helana, if she was trying to protect her, then she would have attacked us by now.

"Alright," I eventually say. "Do what you have to do, if any more of my people turn up direct them to the fight." I know after Kerry text Rick that he is bound to show up at some point. Sharon nods and quickly heads off out of the library.

"I think you're making a mistake with that one," Gideon says off-handedly as he starts to walk over towards the far door, he might be right but I have to go with my gut instinct.

"What should we do now?" Kerry asks. I turn and see her brandishing a machete and smile.

"Now?" I reply as I start to head towards the door. "Now we kill them all."

We quietly make our way down the stone stairs and towards the meeting room. The large wooden door has been replaced and is slightly open, so I can just say make out the group inside, they are all stood in a circle chanting, I can't quite hear what they are saying but honestly I don't particularly give a shit. I watch them for another minute until I spot Helana, she stands at the centre of the circle with her back to me, but I know it's her. I pull one of the guns from my belt and take off the safety then grip it ready to fire. Helana suddenly stops and I instantly get a bad feeling.

"Shit!" I say quietly.

"What's wrong?" Kerry asks from behind me.

"I think she knows I'm here," I reply.

I have no more time to think, I quickly kick the door open, aim the gun and fire. Helana turns and sees me as the bullet flies through the air, she tries to move but isn't quick enough. The bullet hits her shoulder, and she cries out before hitting the floor. The members of the coven turn towards the door and in that moment I know that the shit storm is about to begin.

Everything happens so fast, we get rushed by people, Gideon and Tristen run in to the room, I watch as Gideon swings the sword towards the closest person he comes across and then I see a glint in his eye as blood spurts from a massive wound across the person's chest before they drop to their knees. Tristen tackles another member and quickly snaps their neck before grabbing a second person and sinking his teeth deep in to their throat.

Kerry grips the machete and attacks also, I spend a moment watching her as I've never seen her fight before. I smile, see is quick, it must be those cat like reflexes she has, it is quite surprising. I'm suddenly knocked off my feet and pinned to the ground by someone in a hood, I don't know any of these people but if they stand with Helana I will try to kill them.

I use my power to force them off me, I launch them with such force that I am momentarily stunned by how easy that felt now, then I grab my gun and shoot. I don't even know if I am getting kill shots, I just fire it at as many of them as I can to give myself enough space to get back to my feet. There are far more of them than I expected tonight, easily double what was in here last time. Just as I get back to my feet and find my next target, I feel something slash across my thigh, I look down and see a deep gash a couple inches across at the top of my leg. I groan as pain shoots through me as I look up to see Helana standing smiling in front of me. I don't quite understand what happened, she doesn't have a weapon that I can see.

Helana grins and flicks her hand then I feel another sharp pain, this time across my chest. I stumble and lose my footing slightly as the pain catches me off guard, my own eyes are drawn down to see blood flow down my top and I grab my chest in an attempt to ease the discomfort.

"What the fuck?" I say to myself as I gasp for air. I lift my arm and point the gun at Helana, but she just laughs at me and forces the gun out of my hand, I can't even see where it went. There are people everywhere and it is very easy to get distracted by the noise of them fighting.

"You are a hard one to kill," Helana shouts over the sounds as she walks towards me clutching her shoulder. Just the sight of her sends panic through me, I thought I could face her and be strong, that I knew what I needed to do, but she scares me and at the moment that gives her the upper hand. She raises her palm to me and I feel myself being lifted off the floor by my neck. I glance around and see that Kerry, Gideon and Tristen are all out numbered, I start to panic more and think that it was a really bad idea to come here, I should not have allowed my friends to come either as I have put them all in harms way. I can't help them if they are in trouble, and they can't help me as they are overpowered.

"I... hate... you!" I manage to say as her grip on my neck tightens, I struggle to breathe as my feet dangle below me unable to reach the ground.

I don't know if it is the fear that I have for her or that I can't breathe that is making me lose focus, but I feel like I can't defend myself against her, what if I am not strong enough? Helana ignores my words and smiles as she stands in front of me, she reaches up and lightly strokes my face.

"Don't worry, you will be dead soon," she says to me smiling.

I feel another immense pain and then blood trickle down my back as she uses her power to slice my flesh, it just makes me think about what the General did to me and then all the nightmares come flooding back. I need to get out of my own mind and believe in myself, or I am going to die without even being able to touch her. My lungs start to burn as I try to breathe but my windpipe is being crushed under her grip and my eyes water uncontrollably as Helana starts to laugh.

My head starts to roll back as I hear screaming from over near the doors then from out of nowhere, a large ginger wolf pounces on Helana, as soon as it hits her I drop to the ground as she loses her focus on me. I gasp for breath and refocus my vision then I look up and see two more wolves ripping people to shreds over near the doors, I smile as Ranulf and Tiffany are both here as well as Conall.

I push myself up as the ginger wolf comes over to see if I am alright.

"Velvet? Are you OK?" I hear Conall say in my head, I nod then look around rubbing my throat as it is so sore.

"Where's Helana?" I ask him as he places his head under my hand to try to help me stand. My legs are a bit shaky but I need to concentrate on just killing her instead of thinking about what she can do to me.

"I don't know, she got away from me," Conall says. I moan slightly as my wounds hurt but I try to ignore it and pull the other gun from my belt. I get a sudden flash feeling of being afraid, I know it is not coming from me, so I look around and notice someone has Kerry pinned to the ground, so I quickly aim at them and fire, they drop instantly as the bullet goes right through their skull and splatters blood on exit out the other side.

"Thanks," Kerry shouts, a little out of breath as I turn and shoot another coven member who runs towards me, I am not a perfect shot but the bullets seem to be dropping a couple of them.

Something hits me hard on the back of my head and I fall to my knees disorientated, but before I get a chance to look around to see who is attacking me, Conall jumps over me and strikes. I can't focus straight and the room around me starts to spin as shouting fills my ears and my head throbs. I reach up and can feel blood in my hair, whatever I was hit with has caused a little bit of damage but I can't let it stop me. A few coven members run for the doors and try to escape, they don't want to be involved in the fighting so that is fine with me, whilst some others form small groups to attack in.

Kerry and Tiffany are working together to fight a small group at the far side, they seem to be doing well until more coven members join in, and they quickly get cornered. I know they need help, so I try to get over to them. I force myself up and start to run towards the fighting but then I suddenly hear Kerry scream. I focus as much as I can, as though I am grabbing on to their robes and I pull the coven members away from them with my power, sending them skidding across the floor and clearing a path to the girls as I run over to offer back up. Ranulf also notices what's happening and gets to them before I do. I can see blood dripping down Tiffany's front leg as the wolf limps towards Kerry, who has dropped to the ground.

I almost skid to her side as I see a large knife wound across her neck, I instantly try to apply pressure to stop the bleeding as her blood gushes from the cut, no matter how much I try and stop it, it just flows through my fingers and pools beneath her.

"Kerry?" I shout as I hear her struggle for air. "You're going to be OK." I panic, my hands shaking as she grabs my wrist.

"It's just a flesh wound," she says to me smiling wildly then I hear the blood fill her airways as the sounds of her breathing become gargled and blood fills her mouth.

"Kerry, stay with me... you can't die again," my voice shakes as she forces a smile, her chest heaves a couple of times as it tries desperately to suck in oxygen then her eyes lose their colour, after just a second her grip on my wrist fails and her arm drops to the floor... she is gone. I sit for a moment holding her body, my hands covered in her blood.

"Velvet, I'm sorry... I tried to stop them," I hear Tiffany in my mind but I shake my head and look at her.

"No," I take a deep breath and regain my composure. "It's not your fault, Kerry will be fine." Tiffany collapses as her leg gives way under her weight. "Ranulf make sure Tiffany is OK. Don't worry about Kerry," I say to them both. "She should be fine in a couple of hours... She has like, 6 more lives left I think." Ranulf and Tiffany seem a little confused but I gently leave go of Kerry, lying her back down and grab the machete that she was carrying before I turn to the group of coven members who are now getting back to their feet. I watch them all with growing distaste, I can feel anger and darkness inside of me and for the first time I am so tempted to fully let go, to let it consume me entirely and not give a fuck about any of the consequences.

"Oh! I'm going to enjoy this," I say to myself as I grip the machete and run towards the group, the closest person I come to puts their hand up to try to stop me but I swing the blade, and they scream as the metal goes straight through their wrist, slicing the hand off in one motion and I catch some blood splatter across my face. I smile as I kick one guy in the crotch, and he falls to his knees before I swing again and catch him in the back of the head, I feel his skull split under the blade as his brain oozes out when he hits the floor. There are far too many of them and I feel like I am blindly swinging and hacking at people as more and more come at me, not that I am not enjoying this feeling right now. I want to kill them all.

I'm forced backwards by a blast of power and the machete leaves my hand then I skid across the floor, I don't even think about where that came from I just grab the knife from my boot and stab it in to the chest of another coven member then I turn and receive a hard punch to the face. Blood fills my mouth as I am suddenly surrounded by people and I know I can't fight them all off. I am blindly swinging the knife and throwing punches, there is too many people.

Just as I think that all is lost I hear the sound of gunfire fill the air and I watch as the person in front of me drops to the ground as they are shot in the head. I couple of the group members notice what is going on and decide to run instead of fighting any more. I look across to the door and see about 5 or 6 men head inside with guns, dressed all in black, Rick looks directly at me and I smile at him in appreciation before he turns and joins the fight.

I take a moment to look around, although the hunters are here, the witches are strong and many of them have power far greater than a normal human, it doesn't take them long to disarm a couple of the hunters and ensure quick deaths for them. I shake my head to clear my thoughts and try to find Helana in the sea of people but I can't see her anywhere in the room, she is my target, the only reason I came here, I don't think she got out, we would have seen her. There's no point leaving if I haven't ensured that she's dead because then what would have been the point in coming here in the first place?

I'm tackled to the ground again, this time I recognise the face, it's the blond guy I saw in Gideon's club, he's so strong that he quickly over powers me and knees me hard in the ribs, I inhale sharply trying to catch my breath, but he forces me on to my back, one hand around my throat whilst the other punches me in the jaw. I can't focus on getting him off me as he grips my throat tighter, I can't even shout for help as my head rolls. I try to claw at his hand but my vision is blurred and I can already feel my head swimming.

Just as I feel myself drifting to sleep, my face gets splattered in blood and the head of the guy pinning me down flies off as his body collapses on top of me. I'm not quite sure what happened but I know I didn't do that. I push his body off me and wipe the blood from my face, then I look up and see Gideon standing over me holding the machete, blood dripping from the blade as he smiles down at me.

"Need a hand?" Gideon asks as he stands over me, I smile then nod my head as I reach up to take his hand. Even after everything that has happened between us, I'm so thankful to have him in my life, seeing how much passion he has inside of him just makes me love him more, I didn't think that was possible, but when he showed me how much our child meant to him, even though he never got to meet him makes me wonder what kind of life we could have had together.

"You're like my hero," I say jokingly as Gideon starts to help me ... but then he stops.

His face changes to a look of pain and surprise as my eyes leave his gaze and are drawn down to a gagged piece of wood protruding from his chest.

"Velvet?" Gideon forces out as his breath hitches then he stumbles, his legs not wanting to hold him up any longer.

"No!" I scream as he falls, I try to catch him, but he's heavy and I collapse to my knees beneath his weight. I sit cradling him in my arms as I feel sheer panic rise inside of me. "Gideon stay with me," my hands are shaking as I run them across his face, his skin losing colour and turning to a leather like texture under my touch. This isn't happening, it's not real. I don't know what to do, I don't even know what happened. "GIDEON?" I scream as I see his eyes start to turn a murky black. I can't breathe, I can't lose him. I shake his body to desperately try to wake him up as his life slips away. "No... NO!!"

The room around me no longer seems to exist, I can hear the distant shouting and screaming as the fighting continues. But I just zone out, this can't be really happening. Gideon can't die, I just told him that I loved him, he can't leave me, not like this. My heart was already broken after losing Marcus, I can't have him gone as well.

"NO!" Tristen shouts. "What the fuck happened?" I look up as Tristen comes to Gideon's side, I don't know what to say, I can't even remember how to breathe any more, the air in my lungs is non-existent. I watch as Tristen looks at Gideon, he notices the wooden stake that has been driven straight through his back and out his chest then he looks directly at me. I try to speak but no words come out, I feel completely numb and empty. This is all my fault. Rick comes to stand behind Tristen and without saying a word to us he starts shouting to his men.

"Get everyone out, we need to retreat... NOW..."

I look back down to Gideon's body as Rick pulls Tristen to his feet then two of his men take Gideon from my arms and head towards the exit, I just sit on the ground feeling lost.

"Velvet, we need to leave now," Rick says firmly and I just nod my head at him then he turns to leave, directing another one of his men to get Kerry's body. Ranulf is already back in human form and carries Tiffany out through the door. Some of the hunters are still fighting various witches around the room and for a moment I just sit in the middle of the carnage, blood covering the floor and my heart is now completely empty.

"Velvet?" I hear in my mind and I look up to see the ginger wolf standing in front of me. "I'm so sorry," Conall says as he places his head in my lap to comfort me then I run my fingers through the soft fur as tears start to escape my eyes.

"We need to leave," I manage to say quietly, the wolf looks up at me then starts to walk away as I get to my feet and follow him. What made me think I could do this? Running head first in to a room full of at least 50 people and thinking I could win...

"Leaving so soon?" Helana bellows behind me. I stop and Conall turns to look at me. "Just when we were starting to have some fun."

"Velvet, let's go," I hear Conall in my mind and I nod again at him, we have already lost too much. I stand for a moment, my heart in agony and my soul totally consumed by hate.

"If you leave now I will never stop hunting for you," Helana shouts at me. I focus on Conall, he is right, I need to leave so continue to follow him out.

"I'm leaving," I say quietly, ignoring the fact that she is watching me. I can't risk losing anyone else.

"Shame about the vampire king," Helana shouts after me. "When I drove that spike through his heart I never imagined it would feel so good."

"Velvet don't listen to her," Conall says to me, I nod my head and keep walking. He stands in the doorway waiting for me to catch up, I am so close when Helana shouts again.

"I heard a rumour that there was a young woman stabbed during the, so called, terrorist attack in Newcastle a couple of weeks ago..." I can hear the maliciousness in Helana's voice but I just block it out. "They say that she was pregnant," I stop. Conall notices and slowly starts to head back towards me, I know that he will try to stop me fighting her.

"You don't know what you're talking about," I say to Helana, my voice quivering as I speak.

"I think I know exactly what I am talking about... How did it feel knowing that not only did I murder your whore of a mother but I also killed your only child?" She laughs behind me.

I stand in silence, I know I need to leave, we have lost the battle. But deep down inside of me that darkness is trying to claw its way to the surface. I told Gideon that I feared it, that I know my mothers power came from a place of evil and I didn't know if I could live with myself if I fully gave in to it. I am so angry with her, she has taken everything from me... I can't leave unless she is dead. I look up at Conall, his gaze meets mine and for a moment I feel happy looking at him, but it's not enough any more.

"I love you," I say to him. I see panic instantly rise in his eyes as I force a smile, then I take deep breath and push my palms forward slightly. As though a bolt of energy leaves my hands, fire starts to burn on the floor forming a large ring around myself and Helana. I briefly see Conall through the flames before they burst upwards creating a burning wall.

"That's more like it," Helana says as I eventually turn to look at her. She stands smiling at me whilst clutching her shoulder, her face is already bloodied and bruised, her robes ripped from claw marks off Conall, but I am not just going to walk away now. I can feel the fire burning inside of my soul as pure hatred takes over. I grab the knife from my thigh holster and run at her, she doesn't move and just as I get close I feel pain shoot across my back and I fall to my knees in agony.

"Hurts, doesn't it? I don't need a knife to kill you. I am more powerful than you will ever be." Helana flicks her hand and I feel another sharp pain this time straight across my face as though invisible blades cut in to my skin. I can instantly feel my blood flow down my face as I push myself to me feet and concentrate on Helana's neck, I catch her off guard as she inhales sharply, unable to breath then wipe blood from my eye as I feel Helana trying to fight back against my hold on her, I struggle to maintain my invisible grip as she suddenly forces me back then drops to the floor before lunging towards me.

I land on my spine and drop the knife as Helana pins my arms to the ground, I try to fight her, but she has such a strong power that I feel as though my chest is being crushed as she sneers down at me. She puts her hand out to the side as the knife I dropped hits her palm, and she grasps it tightly then raises it ready to kill me.

I use everything I can muster to force my hand free and punch her as hard as I can in the face, knocking her to the side. Using magic is one thing, but at least after everything I've been through, all of the fights I have been in, I've learned how to throw a decent punch. I force myself up as my chest starts to burn, the flames that I made to just encase me and Helana have kind of got out of hand and now engulf the full room, only leaving a tiny circle where we now stand. I don't even have time to think about if everyone else has got out safe, my only focus is this fucking bitch in front of me.

Helana starts to get to her feet, as she tries to push up on her hands from the floor I run forward and ram the top of my knee in to her face, I know myself it's hard to concentrate on using your powers when you're getting the shit kicked out of you. My face is still bleeding, so I try to wipe more blood from my eyes and then grab Helana's robes and drag her to her feet.

It's strange, even though Helana's power is stronger than mine, she has the actual physical strength of a normal human, which works to my advantage because if I can stop her using magic, I should be able to beat the crap out of her the old-fashioned way. She barely gets a chance to stand upright and I punch her again sending her face first back to the ground then step forward and roll her over so that I can see her eyes, she is covered in blood, can hardly see out of one eye, blood gushes from her nose and mouth but all I can do is smile.

I kneel, forcing one of my knees in to her chest and I push it down, she flails her arms trying to push me off but I punch her again... And again... And again until my own fists are bleeding and I can feel the sting of tears in my eyes from all the emotions inside of me. I hear Helana try to mumble something through the blood, so I lean down to listen.

"Please," she says through rasping breaths. "Show mercy."

I almost laugh in her face, she can't be serious! She didn't show mercy when she killed my mother, murdered Ethel, tried to kill me and ended any chance I would have had for a happy life with my baby... And Gideon, I thought my life couldn't get any worse until I watched him die in my arms.

"Mercy?" I say in disbelief. "You don't deserve mercy."

I will the knife from the floor in to my hand and as soon as the hilt touches my palm I take my chance and drive the blade down as hard as I can, I watch as it glides through her forehead almost effortlessly, her skull crunching beneath the force and after a few seconds her body goes limp under mine. I slump forward as relief washes over me then roll off her, I lie on my back on the stone floor at Helana's side, just letting the world around me keep moving as I try to come to terms with what has happened. My heart hurts so much that I feel like I might die from sorrow.

The flames start to consume the meeting room, and I am finding it increasingly difficult to breathe as thick black smoke fills my lungs. I could just lie here and let the flames sweep me up, I close my eyes as I start to cough more, the fire burning all around me.

"Velvet?" I hear quite distant, I know it's Conall trying to connect with me. "Velvet please, if you're still alive, answer me." I don't respond, instead I sit up and look down at Helana next to me, I thought killing her would make me feel better but the emptiness is so overwhelming.

"Praise be to your dickhead Dark Lord," I say sarcastically down at her dead body.

I look around and see that the wooden beams holding the ceiling in place are on fire and the door at the far side is engulfed. The flames look as though it has spread up the stairs and possibly through the remnants of the old castle.

"Velvet," I hear Conall in my head again. "The building is ablaze, I don't know if you are still alive... I don't know if you can hear me at all, but I just want you to know that I'm sorry... I'm sorry that I didn't stand by you from the beginning, I'm sorry for not protecting you... I'm so so sorry for everything you have lost." I get up off the floor and I start to cry listening to his words. "I just want you to come outside, because everything you are feeling... I'll be feeling if I lose you, and I don't think I am strong enough to deal with thinking that you might be dead... Please, I love you so much."

I nod to myself, I need to leave, I didn't go through everything I have to burn here now. I concentrate on the flames and push them back clearing myself a path through the fire and start to walk away. I briefly turn back towards Helana as I get near the wooden door and watch as the flames take her body. I hope her soul burns in hell forever for what she has done.

It takes me a little bit of time to get out of the castle, the fire is quite out of control but at least my power helped keep the flames at bay, so I could get upstairs and through the library. It's devastating and not a single part of the castle is untouched by the flames. As I reach the main gates I can see the hunters starting to leave in the SUV's, I only seemed to see a few of them in the main room, there must have been more fighting outside as well. There are random members of the Midnight Church who escaped the fighting huddled on the grass and some starting to make their way off the grounds. Just down the driveway I see Kerry's body carefully wrapped in a blanket with Tiffany sat next to her holding her lifeless hand. Ranulf is sat next to her with his arms around her shoulders, her arm covered in blood.

Rick is standing with his hand on Tristen's shoulder as he sits on the ground holding Gideon's body and sobbing for the loss his brother. I've tried to keep strong, to suppress my emotions so that I could do what I needed to in the fight with Helana. But now I just feel consumed by guilt because if I hadn't have been so certain in my desire to kill her, then Gideon would still be alive.

"Velvet?" I glance up at Conall as tears stream down my face, he notices me standing in front of the burning building, his face also showing the remnants of his emotions.

I can't talk, I don't even know what words to say to make things right. I start to walk towards him as he runs at me, but my legs buckle under me as I am overcome with grief. Conall catches me as I fall to the floor and sits holding me as I cry, his arms wrapped around me tightly as he tries desperately to comfort me, but all I can think of is how much we have all lost tonight.

...

The next few days were all a blur.

I haven't seen Tristen much, I asked him if there was anything I could do to help him, but he won't even speak to me. I feel like everyone else is walking on eggshells around me, unsure of what to say in case they upset me, I know they all blame me for what happened.

Kerry grips my hand tightly as the sun begins to set, we all stand waiting for dusk, the time between day and night, when the last of the sun sets and twilight starts.

"Velvet, can I stand with you?" I look down and force a smile as Emily takes my other hand, and we wait quietly for Gideon's coffin to be removed from the back of the hearse, the air is crisp as I try to fight back the tears.

As soon as dusk arrives his funeral will begin. He is being laid to rest in his family's mausoleum, it's clearly old and been in place for many years but it's all made of marble and it's grandeur is beautiful. Above the front door is what looks like a Ankh carved in the stone, its edges flared to symbolises eternal life, something that has sadly now ended for Gideon. The mausoleum has small stained-glass windows that let light inside and although it is a small building it looks very expensive, a perfect resting place for a King.

I take a deep breath and wrap my arm around Emily as Tristen, Greg and a couple of his other men step forward and remove the casket. It's an unusual ceremony, it's not like a priest or anyone says anything, it's not your average funeral at all. The men hoist the coffin on to their shoulders and as soon as the night sky turns dark they start to walk Gideon on his final journey to lie at his parents side. They disappear inside the building, and we can hear him being placed inside his marble tomb, before all the men leave and wait for Tristen to finalise the committal and seal Gideon in to his eternal resting place.

Everything is so quiet around us, I look down, Emily buries her head in to my side as she cries for the loss of her brother. I try to stay strong for her, she lost her parents so young and then Gideon... No child should have to go through this.

There's a lot of people here that I don't recognise, I assume a lot of them are vampires that Gideon's family has allied with or ruled over, friends that he has known and what little family he might have left. Rick is here, he decided it would be best to stand back and slightly out of sight as he has a reputation for being a much feared hunter when he ran the council, he's probably fought many of these people in the past. Conall, Ranulf and Tiffany all came for support, as did Dee and Ben. Although I don't deserve their support, I've been racked with guilt over Gideon's death and every time I hug Conall or feel that slight bit of happiness, I feel like I am betraying Gideon, as though I shouldn't be allowed to feel happiness any more now that he is gone.

"Firstly I want to say thank you to everyone for coming," Tristen says as he emerges from the building and stands on the steps to the family's mausoleum, I can see that he is struggling to hold it together but it's now his job to be strong. "My parents were immensely proud of Gideon, when father made the decision some years ago to step down as our leader, my brother took this opportunity to try to change our world for the better... His passion and dedication to his people saw us thrive in a world full of prejudice," Tristen pauses slightly to regain his composure. "He always said he would never go down without a fight... And now we are in the wake of what may become the biggest fight any of us has ever faced... And that is to carry on without him." I try to control my breathing as tears begin to flow down my face. "I've always had my brother by my side and now I feel lost without him... I am going to keep things short because I'm not one to waffle on." There's a slight chuckle throughout the group and Tristen forces a smile. "Gideon would have appreciated every single one of you being here tonight, as do I... You honour his life by your presence... So thank you again," Tristen nods his head and nervously walks down the steps. I watch as people start to walk towards him and shake his hand to show their respect.

Eventually everyone starts to filter away, Conall, Rick and the others are meeting us back at the apartment. Kerry stays with me as I stand with Emily. The hearse leaves and after some time there is only us and Tristen left. Emily clings to me as Tristen sees that we are the last ones here and reluctantly walks over to us, he looks towards Emily and forces a smile for her as I stroke her hair.

"Thank you for coming," Tristen says quietly to me, I nod my head, I am not sure what to say for the best.

"Emily why don't we go for a walk and let your brother and Velvet talk for two minutes," Kerry says gently to Emily. She smiles at Kerry and takes her hand before walking away. Myself and Tristen stand awkwardly not speaking for a few moments.

"I'm sorry," I finally say to him. "This is my fault, I shouldn't have..."

"No," Tristen interrupts me. "You didn't force Gideon to go, he made up his own mind. No one could have forced him to do anything he didn't want to." I look up at Tristen and nod.

"I just wish there was more that I could have done," I reply.

"You killed Helana... So I think that is payment enough," Tristen sighs. "I don't blame you... for his death I mean. Gideon loved you." I take a deep breath and wipe away more tears from my face.

"I loved him too," I say trying to stop myself crying. Tristen smiles at me then steps forward and wraps his arms around me, he holds me tight as I hug him back. Both of us trying to comfort each other after such a massive loss.

"What will you do now?" Tristen asks me.

"I don't know... Probably take some time out, go home with Conall," I try to smile slightly as we part and Tristen looks at me.

"Promise me that you will be happy," he says gently. "My brother would have wanted you to be happy."

I nod at him as he takes a deep breath then walks away. I stand by myself for a moment in the cemetery, the world shattered around my feet then after a while I turn and leave.

Chapter Fourteen

"How are you feeling today?" Ben asks me as I sit down on the sofa opposite him.

"If I told you that I was fine, would you believe me?" I ask cautiously. Ben sighs then he gives me a concerned look. "I feel like things are getting worse," I say truthfully, looking down at the floor.

We are sat in the den at the Lookout, he keeps trying to encourage me to go and see a proper therapist but I don't trust anyone else. We have been having private sessions every week for a little while now, he regularly reminds me that he is not psychologically trained, but I don't care, he knows everything that I have been through and it makes it easier to talk to him about the things that are in my head.

Its been a few months, since the fight at the Midnight Church where we lost Gideon. So much has changed in that short time that it's now like living in a different world. Tristen has disappeared, he was next in line to take control of the vampire clans but shortly after Gideon's funeral, he left and no one has seen him since and I have no idea what happened to Emily. Because of Tristen leaving, Claudia came back and claimed power, she's ruthless, the streets at night are no longer safe as she has changed all the rules and laws that Gideon set in place to try to keep peace between the people. Humans are being attacked every day, their bodies drained of blood and left in the streets like nothing more than fast food. The General took control of the specialist units for the supernatural presence as Gideon was no longer there to run against him, so anyone of a supernatural origin is being hunted and sentenced to imprisonment until such a time that they are deemed safe. But knowing the General and the way he's running the Bird Cage, that means certain death. Everything has gone to shit.

A few days after Gideon's funeral I left Kerry in Newcastle then headed back to the Highlands with Conall and the wolf pack. I've tried to move forward with my life, I've wanted to make things work and have that happy life that I originally set out to find. I can't fault Conall at all, he has been amazingly supportive for me, he has been by my side through every dark day and every time I cried he was there to hold my hand. He knows I still had feelings for Gideon when he died, but we haven't spoken about that, instead he just doesn't mention his name. But I'm happy, and that is what is the most important thing right now... or so that is what I keep telling everyone else.

"Have you been taking the medication I gave you?" Ben says, forcing a small smile.

I learned very fast when I came back to the pack to try to control what thoughts I had in my head when Conall was around me. He is the only one out of all the family who can literally hear everything I think, I guess we are so close that I find it hard to block him out. I have had a lot of dark thoughts and the only person I have spoken to openly about everything is Ben. But only in a professional capacity as my Doctor. In front of everyone else I have to make it look as though nothing is wrong with me, I just feel like they wouldn't understand.

"I don't like them. The meds make me feel really spaced out," I explain. "They make me feel exhausted, but yet I can't sleep. Some days I feel OK, others..." Things have been hard. I am not going to lie, some days I struggle to just get out of bed.

"Are you eating or sleeping at all now?" Ben says as he takes a drink of his coffee.

"Not really. I just don't feel like eating most days and every time I close my eyes to sleep, the nightmares take over," I explain.

"I don't like having to keep prescribing you sleeping tablets, but you need something to help you..." Ben sighs. "I am worried about you, Velvet. I am sat watching you spiral down before my eyes and there is only so much I can do if you refuse to take the medication I give you. You need professional help."

"I have you, that's all I need," I reply.

I have been on a slow decline following Gideon's funeral. At first, I was just sad and then as the days went on I slipped more in to despair and now...

"You are in denial, Velvet," I can see Ben is frustrated with me.

"I'm fine," I reply quietly. Ben sits and watches me for a few moments whilst he thinks of something else to say.

"When we first started these sessions you told me that you thought you were having panic attacks. Tell me truthfully when was the last time you experienced one and what happened," Ben waits patiently for my answer but I don't want to give him it. I look up, and he nods at me to encourage me to speak.

"Yesterday," I sigh. "It was a bad day. I was supposed to go and meet Tiffany but the thought of leaving the house just got too much. I don't even know where it came from I just..." I take a deep breath, the thought of what happened is enough to make me feel as though I am panicking again.

"It's OK, this is a safe space, remember," Ben says gently.

"I know," I nod at him whilst trying to relax. "I told her I was sick, that I was sorry that I couldn't meet up with her but I just... I was terrified to leave the house. The more I thought about going outside the more I started to panic and I ended up curled up in a ball on the floor. Then later in the day I was watching TV, it wasn't even anything serious but there was a baby playing with some toys... It hit me hard and all the memories of losing Marcus consumed me. I just broke down."

"I've brought a stronger anti-depressant for you to take alongside the sleeping tablets. I need you to promise me that you will actually take them," Ben says forcefully, I glance at him and shake my head.

"I don't need more tablets," I snap back at him.

"Well that is where we disagree," Ben replies. "I know that you are heavily drinking again, you have severe anxiety... In the past you have shown suicidal tendencies..."

"That was different," I interrupt him.

"Did you or did you not slit your own wrists and try to kill yourself?" Ben watches me, he can see I am uncomfortable about this already, but I don't reply, I don't know what to say, so I just nod. "And since then how many times have you thought about trying something again? Hurting yourself to take away the pain?"

"I, erm..." I avoid making eye contact with him, I know he is right but I don't want to admit it. Everything in my head is pretty bad.

"Have you spoke about this properly with Conall yet?" Ben watches me waiting for a response. "You can't keep denying how you are feeling. There is nothing to be ashamed about, you have been though some terrible things and lost so much.

But you also have a man who would do anything for you, you hiding this from him is only going to make things worse."

"I know," I say quietly. "I just feel like he might not understand." Ben sighs and leans over to his bag, he takes out a couple of boxes of medication and places them on the arm of the chair.

"Try these for a couple of weeks and hopefully things will start to improve. I want you to try to speak to Conall at some point and I want you to stop drinking." I give him a look. "I'm serious Velvet, alcohol is only going to make things worse." I know Ben is right, but I am just not ready to share with Conall yet, I need to work out what I am going to say and how best to bring the subject up.

"Conall is home tomorrow, I promise I will try to speak to him at some point," I say, telling Ben what he wants to hear.

I talk with Ben for a another hour about everything that is on my mind, and he leaves. I have been alone in the Lookout for the last couple of weeks as Conall and Ranulf have been away on business. They have been working with Rick and I've had Tiffany keeping me company, she does take my mind off things sometimes and it has been fun working through that book of hers, I try so hard to seem normal.

I am very excited for Conall coming home, I seem to feel worse when I am by myself. Just me and my thoughts. I do love Conall, I love him more than anything, and he makes me so happy, he lights up my heart, and he is probably the only reason I get out of bed each morning. But I can't deny that my soul feels lost. When everyone else is around me I feel so fake, like my whole life is a lie because I spend all my time trying to be the Velvet that they know and love, instead of the empty shell I feel like now.

The next day I drag myself out of bed around lunch-time, I know I need to be on my best form today as we will have a house full tonight with everyone being back home. I took a couple of the sleeping pills with the other meds that Ben gave me last night, they knocked me out and I slept but I don't feel refreshed, instead I just feel numb.

"Hey," Conall says as I walk in to the living room, I am a bit startled as he wasn't supposed to be back until later on tonight, but he must have returned whilst I was in the shower, I've been looking forward to having him back with me, the bed feels empty now when he is not here.

"Hi," I look around the den. "You're back early, where is everyone?" I could have sworn he said we would all be having a late family dinner when they got home.

"I thought it would be nice to have some time, just the two of us, we haven't had that chance for quite a while," Conall replies as he sits on the sofa smiling at me. I can't help smile back when I look at him, he's my shining light. "So... Ranulf is staying with Dee tonight to give us some alone time." I casually walk over to the sofa, and he watches me intently as I straddle his lap. If I had of know that we would be alone tonight I might have made more of an effort to dress in something a bit more sexy than sweat pants and a Care Bears t-shirt.

"And what exactly did you have planned with this... alone time?" I ask playfully as Conall places his hands on my hips and watches me.

"Well..." He says standing up from the sofa and lifting me up with him, I quickly place my arms around his neck so that I don't fall and laugh slightly at my surprise. "The first part of the plan includes making love to you," he smiles as he kneels in front of the burning fire on the thick fur rug, my legs around his waist as he gently kisses my neck. "Right here should do it," he smiles more as he lies me back and runs his hands around my thighs as he leans over me and moves his mouth to my lips then kisses me deeply. I can feel that he is already hard as his crotch rubs against me through my pants as he slowly grinds on me. I moan slightly as he presses between my legs a little more firmly wanting to feel me against him.

"I missed you," Conall says down at me as he runs his hands up and under my t-shirt, his palms warm on my skin. I grab the bottom of his shirt and pull it up, I am instantly turned on by him and I want him now. Conall smiles and quickly takes over to remove it, discarding it to the floor next to us. He then moves from on top of me to enable him to remove my pants and underwear, I let him, just lying in the thick fur watching him become more aroused by seeing me half naked.

He pushes up my t-shirt and starts to seductively kiss my stomach, I feel his tongue tease my skin as he trails the kisses down and across my mound. Conall gently spreads my thighs and positions himself between them so that he can slowly play. His mouth isn't even on my clit yet and I can already feel myself wanting him, needing him in me then I feel his fingers tease me slightly and I inhale sharply as they work their way towards my hole, the anticipation of feeling him inside of me is already starting to make me wet as his fingers glide between my moist lips then his tongue suddenly flicks across my clit and my body shakes beneath him.

I close my eyes and relax as his lips touch me, moaning as his tongue stimulates my bud then his fingers slowly slides inside of my pussy. I know it's only been a couple of weeks without him but it feels like it's been forever since I was this close to another person. I mean, it's not like I've been alone all the time, I've been trying to keep busy in town and helping with some of the chores, when I am not hiding in my room that is. I don't like being by myself, because my mind wanders and the places it goes to are too dark for me to deal with alone.

I moan louder as Conall slides another finger inside my pussy, filling my hole and making me beg for more. As much as his mouth and fingers feel so good playing with me, I want his cock, I want him to fuck me so that I forget about everything else. I want to feel him inside of me and cum so hard that I scream.

"Is that really what you want?" Conall says playfully as he moves up from between my legs and looks down, his fingers still inside of me.

I smile as he heard those thoughts again, I know I have to be careful what I think as he has a knack of hearing literally everything. Conall leans down and kisses me again as he moves his fingers more inside of me, even my mouth wants him completely, to dominate me. He pulls his fingers out slightly, the penetration feels shallow as he concentrates on only one area near the front of my opening. He starts to play above my g-spot and suddenly everything feels different. An intense pressure starts to build within me as my body moves against his hand, almost bucking as my loins throb for him to be inside of me.

"You're going to have to wait for my cock because I am having way too much fun watching you squirm," Conall whispers in my ear then starts to kiss my neck. I grab on to the fur beneath me as his fingers continue to play.

"Oh... god," I moan as I realise what he is doing, my breathing changes as the pleasure builds deep inside of me. I can feel Conall smiling to himself as he kisses my skin. "Fuck!" I cry out as his fingers move a little faster and rub my g-spot more. His touch getting firmer and sending me reeling.

"Are you going to cum for me?" Conall says playfully in my ear as my hand moves to his, I grab his wrist as he plays roughly. I suddenly find it hard to breathe as the pleasure becomes all consuming. He watches me as I try to hold back, I've felt this before and I know that things will get quite messy if he caries on because he will make me squirt. "That's entirely the point," he says hearing my thoughts again, "nothing would turn me on more right now than watching you cum all over my hand." My back arches as I feel like I am literally going to explode, Conall maintains eye contact with me as I bite my lip to stop from crying out as I can't resist it any longer and Conall knows it as he smiles wildly.

"Shi..." It feels so amazing that I can't even get my words out. The sensations that he is giving me are so intense that I forget that I actually need oxygen and catch myself holding my breath. I'm struggling to keep my eyes focused on Conall as I throw my head back, I feel myself explode in orgasmic pleasure and my cries echo around the room.

"Yeah... Just like that," Conall says watching me as I gush, making his hand soaking wet and my pussy dripping. I can see he is so fucking aroused that he is already breathing heavily just from watching me cum for him. He leans down and kisses me passionately as he moves his hand to unfastened his own jeans, I help him push them down as he pauses briefly to remove them then grabs me and rolls me over until I am lying on top of him. I can feel his cock between my legs as I sit back and take off my top and then remove my bra. Conall's hands go straight to my breasts, caressing and gently squeezing them as he watches me move and slide his dick inside of me.

I can tell that Conall likes when I'm on top, as much as he enjoys making me cum he loves to watch me be in control, he gets off on watching me climax as well, he is definitely a giver. I grind on him, pushing my hips forward as Conall groans loudly.

"Oh, fucking God, I love you so much," he says as he grabs my thighs and thrusts up every time I move. I grab his hands as I feel the pleasure build inside of me again and I know that it is not going to take me long to cum again if he starts to fuck me.

"I love you too," I reply as I push my hips forward more forcefully, I want to be fucked, I want cum again. I see Conall grin then he sits up slightly and wraps his arm around my waist and flips over until I am on my back, Conall pulls me in closer to him and puts my leg over his arm to allow him to drive his cock deeper in to my pussy.

"You like that don't you?" He asks as he starts to fuck me hard. "You like it when I fuck you?"

I can't do anything but nod my head as pure lust takes over, I grab his arm as he thrusts deep and hard as I swiftly cum loudly again, as I do his face changes, and he cums with me, still driving hard in to my pussy as he empties himself inside of me completely. I run my hand up his arm then around the back of his neck and pull him down to kiss me, our tongues playing wildly together as he continues to grind in and out of me slowly until our bodys begin to relax. After a moment our lips part and Conall smiles down at me.

"I missed you so much whilst you were away," I say as I get my breathing back under control. "And I am definitely liking your plans for this evening so far," I laugh slightly. Conall kisses my lips gently again then leans back to get up from the floor.

"So, what have you been up to whilst I've been away?" Conall asks as he picks up his jeans and puts them on then playfully throws my t-shirt towards me. I sit up and pull it over my head and grab my pants.

"Nothing much," I reply not wanting to give too much away, I don't think tonight is the right time to speak to him about everything that I have been feeling, I just want one last night where everything feels perfect before I hit him with that bombshell. "I've just tried to keep myself busy." I get up from the floor and put on my bottoms then turn back to Conall, I need to change the subject. "Are you hungry? I can make you something to eat of you like."

"Yeah, that would be nice. I'm starving actually... think I have worked up an appetite," he says smiling as I nod and head off in to the kitchen. I open the fridge to have a look at what to make.

"What do you fancy?... Apart from me, that is," I call to Conall, laughing at myself for what I said.

"Not sure, give me two seconds whilst I go and put some shorts on because I am quite warm and I'll come and have a look," he shouts back. I nod to myself and grab a glass from the cupboard then pour myself a large drink of wine and just stand for a few minutes waiting for Conall to come in.

"Hey," he says as he enters the kitchen, I fill my glass again as I drank it whilst I was waiting. He stops and watches me take another sip. "When did you start drinking again?" I look down at the glass and realise that Conall thinks I haven't touched a drop of alcohol since I found out I was pregnant.

"It's just a glass of wine," I explain, trying to brush it off.

"It's not though, is it?" Conall takes the glass from my hand and places it on the breakfast bar. Conall doesn't drink much at all and I tried so hard to live a bit more healthy since coming back here, but things have been a bit up and down for me so alcohol had always been my go-to coping mechanism. Whilst he was away it was pretty much all I did when I was alone.

"I've had a couple of drinks," I explain. "Nothing excessive, just... enough to take the edge off," I swallow and look down, I know I am lying to him, I don't like doing it but I don't know how to tell him the truth. I don't know why but it makes me feel ashamed of using it as a crutch. With Conall being gone these last couple of weeks and being alone with my own thoughts, my mind has gone to some pretty dark places, Ben told me I should have spoken to him about this ages ago in case something like this happened. I feel sick, I don't know where to look.

"What's going on?" Conall stands watching me, I go to say something but I don't have any words. "And what are these?" He takes a couple of boxes of medication out of his back pocket and places them on the counter. I just stand with my mouth open slightly, I feel like a deer in the headlights and I can feel myself starting to panic.

"Erm... I..." My chest feels so tight, I can't have an anxiety attack right now, not in front of Conall.

"I want to give you the chance to tell me the truth, I would rather hear things from you," he says gently. My heart is racing, I don't know what to do.

"Ben gave me those ages ago, I forgot I had them. I swear everything is fine," I know as soon as I say those words that I shouldn't have, I have just blatantly lied to Conall's face, and he knows it. He sighs and sits down at the breakfast bar, turning the boxes over in his hands to keep occupied. I just stand in silence and watch him, he doesn't even look at me.

"I know that you and Ben have been meeting in secret pretty much every week," Conall says cautiously. "Dee noticed before I did, she knew that you two were close and assumed the worst..."

"I would never... we have never... it's nothing like that," I quickly explain.

"I know," Conall glances up at me. "But Dee was worried, so she confronted him about your meetings with each other. For the sake of their relationship he told her the truth... And she confided in me, our family has no secrets, even when they involve each other." I feel so nervous.

"What did she tell you?" I ask as my voice begins to shake.

"Enough," he replies, I try to breathe deeply but I can feel my hands start to shake. "I have known things have been wrong for a while, I had hoped that you would talk to me, that you would allow me to understand what you might have been going through... I am more disappointed that I just asked you directly about it and you lied to me." We both fall silent, I know I should say something, anything to make things better. "How much have you been drinking? The recycling bin is filled with empty bottles and I know that they are not off Ranulf... Are you going to tell me what the medication is for? Or are you going to continue denying everything even though I have already been told." I literally can't find the words to explain what is going on at all. "I know I can't stop you doing what you want, but I don't like that you can't just talk to me about what you are feeling instead of hiding it away," Conall says to me then he waits for me to respond.

"I can't," I reply. "I can't say how I am feeling deep inside because if I do I am scared that bad things will happen." I try not to think, I don't want to let those thoughts and feelings in right now, especially not when I'm with Conall. He's my light, he keeps me from being consumed by the darkness that is trying to claw its way to the surface.

"Please talk to me," Conall pleads, he gets up from the stool and walks around the breakfast bar then takes my hand. "I want to help you, to make sure that you are OK, but I can't do that if you don't speak to me." I shake my head and take a deep breath, I can't do this. There is war raging inside of me and if I ignore it, eventually it might just go away. God I need a drink, I think to myself and then I hear Conall sigh.

"I'm sorry," I say quietly. I don't know what I'm sorry for but I feel like I need to say it.

"This is still about Gideon, isn't it?" Conall blurts out, his attitude has changed and this is not a conversation I want to be having right now.

"No," I lie. "It's just me... Over thinking things." I pull my hand away from Conall and take a step back to try to distance myself from the topic. "So, how was your time away? Did Rick ask about me?"

"Don't try to change the subject," Conall says. "It's been about three months, you won't talk to anyone about what happened inside the church, you won't even say his name around anyone." I shake my head, I don't want to talk about this. "I think you need to talk about this Velvet, all this bottling up of your feelings and thoughts is not healthy for you. We, as a couple, can't move forward until you accept that things are different now, we have a life together here, a good one... But you need to let Gideon go."

"What if I don't want to let Gideon go?" I snap at him. I try to slow my breathing as I feel rage rise inside of me and I know that I can't let Conall see it.

"He's dead, Velvet," Conall says bluntly. "I'm not going to spend my time walking on eggshells around you any more," he laughs to himself in frustration. "I've done everything I can to make you happy, to give you a good life, but you lie to me about the drinking and you're keeping things from me, these drugs... you won't just tell me what they are for. Clearly you are speaking to Ben more than you are speaking about things with me... You've changed and I don't know what to do for you any more."

"It's not like that," I try to explain. "I just don't want to talk about these things, I don't want to remember it all... but I can't just forget about losing my baby and how it felt to be consumed with pain. You don't understand what it is like to lose a child... And close friends." I grit my teeth and try to push the darkness back. I don't want to feel it.

"I know you are hurting still, I know that the pain won't just disappear overnight, but you have to live your own life now... Fuck! Velvet, I feel like you are more concerned with that bastard vampire than noticing that it is me that is stood right in front of you." I stand in shock as Conall seems like he is staring to lose it, and we never fight, I have never seen him like this. "I'm here! It is me that you love and who cares for you. It's me that is now having to deal with the aftermath of this shit with the General, Claudia and every one else you have pissed off. Gideon is dead, he is not in your life any more, you need to fucking get over it." I scoff to myself and nod my head, slowly taking in everything he has just said to me.

"I need to fucking get over it?" I ask him, I can see it in his eyes that he instantly feels guilty about saying that. "You want to truly know how I feel?"

"I didn't mean what I said, I..." Conall tries to explain but I stop him.

"No, you meant exactly what you said. You seem to forget Conall, that I had a life before you came along, no matter how much of an arsehole you think Gideon was, I loved him... is that what you want me to say? I fucking loved him so much it hurt, he was the father of my unborn child, he was passionate, and he stood by my side when no one else would." I feel so fucking angry. "And then I watched him die in my arms, and I was helpless to stop it from happening, just like his son, I lost my world... You Conall, you are the light in my life, the one thing that keeps me sane... But there's something else inside of me and it's dark, the pain and the darkness will not go away because it is part of me. Yes, I drink a lot. I drink to numb that pain, to escape the possibility that I will never be free of it."

"Velvet, I am sorry, I didn't mean to..." Conall says trying to take my hand again but I push him away.

"I told you that I didn't want to talk about it, I said that I didn't want to think about all this, but you kept pushing and pushing and right now... I don't even know... I'm confused... I can't do this," I say quickly and walk away from him.

"Where are you going?" Conall tries to call after me.

"Bed!" I snap back. "I think I need to be alone." I almost run up the stairs and jump under the duvet. I've tried so hard to act like I am doing good but even though there is so much love between me and Conall, my heart still feels torn to shreds and it aches every single day.

This power that I have inside of me, the abilities that I received from Lena feel evil and it terrifies me that if I let myself be consumed by it, combined with the darkness I feel inside of myself, then I am scared of what I might do. I didn't want to hurt anyone, I just wanted to be normal but I feel like I am going crazy, my mind won't let me rest, constantly making me see death and destruction everywhere I look. I've gone as far as not wanting to go after the General or Claudia because I want to stay in the light, I want to keep my humanity. If I give in to the darkness I might become a monster.

I drift in and out of sleep, I am too angry to fully rest, all those emotions that I pushed down after I killed Helana are coming back with vengeance, it's everything that I've been trying to avoid. I lie in the bed as my heart starts to race and I feel like I am going to have a panic attack as the thoughts take over, my pulse is pounding in my ears. I feel like I am screaming inside, I put my hands over my head and curl up in a ball trying to feel safe from the outside world and all those demons that are trying to drag me down. Conall doesn't understand what it's like to feel this way, his heart is pure and good, there is not an evil bone in his entire body.

I was told I was born from both the dark and the light, both good and evil... And no matter how hard I try to stay in the light, to fight for good and keep hold of my humanity, my soul is so tempted by the other side.

"Hey?" I hear Conall say quietly from the bedroom door. "Are you still awake?" I take a moment to control my breathing before speaking.

"Yes, I'm awake," I say nervously. "I can't sleep." Conall comes in to the room and climbs in to the bed behind me, I've got my back to the door so that he can't see my face, but he gets close to me and places his arm around my waist.

"I'm sorry," he says gently. "I shouldn't have pushed you like that, I just feel like I'm losing you, like you're slipping away from me." I nod my head slightly as he holds me tight, I think he can hear the panic coursing through my body.

"I just feel... I am so lost Conall," I say as my voice quivers. "I don't want to hurt you, but I can't help what I feel inside."

"I know," he says as he kisses the back of my neck gently to comfort me. "Things got bad, I understand that. I just hate seeing you miserable and sad." I sigh, and we lie is silence for a moment before I speak again.

"I was thinking I might go and visit Kerry, stay with her for a few days, just to clear my head," I say cautiously.

"If that's what you feel you need to do," Conall replies reluctantly, I can tell he doesn't want me to go. "Do you want me to come with you?" He asks hopefully but I shake my head.

"No," I say. "Maybe a bit of girl time will do me good, allow me to work through some things and then I'll feel better... I won't be away too long, I promise," I add. The silence fills the room again and after a while Conall starts to fall asleep. I lie in the dark and eventually drift off also, consumed by dreams again.

"Velvet?" Gideon forces out as his breath hitches. I know this is a dream and I've seen it nearly every time I close my eyes but it never gets any easier.

"No!" I scream as he falls, I try to catch him, but he's heavy and I collapse to my knees beneath his weight. I sit cradling him in my arms as I feel sheer panic rise inside of me. "Gideon stay with me." My hands are shaking as I run them across his face, his skin losing colour and turning to a leather like texture under my touch. This isn't happening, it's not real. I don't know what to do, I don't even know what happened. "GIDEON?" I scream as I see his eyes start to turn a murky black. I can't breathe, I can't lose him. I shake his body to desperately try and wake him up as his life slips away. "No... NO!!"

I sit bolt upright in the bed gasping for air then look down to my side as Conall is fast asleep. He is quite a heavy sleeper once he is comfortable so the times when I have been awake all night he hasn't noticed. I like it when he is asleep sometimes because it's the only time, apart from when I am alone that I am able think what I want and not have to worry about trying to close my mind off to the pack. It's the only time I can let my true feelings show, because even though I act happy and content, my heart is still empty, I feel as though I'm trying to create this version of me that is a total lie.

I glance to the clock and see it's only 11pm, it's still super early, I know I am not going to get any sleep tonight now, so I carefully get out of bed without waking Conall and get dressed into black jeans, a black hoodie and some boots. I keep an eye on him in case I make enough noise to disturb him as I pack a bag then take out my phone and text Kerry to say I am coming for a surprise visit and that I'll see her tomorrow. I need to clear my head, spend a bit of time being able to think properly and decide what it is I want to do next.

When I am ready to leave I lean down and gently kiss Conall on the forehead, he stirs slightly and rolls over to go back to sleep. I feel a little bad for leaving in the middle of the night but at least I don't have to explain more or give him the opportunity to talk me in to letting him come with me. I go to leave and notice my meds on the bedside table, he must have brought them back upstairs with him when he came to speak to me. I know I need to take them, I promised Ben that I would but after the discussion with Conall tonight I feel now more than ever that a few pills are not going to help me.

The journey down to Newcastle is quiet, the roads are clear and I get in to town before 5am. The streets are empty as I drive around, it never used to be like this but people are afraid to leave their homes during the darkest parts of the night for fear of all manner of monsters roaming around.

I had intended on going straight to the apartment, I have a spare key, so I could have let myself in and made a coffee or three before Kerry woke up. But instead I am sat in the car at the entrance to the cemetery where Gideon's family mausoleum is. The main gates are locked at this time of night for cars, so I get out and go through the small side gate. The walk to where Gideon lies is the hardest I've ever had to do by myself, I haven't been back here since his funeral and as I approach the front I realise that I didn't go inside, so I don't know what to expect.

There's a heavy chain and padlock on the metal railing door, so I gently take hold of the lock and use my power to open it, removing one side of the chain to allow the door enough room to open so that I can go inside. The mausoleum seems a lot more peaceful than I thought it would be, I know that sounds stupid with it housing the dead, but it's unusually calm. The inside itself is small, but still big enough to walk around in. Everything is white marble and gold accents, the wall to the right of the door has 9 large squares carved in it, I see Gideon's name on an inscription instantly in the one on the left in the middle row. Beneath him I see Marcus carved in the stone and next to it the name Lillian, both dates of death are the same on the bottom ones, so I assume these are Gideon's parents. There is also writing on the far upper right square but don't want to read any more names, I am not ready to think about how many lives have been laid to rest here.

There is a small bunch of red flowers placed in a vase attached to the wall next to Gideon's name, they seem fresh so someone must have been in here very recently. I should have brought flowers, that's what people do, isn't it? I notice a white leather armchair in the corner then go and sit down. The moon shines through the small stain glass windows making patterns on the floor and I sit watching them for a few minutes.

"I kept meaning to come sooner," I say, I know I am most likely talking to myself but maybe if I speak the words that are in my head then I'll feel better. "This place is... Nice... Sorry, I am not sure what to say... Everything happened so quick that I didn't even get a chance to say goodbye to you." I take a deep breath and think. "I miss you Gideon. Even after all the fights and arguments, you still had hold of my heart. I just wish so much that I had told you sooner." I close my eyes slightly as I feel the sting of tears in my eyes. "I don't even know where you are... When I died I saw my mother and Marcus... But it kills me inside to think that you won't be with them... When you died I felt like my entire soul had been ripped out of my body and crushed, and I've tried so hard to carry on... But I just can't do it, I can't live without you in my life." I shake my head at myself as tears stream down my face. "Tristen told me that you would have wanted me to be happy, and I am... I think. Conall is good and kind, he cares deeply for me but I feel like I am living a lie, because he's not you..." I sit in silence for another 10 minutes before I get up out of the chair and walk over to the wall, I place my hand on the cold marble as my fingers gently trace the carving of his name. "I love you Gideon, I always will," I say softly and then lean forward slightly and gently kiss the stone as I can't fight back the tears any more. I pause for a moment and take a breath before leaving then close the metal grated door and relock the chain. Once outside I inhale the crisp morning air and get the feeling that I am being watched. I look around but I can't see anyone, my thoughts think it might be Tristen, but he hasn't been seen in a while and if he wanted me to know he was here he would show himself. I stand for a moment waiting to see if anyone makes a sound, but nothing happens so I take a slow walk back to the car.

I drive around for a bit and find myself parked up in the car park opposite Gideon's club. The doors are all boarded up, when I get out of the car and wander over, it looks as though the place is trashed, probably no one has been here properly since Gideon died. I glance at my phone and it's not even 6am yet, it's still pitch dark, and I could murder a drink.

I leave the Camaro parked up and decide to walk the 5-minute journey to The Makers Forge, I haven't been here since the night I first met Tristen, and it's the only place I know around here where it's always quiet and open all the time. I walk inside and it's the same dimly lit shit hole it has always been, there's a couple of people dotted about and the exact same older gentleman with his magnificent beard sitting behind the bar reading. I walk down to the far side of the bar and climb on to a barstool then grab my wallet from my back pocket and open it. Just as I go to get some money to order a drink, a glass is put down in front of me with a dark liquid inside and a half full bottle of Kraken placed by it. I look up and the old man smiles.

"Haven't seen you in here for a while," he says as he stands and watches me, I pick up the glass and take a sip them laugh slightly.

"Yeah, things got a bit complicated," I reply.

"Bad day?" He asks as he starts to clean the bar counter. I wish it was that simple.

"More like a bad 6 months," I smile. He pauses for a moment as though he is going to say something else but then nods and returns to his seat at the other end of the bar. He hasn't been sat there long when a small group of people come in, it's still early morning, you don't usually get groups heading this way.

"I don't want any trouble," I hear the old guy say, it's none of my business as to what is going on, so I refill my glass and take another drink.

"You got the money?" I hear a younger man's voice ask him.

"No, it's too much," the old guy replies. "She keeps asking for more, for protection from your kind, but I don't have anything left to pay." The younger guy lunges forward and partially drags the old man across the counter top. I glance around and no one else in the bar is paying any attention to what's going on, I look towards the group and get the strong feeling that they are vampires, which means the "she" he was referring to is their new bitch master, Claudia. It's still none of my business... not my pig, not my farm and all that bollocks.

"You know what happens to people who can't pay?" A high-pitched, highly irritating voice says. I sigh heavily and put my glass down then turn in my chair and watch the scene in front of me unfold.

"Please, I can get the money for you, I just need more time," the old guy begs.

"This was the final time," the blond haired slutty bimbo steps forward and grabs his face. I know I shouldn't get involved, I know I should be lying low especially if they are working for Claudia, but the opportunity to knock Bonnie down a peg or two is far too great to pass up.

"Hey, slutty Mcslutface!" I call over to the group. "Things have definitely gone down hill if Claudia sends a little twatting hag like you to do her work. Talk about scraping the bottom of the barrel." Bonnie looks over in my direction, as the three men she is with turn to face me. The younger one drops the old guy, and he backs away behind the bar.

"You!" Bonnie looks shocked to see me. "There's no one here to stop us fighting this time." I smirk at her and drink the rest of the liquid in the glass before I stand. I've only had a couple but the alcohol has gone straight to my head and I feel a little wobbly on my feet with lack of sleep.

"I didn't come out tonight looking for a fight," I reply. "But I am kind of in a shit mood, you see things have not been too good for me lately and maybe what I need to make myself feel better, is now stood right in front of me." I smile as the three men run towards me, but before they get anywhere near, their bodies crumple to the floor. Bonnie looks at them unsure what happened as they all shrivel up and turn grey. Although I haven't really used my powers very much in the last three months it is undeniable that they are growing. They seem to be getting more instinctive, and I am stronger than I have ever been, so killing those three was not an issue for me. I step over the body closest to me and slowly walk towards Bonnie.

"You see," I say calmly as I give in to the power inside of me. "I've always been afraid of what I could do and subconsciously I think that held me back. But now I have nothing to lose, there's just me here, no one else to help... crushing their hearts was too easy and it just makes me want more. I once said I enjoyed the thrill of the kill..." I stand right in front of her and watch her expression change as I gently stroke her face, she stands still, unsure of what to do. "The power inside of me has always been dark, but I never wanted to admit it. The more I tried to be good, the less I could control it... But I am not afraid of it any more." Bonnie jerks back as I focus on her throat, I just stand and watch as she struggles for breath.

"You don't... have to... do this," Bonnie forces out as she claws at her own neck but there's nothing for her to grab on too.

"I know I don't have to... and right now you're lucky, because I am not going to kill you," I say as I stare Bonnie right in the eye. "When I let you go you are going to remove these bodies from this nice gentleman's bar and then you're going to go crawl back to Claudia and tell her that this town is off limits. If she wants to treat it as an all-you-can-eat buffet then she has to go through me first, understand?" Bonnie nods her head then I let her go, she gasps for air as she drops and quickly starts to do as she is told without saying another word. I stand firm and watch her until the three bodies are gone, and she leaves.

After a moment I take out my phone and text Kerry again.

- Hey, got in to Newcastle earlier than expected, fancied a drink, so I am at The Makers Forge. Yes! I know it's Sunday morning but when you get your ass out of bed get over here, oh and bring a map of the UK and some sort of scrying shit thing, I don't know what's it's called but it's important. Love you x -

I sit by myself and drink, I just can't get Gideon out of my head. I lose track of time quite quickly as I drown my sorrows in rum, I keep trying to pay for the amount that I am drinking but the old guy won't accept a penny from me. So, I just sit and think, the place is serene when arsehole vampires are not in here threatening people's lives. I keep mulling over what I said to Bonnie about the power inside of me feeling dark, I've know it was since I first learned who my mother was but I tried to justify it by picturing her as good. But the more I've learned, the more I've come to understand that no one in this world is truly good... How many innocent people did my mother sacrifice to her Lord? What unspeakable things did she do to keep her coven in power? Maybe that was all she had known, that she had been brought up in that life and it's the only way she knew. Or maybe she chose it, maybe she gave in to the darkness and let it take control of her very soul, and she ended up doing exactly what she had to do to feel alive.

"Velvet?" I hear my name and turn as Kerry walks towards me.

"Hi," I say sounding a lot more drunk than I thought I was. I need to tone that down a bit other wise no one will take me seriously.

"How many have you had to drink?" Kerry stands next to me and moves the bottle from the counter. "It's like, 10am on a Sunday morning."

"Hello to you too," I say sarcastically. "Is that any way to speak to your best friend that you haven't seen in weeks?" Kerry sighs and sits down on the bar stool next to me.

"I'm going to guess that you're not doing too good right now," Kerry says giving me a disapproving look. I take a deep breath and shake my head, I tried so hard to push everything down, I tried the whole talking about my feelings thing with Ben. I even tried to pretend I was fine and deny to myself that there was anything wrong. But I am not doing good at all. I'm a little disappointed in myself for drinking so much, so I push the half full glass away from me and look down.

"I went to see Gideon this morning," I explain. "It was weird being in there, knowing that his body was behind that stone slab, just inches from me." Kerry takes hold of my hand and squeezes slightly so that I know she's here to support me. "I should have taken flowers but I didn't think... Do you think he would have wanted me to take flowers? That's usually what people do, isn't it?" I look to Kerry who smiles at me sweetly.

"I'm sure... I'm sure he wasn't bothered about the flowers and that just having you visit was enough," she says gently, I nod my head and inhale deeply. We sit quiet for a few minutes, I run through everything in my head before I speak again.

"Can I ask you a question?" I say seriously. Kerry nods her head and looks at me. "As my familiar, what dutys are you bound too? Like, if I needed your help with something, would you have my back, no matter what?" I can see Kerry instantly understands that the drink is no longer talking and that I am now being deadly serious with my questions.

"I'll always have your back, no matter what... Anything you ask of me, I will do," she replies. I nod and inhale slowly thinking about how to say the next part.

"Did you bring the things I asked for?" I say. Kerry nods and gets a map book out of her bag and what looks like a clear crystal on a chain.

"What do you need these for?" She asks me as I open the map.

"I need to find someone, I think they might have the answers that I need... I want to know more about my mother and my powers." Kerry sits silently as I close my eyes and picture who I want to find, I don't have anything of theirs and I don't even know a rough location. But I know this will work as I can feel it inside of me. The crystal circles the map for a moment then stops on Manchester. I quickly flick to the zoomed in page of the city and repeat the process until it stops on a street name.

"Who are you trying to find?" Kerry eventually asks me.

"Remember at the Midnight Church, there was a woman, Sharon she was called." Kerry nods at me to confirm she knows who I am talking about. "She said she knew my mother, and she has been advising the High Priestess for many years, so I assume she knows a lot more about magic and the way it works in this world, than we do."

"That's not hard," Kerry laughs. "We haven't even scratched the surface. But if you feel like you need to talk to her, then I guess I'm driving because you are in no fit state to do so at all." I smile at Kerry as we get up to leave. I quickly take a couple of notes from my wallet and leave them on the counter, even if the old man won't take my money, I am still going to leave it.

I don't remember the drive down, I remember we walked to the car then after that nothing until Kerry is nudging me awake as she pulls up in some random street. I shake my head to wake myself up as Kerry hands me a bottle of water, I don't even ask where she got it from, instead I just drink it whilst I look around. The street is lined with office blocks, a small bed and breakfast kind of thing, coffee shop, the usual. Nothing stands out to me.

"Anything?" Kerry asks as I rub my eyes and yawn. I watch as a smartly dressed guy in a suit leaves the bed and breakfast then walks away down the street.

"I want to try in there," I say pointing to where he has just emerged from, I don't know why, but I get the feeling that's no ordinary hotel. We get out of the car and walk across the road, it looks pretty posh actually but as soon as I open the front door and walk in I can sense the bad energy here.

"Hello, can I help you ladies?" A smartly dressed woman in a blue trouser suit says from behind the front desk.

"Yes," I reply having a look around, everything seems so sterile and clean. The sofas in the lobby are leather and the entire place is immaculate. "I have a feeling that I need to speak to your boss." The woman looks me up and down then smiles.

"I'm sorry, she's in a meeting at the moment. By all means you are more than welcome to leave a message and I'll pass that on to her when she has the time to respond," the woman says very professionally. I shake my head and lean on the front desk.

"Yeah, that's not going to happen," I reply and smile back. "What room is she in?" I say firmly. The woman shakes her head at me.

"Like I said, unfortunately she is in a meeting..." I don't wait for her to finish, instead I use my will to push her back in to her chair and force her to stay there, the chair rolls across the floor on its wheels and hits the wall behind her. She goes to speak but I just smile and stop her from talking, the surprise on her face is priceless. Although I am also surprised how easy I am finding using my powers when I don't give a fuck any more. I lean over the desk and look down at the appointment book, scrolling through the room numbers, one in particular catches my eye. I smile and look back at the woman.

"Thank you for your cooperation, it is much appreciated," I say sarcastically before walking off towards the rooms. I'm looking for room 7 which is up some stairs, as we approach I know that I am in the right place. I don't know how I know, but I do.

"Shall we knock?" Kerry asks from behind me but I shake my head and smile.

"Na, it would ruin the surprise," I reply. I stand for a moment and then with all my force I kick the door open, the wooden frame smashing as the door comes off its hinges.

"What the fucking shit?" I hear a woman's voice scream as I walk through the busted open door then stop.

"Holy fuck! This is not what I was expecting," I say trying not to laugh. The room itself is very white and clean, however on the far wall is a black wooden support with a half naked man gagged with a red leather ball in his mouth, he is strapped to the wall with leather cuffs and padlocks. I try not to make eye contact with him as he looks awkward as fuck. Sharon is dressed in a black leather corset and leather trousers with a whip in her hand, I can't really look at her either, so I look down and try desperately not to cry with laughter.

"Velvet?" She says both scared and in utter shock. "I did what I said, I promise you..." She puts her hands up and steps back obviously afraid for her life, she knows what I did to Helana.

"Take a chill pill Sharon, I'm not here to kill you... I just want to talk," I can't help it, I chuckle to myself as the man starts looking confused. Sharon nods her head nervously and puts down the whip on her little side table, I smirk again as I notice an array of toys, but she doesn't relax just yet.

"OK, what do you want to talk about?" She asks nervously.

"Tell me more about the coven," I say inquisitively. "I want to know what made this particular one so powerful." Sharon thinks for a moment then starts to talk.

"A coven is only as strong as it's High Priestess," she explains. "Not all coven members are born with magic in their veins, yes, some are born from blood lines like yourself but the majority of its members are normal humans who are gifted power when joining." I think for a moment then have another question.

"So, when I killed Helana, many of the coven members lost that power?" I ask and Sharon nods. I never gave any thought previously as to where everyone's power and abilities came from.

"Yes, everything in the coven is connected. The more members it has, the more powerful it is and the stronger its High Priestess becomes." I can tell Sharon is cautious by what she says but I have no reason to think she is hiding anything from me.

"But you guys worshipped the devil?" I inquire and Sharon smiles slightly.

"Kind of, it's not so much that we worship him but more we acknowledge his existence and are thankful for the gifts he gives us. For he has the ability to give and take power, much like any Lord, our religion does not define us but it is the root of our abilities. Our coven has always practised dark magic, and that only comes from one place," she replies. I nod my head, the existence of the Devil is not something I had given much thought to. I mean, if there were such things as God's or Lords or whatever, why would they bother their arses in dealing with us little people on earth or is it just a bunch of over achieving arseholes on a power trip playing games, and we are their pawns? I don't honestly believe he actually exists.

"If you don't mind me asking," Sharon says after a moment of silence. "But why are you wanting to know all this? Why now?" I swallow and look at her. My answer will change everything, but it feels like this it is what I need to do, it's the only way I can live with myself. It's been mulling over in my mind for quite some time and I had always pushed it away but I can't fight the darkness any longer, after all, it is who I am.

"I want to know how to resurrect the dead," I say bluntly. Sharon shakes her head and laughs.

"You're joking right? Resurrection?" She says stunned, but soon her laughter stops when she sees how deadly serious I am about my statement. "You're not joking are you?" I shake my head.

"You want to bring back Gideon?" Kerry sounds shocked by my statement.

"Yes," I reply confidently. "I feel it is what I have to do." Sharon thinks about what I've said then tries to explain more about it.

"It's not easy, in fact I don't know a single person who has successfully done it. And for someone like you who is a solitary witch, even just contacting the dead is hard enough, never mind raising them... That sort of thing takes unimaginable levels of power and a very strong support group... And then there is the matter of finding their soul... That is if it's easily accessible." I nod my head as I listen to her then take a piece of paper from my back pocket and place it on the side table next to her.

"So, you are saying I can't bring someone back from the dead by myself?" I want her to confirm that. I believe what she tells me is the truth. Sharon shakes her head in response. "Then I guess I need more power, don't I?" I say, I've never been more serious about anything before. "I have a vampire that I need to raise from his tomb... I know it won't be easy and I have a lot to learn, but I am prepared to do pretty much anything, even if it means blackening my soul." Sharon sighs and nods at me, unsure as to what I am going to do next.

"What's that?" She inquiries as she looks down at the small piece of paper now laid in front of her. I stand back and smile, I have given this a lot of thought, this is it.

"That's my phone number," I reply smiling wildly at her. "You have 14 days until the next full moon, so I suggest you ring all your bitches... After all I am Lena's daughter and the rightful leader of the Midnight Church. So, I think it's about time that I introduced them all to their new High Priestess."

To Be Continued ....

Velvet Darkness
The Velvet Chronicles – Book 4

Printed in Poland
by Amazon Fulfillment
Poland Sp. z o.o., Wrocław

53973397R00146